Revolver

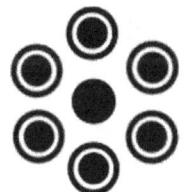

A Johnny Spicer Caper

by

H. P. Oliver

MYSTERIES IN HISTORY

HPO Productions
8698 Elk Grove Boulevard
Suite 1-271
Elk Grove, California 95624

Cover art and design by Steve Eitzen

Back cover author photo:
1937 Chrysler Imperial Business Coupe owned by Camela and Dave Labhard and displayed at the California Automobile museum in Sacramento, CA. Photograph by Tim McCoy.

Printed in the United States of America

ISBN-10: 0988833131

ISBN-13: 978-0-9888331-3-5

DEDICATION

Revolver is dedicated to the motion picture industry's screenwriters.
Without them the movies would have no stories to tell.

ACKNOWLEDGMENTS

The author wishes to thank the following people and organizations for their valuable assistance in the writing of Revolver: Tim McCoy for helping me see the locales in Revolver as they were eight decades ago; Ty Hamby for sharing his extensive knowledge of firearm history; the California Automobile Museum for access to their collection; E. J. Stephens and Marc Wanamaker for their book, *Early Warner Bros. Studios*; Warner Bros. Entertainment for preserving the legacies of Harry, Albert, Sam, and Jack; and Suzanne Cox for the application of her substantial editing skills.

PLEASE NOTE

This book occasionally refers to individuals and groups with terms that are considered inappropriate in today's society. These terms, however, were in common usage during the historical period in which this story is set and are included here solely for the purpose of accurately depicting the attitudes and customs of the era.

Revolver

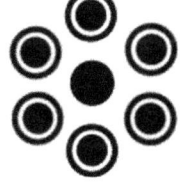

One

Warner Bros. Burbank Studio Lot
9:30 A.M. – Monday – November 20, 1939

Many who should be in a position to know about such things are of the opinion that Jack Warner is a scheming bastard. Despite having this opinion, the same people still invite the scheming bastard to their ritzy parties, cheerfully cash the paychecks he signs, and write nice things about him in their newspapers and magazines. That's Hollywood for you.

Having done a few discreet and confidential investigations for Jack Warner, I too am in a position to have an opinion about the man's character. Truthfully, though, I don't care one whit how Warner conducts his affairs. As long as his checks don't bounce—and so far they haven't—Warner's ethics are no concern of mine. That being the case, I had no qualms about agreeing to meet the youngest of the three remaining Warner brothers at the Burbank studio he commands with the tyrannical authority of a Prussian general.

From my office in Hollywood, I followed Highland Avenue north to Cahuenga Boulevard and turned left to head over the pass toward the sprawling San Fernando Valley. Just past the summit, I made a right on Barham Boulevard and followed it down to the sixty-some acre facility in which Warner Bros. studio employees go about the business of making movies.

Actually, the gigantic sign spread across four huge buildings along Barham says, "Home of Warner Bros. – First National Pictures." It is said, however, that the "First National" part of that sign is merely a concession made by the Warners in their agreement to buy the studio lot. No one who does business with the Warner brothers has the slightest doubt as to who owns and runs the place.

I turned right through what's commonly known as the Warner Barham Gate and stopped at the command of a uniformed security guard perched atop a wooden stool in front of the property department on my right. As he approached, I rolled down the passenger-side window and said, "Johnny Spicer to see Jack Warner."

The guard, an older fellow who was probably a retired cop, consulted a list on his clipboard and said, "Mister Warner's secretary left a message that you're supposed to meet Mister Warner in Sound Stage Fifteen." He pointed up the street beyond the gate and added, "You go up this way . . . ."

Interrupting him, I said. "I know where it is. Thanks."

I proceeded slowly—there's an eight-mile-per-hour speed limit inside the gate—through a narrow canyon of towering sound stage buildings. Warner's sound stages all look more or less the same—three-story pinkish monstrosities ranging from about a hundred feet to more than two hundred feet in length. Most of them have no windows and are topped by arched roofs. Warner Bros. has more than thirty of these giant edifices and the only way you can tell one from another is by large numbers painted on each corner of the buildings.

The lot, as studio facilities are known in this part of the world, was surprisingly quiet on this Monday morning. Typically the streets are fairly humming with vehicles and pedestrian traffic bustling back and forth between sound stages, the prop warehouse, and other buildings crucial to the creation of motion picture magic. On this particular day, however, the only activity I encountered on my way to Sound Stage Fifteen was a group of four World War One infantry soldiers taking a smoke break outside Stage Six.

At the corner of Third Street and Avenue E, I turned right and a block later pulled up behind three cars and a small truck already parked alongside the warehouse-sized building with "15" painted on its corners. There are two entrances at that end of the building. The first is a wide roll-up designed to accommodate small truckloads of props and equipment. The second door is smaller, designed to accommodate people. The roll-up door was closed and the people door had an armed security guard stationed next to it. That was odd, and I wondered who or what might be inside that was so precious it required guarding.

As I got closer to the door, I recognized the security guard. Unlike the older, retired cop-types, this fellow was young and fit. He was also a former competitor of mine. Will Gardner was forced to close down his one-man detective agency about a year ago when the state yanked his P.I. license. It was a bum deal because Will didn't do anything the rest of us don't do on a regular basis; he just had the bad luck to get caught doing it by an overpriced L.A. shyster with good pals in high places.

"Hi, Will, how's things?"

"Pretty good, Johnny. How 'bout you?"

"I can't complain. Say, I'm supposed to meet the head man here. You got me on your list?"

"Yeah, I noticed you were on today's list. I'll check ya in."

As Will checked my name off on his clipboard, I gave in to curiosity and asked, "How come they've got you standin' guard out here? That's kind of unusual, isn't it?"

"Yeah, it is. I'm not sure what's goin' on." With a grin, he added, "All I know is the chief of lot security told me to plug anybody who isn't on the list and tries to get in."

Returning Will's grin, I said, "Damn! I'm sure as hell glad I'm on your list."

Will looked up to make sure the red wig-wag light that indicates cameras are rolling inside wasn't lit and opened the door for me. As I walked in, I glanced at the paper notice thumbtacked to a bulletin board next to the doorframe. It said, "Shooting Today: Thunderstruck!" Below that in neatly printed, inch-high letters were the words, "CLOSED SET."

If you've never been inside a sound stage, your first visit can be a little overwhelming, sort of like walking into L.A.'s new Union Station for the first time. These joints are huge.

The building's cavernous interior was mostly empty save for a small area at its center that was brilliantly lit by large carbon-arc spotlights—called Klieg lights—hanging from the maze of rafters and catwalks nearly three stories above the floor. As always, I felt a little nervous walking under those damned big lights. Some of them are more than three feet in diameter and heavy enough to put a good-sized dent in your fedora if the electricians didn't tighten the mounting bolts securely.

The area the Klieg lights were illuminating inside Sound Stage Fifteen was a set designed to replicate what looked to my eye like a parlor or drawing room straight out of the 1800s. Two actors I didn't recognize—a young fellow in chin whiskers that probably weren't his and a pretty blonde—were standing in the middle of the set listening to another fellow who was most likely giving them last-minute instructions on how to play the scene about to be shot. I guessed this because the guy was doing a lot of pointing and gesturing and because I recognized him as one of Warner Bros.' more colorful directors, Dmitriy Volodin, who is more commonly known around the lot as the Mad Russian despite the fact he hails from Poland.

The set was surrounded by the accoutrement of filmmaking: a camera mounted on a moveable, elevated pedestal; a boom extending out over the set to dangle a microphone above the actors' heads; and various and sundry lighting gadgets to supplement the overhead Klieg lights. All of this equipment, in turn, was surrounded by about twenty people. Most of them were crew members in work clothes, but there were also a few big shots watching the proceedings. The big shots were easily identified by their expensive custom-tailored suits.

I recognized one of the suit-types as Jack Warner. He spotted me, gave me a quick wave, and followed that gesture with an elevated index finger meaning he would be with me in a minute. Then Warner returned to the animated conversation he was having with two other suits. They didn't look pleased to be there.

On the set, Volodin finished his instructions to the actors and walked toward the camera, shouting in his high-pitched voice, "Quiet on the set! Quiet on the set! Get in your places! We are shooting this scene now!"

There was a brief flurry of activity as crew members took their positions, and then the big sound stage was suddenly quiet as a tomb. Volodin took a long look at the set, and apparently satisfied with what he saw, calmly said, "Camera . . . action."

I was standing at the side of the open-ended set, so I had a ringside view of the male actor as he emoted, "Caroline! What does this mean?"

The woman replied, "It quite simply means, Samuel, that I am going to have your baby."

Samuel, whoever the hell he was supposed to be, said something in response, but I missed it because a movement up in the sound stage rafters caught my eye. It was hard to see beyond the glare of the lights up there, but I thought I could make out one of the larger Klieg lights, an unlit one, swaying. For a brief moment I thought we were experiencing one of our famous earthquakes, but that didn't make sense because Klieg lights were supposed to be securely mounted; they shouldn't sway, even in an earthquake.

I looked harder and saw the misbehaving spotlight rise a couple of feet, then drop back down and jerk to a stop. Suddenly the meaning of what I was seeing became very clear. Somebody was up there in the rafters trying to unhang one of the hanging Klieg lights. The fact that the Klieg light in question was directly over the male actor's head made me think I ought to do something about the situation, and quickly.

As the light rose vertically again, I shouted, "Look out!" and launched myself across the set at the male actor. I hit him like a lineman tackling a quarterback—a very startled quarterback. He yelled, "What the hell?" and we landed in a heap on the set's carpeted concrete floor a little more than six feet from where he'd been standing a second earlier.

At that precise moment, the Klieg light crashed to the same floor only inches behind my outstretched legs. It sounded something like a garbage can full of broken glass being tossed out a third-story window. The crash was followed by shouts of alarm from the crew and a shrill shriek from the actress at whose feet we ended up.

The actor and I untangled ourselves and I helped him to his feet as several crew members jumped to our aid. Once upright, we all stood there for a moment staring at the Klieg light, which was now little more than a dented three-foot diameter cylinder with a lot of broken glass around it.

Somebody yelled, "Call an ambulance! Eddie's face is all cut up from the glass!"

The actor standing next to me calmly said, "Now that's what I call a close one." Turning in my direction, he offered his hand and added, "Hi, my name's Humphrey Bogart. My friends call me Bogie, and since you just saved my life, I'd say you definitely qualify as a friend."

Two

I introduced myself to the actor, Bogart, and we were still shaking hands when Jack Warner shouldered his way through the crowd of crew members surrounding us. "Bogie . . . Bogie . . . are you okay?"

Bogart fixed him in what a screenwriter might call a "steely-eyed stare" and said, "I'm fine, thanks to my new pal, Johnny, here, but no thanks to your damned electricians!"

Warner said, "I know, I know. I'll find out who's responsible and . . . ."

While all that was going on, I was looking up into Sound Stage Fifteen's rafters. Of course, even if I could have seen him through the glare, whoever tried to drop a Klieg light on Humphrey Bogart's head was long gone. Bogart and Warner saw where I was looking and they, too, scanned the superstructure over our heads for some explanation.

Since there was nothing to see up there, however, Jack Warner did what he does best. He began shouting orders. "There will be no more shooting on this set today! Electricians, get your boss over here and stay put! I want an explanation for this immediately! Everyone else, clear the building, but no one is to leave the lot until quitting time!"

The film's director, Volodin, was standing a few feet away, seemingly transfixed by the smashed Klieg light on his set. Warner jarred him out of his trance. "Dmitriy, I will tell you when to resume shooting. It will be soon, I promise."

The director looked as if he wasn't quite sure Warner's promise was a good thing. I had the same thought.

Turning to the actress, who was cowering in a far corner of the set as though she expected the rest of Sound Stage Fifteen to fall on her head at any moment, Warner said, "Diana, my dear, you should go and change. There will be no more shooting today. But, please, do not leave the lot right away. We, Mister Spicer and I, will want to discuss this with you later. Okay, my dear?"

She nodded and hurried off toward the sound stage door with two older women in her wake, and I considered what Warner said about discussing the incident with her later. It sounded a lot like a clue as to why he called our meeting in the first place. If so, it meant he was already anticipating trouble when his secretary called me late last Friday afternoon to make this morning's appointment.

As crew members secured their equipment and headed for the door, Warner said to Bogart, "Bogie, I can't tell you how sorry I am that this awful thing happened. Please go change and relax for a bit. Nothing like this is going to happen again; I'll see to that!"

The actor took a quick glance toward the rafters and said, "Sure, Jack. Whatever you say."

Dmitriy Volodin chose that moment to call Warner aside for a conversation, so I took advantage of the opportunity to catch up with Bogart as he headed toward the exit. "Bogie, I'm not sure, but I'm guessing Warner called me out here because he was expecting some kind of trouble. I'm a private investigator, and . . . ."

"No kiddin'? A real live shamus? Now that's something!"

"Yeah, ain't it? Anyway, if I'm right about why Warner called me, I'm gonna need to talk to you about this thing. Where can I find you later after my meeting with him?

Bogart said, "Well, it's gonna take me about an hour to get out of this costume and scrub off the makeup. How long you figure to be talking to Jack?"

I shrugged. "Hard to tell. Like I said, I don't even know if what happened here has anything to do with why he called me."

Looking thoughtful, Bogart nodded. "Tell you what. I'll go get changed and meet you in the administration building lobby when you're done with Jack. It'll be about lunchtime by then, so we'll go over to the commissary and talk. Lunch is on me; it's the least I can do after you saved my hide. Fair enough?"

"Fair enough. See you in the lobby."

8

Then a young, freckle-faced fellow who didn't look old enough to be out of school came up and said, "Here's your hat, mister. It just missed getting squashed by that Klieg light!"

I gently worked a dent out of my fedora and said, "Thanks, kid." Then, curious, I asked, "What's your job in this three-ring circus?"

He stood a little taller and with a note of pride in his voice said, "I'm the apprentice best boy on this film. My uncle is the gaffer and I'm gonna to be one, too!"

"Well, good for you, son, and good luck with your motion picture career."

Apparently pleased with my acknowledgment of his ambition, the boy grinned and said, "Thanks, mister!"

He trotted off to do whatever apprentice best boys do and Jack Warner showed up at my side. "Spicer, you got your car here?"

"Yeah, it's right outside,"

"Good. I'll ride with you back to my office."

He steamed off for the sound stage door, and I followed in his wake after turning to take a last look at the set. The powerful carbon-arc lamps were now off, leaving the job of lighting the sound stage interior up to a few incandescent bulbs mounted on the walls. All that remained of the crew were three fellows I guessed were the electricians Jack Warner instructed to stay put until their boss got there and they figured out why the Klieg light fell out of the rafters. I was pretty sure I knew what they'd find when they got up there to the scene of the crime. I also had no doubt that the rafters of Sound Stage Fifteen were exactly that—the scene of a crime.

At the door, Jack Warner was just finishing his orders to security guard Will Gardner. ". . . and you tell your boss I want a full report about this on my desk before five o'clock! No excuses!"

Will nodded meekly and Warner headed out into the bright sunlight. As I passed Will, I said, "I may need to talk with you later. Where can I find you this afternoon?"

Glumly, he said, "I might still be here. If not, the secretary in the security office will know where to find me."

Nodding, I trotted after Warner who was standing in the middle of Avenue E trying to guess which of the two remaining vehicles out there was mine. I steered him toward my maroon Chrysler Royal Business Coupe and we climbed in.

Since we were pointed in the wrong direction for the administration building, I executed a Y-turn in the narrow confines of Avenue E and headed north. In the seat next to me, Jack Warner looked deep in thought, so I concentrated on finding my way to our destination. My route took us to the north end of Avenue E where I turned left and jogged over to Avenue D via a short street between Sound Stage One and the studio commissary. I turned right onto D and a block later turned left at First Street, which took us to the rear of the administration building.

Under its Spanish tile roof, the two-story, U-shaped building housing the offices of the studio's executives had recently been remodeled in the streamline/moderne' style with a snazzy entrance on the other side, facing north on Warner Avenue. We entered through a back door, climbed a flight of stairs, and walked into a spiffy outer office behind a door with a snazzy bronze plaque that said, "Jack L. Warner" and, below that, "President."

As Warner chugged past his secretary, a well-dressed older woman named Esther whose demeanor gave the impressions of competence and efficiency, he said, "Hold all my calls. I don't want any interruptions."

Then Warner went through a doorway marked "Private." As I followed, Esther gave me a nod. We'd met before on my previous visits to Jack Warner's inner sanctum, and her nod was acknowledgment of my status as a fellow confidant to her boss.

In what always struck me as a fairly Spartan inner office for a big shot studio executive, Warner said, "Close the door and take a seat, Spicer."

I did as ordered. and the head man settled in behind the only real adornment in the room—a desk of sufficient mass to be worthy of a fellow who regularly made multi-million dollar decisions. The fellow himself looked equally worthy of multi-million dollar decisions. Below a receding hairline that left the front half of his head bald, Warner's most distinguishing features were a pair of bushy eyebrows, a thin Adolphe Menjou-style moustache, and two intense dark eyes, the left of which had a habit of occasionally wandering off independently of his other eye. Whether his expression was friendly or frowning, it took only one look at Jack L.

Warner's face to know you were in the presence of a man you definitely did not want to cross.

Warner pushed some correspondence aside and leaned his elbows on the desktop. Looking me squarely in the eye, he asked, "What do you make of the accident we just witnessed?"

I was expecting this question and had my answer ready. "It was no accident; I can tell you that much. I couldn't see anybody up there in the rafters because of the glare from the lights, but that Klieg light definitely behaved in a manner contrary to the laws of gravity before it fell. Somebody up there intentionally dropped that thing."

His expression darkened. "That's what I thought. And it's the reason I called you in. I want you to find out who's sabotaging my picture so we can put a stop to it."

"What makes you think it's sabotage and not just somebody who doesn't think very highly of that actor?"

"Because this is the third time we've had trouble on Thunderstruck since we began shooting eight weeks ago, and the first two times had nothing to do with Bogie."

Slipping my notebook and a pencil from my inside jacket pocket, I said, "What kind of trouble?"

Warner leaned back in his executive chair. "The first time they sabotaged a can of film from one of our early shoots. It came back from the lab completely black, like it had never been through a camera."

"Are you certain the cameraman didn't screw up?"

"Of that I am certain," he said emphatically. "The cinematographer on Thunderstruck has been with us since the silent days over on Sunset Boulevard. He's one of the best in the business. He doesn't, as you put it, screw up."

"What's this fellow's name? I'll need to talk to him about that incident."

"Ollie Glick. And be sure you show the man the respect he deserves. Don't go accusing him of any wrongdoing!"

"I won't. What was the second problem you had with this picture?"

"The scene with the bad film was an exterior shot out on our New York Street set. While Dmitriy was re-shooting it somebody started a fire inside the building facade they were using as a backdrop.

"Those sets are like tinderboxes! We were damned lucky the whole back lot didn't go up in flames. Thank God for our fire department!"

"And how do you know the fire was intentional?"

Jack Warner doesn't like it when what he says is questioned, and this was the second time I'd committed that particular sin. His face turned beet red, and he exploded, "Damn you, Spicer! If you're going to argue with everything I say, I'll find someone else to do this job!"

Calmly, I replied, "I wasn't arguing with you, Mister Warner. I have to ask these questions to get a clear picture of what's been going on. Remember, you've been in on this from the beginning, but I just got here."

Warner leaned back in his chair again and took a deep breath. Finally, he said, "I know the fire was intentional because the chief of our fire department found evidence of gasoline-soaked rags and a gas can. He says that's how the fire was started."

Jotting those details in my notebook, I said, "What's your fire chief's name?"

"His last name's Frawley. I don't remember his first name. If you need to talk to him, you'll find him in our fire department on Third Street between Sound Stage Three and Four."

When I finished my notes and looked up, Warner was leaning forward in his elbows-on-the-desk posture again. He said, "Okay. Now you know what's been going on. What's our next step?"

"Our next step is to report all this to the police."

Warner bristled again. "I have you . . . I have my own security department . . . what do I need the police for?"

"For the record, Mister Warner. What happened in Sound Stage Fifteen this morning was attempted murder, and that's a crime. I don't expect the police to find our culprit for us; we can do that. When we do, though, the best way of preventing more trouble is to hand this fellow over to the cops, but if we want them to lock him away, there has to be some record of a crime being committed in the first place."

Warner shook his head vehemently. "Absolutely not! This is our business. Once the cops know about it, our business will be front page news in every newspaper within a hundred miles. I don't want that kind of publicity! When we find the person responsible, we'll take care of him ourselves."

That put me in a bad spot. As a licensed private investigator, I'm required to report crimes I discover during the course of an investigation. Not doing so could cost me my photostat. To make matters worse, I didn't know exactly what Warner meant by "we'll take care of him ourselves." Strong-arming and murder-for-hire are definitely not on the list of services I'm willing to provide my clients.

Since it didn't seem likely Jack Warner was going to change his mind about the cops because of my problems, I put those problems on the back burner for now, but sooner or later I would have to deal with them. To answer his original question I said, "Okay, then my next step will be to talk to that actor, Bogart. He's going to meet me down in the lobby when you and I are through here. Then I'll find Dmitriy Volodin and see if he can add anything to what we know."

"You'll probably find Dmitriy in his production office across the street."

"Okay. After Volodin, I ought to talk to that actress who was on the set. What's her name, Diana something?"

"Diana Dean. She'll probably be in her dressing room in Dressing Room Building Two next door." He gestured to the east and added, "But watch out for her mother, Gladys Grebb. She's a real shrew if there ever was one.

"That woman almost drove me to drink when we signed Diana for this picture. She didn't like the script; she didn't like Diana's dressing room; she didn't like Dmitriy; she didn't like anything!

"I was finally forced to ban her from all shooting because she was so disruptive. That's one of the reasons for the closed set this morning."

"I wondered about that. When do you figure on resuming the shooting on . . . what is it? Thunderstruck?"

Warner looked determined as hell. "We will resume shooting tomorrow morning where we left off today. I will not allow whoever is trying to sabotage us run this studio!"

"It might be better to give me a little time to find this guy. God only knows what he's got in mind next."

"I considered that, but I need Bogart for an Errol Flynn project that starts shooting right after the holidays. Thunderstruck must be in the can by the end of this year."

"Then I hope you plan to tighten security on Sound Stage Fifteen."

"I do. I'll have everybody we've got in security except the gate guards in there tomorrow. I trust you'll be there, too."

"Count on it. And now, if we're through here, I'd better get busy. I'll check back with you after I talk to that actress this afternoon. Maybe you'll have the reports from your electricians and your security chief by then and we'll know how that Klieg light got unhinged."

"Yes. Now go find this saboteur, Spicer, and find him quickly!"

Three

It was few minutes before noon when I arrived in the administration building lobby, and I was thinking I might have to wait for Bogart when I spotted him chatting with a cute receptionist behind the glass and chromium reception counter. He spotted me, too, and headed in my direction.

His appearance was quite different without the beard and sideburns, and as he approached, I was struck by the thought that Bogart was an unusual choice for a leading man. He was on the short side—no more than five-nine or ten—and he wasn't particularly handsome, at least not in the same sense that Gable, Flynn, and Cary Grant are handsome. This guy's features, including a scar on his upper lip, gave him more of a rough-and-tumble look. That overall impression was accentuated by a gruff voice with a slight lisp.

No, Humphrey Bogart didn't seem a likely candidate for stardom, but if Jack Warner gave him a starring role in a film, the guy must have something going for him. I made myself a mental note to see one of his films and find out what Warner saw in this fellow. Personally, I hoped he made the big time because, unlike the few leading men I'd personally encountered, he seemed like an alright guy.

Bogie stuck out a paw to shake and said, "Hiya, Shamus. You get on with the boss alright?"

"Yeah, Warner and I get along okay. I don't argue with him, and he signs checks that don't bounce."

Bogart grinned. "You must be pretty good, Shamus. Not many can say they get along okay with Jack Warner. Let's go put on the feedbag. Damn near gettin' killed makes a fellow hungry."

We left the administration building by the same backdoor Warner and I used coming in. Then we turned left and hiked about a block-and-a-half up First Street to the studio commissary—a single-story building with lots of windows and a long striped awning covering a few outdoor tables and the main entrance.

Inside, the main dining room was a large open space crowded with about a hundred tables under a beamed ceiling supported by wooden columns. The window-lined walls were painted white, which gave the place an airy feeling and kept it from seeming cramped despite the closely spaced tables. It was also a noisy place. At least three-quarters of the tables were already occupied, and all those conversations bouncing off the walls and ceiling created quite a racket.

Bogart steered me toward a smaller dining room with Venetian blinds over the windows and eight-by-ten glossies of Warner Bros. stars lining pale green walls. A tall woman with a very business-like appearance stood guard at the entrance, but stepped aside as we approached. "Good afternoon, Mister Bogart. Enjoy your lunch."

We grabbed a corner table and Bogart said, "We'll be able to talk better in here. In case you're wondering, this is the 'Green Room.' It's reserved for studio big shots and stars. Getting in here is one of the privileges that goes with finally landing a leading role."

I took a quick glance at a surprisingly large menu for a studio commissary and decided on stuffed halibut. Bogart ordered a steak sandwich—rare with onion—and a green salad.

With the business of ordering lunch out of the way, Bogie leaned back in his chair and, tenting his fingertips in front of his purple paisley necktie, said, "It really isn't any of my business, but I admit to being curious. Did Jack hire you to look into the trouble we've been having lately?"

"More or less. Tell me, Bogie, you got any idea why anybody would want to drop a fifty pound spotlight on your head?"

The actor's grin was contagious with a hint bashfulness around the edges. He flashed it at me. "I don't remember pissing anyone off that bad lately, unless you count those newspaper critics who say I can't act my way out of a wet paper sack."

16

"Can you?"

He looked puzzled for a moment. "Can I what? Oh, act my way out of a wet paper sack? Sure! That's one of my best roles." Then he put on a hurt expression and added, "You mean you've never seen any of my films?"

"Don't take it personally. I'm just not much of a movie fan. How many films have you made?"

Grinning again, he said, "Now, don't that beat all? A Hollywood shamus who doesn't like movies!" After a pause, he answered my question. "I guess I've been in a couple dozen feature films since I came out here from New York. Some pretty good ones, too, like Dark Victory and The Roaring Twenties with Jimmy Cagney. Those just came out this year, and I got third billing in both of them."

"Well, you must be doing okay if Warner gave you a starring role in Thunderstruck. What's it about, anyway?"

"Don't be too impressed. I mean, I'm happy to get a leading role, but I'm afraid Thunderstruck is gonna end up a B picture. It's a biography of Sam Colt."

"The fellow who invented the six-shooter?"

"Yeah, that's the guy. He was quite a character, a little on the shady side, though. The writers tried to clean him up some, but he still doesn't come off as an upstanding guy like Alexander Graham Bell or Wyatt Earp. And Jack sure as hell isn't spending a bunch of production money on the thing, either. But, like I said, it's my first leading role, and I'm glad for the opportunity."

I was deliberately going around Robin Hood's barn getting to the details of the near disaster in Sound Stage Fifteen this morning. I wanted to learn all I could about the film and its cast in case any of those particulars had something to do with why somebody was trying to sabotage the project.

As I was framing my next question, our lunches arrived. They were served by a pretty, young blonde with all the earmarks of a gal who came to town in hopes of making it in the movies, but wasn't getting very far. After setting our plates down, she gave Bogart a sultry look and said in an even sultrier voice, "Can I bring you anything else, Mister Bogart?"

Stifling a grin, Bogie said, "No thanks, doll. We'll be just fine."

Looking just a little disappointed at his response, or lack thereof, to her sultry act, she walked off, and we took a moment out from the questions to taste our lunches. Bogart seemed happy with his steak sandwich, but my fish was overcooked and dry. I set my fork down and asked, "Who else is in the Thunderstruck cast?"

Between enthusiastic chomps of steak, Bogie said, "Well, there's the little gal you saw this morning, Diana Dean. She made a couple of pictures over at Universal—nothing great, but Jack went out of his way to steal her from Laemmle for this role, so he must think she's got potential.

"Then there's Gale Sondergaard, who plays Colt's second wife. Gale's an experienced pro with a Best Supporting Actress Oscar she won a few years ago for Anthony Adverse. She's a little too stuck-up for my taste, but she's good at what she does.

"The other two main supporting roles are played by Bob Armstrong and Henry Stephenson. Armstrong plays Colt's brother, and he's another pro who's been in films a while. He was in King Kong at RKO a couple of years back, but that won't mean anything to you since you're not a movie fan."

"Actually," I said, "King Kong is one of the few films I have seen. I was rooting for the ape."

Bogart grinned. "So was I! He got a bum deal in that one."

"What about this Henry Stephenson?"

"I guess you'd call him a character actor. He's a British import, and he seems to keep working regular. Stephenson's done some period stuff here with Flynn—usually plays dignified roles as a lord or a duke or something along those lines. In Thunderstruck he plays a guy named Sam Walker who was a partner in Colt's gun business for a while."

I'd taken my trusty notebook from my jacket pocket and was busy jotting down the details Bogart was providing. He noticed my lack of interest in the stuffed halibut on my plate and said, "Something wrong with your fish?"

"It seems a little dry, but that's probably just me."

"Say, if it isn't good, we oughta send it back!"

"Naw, I had a big breakfast this morning. I'm okay."

That's when the Grande Dame of Warner Bros. arrived at our table in all her glory. She was accompanied by an older fellow in a suit who might have been a studio executive or maybe her agent. Either way, he had a definite air of impatience about him as he went on to wait for her at the Green Room entrance.

Resplendent in a casual checked frock of brown and white, she exhaled a cloud of cigarette smoke and emoted, "Bogie! I heard what happened this morning. It was shocking! Those electricians are such a careless bunch. Jack ought to fire the whole damned lot of them! I'm so glad to see you're none the worse for the accident."

We both stood and Bogart said, "Hiya, Bette. Yeah, I'm just fine thanks to this fellow. He saved me from an untimely end to a brilliant acting career. Bette Davis, meet Johnny Spicer. Johnny, this is Bette Davis. You might have heard of her."

I gently shook the dainty hand she offered. "Pleased to meet you, Miss Davis."

She nodded with a smile that might have even been sincere. Bogart said, "Johnny here is a real live gumshoe, just like Sam Spade."

Davis looked at me with what appeared to be new appreciation, like maybe she had a soft spot in her heart for gumshoes. "Are you really, Mister Spicer?"

"Well, I'm a licensed private detective. That part's true, but there isn't much similarity between what I do and what they write in the pulp fiction stories."

Sounding a little disappointed, Bette Davis said, "I see. Well, Bogie, I'll leave you two to your lunches. You be careful!"

Bogart promised he'd follow her council, and Davis set sail for the exit, leaving a room full of stares in her wake. We reseated ourselves and Bogie said, "That's one hell of a lady there. I'm very happy to be on her good side. Those who aren't don't seem to last long around here."

I said, "I'll remember that. Now, getting back to this morning's incident, did you happen to notice anything or anyone unusual around the set?"

He thought for a moment. "Nothing that comes to mind, but don't put much stock in that. I'm usually concentrating on my lines before a shoot. There could be a whole gang of desperados causing mayhem on the set, and I probably wouldn't notice 'em." He paused for a moment, then added, "Tell me if I'm wrong, but I'm getting the idea you think that Klieg light didn't fall out of the rafters by accident."

"Then you're getting the right idea. There was nothing accidental about it. I saw the light moving strangely just before it fell. Somebody up there tried damned hard to drop that thing on your noggin. That's why I asked if you knew anybody who had it in for you."

Bogart nodded solemnly. "Like I said, there's nobody like that I can think of. Do you figure this is personal, or is somebody trying to sabotage the film and I just happened to be a handy target?"

"In light of the two previous problems—the ruined film stock and the fire—I'm inclined to think it's something to do with the film, but that doesn't let you off the hook. Whoever is behind this is getting desperate. Each incident has been more violent than the last. If that Klieg light had hit you, it's a sure bet you'd be playing your next scene in the great hereafter. Someone who's willing to risk committing murder just to stop a film from being produced is a serious danger to everyone on the set."

"So I'm guessing Jack told you to find the guy quick so we can get back to shooting Thunderstruck."

"Warner's not waiting for me to find the culprit. He told me shooting resumes tomorrow morning with every security cop on the lot standing guard."

Bogart nodded. "Yeah, that sounds like Jack alright. Full speed ahead and damn the torpedoes or however that goes." After a thoughtful pause he asked, "You gonna be there tomorrow morning?"

"Yup, I'll be there."

"Good. Keep a sharp eye on the rafters, will ya? My wife prefers her husbands with a head on their shoulders."

"Don't worry. You concentrate on your performance. I'll make sure you've still got a place to wear your hat."

With that, Bogart paid our lunch tab and we left the commissary. Since he was going in that direction anyway, he escorted me to the office building on First Street where I would presumably find Thunderstruck's director, Dmitriy Volodin.

Outside the building, I thanked Bogart for lunch. He said, "I still owe you a meal, Shamus. I don't pay off my debts with bad fish."

Four

I found Dmitriy Volodin's office on the building's second floor. His domain was identified by black letters on the door's frosted glass: "D. Volodin – Director."

After knocking twice, I heard a high-pitched and accented voice from within say, "Yes, come in."

I did, walking into a reasonably large space made cramped by stacks of paper, books, and photographs on every horizontal surface. The Mad Russian was a short, slender fellow in his mid-fifties with a pink face and a white fringe of hair around a bald pate. Dressed in black slacks, a white shirt, and a gray pullover sweater, he was one of those nervous types who always seem to be in motion even when they aren't.

Volodin peered at me from behind his cluttered desk with large, pale blue eyes. He recognized me, but couldn't quite remember where from. I said, "Hello, Mister Volodin. My name is Spicer. I'm a private investigator. Jack Warner hired me to look into the trouble you've been having on Thunderstruck."

That did the trick. Now he recognized me. The director jumped out of his desk chair and offered his hand, saying, "Yes, hello, Mister Spicer. I am seeing you this morning on the set, yes?"

"That's right."

"You are being the fellow who is saving Humphrey Bogart from the falling Klieg light, yes?"

"Right again."

He rushed around his desk and cleared one of his guest chairs by dropping its stack of stuff on the floor. "Here, Mister Spicer, please be sitting and telling me how it is I can help you."

I sat and said, "Thank you, Mister Volodin. Let's start with whatever you can you tell me about the trouble you've had shooting Thunderstruck."

He settled back into the chair behind his desk again and began tapping an engraved, silver letter opener on the blotter. "Yes. Well, the first trouble we are having is about the film we are shooting on scene twenty-four. We are filming on the New York Street and we are getting good performances, but the film is coming back *pusty* . . . ah, you would say blank, as if it was never being exposed."

"How could something like that happen?"

"This I am also wondering myself at that time. If the camera operator was not being Oliver Glick, I would be thinking he is making a mistake, but I am knowing Oliver is not making such a mistake. Then I am thinking that some *glupi* in the film laboratory is mixing up our film with unexposed stock. This I am now believing is the way it must have been."

Jotting Volodin's thoughts in my notebook, I asked, "Alright, what happened next?"

"Then we are reshooting scene twenty-four on the New York Street set and smoke is suddenly coming out of the false buildings. There are much flames and the firemans are coming to be making the fire go out. Now we are having to be waiting for the builders to make new the buildings so we can be shooting scene twenty-four for a third time. I am being very upsetted by the delays!"

"I can understand that. What about the incident this morning. Do you have any thoughts on how that happened?"

Volodin had lost interest in the letter opener and was now unscrewing and re-screwing the cap of a dark green fountain pen. "I am having no ideas about how such a thing is happening. All I am knowing is that Klieg lights are not falling down out of the sky all by themselves."

I looked up from my notebook. "So you think someone intentionally dropped the light?"

Pen still in hand, Volodin gave me an exaggerated shrug and said, "There is being no other way such a thing is happening!"

"Do you have any thoughts about who might be trying to sabotage Thunderstruck?"

He gave me a puzzled look. "Sabotage? Oh, you are meaning trying to make us be stopping the filming? No, I am knowing of no such person. Why would any person be doing such a thing? It is making no sense to me."

"Then you don't have any enemies who might like to see the project fail?"

Volodin took a deep breath and spoke as if he were trying to explain something to a child. "Mister Johnny, all of creating persons are having enemies because there are always being people who are *zazdrosny*—you would say envying—of our talents. This is being the way of things, but I am knowing of no persons who would be doing such evil tricks."

"What about former employees who might be bitter about being fired?"

He thought about this for a moment. "No, no, there is nothing like that." The director dropped the green fountain pen and picked up his letter opener again. "I am telling you this: If I am not knowing she is too fat to be climbing up into the rafters, I would be suspecting that evil woman who is the mother of Diana Dean."

I took a quick look back at my notes from Jack Warner and said, "You mean Gladys Grebb?"

At the sound of the woman's name, Volodin's face got even pinker than its natural shade. "Yes, yes. That is her name." He snarled, "She is being a *zła jędza* if there is ever being one!"

I had no idea what *zła jędza* meant, but from the expression on Volodin's face, I felt safe assuming it wasn't a term of endearment. I said, "But why would the mother of one of your leading ladies want to cause the film to fail?"

Clearly agitated, the Mad Russian's shrill voice went up another octave and he pounded the desk with his fist. "Only God or *diabeł* would be knowing the answer to such a question! I am only knowing this woman is being evil, evil, evil!"

Not wanting to be responsible for Dmitriy Volodin having a siezure, I decided to end our interview on that note. I'd probably learned all I could from him for the moment anyway. "Alright, Mister Volodin, thank you for your thoughts. Is there anything else you would like to tell me before I let you get back to work?"

"Yes, yes! I am receiving . . . ." He rummaged through the clutter on his desk and, finding what he was looking for, waved a sheet of paper at me. "I am receiving this a short while ago. Mister Warner is saying we are to be filming again on tomorrow at the Sound Stage Fifteen. This news is being very upsetting to me! I am not wanting someone to be dropping a Klieg light on my head, also!"

I took a shot at reassuring him. "Jack Warner told me he would have plenty of studio security people there to make sure there are no further problems. So I think it should be alright."

Volodin didn't look convinced. In a slightly calmer voice he asked, "Will you be being there, Mister Johnny Spicer?"

I said I would, and the director nodded in a way that made me think he thought my being there would make everything okay. Bogart had done pretty much the same thing. I hoped to hell I was worthy of all the faith these folks had in me.

Then I shook Volodin's hand and headed for my next interview. Crossing First Street, I walked half a block east to Dressing Room Building Number Two, which was where Jack Warner told me I would find Diana Dean and possibly her mother. If Gladys Grebb was indeed with her daughter, I was about to learn firsthand what the hell *zła jędza* meant.

My destination was a long, two-story building paralleling First Street opposite Sound Stage One. Like most of the support buildings on the Warner lot, this one was designed in the Spanish mission style complete with a red tile roof. The side of the building along First Street was lined with casement windows, and its entrances were on the building's west end facing the administration offices. An exterior stairway provided access to a second story entrance above the first floor entry doors.

Since Warner hadn't told me where in Dressing Room Building Two I would find Diana Dean's dressing room, I walked through the first floor entrance in hopes of finding a directory that might save me some hunting. There was no such directory, so I started down the long hall, checking five-by-eight cards inserted in brass frames alongside the doors lining the corridor. About halfway through the building, the card next to door number one-fourteen informed me I'd found the dressing room of Miss Diana Dean. I knocked and waited.

The woman who answered my knock looked to be in her late thirties or early forties and wore a business-like, white apron over her gray dress. I recognized her as one of the two women who'd followed Diana Dean out of Sound Stage Fifteen that morning. She said, "Yes?"

I said, "My name is Spicer. I'm here at Jack Warner's request to see Miss Dean."

She gave me the once-over and replied, "May I tell Miss Dean why you want to see her?"

Since the reason for my visit was none of her business and because I possess a particularly strong dislike of nosey people, I said, "No, you may not. Just tell Miss Dean I'm here."

The woman gave me a glare that might have been hot enough to melt a polar icecap or two and said, "Wait here." Then she closed the door in my face and I waited, although none too patiently.

In less than a minute the assistant wardrobe mistress, or whatever the hell she was, returned and held the door open for me. In a tone that would have easily refrozen any damage done to polar icecaps by her earlier glare, she said, "You may wait here in the sitting room. Miss Dean will join you in a moment."

With that, she stomped off through an interior doorway in the wall opposite the hall door. The sitting room, as she called it, was a cozy space furnished with a small loveseat set against the back wall, two stylish club chairs, a glass-topped coffee table, and a mahogany bar cabinet on the wall to my right. The decor was moderne' and very mauve, that being the predominant shade of purple in the room's vertically striped wallpaper. The loveseat and chairs were upholstered in a geometric pattern of colors that sort of went with the wallpaper.

A chromium and frosted glass ceiling fixture illuminated the room and the art prints on its walls, which were clearly chosen for their ability to get along with the wallpaper rather than for any artistic merit. The coffee table held the latest edition of Photoplay with a rather dramatic picture of Hedy Lamarr on its cover. Next to the magazine were a white and green pack of Kool cork-tipped cigarettes and an amusing chromium ashtray featuring two toucan birds with their beaks open to hold lit cigarettes.

Just as I was running out of amusing things to look at, Diana Dean sauntered into the sitting room. She was a petite woman with vivid green eyes and strands of wet blonde hair poking out from under a towel she wore wrapped around her head. The rest of her costume consisted of bare feet and a loosely tied, purple terry cloth robe monogrammed with white, overlapping Ds above her left breast.

Diana Dean flopped onto the loveseat, removed a cigarette from the pack on the coffee table, and hunted for something with which to light it. With fedora in hand and an elbow propped on the top of the bar cabinet, I watched Miss Dean's performance and waited for her to acknowledge my presence in the room.

After she'd searched the coffee table and the pockets of her robe for a lighter or matches, Miss Dean looked up at me and said in a high-pitched, almost squeaky, voice, "Hey, you gotta light?"

Removing my trusty Zippo from a jacket pocket as I casually walked over to the loveseat, I flipped the spark wheel and held the flaming lighter out. Diana Dean leaned forward and placed her hand over mine as she pulled the flame closer and lit her Kool. She took a long drag, exhaled the smoke, and said, "Thanks."

I returned to leaning on the bar cabinet and watched her look me over from head to toe. Then she realized who I was. "Say, aren't you the guy who saved Bogie from gettin' conked on the noggin this morning?"

"That's me. My name is Johnny Spicer. I'm a private investigator hired by Jack Warner to look into some problems, but before we get into that, call your wardrobe woman in here and tell her to take a hike."

Cocking her toweled head to one side and putting on a suspicious expression, Diana Dean said, "Why would I want to do that?"

"Because the subject of my investigation is confidential and because she's in the next room with her ear to the door trying find out what's up so she'll have some juicy gossip to share with her cronies."

With the hint of a smile on her lips, Miss Dean raised the volume level of her voice a couple of decibels and commanded, "Bessie, come in here."

The door opened almost immediately, confirming my hunch about what Bessie had been up to in the next room. Stepping into the sitting room, the woman said, "Yes, ma'am?"

"Bessie, I need to have a private conversation with Mister Spicer here. Please get lost for a while."

I got another ice-melting glare before Bessie said, "Yes, ma'am," in an annoyed tone and stomped out through the hall doorway. I was pretty sure that, if I opened the door, I'd find good old Bessie lingering out in the hallway in hopes of overhearing our conversation, but I really didn't care. She'd been properly put in her place.

Setting my fedora on top of the bar cabinet, I settled into the nearest mauve club chair and pulled out my notebook. As I opened it to a fresh page, Diana Dean flicked a carefully aimed cigarette ash between the two toucan heads and said, "Are you going to tell me what the hell this is all about, or do I have to guess?"

I looked her square in the eye and said, "What the hell this is all about is the same thing that had you screaming your fool head off on Sound Stage Fifteen this morning. Tell me what you think about that 'accident.'"

She shrugged. "Some damned electrician messed up and a spotlight fell on the set. Bogie was damned lucky you saw it coming." Shrugging again, she added, "That's what I think."

"Then it would come as a big surprise if I told you somebody intentionally dropped that Klieg light out of the rafters?"

I finally had Diana Dean's full attention. She stubbed out her cigarette and showed me her first honest expression since she arrived in the sitting room. That expression was fear. There was also fear in her voice when she said, "Who did that?"

"That's what Jack Warner would like to know. Presumably it was the same person who sabotaged a can of film stock and set fire to New York Street while you were shooting scene twenty-four out there."

That particular piece of news hiked Miss Dean's fear factor up another notch. "You mean somebody did all that stuff on purpose? Why?"

"That's the other thing Jack Warner would like to know, and he hired me to find the answers to both of those questions. It would seem someone is trying to sabotage Thunderstruck. You have any ideas about who might want to do that?"

She shook her head vehemently. "Good heavens, no!"

"Can you think of anyone who might have it out for you or someone else in the cast?"

Diana Dean was much too upset to give my questions any serious thought. She just kept shaking her head. "No, no, I can't."

I spent a moment making some worthless notes in the hope that a short time-out might calm her down and inspire a thoughtful answer or two. It didn't work. In a shrill voice she put words to the only thoughts in her mind at that moment. "I just got a memo. We're supposed to shoot the scene again tomorrow! What if something else happens? Somebody could get hurt or killed!"

"Mister Warner is taking precautions. He'll have lots of studio security people on the set to keep an eye on things. And I'll be there to do the same."

Unlike Bogart and Volodin, Diana Dean didn't find the fact that I'd be on the set reassuring. She squeaked, "No! I won't do it! I don't want some crazy guy dropping a spotlight on my head. That's just nuts!"

In the calmest tone I could muster, I said, "I'm certain you'll be perfectly safe. By now this guy knows we're wise to him. Whatever he does next, if he does anything next, won't be during a shoot. Whoever he is, he's not going to risk getting caught in the act, and that's exactly what would happen if . . . ."

She jumped up from the loveseat, losing the towel from her head in the process, and shouted, "I don't care! I'm going to get dressed and get the hell off this lot. But first, I'm going to call Jack Warner and tell him exactly what I think of him for putting my life at risk over a stupid movie!"

The last glimpse I had of Miss Dean was a headful of wet, straggly hair and the back of her purple robe before the interior door slammed behind her. I gave a moment's thought to sticking around and trying to calm her down, but decided that was a hopeless cause. Instead, I tucked my notebook away, donned my fedora, and departed the premises.

I was surprised to find the hallway outside dressing room one-fourteen empty. Apparently Bessie had given up on overhearing any good gossip, or maybe she figured just my presence in Diana Dean's dressing room was juicy enough to blab about.

Outside Dressing Room Building Two I glanced at my wristwatch. It was a few minutes before three o'clock. Figuring ample time had passed for Warner's chief of security and the head of his lighting department to give him their reports on the Klieg light incident, I headed for the administration building's rear entrance. I also figured I probably had some explaining to do if Diana Dean made good on her promise to give Jack Warner a piece of her mind.

Five

Cutting across the neatly mown lawn between Dressing Room Building Two and the administration building, I was contemplating my less-than-successful interview with Diana Dean when a distinctly recognizable voice hollered, "Hey, Shamus!"

I turned toward First Street and saw Bogart on, of all things, a bicycle. He was stopped on the street next to the lawn, and as I walked toward him, I said, "You out getting your daily exercise?"

"Hell, no! A bike is the only way to get around on these narrow streets, especially when the place is busy. You find our culprit yet?"

"Nope. The clever detective doesn't figure out who dunnit until much later in the picture. So far nobody knows nothin' about nothin'."

Bogie grinned at my movie analogy and asked, "You talk to Diana?"

"Yeah. That was pretty much a waste of time. All she's thinking about is her own hide."

Bogie flashed his grin again. "With a hide like she's got, I can't say I blame her!"

"I suppose, but this thing's got her pretty upset. She was damn near hysterical by the time I left."

"Don't put too much stock in that, Shamus. Remember, Diana is well paid to be hysterical, or whatever overreaction the situation calls for."

"Well, if she was acting back there in her dressing room, it was a performance worthy of an Oscar. Anyway, I was just on my way to

Jack Warner's office to see what, if anything, he's learned about this morning's incident."

Bogart nodded. "Well, I won't keep ya, but I'm glad I ran into you. If you're not doing anything Wednesday night, Mayo, that's Missus Bogart, and I are throwing a little Thanksgiving Eve dinner party at Chasen's—not a big deal or anything, just a few friends. Think you could make it?"

"I believe so. Okay with you if I bring a friend?"

Bogart cocked his head slightly to one side, and his expression changed to something I couldn't quite read. "Ah . . . Would that be a lady friend?"

"It would."

He looked relieved. "Then, sure, bring her along! We'll kick things off around seven. Dress will be casual—wear a tie, though. Chasen's won't let you in without one."

"Alright, we'll be there. Thanks for the invite."

As Bogart climbed back aboard his bike, he said, "Sure thing, Shamus. Now you go see Jack, and I'm gonna get the hell out of here. It's been quite a day."

Giving Bogart a wave as he rode off, I resumed my trek to Jack Warner's office and contemplated the invitation I'd just received. His question about the gender of the friend I wanted to bring to his party raised my curiosity.

The movie business seems to attract homosexuals, and although that's a secret studios work hard to keep under wraps, there are always rumors about this actor or that one being a fag, the most common derisive name given to homosexual men. Righteous move fans would be shocked as hell to hear that some of their favorite leading men—guys like Tyrone Power and Cary Grant—were said to prefer male sexual partners over women. I had to wonder if Bogart's question was prompted by some bad experience in the past. Maybe he wasn't quite the casual, easygoing guy he appeared to be.

Walking into Jack Warner's outer office, I hung my fedora on a coat rack next to the door and said, "Hi, Esther. Is Mister Warner in?"

"Yes, I'll let him know . . . ."

Esther was interrupted by the man himself. He stuck his head through the inner office door and said, "Spicer! I thought I heard you out here. What the hell did you say to Diana Dean? I just got through talking to her on the phone. She was having a fit!"

Following Warner into his inner office, I said, "Well, she got a little upset when I told her the 'accidents' you've been experiencing weren't accidents."

Dropping into his desk chair, Warner said, "A little upset? Hell, she told me she was going home and she wasn't going to set foot on the lot again until whoever tried to kill Bogie this morning was behind bars or words to that effect. I had to talk like a Dutch uncle to convince her it was safe to start shooting again tomorrow morning."

"So she'll be on the set tomorrow?"

"She said she'd be there, but she wasn't happy about it."

"I guess that's understandable. Have you heard from your lot security chief and the head electrician yet?"

"Yes, they just left."

"And what brilliant conclusions did they come up with?"

Warner picked up what looked like a typewritten report and leaned back in his chair. Referring to the paper, he said, "You were absolutely right about it being no accident. The Klieg light mounting bracket was intact. The particular type of bracket they use for mounting overhead lights clamps onto a pipe running along the catwalk. The clamp is a heavy-duty gizmo that's held closed by a couple of large bolts that would have had to be loosened with a wrench. When the clamp is removed, the mounting bracket just hangs from the pipe. A good push is all it would take to drop the whole shebang to the floor.

"Well, both bolts and the clamping device are missing; they couldn't find them anywhere. According to Harry Reid, our head electrician, the intact mounting bracket and the missing clamp pieces prove someone deliberately dropped the Klieg light."

I was busy making notes in my trusty notebook again. I looked up and said, "Did they find anything else out of whack?"

"Looking at the sheet of paper again, Warner said, "Yes. There's one other item here. Those Klieg lights have three-foot power cords that plug into junction boxes on the mounting pipes. Reid noticed the power cord on the one that fell is missing its male end—the end that plugs into the junction box. He said it looks like the cord was just jerked out of the plug, but it would take a lot of force for that to happen. Then he found the missing plug jammed into a joint in the catwalk. He figures the plug got jammed in there when the light was pushed off its mounting pipe, so the guy had to jerk it loose to get the light to fall."

I said, "That explains the strange movement of the light just before it fell. When I looked up, I saw the Klieg light actually move up and then drop back down. That must have been when our culprit was trying to get it loose. Did your security chief have anything to add?"

"No, that bastard was too busy protecting his own ass. He claims all of Sound Stage Fifteen's doors were locked from the inside and he had a man on the front entrance when shooting started. But there were a lot of people going in and out when the set was being assembled early this morning—electricians, camera crew, prop movers, carpenters, and like that. He says nobody told him to watch what went on then. Technically he's right about that. I just gave him orders to close the set."

"I assume you gave him a different set of orders for tomorrow."

"You bet I did!"

"We're probably closing the barn door a little late on that horse because I don't think our culprit will risk pulling anything else on Sound Stage Fifteen. Still, better to be safe than sorry."

"Then what do you think this guy will do next?"

I answered his question with one of my own. "What would have to happen for you to shut down Thunderstruck for good?"

"I won't do that, no matter what!"

"You might not have any choice if one of your actors—say, Diana Dean—refuses to go on with the picture."

"She has a contract; she has to make Thunderstruck!"

"That contract would be hard to enforce if some shyster convinces a judge that working on Thunderstruck is dangerous. Right now you'd have a hard time proving him wrong. What's more, if something like that ends up in a courtroom, the publicity sure wouldn't do the studio any good."

Jack Warner stared at me across his desk for a long moment. Then he smacked his fist on the desk top hard enough to make his telephone handset jump. "Then you gotta find this guy and fast!"

"That's my intention. What time does the shoot start tomorrow?

"I sent a memo out scheduling it for nine."

"Okay, I'll be there by eight so I can talk with some of the people I didn't see today. You might be able to speed the process up by getting your security people to interview everyone who was working on the set this morning before it was closed—find out if anyone saw anything unusual or anybody who didn't belong there."

Looking pleased with himself, Warner said, "I'm way ahead of you. I already told Hanson, the chief of lot security, to do exactly that. He gave me a bunch of crap about how that would be a waste of time, but I told him to do it anyway."

I made a mental note to watch out for Warner's lot security chief. Circumstances were making him look bad, and that sure as hell wasn't going to engender a cooperative attitude, especially toward a private eye his boss called in.

Warner said, "What else can we do to help you find this guy?"

"The biggest help would be coming up with a motive. Our culprit isn't doing this for fun. There has to be something in it for him—money, revenge, or something else. Knowing the why of it would make figuring out the who part a hell of a lot easier."

"I haven't been thinking about anything else since this morning. I can't think of anybody who stands to gain anything if we're forced to shut down the film."

"Well, please keep thinking about it. There has to be a reason behind all this."

Warner nodded, and in that moment I got the definite impression there was something else—something he knew or suspected—he wasn't telling me. I can't say exactly what made me think that, but I filed the thought away for future reference.

"Okay, Mister Warner, I'm gonna find the guard who was outside Sound Stage Fifteen this morning and have a talk with him.

After that, I'll go back to my office and try to fit some of the pieces of this puzzle together."

"Did Bogie or Dmitriy have anything useful to tell you?"

"No. What I got from them was mostly background—call it a feeling for what's been going on."

"And that helps?"

"It does. Oh, and please make sure I'm on the gate list for tomorrow morning."

"I've already done that, too. You are on the list until I tell 'em to take you off of it."

Standing, I said, "Thanks. We'll figure this out. You can count on that."

Warner remained seated, but he looked up at me and said, "I sure as hell hope so. And the sooner the better!"

I wished Esther Smith a pleasant evening and retrieved my hat on the way out of Warner's office. Then I got my car, cut over to Third Street, and drove west toward the Barham gate. Just before I got to the gate, I pulled to the curb behind Sound Stage Twenty-Two and walked across the street to the security offices in the north end of the property department building.

Inside, I asked the young woman behind the counter where I might find Will Gardner. She looked up at me with something like embarrassment on her face and said, "I'm sorry, sir, but Will Gardner doesn't work here anymore."

That one took me by surprise. "He sure as hell worked here this morning. What happened?"

She hesitated, looked sincerely sad, and finally said in a quiet voice, "Mister Hanson fired Will a little while ago."

"Is that so? Well, I need to talk with Gardner, so please jot down his home address for me."

She was reaching for a pad and pencil when the door to a glass-walled office on my right flew open and a big, red-faced fellow with a well-developed beer gut stormed into the reception area. He said, "Hey, you're that keyhole peeper Warner hired, ain't you?"

I casually turned toward the guy and looked him straight in the eye. "Well, I might put it a little differently, but yeah, you have the general idea. My name's Spicer. Who might you be?"

"I'm Don Hanson, and you're standing in my security department. Spicer, huh? I've heard of you. You've got a smart mouth and a reputation for sticking your nose where it ain't wanted. Well, just so you know, you ain't wanted around here, and you ain't gettin' no cooperation from this department!"

I continued looking him in the eye and said nothing. His face got a few shades redder. Finally I said, "You might just want to give that decision a little more thought, Hanson."

"Yeah? What makes you think so, wise guy?"

"Well, for one thing, what you said a minute ago isn't quite right. I'm not standing in your security department; I'm standing in Jack Warner's security department. You're wrong about something else, too. I am wanted here. Jack Warner wants me here, and I'm pretty sure he also wants you to cooperate with my investigation."

If our conversation had been taking place in a Warner Brothers cartoon, the artist would have drawn steam coming out Hanson's ears at that point. "We'll damned well see about that! I can solve this problem without any of your meddling!"

"Hanson, if Jack Warner believed that, he wouldn't have hired me in the first place."

Apparently glaring is a favorite pastime on the Warner lot. Hanson's glare reminded me a lot of the glares I'd gotten from Diana Dean's wardrobe gal, and it occurred to me I wasn't making many new friends today.

Hanson spun on his heels and stormed back into his office, slamming the door behind him with enthusiasm. I watched through the glass as he returned to his desk and busied himself with a stack of paperwork. While I guess I should have been pleased with myself for getting the better of Hanson, I wasn't. Now I would have to do his job as well as mine because he sure as hell wasn't going to tell me anything he found out, if he was indeed smart enough to find anything out.

Turning back to the young woman behind the reception counter, I noticed her expression looked a little more cheerful now. I gathered she approved of the way I'd handled her boss. I said,

"You were about to give me Will Gardner's home address. While you're at it, jot down his phone number, too."

Back in my car, I unfolded the receptionist's note to see where Will lived. Below a telephone number and an address on Olive in Burbank were the words, "Thank you, Mr. Spicer!" The note was signed, "Betty R." I smiled. It seemed I'd made at least one new friend after all.

Olive Avenue was one of Burbank's main drags, and it ran right by the studio, but I decided to hold off on seeing Will. Having just gotten the sack, I didn't figure he needed a visit from me right then. I'd give him a call later from my office.

Six

The Cahuenga pass near the eastern end of the Santa Monica mountain range is the oldest and most-traveled road between the Los Angeles basin to the south and the vast San Fernando Valley to the north. In fact, the route was originally established by the local Indians long before the Spanish arrived in the area.

Spanish missionaries made the Cahuenga—if you care, it's pronounced ka-WENG-gah—Pass part of the El Camino Real which extends from San Diego on up the coast of California to San Francisco and beyond. The first actual road was built over the pass just after the turn of the century. Now, because of the heavy traffic between Los Angeles and the San Fernando Valley, the great state of California was turning the old road into a modern highway.

That construction is why I was inching my way over the pass as I headed back to Hollywood. Sitting there amidst the exhaust fumes and dust clouds raised by large, noisy construction equipment, it occurred to me I might be in a little Dutch when I got back to my office.

The love of my life, Tess Gallagher, who was also my downstairs neighbor at the Montero Apartments on Yucca, had some rare free time on her hands because Betsy Lind's all-girl orchestra, in which Tess plays the trombone, wasn't booked again until Saturday night. When Tess kindly offered to spend some of her time off helping me catch up with my filing and correspondence at the office, I didn't hesitate to take her up on the offer.

Thus, I'd left Tess up to her ears in cardboard boxes of stuff that was long overdue for filing when I headed out for my appointment with Jack Warner nearly eight hours ago. The reason I thought I might be in trouble is I fully expected to be back by lunchtime. When things didn't work out that way, I wasn't concerned because Tess has known me long enough to understand things don't always go as planned in the detective business. What might have me in trouble, however, was that I didn't think to call her and explain the change in plans. My only excuse was that it's been a long time since I had anybody around who cared enough to be concerned about where I was.

That particular change in my life would take some getting used to, but one quick look at the mental picture of Tess I carried in my head was enough to convince me that having her in my life was well worth the effort. She's tall and slender with shoulder-length auburn hair that seems to glow a little when the light is just right. Tess also possesses the sort of deep green eyes, prominent cheek bones, and gentle line of jaw motion picture cameras were made to paint on a canvas of film. More important from my point of view, she has patience, a sense of humor, and a contagious smile that never fails to brighten the day, no matter how grumpy my mood. Yeah, Tess was definitely worth the effort.

So when I finally pulled into the parking lot behind the First National Bank Building at Hollywood and Highland, I was prepared to deliver the apology Tess deserved. I climbed the back stairs to the second floor, and as I walked down the hall toward my office, I detected an unusual odor. It smelled like fresh paint, and it got a whole lot stronger when I opened the hall door to my outer office. Sticking my head into the inner office, I discovered the reason for the smell; instead of the dingy shade of gray they'd been for years, my office walls were now a brilliant shade of bluish-white. Being the clever detective type that I am, I immediately detected some clues as to how this miraculous transformation had occurred. Those clues included a couple of gallon-sized paint cans in the middle of the floor, an A-frame ladder, and next to the ladder, Tess in coveralls that were at least three sizes too large for her.

She had her back to the door, apparently admiring her handiwork, so I announced my arrival by saying, "Wow! Am I in the wrong office?"

Tess turned and gave me that wonderful smile. "There you are! No, you're in the right office. It's called Snowfall Blue. What do you think?"

"It looks great! How did all this come about?"

Taking care not to trip over pant legs, which even rolled up about six inches were still dragging on the floor, Tess came over to stand next to me and said, "Well, I finished your filing in about an hour, then I looked around to see what else I could do to be helpful, and it seemed to me the place could use some sprucing up. So I called the building manager and told him the place was badly in need of a paint job."

I cringed at that piece of news. The building manager and I had an unwritten agreement by which I didn't complain about anything and he didn't raise my rent. The new paint job looked like it could easily cost me five bucks a month.

Tess continued her explanation, saying, "I offered him a proposition. I said I'd do the work if he'd buy the paint. He seemed to think that was fair, so he told me to have you deduct the cost of the paint from next month's rent, and I went to work. The receipt for the paint and supplies is on your desk."

Putting an arm around Tess's waist, I pulled her close and said, "Tess, you never cease to amaze me!"

She gave me a peck on the cheek and said, "Good, then you won't be upset with me for buying you a couple of new office chairs. The Hollywood Hotel across the street had an announcement in the Times about selling some used furniture, so I stopped by to see what they had when I went out to get the paint. I picked out a couple of nice, comfy chairs that go with the new paint and hardly show any signs of wear. I got the pair for five dollars. The bill is on your desk next to the paint receipt. The hotel even agreed to deliver the chairs. They'll be here tomorrow morning."

"You're just bound and determined to make me look reputable, aren't you?"

With her smile turned up to full power, Tess said, "That's my mission in life. Now, tell me all about your exciting day at the movie studio."

Lighting Lucky Strikes for both of us, I leaned against my desk and said, "Actually, it started out a whole lot more exciting than I expected. That's why I'm so late getting here." Then I gave her a condensed version of the morning's events in Sound Stage Fifteen.

When I finished the tale, Tess cocked her head a little to one side and said, "What was the name of this actor you saved from getting conked on the head?"

"Some fellow I never heard of by the name of Bogart—Humphrey Bogart."

In a tone of utter astonishment, Tess blurted, "You saved Humphrey Bogart's life?"

"Yeah, why? You heard of him?"

Shaking her head in amazement at my lack of motion picture sophistication, she said, "Have I heard of him? Only in every fan magazine at the newsstand! They say Bogart is the next Spencer Tracy and James Cagney rolled into one! He's really good at playing tough-guy and gangsters."

Grinning at her enthusiasm, I said, "I'm sure Bogie will be very pleased to hear all that. In fact, unless you have other plans for Wednesday night, you can tell him yourself."

"Why? What's happening Wednesday night?"

"Oh, nothing much. Bogie just invited us to a Thanksgiving Eve party he's throwing at Chasen's, but if you don't want to go . . . ."

"If I don't want to go? Johnny, you rat! Of course I want to go!" Tess demonstrated her excitement at the prospect of going to Bogie's party with a hug and a kiss on the lips that damn near knocked me over. Then she stepped back and, giving me a suspicious look, said, "Did you happen to meet any other movie stars you never heard of?"

"Well, Bogie introduced me to Bette Davis at lunch. I've heard of her, but she kinda lost interest in me when I told her my life as a private detective wasn't nearly as exciting as Sam Spade's."

Tess shook her head again. "You met Bette Davis? Unbelievable! Anyone else?"

"Yeah, I met a kid named Diana Dean. Bogie says she's only done a couple of small roles up at Universal, but Jack Warner apparently thinks she's got promise."

Tess repeated Diana Dean's name and said, "I don't think I've heard of her."

"Don't worry about it. She won't be inviting us to any parties. Now go clean the Snowfall Blue freckles off your nose, and I'll take you to Pig 'N Whistle for dinner and a hot fudge sundae." Gesturing toward the gleaming walls, I added, "That's the least I can do considering all this respectability you've given the joint."

Tess said, "Deal! I won't be a minute," and trotted off to the tiny washroom built into one corner of my office.

While she was cleaning up, I sat at my desk and dialed THorndike-three-one-two-nine, the telephone exchange Betty, the security department receptionist, gave me for Will Gardner. Will answered after two rings and I said, "Hi, Will, Johnny Spicer here."

"Hi, Johnny. I've kinda been expecting you to call. Betty telephoned a while ago and told me she'd given you my number."

"Yeah, and she seemed pretty upset about you getting the sack."

Sounding depressed, Will said, "I'm not surprised. We're engaged to be married, but now we'll have to put that off until I find another job."

"Don't sound so glum, chum. Your former boss is a jerk of the highest order. You didn't do anything to justify him firing you; you were just a handy scapegoat. We might even be able to do something about that, but even if we can't, you're a pretty sharp guy, so it won't take long for you to land another job."

"Thanks for the vote of confidence, Johnny. From what Betty said, I take it you gave Hanson a pretty thorough trouncing. Thanks for that, too."

"He had it coming."

"He did, but not many people have the nerve to set him straight. You'll have to watch your back from now on, though. You made Hanson look bad and he'll be out for revenge. That guy is pure snake-mean." Then changing the subject, Will said, "I guess you called to find out what I know about what happened this morning."

That's when I made up my mind. Warner was paying me seventy-five per day plus expenses. I decided I could part with a little of that money to help out a guy who'd gotten a couple of raw deals. I said, "Actually, no. We can talk about that later. I called to see if you were available to give me a little help with this case. I can't afford to pay you what you're worth, but I can give you twenty a day. What do you say?"

Will's tone brightened considerably. "Gee, Johnny, that's really swell of you! I can sure use the money, but only if I can actually do something to help. I don't want any charity."

"Hey, this is Johnny you're talkin' to, not the dang Salvation Army. If you help me out here, you'll earn every dime and then some."

"In that case, you've got yourself a helper. When do I start?"

"Tomorrow morning. Warner rescheduled the shoot on Sound Stage Fifteen, and I need to be there around eight. How 'bout I pick you up about seven-thirty?"

"I'll be out front ready to go. You have my address?"

"Yeah." I looked at the note Betty gave me and added, "I have twenty-seven-fifteen West Olive. That right?"

"Yes, it's the Rancho Burbank Apartments—on your right as you head east, a couple of blocks past Alameda."

"Got it. See you tomorrow morning."

Placing the receiver back in its cradle, I looked up and saw Tess standing outside the washroom door. She said, "I didn't mean to eavesdrop, Johnny, but I couldn't help overhearing. This must be a pretty tough case if you're hiring someone to help. You usually like to work alone, don't you?"

Nodding, I said, "I do, but this is a special situation. The guy I was talking to just now is Will Gardner. He's a former private investigator who's gotten a couple of rotten breaks. First, he stepped on the wrong toes and got his state license pulled for doing something we all do. Then he went to work in the Warner Brothers security department, and he just got the sack over that incident in the sound stage this morning. Will didn't deserve to lose his job over that. His boss just needed a scapegoat and Will was handy.

"Anyway, Will is planning to get married, and I know he could use a little extra money right now. I figure I'm making enough off Warner that I can afford to put Will on the payroll for a few days. But don't worry; he'll earn his keep."

Tess came around to my side of the desk and gave me a kiss on the forehead. "Johnny, you try real hard to come off like a tough guy, but you're actually just a soft-hearted teddy bear." With a wide smile, she added, "That's one of the few reasons I put up with you!"

Standing, I said, "Yeah, I'm a real sweetheart, but don't let it get around, okay? Now let's go get some dinner. The fish I had for lunch at the Warner's commissary wasn't worth eating, and I'm starved."

Still smiling, Tess said, "Sure, Mister Hardboiled Private Eye; whatever you say."

The Pig 'N Whistle is next door to Grauman's Egyptian Theatre, about a block-and-a-half east on Hollywood Boulevard from my office. "The Pig," as it is affectionately known by locals, is a different kind of joint—a first-class eatery with a soda fountain up front. That's definitely unique in a town that runs on hundred-proof booze.

Inside, The Pig is all snazzied up with fancy wood carvings on its beamed ceiling and classy wall decor that gives the place a ritzy look without making it so snooty regular folks feel uncomfortable there. The joint does a land-office business on Friday and Saturday nights because of the Egyptian next door, but the rest of the time it's a quiet, intimate sort of place where you can get a decent meal at a reasonable price.

Marco, a hefty, jolly chap who's on a first name basis with every bigwig in town, has been a fixture at the Pig 'N Whistle since it opened more than a decade ago. Being as how he is also on a first-name basis with some of us lowbrows who frequent the joint when we can afford to eat out, Marco greeted us at the entrance with a cheerful, "Good evening, Miss Tess . . . Johnny. How are you folks tonight?"

Tess replied, "We're great, Marco. This big lug is treating me to dinner, so roll out the best you've got!"

"Sure thing, Miss Tess. Step right this way."

Seven

Montero Apartments – #201, Hollywood
3:45 A.M. – Tuesday – November 21, 1939

My apartment telephone has a little built-in niche all its own out in the hall near the living room, but it rings plenty loud enough to jar me awake in the bedroom, even at the ungodly hour of three-forty-five in the morning. I groped my way down the hall, picked up the handset, and said the most coherent thing I could muster, "Spicer."

"Hi, Johnny, this is Bob Winfield. Sorry to get you out of bed at this hour."

I thought about telling the L.A.P.D.'s Hollywood Division chief of detectives he damned well should be sorry, but in the interest of maintaining a working relationship with one of the few L.A. cops I could almost call a friend, I said, "That's okay, Bob. What's up?"

"We received a missing person call a little while ago, and the subject is tied in with a case you're working. I need to hear whatever you can tell me about it."

Even in my sleepy state I was able to figure out Winfield had to be talking about the Warner case, Jack Warner was the only client I had at the moment. I said, "Who's missing?"

"An actress by the name of Diana Dean. Does that ring any bells with you?"

That piece of news sucked the cobwebs out of my brain like an Electrolux. "It does. What's the story?"

"I'll give you the details when we talk. Shall I come over to your place, or would you prefer to meet me at the precinct?"

Actually I preferred neither, but I picked the precinct option. "I can meet you at your place in about an hour. Will that work?"

Winfield didn't answer right away, and I could hear snatches of a muffled conversation going on at his end. Finally he said, "Sorry, we're in it up to our ears here. Yes, that will work, but make it sooner if you can. We need to move quickly on this one."

I washed away the rest of my grogginess with an intentionally cold shower, and as I dressed for what promised to be a long damned day, my brain shifted into high gear and asked a particularly relevant question: How the hell did Winfield find out at three o'clock in the morning that I was working for Jack Warner?

It figured that the missing person call came from Diana Dean's mother, and it wasn't likely she knew or would have mentioned my name. That meant Winfield talked to somebody at the studio. I hoped to hell it wasn't Jack Warner. The news that one of his stars was missing wouldn't make him happy, especially if the cops woke him up in the middle of the night to tell him about it.

In the kitchen, my percolator had finished gurgling, so I sat at the table with a cup of coffee in one hand and a pad of paper in the other. Between gulps of java, I wrote a brief note to Tess. She was scheduled to help out in the office again today, so I needed to let her know where I was and why. I told her I had no idea when I'd get back to the office, but I would check in with her when I could.

At four-thirty I donned my fedora and headed out, pausing to slip my note to Tess under the door to apartment number 101. Precisely ten minutes later I strolled into the L.A.P.D.'s Hollywood Division on Wilcox, a block-and-a-half south of Sunset.

On my way to Lieutenant Bob Winfield's second-floor office, the level of activity made it clear he hadn't been exaggerating; L.A.'s finest were indeed up to their ears. Diana Dean's disappearance definitely had their full attention.

I poked my head into the chief of detective's office and saw Winfield, his tie loosened and shirtsleeves rolled up, standing behind his desk with his ear to the telephone. Judging by his frown and the gestures he was making with his free hand, the subject of the conversation was something a far sight more intense than the Bruins' chances of making it to the Rose Bowl this year.

Just as I was about to back out and wait in the hall for him to finish his call, Winfield looked up and pointed toward the two chairs opposite his desk. I sat myself in one chair and tossed my hat on the other. Watching the lieutenant, I was struck by the same thought I have each time we meet. I know for a fact the guy is nearly ten years older than I am, but he looks ten years younger. That's because he has one of those faces that never seems to age. That face was, however, showing a good deal more stress than usual at the moment.

His telephone conversation lasted another minute or so. When it was done, Winfield came around to my side of the desk to shake hands and close the office door, thus shutting out some of the racket coming from the detectives' room across the hall. Then Winfield flopped into his desk chair and said, "That was the missing girl's mother on the telephone. I swear she calls every fifteen minutes to ask if we've found her darling daughter yet."

"And I take it you haven't?"

"You take it right. That's why I called you. I need some leads—something to go on. Right now I've got practically nothing. You have any ideas about what's happened to her?"

"Not yet, but I can give you some background that might have some bearing on the case."

Winfield's expression got a little brighter. "What do you have?"

"First, I have a question for you. Who told you I was working on a case for Warner?"

"Don Hanson, Warner's lot security guy, who, I might add, is not one of your biggest fans. Why do you ask?"

"I was just curious. I thought you might have talked to Jack Warner."

"No, I haven't. Should I?"

"Probably not, and definitely not at this hour. Let me tell you what I'm working on, but I need your word you'll keep as much of it under your hat as you can."

"That might be hard to do, but I'll try."

I spent the next ten minutes telling Winfield why Warner hired me and the attempts to sabotage Thunderstruck. Under normal circumstances I wouldn't be nearly so forthcoming with the cops about a client's business, but Winfield was unknowingly doing me a favor by calling me in.

Jack Warner's vehement orders that I was not to inform the police about his problems had been worrying me because following those orders put me in violation of the law that says licensed private investigators who have knowledge of a crime are required to report it to the authorities. I had knowledge of at least three crimes, one of them being attempted murder, and visions of the state yanking my license like it had Will Gardner's were doing nothing for my peace of mind.

Now I was off that particular hook. Warner, if he found out what I told Winfield, wouldn't be happy about his studio's business becoming a matter of public record, but he couldn't very well blame me for spilling the beans. Well, he could, but Winfield was my out.

When I'd told my story and Winfield finished the notes he was taking, he looked me in the eye and said, "So I gather you think Miss Dean's disappearance might be another attempt to sabotage this motion picture?"

"I can't say that with any certainty, but her disappearance certainly fits the pattern. There aren't many things that could bring the production of a motion picture to a screeching halt faster than snatching the film's leading lady."

Winfield nodded and seemed to be giving my point some thought. Finally he said, "Okay, that opens up a new direction for us, but you don't have any suspects yet?"

"C'mon, Bob, I only got the case yesterday. So far I've only talked to a couple of the film's actors and the director, and they didn't toss me any clues. I'd planned to do more interviews today, but now it seems my time would be better spent looking into Diana Dean's disappearance. Can you tell me what you've got so far?"

It's at this point that most cops clam up and tell a private investigator to get lost because they don't want anyone horning in on their cases and making them look bad. Fortunately, Winfield isn't most cops. While I wouldn't call us bosom buddies, we respect each other and he knows me well enough to feel okay about letting me in on a case.

Winfield said, "Sure, Johnny." He picked up what looked like an official L.A.P.D. complaint form and said, "The initial call came into the precinct at twelve-thirty-seven this morning. The caller said her name was Gladys Grebb and that she was calling to report the disappearance of her daughter, Mildred Grebb—an actress who goes by the stage name Diana Dean. Miss Dean lives with her mother at eight-two-one-three Monteel Road.

"Missus Grebb reported that she'd last seen her daughter around six-thirty Monday evening when Miss Dean left the house to meet a friend for dinner at Barney's Beanery. Miss Dean . . . ."

I was busy making notes, but his mention of Barney's stopped me cold. "Whoa! Hold it a minute, Bob. You're saying Diana Dean was meeting her friend at Barney's Beanery? That joint out on Route Sixty-Six in West Hollywood?"

"Yeah, that seemed a little odd to me, too. Barney's isn't exactly the sort of first-class establishment that attracts movie stars."

"More like a first-class dive. It's nothin' but a roadside shack for tourists."

With a hint of humor, Winfield said, "Yeah, but they serve best chili in Los Angeles."

"So they tell me, but Diana Dean ain't a beanery type of dame."

Winfield shrugged. "Maybe she and her pal were out slumming. That's something you can ask her when we find her. Anyway, Miss Dean told her mother she would be home before too late because she had to be at Warner Brothers in Burbank early Tuesday morning." Referring to the complaint form, he added, "The name of the friend she met for dinner is Ruth Barnes.

"Missus Grebb stated she became concerned when her daughter had not returned by midnight. At that time she called the home of Ruth Barnes and learned that Miss Barnes had last seen Miss Dean outside Barney's Beanery around nine o'clock Monday night."

He scanned his eyes over the form. "The only other item here is the mother's description of Miss Dean—five-two, one-hundred-ten pounds, blonde hair, and green eyes."

Winfield looked up and said, "That's pretty much the gist of Missus Grebb's initial call. After the complaint desk officer finished talking to her, he called me. Standard department policy these days is to have the highest ranking detective available immediately brought in on high-jingo cases . . . cases involving well-known people, and especially motion picture actors.

"I went straight from my home to Missus Grebb's residence, which is just off The Strip up behind the Chateau Marmont. There I reviewed Missus Grebb's story with her a couple of times to be sure we had everything. Then I stationed a detective in an unmarked car at the house in case the gal showed up or there was a ransom call. After that I came here to start things moving on the investigation."

I was jotting notes as fast as I could go, and Winfield paused a moment to let me catch up. When I had it all down, I said, "I take it there hasn't been a ransom call."

"Not so far."

That was no surprise. If I had this thing figured right, there would never be a ransom call.

Winfield went on with his account of the investigation. "I dispatched detectives to interview Miss Barnes—she lives in apartment four at seventeen-ninety-one North Orange Drive—and to the restaurant, although it was closed by that time.

"Then I tracked down your pal, Hanson, to see if he had any thoughts about where Miss Dean might be or who might have kidnapped her. He didn't have any ideas except that I should collar you because you probably kidnapped the woman." With a smile Winfield added, "From the way he talks, you're a prime suspect for every felony committed within a hundred miles of L.A."

I grimaced and gave the detective my best James Cagney. "You'll never take me alive, copper!"

"Say, that's not bad!"

"Oh, I got a million of 'em. Did the Grebb woman say how Miss Dean got to Barney's?"

Picking up his regulation police notebook, Winfield thumbed through the pages and said, "Yes. She drove her car." He flipped through a few more pages and added, "Here it is. Miss Dean drives a 1938 model Cadillac two-door convertible . . . red . . . California plate three-C for Charlie-two-two-seven."

I added Diana Dean's license number to my notes and said, "Got it. Anything else you think I should know?"

Winfield gave my question a moment's thought and said, "Nothing else I can think of right now. Do you mind telling me what you plan to do next?"

"That's a damned good question. Even though we don't know for sure it's part of my case, her turning up missing right now is too much of a coincidence for it not to be connected. You have any problems with me poking around your case a little?"

"No problems at all, as long as you let us in on anything you come up with."

"You know I'll do that."

Winfield showed me another small smile. "I meant *before* you go in with guns blazing to rescue the damsel in distress. I like you, Johnny, but you do have a reputation for being a cowboy."

"Don't worry, Bob. I'll be sure to give you a call before I gun down any desperadoes."

He didn't hide the sarcasm in his voice when he said, "That would be greatly appreciated."

Slipping my notebook and pencil back into my inside jacket pocket, I said, "You know, there's one thing in particular that bothers me about Dean disappearing like this."

"What's that?"

"I interviewed her at the studio yesterday afternoon, and when I told her the incident in Sound Stage Fifteen was no accident, she went hysterical on me, like she was terrified that something was going to happen to her next. She even called Jack Warner and refused to set foot through the studio gate again until she knew it was safe or words to that effect.

"Warner told me he talked her into showing up for today's shoot, which fits with what she told her mother about an early call at the studio this morning. What's bothering me is that going out for dinner with a pal, especially at a dive like Barney's, just doesn't seem like something a gal like her would do if she was scared to death somebody was trying to kill her."

Bob Winfield nodded and said, "That does seem a little strange. On the other hand, these actors tend to be flighty—overly dramatic one minute and real cool about it all the next. Maybe she'd already forgotten about being terrified by the time she decided to have dinner with Miss Barnes."

"Maybe. I think I'll start out by talking with Missus Grebb. Since I know a little more about the situation and Diana Dean's temperament, I might dig up something her mother wouldn't have thought to tell you. Since she's probably still up waiting for word about her daughter, this is as good a time as any to see her. Would you mind clearing the way for me? Maybe tell her I'm a private investigator working for Warner Brothers, but cooperating with your investigation, or something like that?"

"Sure, I'll give her a call. I'll also tell my detective over there you're on the up and up. By the way, his name is Danny Collins. Danny's new to the department and he's still a little green, but he's a good kid. I think he'll make a first-rate detective in the long run."

"Thanks. Oh, and one other thing, I hired a fellow to help me out on this case a little. Do you remember Will Gardner?"

Winfield stared into space for a moment like he was trying to remember something and then said, "The name sure sounds familiar, but I can't place him."

"You might have heard his name being kicked around the department not too long ago when the state pulled his P.I. license. Will got a bad deal on that rap and had to take a job with Warner Brother's security department to earn a living. Then he got another rotten break yesterday when Don Hanson made him the scapegoat for what happened on that sound stage. Will was guarding the entrance, and he did the job he was told to do, but Hanson still gave him the sack.

"Anyway, Will's okay and he's a sharp guy, so I hired him to give me a hand with this one. Since he's working for me, the thing about his license shouldn't be a problem, should it?"

"Well, technically he's not supposed to be doing any 'investigating' for pay, but if you hired him to do research or something along those lines, he should be okay."

I grinned at Winfield. "Yeah, that's what he's doin', research."

The lieutenant grinned back at me and said, "Then everything is just peachy."

Figuring I'd better get a move on, I stood up, grabbed my hat, and said, "Okay, Bob, I'll get out of your hair, but I'll stay in touch."

Winfield shook the hand I offered and said, "I'll do the same, Johnny. Good luck with that Grebb woman. She's quite a character."

"So I've been told. And speaking of characters, I didn't see Detective Sergeant Mackie out there anywhere on my way in. I figured you'd have him in on this thing for sure."

"I wish he was in on it. C. K. is taking the week off. He and his missus took a train ride up to San Jose so they can spend Thanksgiving with her folks up there. I could use his help, and he left a telephone number where I could reach him, but I just don't have the heart to ruin his holiday."

I chuckled. "Knowing C. K., he'd probably be happier working than visiting with his in-laws."

"You're probably right, but Helen Mackie is a kind-hearted woman who is very patient with C. K. and the long hours he works. She deserves a little time with him and her family. I was thinking more of her than C. K."

On my way out, I nodded to the desk sergeant, but he was too busy typing a report or something to notice. The big clock on the wall behind him showed five-twenty—the perfect hour for a visit to the wicked witch of the west.

Eight

Outside the old Six Precinct building—known more commonly nowadays as the Hollywood Division—it was still dark as pitch. There were, however, a few signs that Hollywood was starting to rise, if not shine. One was the Adohr Farms milk delivery van I passed just before turning left off Wilcox Avenue onto Sunset Boulevard.

On Sunset, however, there wasn't another car in sight, which gave me a very strange feeling because the boulevard is one of the area's main east-west arteries, running all the way from downtown Los Angeles clear out to the Pacific Ocean more than twenty miles to the west. For a while I had the spooky sensation I was the only human being left on the planet.

Then good old Van de Kamp's Bakery saved my sanity when one of their big trucks with the familiar windmill painted on its sides turned out of the A & P Market at Fairfax Avenue. I actually felt a small sense of relief at seeing the truck's headlights in my rearview mirror as it followed me the rest of the way out to The Strip.

For those who don't know Los Angeles, "Sunset Strip" is a name given long ago by local folks to the section of the boulevard beginning at about the point where it swings southwest to skirt the Santa Monica Mountain foothills. When I was a kid growing up in Hollywood, The Strip was still mostly farm country with very little else around except a few roadhouses that were said to be dens of iniquity in which gambling, drinking, and sins involving loose women were rampant. Gambling and drinking were both quite legal on The Strip back then because it was in the county and beyond the authority of the Hollywood bluenoses crusading for higher moral values. Prostitution, if it was really practiced to the extent we kids imagined or wanted to believe, was pushing things a little too far, even for the liberal-minded government of Los Angeles County.

Be all that as it may, I was only on The Strip for a block before I passed the famous Chateau Marmont luxury hotel. Just beyond it I turned right onto Monteel Road and began climbing the hill behind the Marmont. Residential areas in any part of the foothills north of Hollywood are ritzy neighborhoods, but the residences scattered up the hillside behind the hotel were some of the least ritzy. Even the most casual observer could see that, because the mansions here only had a dozen or so rooms whereas the mansions in the really high-class neighborhoods all had at least twice that number.

The small mansion at eighty-two-thirteen Monteel was a Spanish stucco job with a red tile roof and lots of artsy arches and exposed beams that were probably supposed to be reminiscent of the grand haciendas from California's rancho days. That illusion, however, was somewhat diminished by an encroaching jungle of overhead utility wires and the miniscule sizes of the high-priced hillside lots that placed the residences in cheek-to-jowl proximity— conditions no self-respecting Spanish don would have tolerated.

I pulled to the shoulder of the road behind a black, four-door, Ford sedan any miscreant worth his salt would immediately recognize as an unmarked L.A.P.D. vehicle. The Ford's two-way radio antenna and chromium-plated spotlights were dead giveaways to its secret identity.

I climbed the curved stairway leading from a street-level garage to a terrace where a straight stairway took me up to a well-lit arched entrance area with a pair of large, roughhewn, solid oak doors. The door on my right had an elaborate Judas window—a six-by-eight-inch wrought iron grille set at about eye-level and backed on the inside of the door by a solid wrought iron panel. The idea was the occupants of the house could open the hinged inside panel and look out through the grille to see who'd come a-knocking on their door. The outer grilled panel was also hinged so it could be opened from the inside, thus allowing the resident to receive envelopes, business cards, and small packages without opening the entry door.

I poked a finger at an ivory button set in the door frame, and that triggered a set of cathedral chimes any Catholic church in the land would be proud to call their own. A moment later the inner panel of the Judas window squeaked, and a young, freckled face topped with red hair appeared in the opening. I held up my photostat and said, "My name is Spicer. I think Lieutenant Winfield called you to say I'd be coming by."

With that, the wrought iron panel squeaked closed and the large oak door was opened by the red-haired fellow who said, "Come in, Mister Spicer. I'm Detective Danny Collins."

As I stepped through the doorway, I offered my hand. "Hi, Danny. Nice to meet you."

Collins shook my hand with a firm grip and said, "Missus Grebb is expecting you. She's in the library. I'll show you the way."

As he closed the door behind me and double-checked to be sure its deadbolt was secure, I asked, "Anything new here?"

"No, it's been very quiet except for occasional hysterical outbursts from Missus Grebb." He lowered his voice and added, "Good luck getting anything useful out of that old biddy!"

"Careful, Danny. You're paid handsomely to protect and serve that old biddy."

Collins turned quickly to look at me, and it took him a second to decide if was I seriously rebuking him or just pulling his leg. He correctly assumed the latter and said, "If I meet many more like her, I might decide to be a plumber instead of a cop."

The library was at the end of a long hallway. There must be something in the county building codes that says you can't build a swanky house without a library. They all have 'em.

The woman in this particular library was sitting at a reading desk on which were a telephone and the fashion magazine she was reading—probably Vogue or one like it. That struck me as odd for the simple reason that this gal couldn't possibly squeeze into any of the slinky outfits on the page she was studying. In a word, the woman was huge.

I don't mean she was fat; she was just big-boned and large all over. If she'd stood up when I entered the room, which she didn't, we'd have been looking eye-to-eye, and I'm a hair over six feet.

Danny said, "Missus Grebb, this is Mister Spicer, the private investigator Chief of Detectives Winfield called about."

The woman looked up from her magazine and stared at me coldly for a few seconds before saying, "Spicer, let's get one thing straight right here and now. The only reason I even let you into my house is because that policeman asked me to cooperate with you."

Taken aback, but never at a loss for words, I said, "And good morning to you, too, Missus Grebb."

She cranked up the intensity of her glare. "Don't you dare get smart with me, Spicer! There's absolutely nothing good about this morning. My daughter is missing, and I'd bet a lot of money that bastard you work for had something to do with it!"

On that note Detective Danny Collins discreetly beat a hasty retreat, and I said, "You think Jack Warner kidnapped your daughter? What possible reason could he have for doing that?"

"God only knows what evil intentions are in that man's head. Now ask the questions that policeman said you were coming to ask and clear out of here."

While thinking I was witnessing some very strange behavior from a woman who should have been grateful to anyone who was helping to find her missing daughter, I dropped my hat on the nearest chair and removed the notebook and pencil from my inside jacket pocket.

"Missus Grebb, what was your daughter's mood when she came home from the studio yesterday afternoon?"

"What sort of mood do you think she was in? After that actor standing right next to her was nearly killed, Millie was terrified!"

It took me a second to figure out who the hell Millie was. Then I remembered Winfield saying Diana Dean's real name was Mildred, and Mildreds are often called Millie for short. "If your daughter was scared for her life, why did she go out to meet a friend for dinner? It seems to me she would have felt safer staying home."

It took Gladys Grebb a second or two to come up with an answer for that one, and I made a note of the delay. It meant something was out of whack here. Up until that point everyone—namely the L.A.P.D.—had been kowtowing all over the place to calm the hysterical woman whose daughter was missing. But I'd thrown her a curve ball by questioning precious Millie's behavior, and Gladys didn't have a ready-made answer for my question.

Finally she said, "If it's any of your business, Millie met Ruthie for dinner because I encouraged her to do it. She needed to relax and get over her fear."

"So you didn't agree with your daughter that she was in danger?"

"I didn't say that! I just meant I thought she would be perfectly safe going out to dinner with Ruthie and that it would take her mind off of the terrible things happening at that studio."

I considered asking Missus Grebb what made her think a dive like Barney's Beanery was a safe place to go for someone who thought her life was in danger, but decided I'd pushed that line of questioning as far as I dared. Instead I asked, "Have you noticed anything unusual in the neighborhood lately? I mean like people who don't belong here or strange cars parked out on the street?"

She shook her head almost immediately, but as I was taking that to mean no Gladys, changed her mind and said, "Well, there are always strangers coming and going from the Chateau Marmont down the hill, so there might have been someone watching us that we took for a guest there."

I made a note in my book and asked the next question that came to mind. "How long has your daughter known Ruth Barnes?"

Having been caught off guard a couple of times, now Gladys seemed to be giving my questions more thought before answering them, as if she was trying avoid stepping into another trap. After several seconds, she said, "Millie met Ruthie just after we moved out here from Wichita in 1936. Millie still had a year of school to finish, and Ruthie was in some of her classes at Hollywood High School. That's where they got to be friends. We were living in an apartment down on Fountain then, and Ruthie used to come home with Millie after school."

"What does Ruth do these days?"

Caution again showed in her eyes before she said, "Ruthie works for Max Factor. She sells cosmetics in their salon on Highland. She hopes to become a cosmetician for the movies."

"A moment ago you mentioned moving here from Kansas. Was that because your husband came out west to work?"

"Mister Spicer, my husband is a good-for-nothing bum. He's hardly worked a day in his life. Millie and I came out here to get away from him and to give her the chance she deserves to become an actress. Millie is a beautiful girl. Even as a small child she won every beauty contest she entered. And she has always had a flair for the dramatic, so we decided it was time for Millie to start her acting career."

The way she said "we decided" cinched it. I now had Gladys Grebb's number. Little Millie was the beautiful woman Gladys could never be, so mama was living her glamorous dreams through her daughter. In other words, she was the perfect picture of a stage mother, pushing and prodding her daughter through countless beauty contests and dragging her to audition after audition until Millie finally got her start in the business. It was entirely possible Millie had been just as eager for an acting career as her mother, but more often than not, that wasn't the case for daughters of stage mothers. I actually felt a little sorry for Diana Dean.

"Missus Grebb, I believe I heard that your daughter came to Warner Brothers from Universal Studios. Am I remembering that correctly?"

I got the impression pride had taken the place of caution in the way Gladys was now responding to my questions. Without hesitation, she said, "Yes, that's correct. Universal signed Millie to a two-year contract and she appeared in three movies there."

While playing on her ego, I continued along the same line of questioning for another reason that had to do with something Bogart said about Warner stealing Dean from Universal. "Really? When did she start at Universal?"

Gladys gave my question a moment's thought, but I didn't think it was out of caution. She was simply trying to remember the date. "Millie signed with Universal at the end of 1937. I remember it was in December because we thought the contract was a wonderful Christmas present."

I did the simple arithmetic and knew I was headed in the right direction. "Then your daughter left Universal before fulfilling her contract?"

Her caution was instantly back in full force. Gladys looked at me for a long moment before saying, "Well, technically, yes. There were a few months left before her Universal contract was up."

"Were there any problems about that? I mean, did Universal just let your daughter walk away from her contract?"

This time the pause between question and answer was even longer. "At first they put up a little fuss, but Mister Warner worked it all out with Universal because he really wanted Millie for his new movie, Thunderstruck."

"I see. But it's my understanding you were unhappy with the Thunderstruck script. I'm wondering why your daughter would leave Universal to appear in a film you didn't like."

The glare returned. Gladys figured I was trying to trap her again. "What are you getting at, Mister Spicer?"

"I'm just looking for reasons someone might have for sabotaging Thunderstruck and kidnapping your daughter. I thought maybe there was some bad blood between her and Universal."

Gladys appeared to make a concerted effort at restraining her anger at having stepped in another trap. Finally, in a calm, controlled voice, she said, "No, I don't believe Millie's disappearance has anything to do with her leaving Universal."

I simply nodded and said, "Can you think of anyone who might benefit in some way from your daughter's disappearance?"

"No . . . unless someone is holding her for ransom."

I didn't bother mentioning the obvious—that thus far there had been no ransom demand for the return of Diana Dean. Slipping my notebook and pencil back into my pocket, I picked up my hat and said, "Well, Missus Grebb, that's all the questions I have for now. Thank you for seeing me."

Gladys didn't stand or offer to see me to the door, but with about as much sincerity as an unsympathetic bookie, she said, "Mister Spicer, I must apologize for the things I said when you first got here. As I am sure you can quite understand, I am very upset over Millie's disappearance, and I'm afraid I was somewhat rude. I do hope you will forgive me."

Putting on my most ingratiating smile, I replied, "I accept your apology. Don't give it another thought," knowing full and well she'd be giving our conversation a lot of thought once I was out the door.

After saying so long to Detective Danny, I walked to my car and headed back down the hill to Sunset Boulevard. I was pretty sure I'd just learned something important from Gladys Grebb, not so much from her verbal responses to my questions, but from her emotional responses. There was also the complete turnabout of her attitude toward me when I left. Her apology was a concerted effort to get on my good side, which could only mean Gladys feared me for some reason. I just wished to hell I knew what that reason was.

Nine

I turned left on Sunset Boulevard, heading east toward Hollywood. The sky ahead was gradually dissolving from black to gray with hints of pink around the edges. This, along with an increase in traffic on the boulevard, said Tuesday, November 21, 1939, was officially underway in our part of the world. That meant it was time to make some telephone calls. If Tess and Will Gardner weren't up yet, it was high time they stopped featherbedding and got to work.

The Flying A service station just passed Genesee was open for the convenience of early risers, so I pulled in and told the white-uniformed attendant to "fill 'er up." While he pumped gasoline, checked my water and oil, and gave my windshield a cleaning, I made use of the station's public telephone booth.

I dropped a nickel into the slot and dialed Tess's number. She answered promptly.

"Good morning, Tess; it's Johnny."

"Hi, Johnny. I thought it might be you. I found your note. Thanks for letting me know what you're up to."

"You're welcome. Are you still planning on going to the office this morning?"

"Yes. I have the trim to paint and I need to clean up the mess from yesterday."

"I appreciate that, Tess. Could you do me a couple of other favors this morning?"

With a smile in her voice, she said, "Sure, but that will cost you extra."

"Okay, put it on my tab. You got a pencil?"

Now sounding very businesslike, she said, "Yes, I have. Go ahead."

"Call the county recorder's office and get the name of the person who owns the property at eight-two-one-three Monteel Road."

"Wait, I'm getting this down. How do you spell Monteel?"

"M-O-N-T-E-E-L. If the owner's name is anything but Grebb—G-R-E-B-B—or Dean, see if you can find a telephone number for them."

"Got it. Anything else?"

"Yes. I need a brief letter of introduction typed up for Will Gardner. It should be on my stationery and addressed, 'To whom it may concern.' After that, it just needs to say something like, 'This letter will introduce Will Gardner as an employee of the Jonathon A. Spicer Investigation Agency. Mister Gardner is herewith authorized to conduct research on my behalf.' I'll sign it when I come in later."

"Okay, I think I've got all that. When do you think you'll get to the office?"

"I really don't know. I've got to see Jack Warner when he gets to the studio this morning. He'll be in a tizzy because his leading lady has disappeared. After I get him calmed down, I need to follow-up on a couple of slim leads to see if I can find said missing leading lady."

With genuine concern in her voice, Tess said, "Do you think Diana Dean was really kidnapped?"

"I'm not sure yet. She's definitely missing, though, and the entire Los Angeles Police force is out looking for her."

"Okay. Well, please stay in touch just in case any calls come in for you."

"Will do, Kiddo. Talk to you later."

I dropped another nickel into the slot and dialed Will Gardner's number at the Rancho Burbank Apartments. He also answered promptly.

"Hello, Will. This is Johnny Spicer."

Sounding a little concerned, like maybe he thought I'd changed my mind about putting him to work, he said, "Hi, Johnny. What's up?"

"We've got a new development in the Warner case."

"Oh yeah?"

"Yeah. Diana Dean disappeared last night. Her mother called the Sixth Precinct a little after midnight and reported her missing. Chief of Detectives Bob Winfield called me before four o'clock this morning because your former boss at Warner's told him I was involved.

"Since then I've had a long talk with Winfield, and I interviewed Diana Dean's mother. I've got more interviews to do, but I'd like to get you started on some other things. Any chance we could move our meeting time up a little?"

"Sure. I'm ready to go anytime."

"Good. I'll pick you up in fifteen or twenty minutes."

The Flying A attendant was leaning against the driver's side front fender of my Chrysler, and as I approached, he said, "Oil and water are fine. She took eleven gallons. That'll be two-ten."

I handed him two dollars and a dime, then rejoined the happy early morning travelers on Sunset Boulevard. I turned left at Highland and followed it north past my office and onto Cahuenga Pass Boulevard. The construction workers were just getting started there, so traffic was still moving right along. I left Cahuenga at Barham and headed down the hill into Burbank. Just past the Warner lot, I turned right on Olive. A few minutes later I pulled up in front of the Rancho Burbank Apartments.

Will was standing at the curb looking sharp in a spiffy gray sport coat and tie—a big improvement over his baggy Warner Brothers security cop outfit. He climbed onto the passenger seat and said, "Hi, Johnny. Where are we headed?"

"To breakfast. I've already been on the job for four hours, and I'm running on one lousy cup of coffee."

"Okay. Virgil's Coffee Shop is just up ahead a couple of blocks at Victory Boulevard. Will that work?"

"If they've got food, it will work."

Virgil's was a bright and airy establishment with counter service and booths. They were doing a pretty good business at that hour, but the hostess found an empty booth and seated us right away. As I perused Virgil's substantial breakfast menu, I said, "Have whatever you'd like, Will. This is on me."

"I had an egg and some toast at home, so I'll just have a cup of coffee with you."

Our waitress, a pleasant, middle-aged woman in a pale green and black uniform with a nametag that said "Cathy," showed up promptly to take our orders. I told her I'd have scrambled eggs with minced ham, wheat toast, and coffee. She returned almost immediately with our coffees, for which I thanked her profusely.

Fortified with a swallow or two of caffeine, I briefed Will on the details of Diana Dean's disappearance as provided by Bob Winfield. Then I gave him a quick synopsis of my interview with Gladys Grebb. I'd just finished when my breakfast arrived. As I dug into my eggs, Will said, "So you think Diana Dean disappearing is tied into the other problems with Thunderstruck? Like maybe the guy snatched her to stop the production once and for all?"

Between bites, I said, "I'm not so sure about that."

Surprised, Will said, "You're not? Her disappearing is too much of a coincidence not to be tied in with the other stuff."

"Oh, it's tied in alright. It's the kidnapping part I'm not so sure about."

Will frowned. "Why?"

"For one thing, the timing is off. It doesn't seem likely the guy would risk a federal kidnapping rap without waiting a couple of days to see if dropping the spotlight in Sound Stage Fifteen accomplished what he intended it to do."

Dubiously, Will replied, "I suppose, but this guy could also be crazy as a loon, in which case logic wouldn't apply."

"That's true, but there's another thing bothering me. Gladys Grebb is up to something. I caught her in a couple of contradictions about what happened last night. After that she got very cautious about answering my questions. She also did a complete about-face in her attitude. Gladys started out mean as a snake, but she was mild as a lamb by the time I left. She even apologized for being rude to me when I first got there. That makes me think my questions worried her for some reason and she didn't want to antagonize me into looking deeper where I might learn something she doesn't want anyone to find out. I know that's speculation, but there's definitely something going on there."

"Okay, I guess we'll just have to wait until Diana Dean turns up to find out what's going on. That is assuming she turns up alive."

"Oh, she'll turn up in one piece. I'd bet money on that."

"Alright, I'll take your word for it. Now what do you need me to do?"

"I want you to concentrate on tracking down any leads from the first three incidents with Thunderstruck—the blank film, the New York Street fire, and the thing yesterday on Sound Stage Fifteen. Start out by talking to Thunderstruck's cinematographer, Ollie Glick. Warner is convinced this guy is too much of a pro to make a mistake with the film, so find out all the other ways the film could have been sabotaged.

"Next, look into the fire. Talk to Warner's fire chief or anyone else you can think of who might know something, like where the gasoline can came from and if the rags used to set the fire can be traced. Just find out anything you can that might give us something more to work with.

"Lastly, for now anyway, go to Warner's personnel department and get the names and addresses of everyone who was fired or laid off or just plain quit during the months immediately before Thunderstruck started having problems. See if you can find anyone in the personnel files who might have a major grudge against the studio."

With a look of concern, Will said, "You know, Johnny, there will probably be some trouble at the studio over my being there after Hanson sacked me. Hell, they might not even let me on the lot."

"Let me worry about that, Will. Jack Warner trusts me and he's anxious to get to the bottom of things. I'm pretty sure he'll go along with whatever will make that happen sooner rather than later."

"Okay, you're the boss. What will you be up to while I'm digging for dirt at the studio?"

"I'm concentrating on finding out where the hell Diana Dean has gotten off to. Even though I'm not convinced finding her will lead us to the guy who's been sabotaging Thunderstruck, I know she'll be at the top of Jack Warner's priority list. And who knows, maybe we'll make the connection in the process."

According to the snazzy chromium and neon clock on the wall behind Virgil's cash register, it was seven-thirty when we headed for Warner Brothers. We were still a few blocks away when Will said, "Johnny, it might be a good idea to go in through the VIP gate off Warner Avenue. That way we don't have to drive right past the security office at the Barham gate. Hanson's gonna be ticked off about me being there anyway—no sense in rubbing it in by parading me right under his nose."

"Okay, we can do that, but stop worrying about Hanson. His goose is about to be cooked."

The appropriately named Warner Avenue is a frontage road running between the studio and Olive Avenue. I turned onto it and then turned right into the driveway that leads to the so-called VIP gate, which unlike the Barham gate, really has a gate—actually, two of them that meet in the middle to block the entire entrance. The left half of the gate was open, and a uniformed security cop stood to the left of the opening with the ever-present clipboard tucked under his arm.

I stopped, and as the cop walked toward my side of the car, Will said, "That's Mack. He's an okay guy."

Turning to my open window, I said, "Hi, Mack. Johnny Spicer."

He consulted his clipboard and said, "Yes sir, you're on the list." Then he leaned down a little for a look at who was in the car with me. Seeing Will threw him. "Ah . . . hi, Will . . . ah . . . I'm afraid I can't let you in. You've been . . . ah . . . your name has been taken off the employee list."

I said, "His name is no longer on your employee list because Will is now my employee. That means he goes where I go."

That baffled Mack. "Ah . . . I'll have to clear that with my boss, Mister Spicer."

"Your boss has nothing to say about it. I report directly to Jack Warner, and when I talk to him in a few minutes, I'll make sure Will gets added to your list."

On that note, I drove on through the gate. I could see Mack in my rearview mirror. He was standing there, hands on hips, wondering what the hell to do next. Will said, "Geez, he's gonna have every cop on the lot after us now."

"I don't think so, Will. He won't be anxious for Hanson to know he let us slip by. Right now he's just hoping to hell this doesn't come back to bite him in the butt."

I turned right on First Street and a moment later pulled up behind the administration building. I shut the engine off, set the emergency brake, and said, "It'd probably be a good idea for you to wait here while I talk with Warner."

He nodded glumly and I took off for Jack Warner's office. On the way, I mentally braced myself for what promised to be an interesting conversation.

Ten

Jack Warner's outer office was empty when I walked in, and I was wondering if I'd arrived too early when I heard Warner's voice through the open door to his inner office. "You hunt down Wallis and tell that SOB I want him in here immediately! Tell him if he isn't here before lunch, he's fired!"

Esther Smith's voice quietly said, "Yes, sir."

"And find that damned detective. Tell him I want to know what the hell's happened to Diana Dean!"

I stepped into the inner office doorway and said, "That damned detective is already here."

Warner looked up, his face pink with anger, and shouted, "Who the hell's made off with my star?"

Standing aside to let Esther escape the lion's den, I said, "I'm not entirely convinced anybody's made off with her."

Collapsing into his desk chair, Warner said, "Then why the hell did that idiot Hanson wake me up before dawn and tell me someone kidnapped her?"

"Because, as you just pointed out, he's an idiot, and because he jumped to the same conclusion the cops did—a conclusion, I might add, that may have been concocted by Gladys Grebb."

Warner took a deep breath and made what looked like a concerted effort to calm himself. Then in a carefully controlled voice he said, "Okay, Spicer. Please sit down and explain what in blue blazes you're talking about."

I sat. "Mister Warner, I interviewed the charming Missus Grebb around five-thirty this morning, and the story she told me—the same one she told the police—has some flaws in it. The cops wouldn't have spotted those flaws, but I did because I know the sort of mood Diana Dean was in when she left here yesterday."

He was leaning forward and watching me intently. When I paused, he said, "Okay, go on."

"Yesterday when I told her the Klieg light incident wasn't an accident she got hysterical, as if convinced she was in grave physical danger. I wasn't sure whether that was an honest reaction or if she was just doing what actresses get paid to do—being dramatic. Her telephone call to you a few minutes later, however, would seem to indicate she really was upset. Would you agree with that assessment?"

Warner nodded and grunted, "I would."

"Then I have to wonder why she went home and made arrangements to meet a girlfriend for dinner at a dive roadhouse out on Route 66. That's just not something a woman would do if she believed she was in mortal danger."

Warner appeared to give that a moment's thought before saying, "Agreed."

"What makes all that even more suspicious is Gladys Grebb's reaction when I made the same point to her. She got flustered, and from that point on she was very cautious about how she answered my questions. That suggests there might be something about Miss Dean's disappearance her mother doesn't want us know. I have no idea what that might be, but something smells very fishy there."

"Spicer, that Grebb woman is a manipulating bitch. It doesn't surprise me at all that she's up to something, but that doesn't rule out the possibility Diana was kidnapped by whoever is trying to shut down Thunderstruck."

"True, but something else does rule it out or at least makes kidnapping highly unlikely."

Warner frowned. "What's that?"

"The timing of Miss Dean's disappearance. Up until now your saboteur has been very meticulous. He sabotaged the can of film and waited to see if you stopped production on Thunderstruck. When you didn't, he set the New York Street fire and waited again.

When you still went ahead with the film, he staged the Klieg light accident yesterday morning, so it doesn't fit his pattern to risk a federal kidnapping rap without waiting to see if yesterday's stunt got you to scrap Thunderstruck."

After giving my logic some thought, Warner said, "So if Diana wasn't kidnapped it means she must have disappeared of her own will. If that's what you're telling me, it doesn't make sense either. Why would she do that?"

"Mister Warner, sometimes being a detective is like working a kid's jigsaw puzzle and finding pieces that fit the puzzle, but not the picture it's supposed to make. When that happens it means the puzzle must make a different picture than we originally thought.

"In those cases it's my job to figure out what picture the puzzle really makes. In other words, I have to make sense out of things that make no sense, and that calls for speculation until I uncover more puzzle pieces that make the picture clearer. Since Diana Dean's behavior last night doesn't fit the kidnapping picture, I'm speculating she may have, as you put it, disappeared of her own will for some unknown reason, and to make sense out of that, I need to find more pieces of the puzzle."

Jack Warner leaned back in his chair and shook his head. "This is all very confusing. What you're telling me is that now we have two separate mysteries to figure out."

"You're right, we do have two mysteries on our hands, but I don't think they're entirely separate. If Miss Dean and her mother did stage her disappearance, I'm sure their reason is somehow related to the sabotage attempts on Thunderstruck."

Starting to turn pink in the face again, Warner said, "All this guesswork is giving me a headache, Spicer. Enough with the speculation. What are you doing to get me some hard facts that make sense?"

"Since, at least for the moment, the investigation is going in two different directions, I've brought in an associate to help me find your facts faster. He'll pick up where I left off tracking down leads that will help us find your saboteur while I hunt down Diana Dean for you."

"Now that makes sense! And with the police involved we need to move quickly before our business is spread all over the newspapers."

Nodding my understanding of the need for a quick resolution to Diana Dean's disappearance, I said, "When I spoke with Chief of Detectives Winfield this morning, I urged him to keep as much of this out of the press as possible. He gave me his word that he would."

What I didn't mention was a detail that made finding Diana Dean quickly even more imperative than Warner realized. If Winfield held to the kidnapping explanation for Dean's disappearance, it was only a matter of time until he'd be forced to call in the feds. That would be a disaster for several reasons, not the least of which was publicity on a national scale.

Instead of opening that can of worms, I opened another one. "There is something I need to tell you about the associate I brought in."

Jack Warner looked at me suspiciously. "Not another headache, I hope."

Giving him what I hoped was a reassuring smile, I said, "Just a small one. My associate's name is Will Gardner, and up until yesterday, he worked for you."

"You're stealing my employees now?"

"Not exactly. Will was the security guard on Sound Stage Fifteen yesterday morning, and even though he followed his orders to the letter, Hanson gave him the ax yesterday afternoon so he could shift the blame away from his own incompetence in not keeping an eye on who had access to the sound stage before shooting began. That has to be when the saboteur got into the sound stage."

Warner grimaced. "I've put too much faith in Hanson. I have to do something about that. I need to know this lot is secure and safe."

"I agree. In the meantime, however, I'm guessing Hanson isn't going to be overjoyed when he finds Will going around the lot asking questions. I already had some trouble bringing him in with me this morning. So would you please see that Will Gardner's name is added to the gate lists? He needs to be able to go anywhere I can go."

Nodding, Warner bellowed, "Esther!"

From her desk in the outer office, she replied, "Yes, sir?"

"Type up a memo to security. Tell them I want a fellow named . . . ." To me, he said, "What's his name again?"

"Will Gardner."

To Esther, he yelled, "A fellow named Will Gardner to have unlimited access to the lot. Type it up right now so I can sign it, and you can give a carbon copy to Spicer here. Then send the original to security. You'd better give them a call, too."

"Yes, sir."

Warner turned back to me and in a quieter voice said, "I hope this fellow is competent. Most security guards don't strike me as being . . . ah . . . well, putting it bluntly, most of them don't seem very bright."

"Will isn't your run-of-the-mill security cop. A few years back he had his own successful detective agency in Los Angeles. Then he got a bad break and was forced to close down his agency. He needed work, and that's how he ended up in your security department."

I got the idea from Warner's expression that he was wondering what sort of bad break puts a private detective out of business. Fortunately, he had more important things on his mind and accepted my sketchy explanation.

Changing the subject, I said, "What do you plan to do with Thunderstruck until I find the missing Miss Dean?"

With vehemence he said, "I'm going ahead with it, dammit! I told my head of production, Hal Wallis, to meet with Dmitriy and reschedule the shooting to work around Diana's scenes." He looked up at me and added, "But don't take too long finding her. There's only so much we can do without our leading lady."

"I understand, Mister Warner. I'll move as fast as possible. I do need to ask you one more question before I go, though."

I could tell I'd just about used up all the time Warner was going to give me. He was already fussing with papers on his desk. He looked up. "What?"

"Yesterday I asked if you had any idea who might have motive for sabotaging your film. You said you didn't. Have you come up with any ideas along that line since then?"

I'm pretty sure I detected a very brief hesitation before Warner said, "No. I don't know anyone who would gain anything by shutting Thunderstruck down."

Pushing my luck a little, I said, "What about Universal? I understand Diana Dean left them before her contract was up in order to make Thunderstruck for you. Any chance someone over there is holding a grudge?"

Warner shook his head emphatically. "No. I worked all that out with Laemmle's kid. Besides, he doesn't have the *chutzpah* or the brains to pull off anything like this."

Standing, I said, "Okay, Mister Warner, I'll get to work. I'll check in with you later."

Jack Warner didn't stand up or offer to shake my hand, but he did look at me and say, "One more thing, Spicer."

"Yes, sir?"

"For crying out loud, stop calling me 'Mister Warner.' It takes too long to say. Just call me Jack like everyone else around here does."

I nodded, but he didn't see me. My new buddy, Jack, had already refocused his attention on other pressing matters among the papers on his desk.

In the outer office, Esther was just rolling the original and two carbon copies of the memo to security out of her typewriter. She said, "If you'll wait just a moment, Mister Spicer, I'll get Mister Warner to sign these and give you your copy."

She walked briskly into Warner's office, and by the time I'd retrieved my hat from the rack by the hall door and returned to her desk, Esther was back. She folded one of the carbon copies and slipped it into an envelope. Handing the envelope to me, she said, "I'll call Betty in security right now and ask her to tell the guard at the Barham gate about this. That way Mister Gardner will be cleared to enter the lot right away."

"Great. There's one more thing. Do you have any idea where I can get my hands on a picture of Diana Dean?"

Esther smiled and held out a thick six-by-nine manila envelope. "Right in here. I thought you might be needing a photo for identification purposes, so I had publicity send a couple up while you were talking with Mister Warner. They sent three copies each of two different photos, a head shot and a full-length shot. Will they do the job for you?"

Slipping the manila envelope into my side coat pocket, I said, "Esther, you are a true gem. Thanks."

Then I donned my fedora and headed back to my car. On the way I pondered the significance, if any, of Warner's slight hesitation when I asked him if he had any ideas about who might be motivated to sabotage Thunderstruck.

Jack Warner had a well-deserved reputation for doing things his way with little regard for, let's say, ethics. Warner Brothers was his damned studio, and he was well known for putting its interests ahead of anything else. While doing things his way usually brought about the results he wanted, it also made enemies—sometimes powerful enemies.

I had to wonder if Warner's hesitation in answering my question was caused by the memory of someone he'd crossed in his enthusiasm to get Thunderstruck produced. If that was the case, I thought I knew someone who would probably have all the juicy details. I made myself a mental note to stop by for a visit with Saul Cohn when I had a minute. His classy digs were up in the rarified air of the First National Bank Building's tower section, eight floors above my humble space.

I arrived at my car to find Will right where I'd left him. As I climbed into the driver's seat, he asked, "How'd things go with Warner?"

"Under the circumstances, they went pretty well. I knew he'd be in a tizzy about Diana Dean, but I calmed him down some when I told him my theory about her disappearance and how we planned to proceed with the investigation."

"What did he have to say about me helping you?"

"He was happy I'd recruited some help. He hardly blinked an eye when I explained the situation with Hanson."

In disbelief, he said, "Really?"

I took the envelope containing Warner's memo to the security department out of my inside jacket pocket and handed it to him. "Here's your authorization to come on the lot whenever you need to. Warner's secretary also called your gal friend in security and told her to let the Barham gate guard know you were cleared, so you're all set."

Taking the envelope, Will exclaimed, "Swell! I'm not going to ask how you pulled that minor miracle off, but thanks."

"Don't thank me for any favors. My motives are strictly selfish. I have to get this thing solved before it all becomes national news, and I need your help to get that done."

"Okay, I'm rarin' to go."

"Will, if you don't mind, I'm going to run you back to your place so you can pick up your own car. That way you won't be stuck at the studio waiting for me in case I don't get back by the time you're through with your interviews. I'm headed back to the office and then across the street to Max Factor's. Dean's pal, Ruth Barnes, works there and she's the next stop on my road to finding our missing starlet."

"That's fine with me. I don't know how long it'll take to talk to the people you want me to talk to, but what are my instructions when I'm done?"

"We'll need to compare notes, so I'd like you to stop by my office. Oh, and if you have any problems getting back on the lot, call me. I'll be in the office for a little while until the Max Factor outfit opens for business. You got my number?"

"I've got it."

"Also, give me a call if you come up with anything hot before then. A friend of mine—her name is Tess—is helping me out in the office for a couple of days, and I'll be checking in with her by telephone, so she can give me any messages you leave."

"Will do."

I left the lot via the same gate we'd come in through because it was the shortest route to Will's apartment. The guard who'd been on duty when we arrived was still there. He eyeballed us pretty closely as I drove through the gate, probably relieved that we were getting the hell off his turf.

Eleven

After dropping Will off at the Rancho Burbank Apartments, I beat it back over the pass to Hollywood and parked my car in the lot behind the First National Bank Building. In the second floor hallway, I paused for just a second to enjoy the little sense of pride I always feel when I read the gold letters on the frosted glass panel in the door to number two-thirteen. They spell out "Jonathon A. Spicer Investigation Agency." It isn't much, but it's mine.

Peeking into my inner office, I found Tess atop a ladder in the corner. Clad in her too-large coveralls again, she was busy applying a coat of stark white paint to the crown molding just below the ceiling. The pure white made a nice contrast that brought out the subtle hint of blue on the walls. She had a good eye for color.

Not wanting to startle Tess from her perch, I knocked my knuckles softly on the inner office doorframe. She looked down and said, "Hi, Johnny! I'll be down in a sec. I'm just about done with the molding up here."

I hung my fedora on the coat rack next to the door and took a look around. It was obvious Tess had been at work bright and early. The baseboards and window frames already wore fresh coats of glossy white.

Carefully descending the ladder, Tess said, "What do you think? Is the trim color okay?"

"It's swell! You are an amazing gal, Kiddo."

She gave me a peck on the cheek and said, "I'm glad you think so. I'm trying to stay in good with the boss."

"You're succeeding."

Looking around at her handiwork, Tess said, "I still have the doors and doorframes to do, but they won't take long." Gesturing toward the canvas drop cloths covering the floor, she added, "I should have all of this clutter out of here by this afternoon. I'd be nearly done by now, but I took time out to take care of those other things you asked me to do."

"Were you able to find out who owns the house on Monteel Road?"

"I was. The info is on your desk. The property belongs to somebody named Ralph Jamison. I wasn't able to find a telephone listing for him, but the county recorder's office has an address for him."

I looked at the neatly printed note on my desk. Ralph Jamison became the legal owner of the property located at 8213 Monteel Road in the County of Los Angles, State of California on April 19, 1934. The address Jamison provided the county recorder's office at that time was 239 South Bristol Avenue, Brentwood Park.

Tess said, "Just out of curiosity, what's so important about that address on Monteel Road?"

"That just happens to be the residence of motion picture actress Diana Dean and her mother. It's a pretty ritzy area in the west Hollywood hills off The Strip, and I wanted to know who it belonged to because that tells me something about Diana Dean's financial standing. If the property was owned by Gladys Grebb or Millie Grebb—that's Dean's real name—it would mean she's doing pretty darn well for herself. Since neither of them owns the joint, it probably means they're renting it, which moves them several rungs down the financial ladder. This guy, Jamison, on the other hand, is loaded."

"How do you know that?"

"For one thing, your research says he has clear title to the house, which means he isn't making mortgage payments. For another thing, he lives in Brentwood Park, one of the more exclusive residential areas in our fair city. All that adds up to a guy who's probably worth a pretty penny."

"I see."

"Would you please start a new case file folder for me? Call it Warner-slash-Thunderstruck, and put these notes in it."

"Will do. Oh, and here's the letter I typed for Will Gardner."

Tess handed me a letter on my stationery. It was neatly typed and said exactly what I wanted it to say with no spelling or typographical errors that I could find. I signed "J. Spicer" in the appropriate spot, saying, "It looks great. Thanks!"

"I made a carbon copy on onion skin paper. Do you want me to put it in the new file folder, too?"

"That's as good a place as any for it, since it's doubtful I'll be using Will on any other cases in the near future. Speaking of Will, he may call with a progress report sometime during the day, and I asked him to stop by later this afternoon so we can compare notes on what he finds out today."

Tess smiled. "Then I'd better get busy making the place neat and tidy so it will make a good impression when he gets here."

"Tess, Darlin', Will is an employee. I don't give a damn whether he's impressed or not. It's the clients we want to impress."

"It never hurts to make a good impression, even on employees."

I looked at my wristwatch. It was nine-forty-five. "I wonder what time Max Factor's across the street opens for business."

Tess said, "Probably ten. Why? Are you thinking of getting a new hairdo?"

"Very funny. The woman Diana Dean met for dinner before she disappeared, Ruth Barnes, works there. Since she was the last one we know of to see Miss Dean, I need to find out what she remembers about last night."

"Well, since you have a few minutes to spare, what are your plans for Thursday?"

"Thursday? I don't know. Why?"

"Thursday is Thanksgiving."

"Oh."

"I'm asking because I know you don't have any family left in the area, and I was wondering how you plan to celebrate."

"I haven't thought about it, but I'll probably just do what I always do on Thanksgiving."

"And what's that?"

"I'll walk over to Eli's deli and get myself a turkey sandwich. What are you doing?"

Tess had one of those looks on her face that tells me something out of the ordinary was on her mind, but she was reluctant to tell me about it, maybe for fear I'd think her idea was silly. I waited her out, and she finally said, "Well, my Aunt Jean—she lives in Compton—is having Thanksgiving dinner for a few people. She invited me and said I could bring a friend. I thought, if you weren't doing anything else, you might like to go to Aunt Jean's with me."

I could only think of about a hundred things I'd rather do than have Thanksgiving dinner with some old gal in Compton, but I kept that to myself. Judging by Tess's hesitation in asking me and the slight hint of nervousness on her face while she waited for my answer, it seemed the invitation was important to her. Resigning myself to a boring day, I said, "Sure, Tess. That's sounds fine. Thanks for inviting me."

Looking relieved, she said, "Oh, good! I was afraid you . . . well, that you might think having Thanksgiving with my aunt was a dumb idea." She paused, then quickly added, "I guess I'd better get back to work."

Grabbing her can of trim paint, Tess headed for the washroom door and went to work painting the frame. Congratulating myself on making what was apparently the right decision, I picked up my telephone handset and dialed the Sixth Precinct.

After a wait of at least two minutes for the switchboard operator to get Winfield on the line, I finally heard the chief of detectives say, "Hello, Johnny. I hope you've got something good to tell me."

"I've got nothin' but a hunch without much to back it up."

"That's more than I've got. Tell me your hunch."

After giving Winfield a condensed version of my conversation with Gladys Grebb, I told him about my feeling that she was hiding something and why I'd come to the conclusion that Diana Dean's kidnapping was a bunch of baloney. When I finished, Winfield said, "So you don't think her disappearance is connected to those problems at Warner Brothers you told me about?"

"I didn't say that. I'm sure it is connected somehow, but not in the way we originally figured. My next step is to interview Dean's pal, Ruth Barnes. With a little luck, she might give me something to support my theory or maybe to prove I'm way off the beam."

"Well, good luck with that. We didn't get anything useful out of her other than confirming she and Miss Dean had dinner at that roadhouse."

"I may not do any better, but I have to give it a shot. Do you have anything new there?"

"Not a thing. The detective I sent over to Barney's Beanery called in almost an hour ago. Some of the employees showed up to get the place ready to open, but none of them were there last night, so we're trying to track down addresses for the ones who were there when Miss Dean and her friend had dinner.

"Beyond that, the only positive thing we've accomplished is getting copies of Miss Dean's picture made so we can circulate them to other precincts and the police departments outside the city, including the county sheriff's office. We're putting out a bulletin with the picture to keep an eye out for her."

Winfield sounded frustrated and I understood why. The case got colder with every minute that passed. I asked, "What else do you have planned?"

"I just dispatched a couple of patrol officers to canvas Dean's neighbors on Monteel Road, but I'm not expecting much there. And as soon as I can spare one of my detectives, I'll send him over to Warner Brothers. I was just about to call Don Hanson to clear the way for that. Any ideas on who my guy should talk to?"

I gave his question a few seconds of thought and decided I had no choice but to give him the straightest answer I could. "Well, I can save you the trouble of questioning Jack Warner. I did that about an hour ago, and I'm pretty certain he doesn't know any more about what happened to Diana Dean than we do. Other than him, the person on the lot who probably knows Dean best is her wardrobe mistress—a gal named Bessie Klein. Be careful what you tell her, though. She's a busybody and anything your guy says to her will end up all over the lot within an hour."

"Got it. Anyone else?"

"You might have your detective nose around Universal Studios while he's out in the valley. Dean has only been with Warner for a few months, but she was at Universal for almost two years before that. Somebody there might know something worthwhile."

Winfield sounded genuinely grateful for my suggestions. "Thanks, Johnny. I didn't know Dean was at Universal. I'll make sure we cover that base. Anything else?"

"Only a question. At what point will you have to call the feds in on this?"

"I've been wondering that myself. Of course, my boss doesn't want them anywhere near the case and, for that matter neither do I, but if we don't come up with something useful by tomorrow morning, I won't have much choice but to get the FBI involved." After a short pause he added, "If you could come up with any hard facts to support your theory that Miss Dean wasn't really kidnapped, it would go a long way toward giving me some justification for keeping this investigation to ourselves."

Bob Winfield was no dummy. He knew damned well FBI involvement and the national attention that would bring to Diana Dean's disappearance were the last things Jack Warner wanted. The implication in what he'd just said was clear; if I wanted to keep my client happy, I'd better come up with something quick. He could have saved his breath, though, because I was already well motivated.

On that note, we finished our conversation. I replaced the telephone handset in its cradle and took a minute to mull things over. The problem was I just didn't have much to mull. That being the case, I walked over to where Tess was industriously slathering paint on the washroom door and said, "I'm going across the street to see what this Barnes gal can tell me. Then I'll probably head out to that roadhouse where she and Dean had dinner last night, but I'll check in back here before I take off."

"Good luck, Johnny. I hope something good turns up."

"Thanks. We need something good to turn up and quick, or we'll have J. Edgar's Junior G-men all over this thing and a very unhappy client on our hands."

Twelve

Leaving the First National Bank Building through the Highland Avenue entrance, I turned left and walked down to Hollywood Boulevard. While waiting for the traffic signal to change, I looked across the boulevard toward my destination. The Max Factor salon took up about half a block on the east side of Highland, beginning with a four-story, deco-style edifice about mid-block. From there it dropped down to a series of five identical, single-floor facades that ended next to a parking lot at the corner of Highland and Hawthorne.

The building has been there for at least a decade, but it stood empty until about five years ago. Then Max Factor lit up his signs and became what I'm told is one of the most exclusive beauty salons in Hollywood. Even though Max himself died about a year ago, his renown as the makeup artist and hairdo doer to the stars still attracts customers in droves, and not just the rich and famous. A lot of everyday dames with dreams of looking like a movie star save up their pennies to pay for a Max Factor style job. Everybody in this town wants to look like a star.

Beyond a pair of glass doors set in an elaborate marble entryway, I walked into Max's lobby, a large oval-shaped room all done up in pink and gold deco with gray marble columns and mirrors all over the place. I showed the classy brunette behind the counter my photostat and said, "I'm here to see an employee named Ruth Barnes."

The receptionist, who was clearly chosen more for her looks than her intelligence, took several chomps on the wad of gum in her mouth, stared at my P.I. license through slightly crossed eyes, and said nasally, "You want to talk to Ruthie?"

"You catch on quick, doll. Now run and find her for me while we're both still young and beautiful."

The brunette looked up at me like she was trying to decide if I'd just paid her a compliment. Apparently failing at that endeavor, she said, "Sure, mister. I'll be back in a sec."

I stood there for quite a while, counting all the Johnny Spicers looking back at me from the mirrors on the lobby walls. There were twelve of me—more than anyone should have to endure for as long as it took the receptionist to return. When she finally showed up again, a short redhead followed in her wake. The brunette said, "Here's Ruthie, mister."

To the redhead, I said, "You're Ruth Barnes?"

She looked nervous and nodded. I pointed to a couple of chairs that looked like they'd been heisted from an ice cream parlor and said, "Let's go over there where we can talk."

The redhead nodded again and walked off in the direction I'd pointed. She was wearing a smockish sort of garment with buttons on the shoulder like the kind of thing doctors wear, except hers was pink instead of white. The rear view I had of Ruthie as I followed her to the chairs wasn't her best side. If she didn't lay off the hot fudge sundaes at C. C. Brown's, it wouldn't be long before young Miss Barnes graduated from pleasingly Rubenesque to downright chubby.

We sat down and I said, "My name is Johnny Spicer. I'm a private detective looking for the missing Miss Diana Dean or, as you probably know her, Millie Grebb."

Ruthie nodded yet again, still not saying a word. Growing bored with our one-sided conversation, I put a question to her: "You were the last person the police know of who saw Miss Grebb before she disappeared. What can you tell me about last night?"

This time she came up with some actual words to go with her nod. "What would you like to know, Mister Spicer?"

"Well, let's start at the beginning. When did the two of you decide to have dinner together?"

Ruthie thought about that for a lot longer than her answer deserved. "It was on the spur of the moment. Millie called me about five-thirty, right after I got home from work, and asked if I wanted to meet her at Barney's for dinner."

Noting this in my book, I asked, "Is Barney's a regular place you two go?"

"It's one of the places we like. Sometime we go to El Coyote, the Mexican restaurant over on La Brea, or if Millie's in the mood to be seen in a celebrity sorta place, we go down to the Formosa Cafe across from Paramount and RKO."

"So you girls have dinner together often, do you?"

"Maybe once a week or like that." After a brief hesitation, Ruthie continued in a tone tinged with embarrassment. "I can't really afford to eat out that much on what I make here, but Millie always insists it's her treat, so I go with her."

I gave Ruthie a friendly smile in the hope of opening her up a little and said, "Millie sounds like a good pal."

"Oh, she is. We've known each other since high school. That was back before she got into the movies."

Ruthie made the three years she'd known Millie Grebb sound like a very long time. From her youthful point of view, it probably was. "So getting back to last night, did she come by and pick you up, or did you meet Miss Grebb at Barney's?"

"I met her at Barney's."

"How did you get there? Do you have your own car?"

"Yes. My dad gave me his old Ford when he got a new one last year. I don't drive it to work or anything 'cuz it's cheaper to take the streetcar."

"That was nice of your dad. What model year is your Ford?"

Ruthie gave my question a little thought and said, "I don't know. It's a gray coupe, and I think Daddy bought it brand new when I was in high school."

"I see. What time did you meet Millie at Barney's last night?"

"We met around seven-thirty. I was nearly starved by then 'cuz I usually fix dinner for myself at six."

I gave her another smile. "You must have ordered dinner right away then."

"Well, not right away. Millie always likes to have a cocktail or something first. Last night we had a couple of beers . . . Barney's has about a million different kind of beers."

Putting on a mildly surprised expression, I said, "They served you beer? You girls aren't twenty-one yet, are you?"

Ruth Barnes realized she'd just said something she shouldn't have said and tried to offer an explanation. "Well, no . . . not quite. The thing is the places we go regular, they know us, and nobody ever asks us if we're old enough. You won't say anything about that, will you? I'd hate to get Barney's in trouble."

I gave Ruthie a conspiratorial smile and said her secret was safe with me. Then I changed the subject. "I hear the food at Barney's is pretty good. What did you have for dinner last night?"

Looking relieved to have the beer issue out of the way, she said, "I love their chili . . . I had a bowl of it with cornbread. They even put cheese on top. Millie had what she always has, a salad. Millie says she has to watch her weight 'cuz of the movies." After a short pause, Ruthie added, "I know I should do the same thing, but I like to eat."

With a smile that was sympathetic this time, I said, "Me, too. So what time did you leave Barney's?"

There was a subtle change in Ruth Barnes's tone, like I'd finally asked the question she'd been waiting for. "We left Barney's at nine-thirty. I remember 'cuz Millie said how she couldn't stay out late 'cuz she had to be at the studio early in the morning."

Her response sounded almost rehearsed. I said, "That makes sense. What did you do next?"

Ruthie took a deep breath and rattled off another canned reply. "We said goodnight in the parking lot, and we drove home. She left first and I followed her. I was behind her all the way to Crescent Heights, but I got stuck behind some traffic then so I didn't see her after that."

"I see. Ruthie, what do you think happened to Millie?"

That one seemed to stump her. It was as if she'd anticipated my questions about the time they'd left the restaurant and the route they'd taken home, but now I'd thrown her one she didn't expect. After a few seconds' hesitation Ruthie said, "I don't know. She just disappeared." Then, as if suddenly realizing she wasn't showing a whole lot of concern for the whereabouts and well-being of her best friend, she added, "I'm very worried about Millie. I hope she's okay."

Ruthie Barnes wasn't much of an actress, and I was sorely tempted to apply some pressure to see if I could shake a little honesty out of her, but I decided Max Factor's lobby wasn't the place to do that. Instead I said, "Don't worry, we'll find her. I'm sure Millie is just fine. Tell me, though, is Millie in the habit of disappearing? I mean, has anything like this ever happened before?"

"Oh, no, Millie's mom would never stand for anything like that."

Putting on my friendliest smile again, I handed Ruth Barnes one of my business cards and said, "Thank you for your help, Ruthie. If you think of anything else that might be helpful, please call me. My office is just across Hollywood Boulevard in the First National Bank Building."

She accepted my card and nodded silently. As I walked toward Max Factor's front door, I caught a glimpse of Ruth Barnes in one of the mirrors. She was still sitting in her chair with my card in her hand and a slightly bewildered look on her face.

Ruthie knew stuff she wasn't telling me, and most of what she did tell me was a pack of lies designed to throw the cops, and anyone else who asked, off of Diana Dean's trail. My conversation with Miss Dean's best pal removed any lingering doubt I had about her "kidnapping." She'd disappeared all on her own, alright, and she'd recruited Ruthie as an accomplice to help pull it off. I was also pretty sure Mama Gladys was in on the gag. Heck, she might even be the one who came up with the scheme in the first place.

Assuming my clever sleuthing had me on the right track, I was now left with two new questions: Why was Diana Dean hiding, and where the hell was she doing her hiding? Besides Miss Dean, I figured there were probably two people who knew the answers to those questions: Gladys Grebb and Ruthie Barnes. Of the two, Ruthie would be easiest to crack. But to make her spill the beans, I needed the right opportunity to confront her and some undeniable facts to use as leverage. So where would I find the necessary bean-spilling facts? The logical place to look was a beanery—to be specific, Barney's Beanery.

Tess was applying the finishing touches to the inner office doorframe when I got back. I interrupted her long enough to find out if there were any telephone calls demanding my attention. There weren't, so I went back down to my car, pulled out of the parking lot, and made a left turn on Highland.

I followed Highland all the way down to Santa Monica Boulevard and turned right. Had I turned left and driven a mere two-thousand-four-hundred-and-some miles, I would have found myself in Chicago, for I was now at the western end of the highway they call America's Main Street—the Mother Road—Route 66.

In the direction I was headed, however, Route 66 only had a dozen or so miles left of its cross-country run. The Mother Road ended at the Pacific Ocean in Santa Monica, but my destination wasn't even that far. I pulled to the curb in front of Barney's Beanery at eleven-fifteen.

With the exception of large signs reading "Chili" and, below that, "Barney's Beanery" stuck atop its mansard roof and an awning advertising French onion soup over its front door, Barney's looked like a small wood-frame cottage—more like a residence than an eatery. The board siding had been painted white sometime in the dim past, and the trim around the front door and a few large windows was dark green.

I pulled into a driveway on the west side of Barney's and parked in the gravel lot. I stood next to my car for a moment watching traffic zoom past on the busy, two-lane highway out front and imagining what it had looked like last night around nine-thirty. I guessed things had looked about like they did now except it had been dark, the traffic would have been sparser, and there were probably more cars in the lot. At the moment, mine was one of only four automobiles there. The lunch crowd had yet to arrive.

Inside, Barney's ambiance was as deceptive as its exterior, only from this point of view, it looked more like a junk shop than an eatery. The wall decor consisted of old automobile license plates from states near and far, signs with witty sayings, a few hubcaps, and a lot of other stuff most folks would have thrown away long ago.

The dining room was small with a typical diner-style counter down one side and tables lining the other side. The entire room was illuminated by floor lamps stuck here and there between the tables. The only sign of life I could see amongst the clutter was an older fellow wiping glasses with a towel behind a short, scarred wooden bar at the back of the dining room. As I approached, I noticed a large cardboard sign stuck to the edge of a bottle shelf behind the bar. The sign was white with large black letters that said, "Fagots – Stay Out!" The guy behind the bar looked to me like the sort who would be proud of such a sign, even after customers no doubt pointed out its spelling error.

He gave me the once-over as I approached and said, "Which are you, a cop or one of them troublemakers from the Treasury Department?"

"More like the former than the latter."

He looked at me like I'd said something that had nothing to do with his question. Rather than wait for him to figure it out, I said, "I'm a private investigator working with the L.A.P.D. on a missing person case."

"All the same as a cop without the badge," he muttered. Then he said, "Who's missing?"

"One of your customers—a gal named Diana Dean."

"Yeah, I know who you mean. What makes you think she's here?"

"I don't think she's here, but I know she was here last night. I'd like to talk with any of the employees who might have seen her then."

He shook his head and muttered, "Always something." After setting the glass he'd been wiping on a shelf somewhere under the bar, he said, "Only one guy here now who was here last night."

When it came to conversation, this fellow and a brick wall had a lot in common. With my patience wearing thin, I said, "Would you mind asking whoever that might be to come out here so I can have a few words with him?"

"Can't do that."

I went another round with him. "Why not?"

"'Cuz he's the chief cook and he's busy gettin' stuff ready for lunch customers."

"Then how about I go back to the kitchen and talk to him there?"

"Guess you could do that."

At that point a young Mexican lad with a tray full of ketchup bottles came through a door at the right end of the bar. From the noises and smells that came with him, I concluded the kitchen was on the other side of that door. I said, "Don't bother; I can find my way."

He didn't look up from the dirty glass from which he was dry-wiping a lipstick smear, and I walked into Barney's kitchen. There were only two guys in there—any more would have crowded the tiny space to overflowing. One of the two was another young Mexican kid, and the other was a slightly older Mexican fellow wearing a drooping chef's hat and an apron that was probably white when it was new.

Walking over to the fellow under the chef's hat, who was conscientiously stirring the contents of a pot that must have held at least two gallons of chili, I held up my P.I. photostat and said, "Hi. My name's Spicer. I'm working with the L.A. cops on a missing person investigation. I'd like to ask you a few questions if you don't mind."

The cook had a round face with a thin moustache and a pleasant expression. He smiled, and with an accent anyone from Los Angeles immediately recognizes, he said, "Sure, mi amigo, what do you wanna know?"

Showing him the head shot photo of Diana Dean Esther Smith gave me, I said, "Do you recognize this woman?"

He leaned forward to take a good look and said, "Sure I reco'nize her. She's in here all the time with a little redheaded girl, her friend. I think this woman is in the movies or something."

"Yes, she is. Her name is Diana Dean. Do you remember when you saw her here last?"

His smile widened a little. "Sure. I seen her here last night."

"Was her friend, the redhead, with her?"

"Si. They was here together."

"Do you happen to remember what time they left?"

"Sure, I remember. Every night I take a break at nine-thirty—you know, to get out of the heat and have fresh air for a while." He jerked a thumb over his shoulder toward a door at the back of the kitchen and continued, "I go out back there to have a smoke, and last night the actress girl and her friend came out to the parking lot while I was smoking my cigarette."

"What were they doing when you saw them?"

91

He shrugged. "They was just standing there talking for a little while."

"Then what did they do?"

"The blonde girl, she got in her car—she's got one of those big Cadillac cars—and drove away. Then the redhead, she drove away."

"So Diana Dean left first and the redhead followed her, have I got that right?"

"No."

"No? I thought you just said the blonde left first and then the redhead left."

"That's what I say, but the redhead, she don't follow the actress woman. The blonde, she turn right to go in the direction of the ocean, and the redhead girl, she turn left, back to town."

Alarm bells were clanging in my head as I asked, "Are you absolutely sure about that?"

"Si, I am very sure. The blonde woman, she is in very much a big hurry, so much she squeal the tires of her big car when she turn on the highway, so I notice which way she goes. The redheaded woman, she is in not so much a big hurry."

"Have you told the police all this?"

"No, I have seen no police."

"Well, you will, and when you do, please tell them exactly what you told me, especially the part about Diana Dean turning toward the coast when she left here."

He frowned. "That is important?"

"It is very important."

The cook's smile returned. "Then I will do as you ask. You tell the police to come see me. My name is Rudy Gutierrez. You tell them police to ask for Rudy, and I will say to them the same as what I tell you."

"Rudy, thank you. You've got a good memory, and you've been a big help!"

Rudy was beaming. "Sure, amigo. I am happy to help you." Then he added, "The blonde woman, I hope she is not in trouble or anything."

I fibbed just a little. "No, Rudy, she's not in trouble. For a while we thought she might be, but now I know she's okay."

"Bueno! For that I am happy. She is very nice . . . and also muy bonito." Then, as an afterthought, he said, "Hey, Mister Spicer, it is lunchtime. How 'bout I fix you up a big bowl of chili? I just make it fresh!"

The fumes from his chili pot were almost hot enough to make my eyes water from five feet away, so I said, "Thanks, but I'll have to take a rain check on the chili, Rudy. It looks very good, but I have some things I need to do right away."

"Sure, amigo. You come back anytime. The chili pot, she is always on the stove."

Thirteen

I turned west out of Barney's parking lot in the same direction Diana Dean was going the last time anyone saw her—at least the last time anyone we know of saw her. Two blocks later I pulled up next to a public telephone booth at the Shell service station just past La Cienega Boulevard.

Dropping a nickel into the slot, I dialed the Sixth Precinct. This time I only had to wait about thirty seconds before the switchboard operator got Winfield on the line.

"Hello, Johnny. What's up?"

"I may have something useful. Do you have your detective's notes of his interview with Ruth Barnes last night?"

The sound of paper shuffling came down the wire. "Yeah, I've got it right here."

"Skip down to the part about Dean and Barnes leaving Barney's and remind me what Ruth said about that."

After a moment of silence, he said, "Here it is. She said they left at nine-thirty. She remembered that because Miss Dean, or Millie as Barnes calls her, said she couldn't stay out late because she had to be at the studio early in the morning. Then Barnes said Miss Dean left the restaurant parking lot first, and Miss Barnes followed her all the way to Crescent Heights Avenue, where she got stuck behind some traffic and lost sight of Miss Dean. That the part you wanted?"

"That's the part. It's almost word for word what Ruth Barnes told me about two hours ago, and it's a big fat fib."

"It is? What makes you think so?"

"I just interviewed a fellow named Rudy Gutierrez. He's the cook at Barney's Beanery, and he was there last night. In fact, he was out in the parking lot taking a cigarette break when Dean and Barnes left at nine-thirty."

"So?"

"So Rudy clearly remembers Dean in her big Cadillac turning right on Route 66 and Barnes turning left. In other words, Dean was heading for the coast instead of her home, and Barnes did not follow her like she claims."

Winfield sounded surprised. "Well, how about that!"

"Yeah, how about that. It doesn't prove Dean wasn't kidnapped, but it sure proves there's something rotten in Denmark with the story her mother and Ruthie Barnes have been handing us."

"It does that alright. What the hell are they up to?"

"I don't have any idea, but I'm damned sure gonna find out. In the meantime, I suggest you get a detective over to talk with Rudy Gutierrez so you'll have it all on the record."

"I'll have someone over there within the hour."

"And if you don't mind another suggestion, it might be a real good idea to let Detective Danny over at Gladys Grebb's in on this. He's in a good position to keep an eye open for something fishy if he knows to look for it."

"I was just thinking the same thing."

"I take it there hasn't been any word of a ransom demand?"

"Nothing so far."

It was time to ask the big question. "Tell me, Bob, are Ruth Barnes' lie and the lack of a ransom demand enough to keep the feds out of this?"

Winfield took a few seconds to think about that. Finally he said, "Yeah, I think I'd be justified in waiting another twenty-four hours to see what turns up."

That was what I wanted to hear. Keeping the FBI out of the case would also keep Jack Warner happy. I asked, "Anything new at that end?"

"No. The patrol officers I sent to canvas Gladys Grebb's neighborhood came back empty-handed. We've sent the sheriff and all the local police departments in the county be-on-the-lookout notices on Dean and her car, but nothing's come back from that yet. I've got a detective out at Warner Brothers talking to that wardrobe woman you mentioned, but I haven't heard anything from him either. His next step will be to follow up on your idea about looking into Diana Dean's background at Universal. That's it so far."

"It seems like you've got all the bases covered."

Sounding doubtful, Winfield said, "I guess so, at least all the bases we know about so far. What's your next move?"

I knew where I was going next, but I wasn't particularly proud of what I planned to do, so I fibbed to Winfield. "I'm not sure yet, Bob. I think I'll get myself some lunch and think all this through."

"Okay. Stay in touch, okay?"

"Sure, Bob. You do the same. If you come up with anything, you can leave a message for me with my secretary."

I could hear the smile in Winfield's voice when he replied. "You have a secretary now? The private detective business must be picking up."

"Well, it's a temporary thing; a friend is helping me out for a few days."

Feigning astonishment, he said, "You have a friend? That's even more amazing than you having a secretary!"

I gave him some of his own right back. "Listen, flatfoot, you keep talkin' like that and I'll let you solve your own damned case. Then where would you be? You'd have to actually do something to earn that big fat paycheck the city gives you every week."

"Oh, no! Even you wouldn't do an awful thing like that!"

"I might. Talk with you later, Bob."

I hung up and smiled to myself. It was good to know Winfield hadn't lost his sense of humor over Diana Dean's disappearance. A cop without a sense of humor just isn't any fun at all.

Adding another nickel to the telephone company's coffers, I called my office. Tess sounded very businesslike. "Good afternoon, Jonathon Spicer Investigation Agency."

"Hey, good lookin', what's cookin'?"

"Oh, hi, Johnny. I finished the painting and your new office chairs are here. They look pretty classy."

"I can't wait to see 'em. Any calls?"

"No, no calls. How are you doing?"

"I'm makin' some progress. I'll tell you about that later. Right now I'm going to get some lunch."

"You didn't have any of Barney's famous chili for lunch?"

"Not on your tintype, Kiddo. I was sweatin' just bein' in the kitchen where they make that stuff."

"And you call yourself an Angelino!"

"Not often. After lunch I'm going out to Santa Monica. I'm gonna pay a call on our old pal, Detective Lieutenant Luther Carson."

It took a moment for Tess to connect the name to a memory. "That awful man? Why on earth would you want to see him again?"

"Because I need a favor from him."

"Well, good luck with that! And please try to stay out of his jail this time."

"Do my best. I'll see you after I get back from Santa Monica."

I could tell Tess wasn't entirely kidding when she said sourly, "That is, *if* you get back from Santa Monica."

Several blocks later, just before I came to Doheny Drive and ritzy Beverly Hills, I pulled to the curb in front of a hole-in-the-wall sandwich shop. Inside, I ordered a ham on rye and a cup of coffee. While munching my sandwich, I gave some thought to my next stop and why Tess was concerned about my going there.

Detective Lieutenant Carson of the Santa Monica Police Department is a crooked cop. I know that for certain because nine months or so ago I'd tangled with Frank Dragna, the boss of L.A.'s number one crime family. Through no choice of her own, Tess was with me when I was forced to do what Dragna called a favor. It was either that or we would end up as fish food in Santa Monica Bay. The entire experience made a lasting impression on Tess.

The favor I'd done for Dragna involved delivering the loot from an unauthorized bank heist to Carson so the lieutenant could square things with the good citizens of Santa Monica and continue looking the other way when Dragna needed him to. The details aren't important, but the outcome is. Carson, who'd sooner have locked me up and thrown away the key, was given to believe I was one of Dragna's boys. To him that meant I was in the know and was a guy who could louse up the profitable arrangement the lieutenant had going with Dragna.

On that occasion, Carson's last words were to get the hell out of his town and stay out, but we both knew that was a bluff. Now I needed Carson to do something for me, so I was about to call that bluff.

What I needed Carson to do was turn his town upside down and shake Diana Dean out of wherever she was hiding. Of course, I didn't know for sure she was in Santa Monica, but it seemed a likely choice for her. Being a celebrity of sorts, Miss Dean was accustomed to her comforts, and Santa Monica, being a resort town, was the handiest place to find those comforts.

Fortified with the ham sandwich and a cup of strong, black coffee, I followed Santa Monica Boulevard to within a few blocks of its terminus at Ocean Avenue in the city for which it was named and turned left on Fourth Street. Then I made a right on Colorado Boulevard, and another left on Main Street, which put me in front of Santa Monica's snazzy, deco-style City Hall. I parked across the street and headed for the first-floor cop coop occupying the northwest corner of the city's monument to graft and corruption.

I gave the duty officer at the counter my name and told him I wanted to see Carson. He made a call and Carson slithered up a moment or two later. He was clearly overjoyed at seeing me again. "Spicer, I thought I told you to stay the hell out of my town."

"That you did, Lieutenant, but I just can't get enough of your charming personality. Besides, we have mutual friends, and I was sure you wouldn't mind me dropping in for a chat."

The "mutual friends" bit made the situation clear to Carson. He glared at me, glanced over at the duty officer who was waiting nearby to see what happened next, and said in a calmer tone, "Alright, Spicer. Come on back to my office."

He closed the door and sat behind his desk. I plunked myself down in a chair opposite him, and he said, "Okay, what the hell do you want?"

"Just a small favor."

"And why the hell should I do you any favors?"

"Come on, Lieutenant, we both know the answer to that question, don't we?"

Carson sighed, resigned to his fate, and said, "Yeah, what do you need?"

I leaned forward and dropped one of Diana Dean's head shots on his desk. He looked at the photo and asked, "Who the hell is this?"

"Her professional name is Diana Dean, aka Millie Grebb. She's an up-and-coming movie actress who might be taking a short vacation in your town—a vacation, I might add, she and her mother staged to look like a kidnapping. You should have gotten a be-on-the-lookout flier about her from the L.A.P.D."

Still staring at Diana Dean's picture, Carson shrugged. "Maybe, but I haven't seen it. So what do you want me to do about this?"

"I just want you to send a couple of Santa Monica's finest around to the high-class hotels and such to find her. If you look for her car, Miss Dean shouldn't be too hard to locate. She drives a brand new, shiny red Cadillac convertible, California license number three-C-two-two-seven. She would most likely be registered under the name Millie or Millicent Grebb. That's with two Bs."

Carson turned Diana Dean's photo over and noted my description of her car and its license on the back. "Alright, what do you want me to do with her if we find her?"

I flipped one of my business cards onto his desk. "Just give me a call and let me know where she is so I can pay her a visit."

He nodded and looked up at me. "I take it you want to find this gal before L.A.P.D. does."

"I do, Lieutenant, but only to have a conversation with her. The important thing here is time. If Miss Dean is in your fair city, I'd like to know about it today. Think you can handle that?"

Carson sighed again and said, "Yeah, if she's in town, I'll find her for you, but this squares us, right? No more favors."

"Sure, Lieutenant. No more favors." I was tempted to add "until I need another one," but didn't. I suppose I should have felt bad about using the Dragna connection that way, but I didn't. I was just making Carson do what he got paid to do—at least what he was paid by the City of Santa Monica to do.

"Alright, Spicer, you'll be hearing from me."

"Soon, Lieutenant Carson?"

"Yeah, Spicer, soon."

Fourteen

Putting Santa Monica in my rearview mirror, I set sail for Burbank. I needed to tell Jack Warner there was little doubt left that Diana Dean's disappearance was a put up job. I could accomplish that chore most quickly on the telephone, but that meant going through a switchboard with ears. Anything I wanted to say to Warner confidentially had to be said in person or it would be all over the lot faster than you could say Jack Robinson.

The shortest route to Warner Brothers was Santa Monica Boulevard back to Hollywood and over the Cahuenga Pass, but given the road construction there, I decided the long way around might be quicker. The long way around involved turning north onto Sepulveda Boulevard in West Los Angeles and following it through the westernmost pass over the Santa Monica Mountains and down into the San Fernando Valley. From there I could take U.S. 101—Ventura Boulevard—east along the northern edge of the mountains, skirt the massive Universal Studios lot, and end up in Burbank.

Traffic was light, giving me some time to think about Diana Dean and the two remaining questions I had regarding her disappearance. If my guess about her holing up somewhere in Santa Monica proved correct, I'd have the answer to one of those questions. That left the matter of why she decided to disappear in the first place.

With what I had to go on at the moment, the only explanation that made any sort of sense was fear. Was Miss Dean really so afraid for her life after the incident on Sound Stage Fifteen that she went into hiding? Given her hysterical reaction to learning someone intentionally dropped that Klieg light on the set, fear was certainly a possibility, but something told me there was more to it than that.

True, Diana Dean knew damned well Jack Warner intended to hold her to her contract and go ahead with the shooting of Thunderstruck. He'd made that clear, so if fear was her only motive for disappearing, she and her mother might have figured lawyers were going to be involved sooner or later and running away to hide might ultimately help convince a jury she really feared for her life. It was a risky move, though, because it put her at risk of losing her first starring role. Worse, crossing Jack Warner was a real good way to end a career in the motion picture business.

Another possibility was that Dean and her mother saw the situation as an opportunity to make headlines, and they thought up a publicity stunt to take advantage of the circumstances. It certainly wouldn't be the first time such a stunt was attempted.

Back in the twenties, popular radio evangelist Aimee Semple McPherson tried something along those lines with disastrous results that pretty much ended a profitable career in the soul-saving business. But even if Diana and Gladys thought they could succeed where Aimee failed, they had to realize Jack Warner would be furious over such a stunt. He had me doing everything I could to keep the Thunderstruck mess out of the papers, and if they screwed that up, the result would again be the end of Dean's career in films.

No, there had to be more to it, an explanation that actually made sense. If I was right about that, the "more to it" might also shed light on the rest of the Thunderstruck mystery.

I walked into Jack Warner's outer office a few minutes before three o'clock and tossed my fedora on the hat rack next to the hall door. The door to Warner's inner office was closed. Esther Smith looked up from her desk and said, "Good afternoon, Mister Spicer. Do you want to see Mister Warner?"

"If he's not too busy, I have a piece of news for him."

Esther used the intercom gadget on her desk to convey that message to her boss, and his tinny response was something to the effect that he could only spare me a few minutes. She said, "You can go right in."

Entering Warner's inner office, I found him looking at a screenplay. There was a stack of five or six more off to one side of his desk. Was one of them the next candidate for a Best Picture Oscar? Could be.

Warner tossed the screenplay aside and said, "What do you have for me, Spicer?"

"It's not a lot, Jack, but it is conclusive proof of something we pretty much suspected—that Diana Dean disappeared of her own free will. In a nutshell, Dean's pal, Ruth Barnes, lied about what happened when they left the restaurant last night. She told the police she followed Dean back to Hollywood, but she couldn't have because they went in opposite directions. Ruth went home to Hollywood, alright, but Diana Dean went the other way on Route 66—west toward Santa Monica."

Warner frowned. "How the hell do you know that?"

"The cook at Barney's Beanery was outside taking a smoke break when Dean and Barnes left last night. He clearly remembers Diana Dean's red Cadillac turning right out of the parking lot instead of left. That throws Ruth Barnes' story into a cocked hat and pretty much proves she was in on a scheme that Dean, and maybe her mother, concocted to make her disappearance look suspicious."

Warner exploded. "That conniving little bitch! This stunt is costing us thousands!" He slammed his fist on the desk hard enough to make the stack of screenplays jump at least an inch. He bellowed, "Esther! Get in here!"

No more than two seconds later the door to Warner's inner office popped open and Esther appeared, steno pad in hand. "Yes, sir?"

"Call Wallis. Tell him to find a replacement for Diana Dean in Thunderstruck. She's out as of right now! Tell him to be quick about it!"

Esther glanced at me, no doubt wondering what the hell I'd told her boss to get Diana Dean canned. To Warner, she said, "Yes, sir. Anything else?"

"Yes! Call Volodin and tell him Dean's out. Tell him I want to see him before he leaves the lot today. And call the head of our legal department . . . what the hell is his name?"

"Ron MacDonald."

"Yeah, him. Tell him I want his butt in here this afternoon, too. I've got a job for him."

Esther Smith simply said, "I'll take care of these things right away, Mister Warner." She took another quick glance at me and closed the door.

Calming a little, Warner shook his head and said, "I give that woman the break of a lifetime, and how does she repay me? By pulling a stunt like this. That's gratitude for you!"

Feeling almost guilty for bringing Jack Warner news that was costing Diana Dean her career, I said, "I hope you're not jumping the gun here. I mean, Diana Dean could have a good reason for disappearing."

"There is no good reason for disappearing in the middle of a production without saying a word. None at all!"

"Still, it might be smart to find out the whole story before . . . ."

"I'm not paying you to question my decisions, Spicer! You just catch the bastard who's trying to ruin my movie!" As an afterthought, Warner added, "And find that Dean bitch so I can have the pleasure of firing her in person! Now what else do you have for me?"

"Nothing specific. On the chance Miss Dean might be holed up in Santa Monica, I have people checking the hotels there. I should hear back on that today or tomorrow morning at the latest.

"And as soon as we're done here, I'm meeting with my man who's been digging deeper into the sabotage attempts. He may have something new to go on. With a little luck I'll have some answers for you tomorrow."

Still fuming over Diana Dean's disloyalty, Warner said, "Yes, do that. I'm sick and tired of you bringing me bad news all the time. Bring me some good news for a change!"

In the outer office, Esther Smith looked at me expectantly. She wanted to know what the hell I'd told her boss that caused such a ruckus. I started to give her a brief explanation, but was interrupted by another bellow from Warner. "Esther!"

She grabbed her steno pad and said, "Tell me tomorrow, Mister Spicer."

Esther disappeared through the inner office doorway, and grabbing my hat, I disappeared in the opposite direction. I was nearly back to my car when I spotted Dmitriy Volodin heading for the administration building. He looked like a competitor in one of those fast walking races, moving as fast as he could without actually breaking into a run.

We arrived at the rear bumper of my Chrysler simultaneously. He was huffing and puffing like an overworked steam engine. His expression was a mask of agitation. "Mister Spicer, you are having just seen Mister Warner, maybe?"

"Yes, Dmitriy, I have."

"Then, maybe, you can be telling me what is happening. His secretary is just calling me. She is saying Diana Dean is fired from Thunderstruck, and I am to be coming immediately to see Mister Warner. Are you knowing why these things are happening?"

I nodded. "Yes, Dmitriy, I know why Mister Warner fired Diana Dean, but you'll have to ask him for the reason because it's confidential and I can't say anything more about it."

Now Volodin's expression was approaching panic. "Mister Spicer, please, you can be giving me, maybe, a hint?"

I would have expected Thunderstruck's director to be upset over the news that his leading lady had been sacked in mid-production, but Volodin's reaction seemed to be more than that. On the other hand, Diana Dean's dismissal could have been the last straw after all of the other problems he'd experienced with the film. I felt a little sorry for the guy, but not enough to violate a client's confidence. I said, "Dmitriy, just go see Warner. I'm sure he'll tell you the whole story."

Volodin said nothing more. He just shook his head in frustration and rushed off. I climbed into the driver's seat and looked back just in time to see the anxious director disappear through the administration building's back door. As the door closed behind him I realized I'd just witnessed a demonstration of the absolute power wielded by Jack Warner.

Dmitriy Volodin is one of the most successful directors in the business. He could write his own ticket at any of the major studios, and yet here he was quaking in his boots like a school kid summoned to the principal's office. I wondered what it felt like to have Jack Warner's kind of clout.

It took me most of thirty minutes to travel the five miles of construction-clogged highway between the Warner Brothers lot and my office. It was already quarter to five by the time I pulled my dust-covered Chrysler into the parking lot behind the First National Bank Building. Making myself a note to stop by Jack's carwash stand tomorrow for one of his twenty-five-cent-special wash jobs, I climbed the back stairs to the second floor.

Walking into my inner office, I found Tess and Will Gardner seated in the new armchairs from the Hollywood Hotel. The chairs were upholstered in a grayish-blue geometric pattern that went well with the new paint on my office walls. Tess and Will were chatting up a storm.

"I see you two have already met."

Will stood to shake my hand, and Tess said, "Yes, Will has been telling me stories about the famous Johnny Spicer."

I shot Will a mock glare and said, "Don't believe a word he says. It's all professional jealousy."

Will feigned a hurt look. "Hey, is that any way to act? I was only telling her the good stuff about you."

Slipping into my desk chair, which looked shabbier than ever next to the new paint and guest chairs, I said in a sarcastic tone, "That must have been a short conversation. Any calls, Tess?"

"Only one. Jack Warner's secretary called about two-thirty to say Mister Warner wanted a status report on the investigation."

"I just came from talking to Warner, so we can cross that one off the list." Turning to Will, I said, "Okay, give me the lowdown on all the clues you picked up on the Warner lot today."

Before Will could answer my question, Tess stood and said, "I'll wait in the outer office while you two talk."

I said, "No reason for you to do that unless Will has more stories about me."

Tess sat again and Will said, "No, no more stories. As for what I learned today, it isn't much. I started off talking with a fellow I know in Warner's fire department. He told me the New York Street fire was started with gasoline from a one-gallon can that could have come from the studio transportation department. All the paint was burned off the can, but it's identical to the ones the transportation guys use to refuel vehicles and equipment that need gas out on the lot. I checked with them to see if they were missing a can, but the guy I talked to said they have so many of 'em, one could disappear and nobody would notice."

Nodding, I asked, "What about the rags found at the fire scene?"

Consulting his notebook, Will said, "Not much to go on there, either. The rags were just about entirely consumed by the fire, but the scraps they recovered appear to be pieces of white cotton with pale blue stripes, the kind of material that might be used to make a shirt or just about anything else.

"Next, I went over to see Oliver Glick, the camera operator. My impression is that Warner was right about him. The guy's a real pro with a lot of experience. I can't see him making the sort of mistake that would result in a can of blank film.

"Glick said that could only happen one of three ways. One is that the film was in the camera, but wasn't threaded right, so it never went past the lens. Glick said he would have noticed any problem of that sort right off.

"The second way blank film could come out of a camera was if the shutter mechanism failed. He said he checked that immediately after learning there was something wrong with the film. The camera was working just as it should. Apparently Glick does all the maintenance himself on the cameras he uses. I get the idea he's a stickler for details."

I said, "That's usually the case with any technician who's really good at his job. What's the third way the film could have come out blank?"

"The third way is the film never went through the camera in the first place, and that's what Glick thinks happened. He figures someone intentionally swapped his can of exposed film for a can of blank film, and it had to be intentional because they use a check-and-double-check system for labeling film cans. He's also certain the swap must have been made in the lab because he personally removed the exposed film from the camera, filled out the labels, and hand-carried the film to the lab.

"So my next stop was the lab, and I can see how the swap could have been done. They store all the unexposed film stock in one room and the film brought in for processing is kept in another room, but the place is full of technicians all running around helter-skelter. It would have been easy for one of them to swap Glick's labels to a can of unexposed film and then to dispose of the film Glick shot."

As I made notes of Will's report in my own notebook, a question occurred to me. "Is there any chance of lifting prints from the film can they returned to Glick?"

"I thought of that, but it's no good. Those film cans are covered with prints because they're legitimately handled by a bunch of people. The culprit's prints are probably on the can, but there's no way of picking him out from all the others."

"I see. What else have you got?"

"Well, I went over to the personnel department last. At first I had a problem getting my hands on the files of the people who'd been recently fired or left Warner's for some other reason. I had to wait for the old gal in charge to clear it with Jack Warner's office.

"Once I started going through the files, though, I knew I was on a wild goose chase. Fifty-some people left the studio just between August and November when they started shooting Thunderstruck, and at least half of those were either fired or laid off. Worse, the personnel files are vague about why most of those folks were let go. Just the same, I went through all of them in hopes of finding something that stood out, but came up empty. After that, I came over here."

I studied the notes I'd made for a moment and then said, "Going back to the rags used in the fire, is there a big enough piece left to show the people in Warner's costume shop?"

Will looked a little surprised. "Yes, I suppose so. I didn't think of that. I'll put it on my list for tomorrow. I'll also take the sample over to props and see if anyone there recognizes it. I take it you think this is an inside job."

"That's a strong possibility. Our culprit obviously knows his way around the lot and must be familiar with how things are done. Also, it seems like a stranger in the film lab would be taking a big chance of being noticed."

Will gave this a moment's thought. "True. He also knows something about Thunderstruck's shooting schedule. Unfortunately, knowing it's an inside job doesn't help us much. A couple thousand people enter and leave that lot every day."

"The thing we need to crack this case is a motive. We have to think more along the lines of who has a reason for wanting the film shut down—either a financial reason or a grudge."

He frowned. "That's the tough part. There are too many people involved. Could Diana Dean's disappearance point us toward a possible motive?"

I shrugged. "Maybe, but we have to locate her first and get her talking." Then I gave Will a summary of my day, beginning with interviewing Ruth Barnes and ending with Warner sacking Dean.

Will said, "Ya gotta wonder what's going in that dame's head. She had to know Warner would blow a fuse if he found out her disappearance was staged to look like a kidnapping or something."

Turning to Tess, who'd been quietly absorbing our conversation, I asked, "What do you think? I mean, does what Diana Dean did make any more sense from a woman's point of view than it does from a man's?"

Tess considered my question. "Well, she has good reason to be afraid. It must seem to her that the studio is a dangerous place right now and that nobody is really looking out for her safety, but my sense of it is there's something deeper going on. Do you know if she's romantically involved with anyone? Love can make a woman— or a man, for that matter—do things that don't make sense."

Will jumped on that idea with both feet. "Tess is right, Johnny! It would be a good idea for us to look into Dean's love life."

"Okay, Will, how do you propose we go about doing that?"

"You could talk to her pal, that Barnes gal, again. If anyone would know about a guy in Dean's life, it would be her. You might try Dean's mother on that subject, too."

I thought about Will's suggestions. "Gladys Grebb is playing things too cagey. She's suspicious of every question I ask her. Barnes is trying to be cautious, too, but she's not nearly so good at it as Gladys, so she might let something slip. I was already planning a visit to Miss Barnes this evening to confront her about the lies she told us. Tess, are you up to coming along with me and observing?"

"I could do that."

Then another idea popped into my head. "I just thought of someone else who would know if Diana Dean has a man or men in her life—Bessie Klein, Dean's wardrobe assistant. Will, take a shot at her tomorrow, but be careful what you say. Bessie has Hedda and Louella beat hands down when it comes to gossip."

Will made a note in his book. "Okay, that's two jobs on my list for tomorrow—talking to the Klein woman and showing the fire rag fragment around. What else?"

"You know anybody out at Universal Studios who could help you get on the lot?"

He pondered my question and said, "No. You want me to go out there?"

"Yes. Diana Dean started out at Universal, but she left a few months before her contract was up to take the role in Thunderstruck at Warner Brothers. There might be something useful to be learned if we get to the right people."

Will said, "Maybe Jack Warner could help us get into Universal."

"I don't think so—at least I don't want to go that route. When I talked with Jack this morning, I specifically asked him if there was any chance someone at Universal was behind the Thunderstruck sabotage, if there was any bad blood there because of Dean bailing out of her contract early. That question struck a nerve with Warner. I don't know why, but there's something there he isn't telling us. It might be nothing, but I don't want to set off any more fireworks with Jack right now."

"Okay, I'll go out to Universal and see if my charm will get me through the gate."

I grinned at him. "Oh, that'll do the trick, alright."

Will grinned back. "Look who's talkin', Mister Personality."

Fifteen

The chimes atop the gothic tower of the Methodist church a block to the north were joyously announcing the arrival of the six o'clock hour as I closed and latched my office windows. Tess had opened them earlier in the day to let the fresh paint fumes out, but now the late November evening breezes were bringing in a chill that would make a Frigidaire jealous.

Below me a long string of headlights inched its way through the intersection of Hollywood and Highland—weary workaday minions returning to the comforts of hearth and home. Nighttime was descending upon the big city.

I thought about Will Gardner out there somewhere in a similar scene on the Cahuenga pass. He'd left for Burbank just in time to join the grand daily exodus to suburbia. There were probably better ways and places to live, but they didn't have what Hollywood had.

Tess moved to my side, buttoning her coat as she said, "I'm ready when you are, Johnny."

"Okay, let's go."

I turned to retrieve my fedora from the coat rack, and the telephone on my desk sounded off. I answered the call and the voice at the other end said, "Spicer, this is Carson. That dame you're lookin' for ain't in Santa Monica. A couple of my boys checked every hotel in town and didn't find hide nor hair of her."

"Okay. It was a long shot and I guessed wrong. Thanks for the search."

"Don't mention it, Spicer, and don't hesitate to never call me again."

I was too tired to think of a snappy reply, but Carson wouldn't have heard it anyway. All that was coming down the telephone line by then was dead air. I dropped the handset back into its cradle and said, "That was our pal, Lieutenant Carson. He says his boys just scoured the whole town for Diana Dean and came up empty."

Tess frowned. "That's a shame. I was really hoping he'd find her."

"Me, too. But that would have been too easy. Let's get out of here."

Down in the First National Bank's parking lot, across the service alley behind the building, I opened the passenger door for Tess, climbed into the driver's seat, and looked at my wristwatch. Six-fifteen. I said, "Ruth Barnes is probably having her dinner right about now. What do you say to getting ourselves a quick bite before we go over there?"

"Sounds good."

The nearest place around to get a decent quick bite was Carpenter's Sandwich Drive-In on the north side of Sunset just east of Vine. Most times of the day I would simply head south on Highland, but in deference to that street's long line of traffic heading toward the Cahuenga pass, I turned east out of the lot and drove down the service alley to McCadden at the other end of the block. Since McCadden doesn't really go anywhere most drivers want to be, it was free of traffic. I shot across the empty street and continued along the service alley to Las Palmas, where I turned right and caught a break in the form of a green light that let me zip right across Hollywood Boulevard. From there, getting to Carpenter's was a simple matter of zigging and zagging in a southeasterly direction until we reached Sunset and Vine.

Carpenter's Sandwich Drive-In consists of a forty-foot diameter octagonal building surrounded by parking places where cars nose in like hogs at a trough. Once parked, a young woman called a carhop shows up to take your order. A few minutes later she returns with a reasonable facsimile of whatever you asked for.

The menu at Carpenter's is painted on signs above an awning surrounding the service counter. They offer a variety of sandwiches, but the best deal for my money is a hamburger that can be had for a mere fifteen cents. If you're feeling flush, you can throw in another fifteen cents and have a beer to wash down your burger. It's the sort of touch that makes Hollywood the glamour capital of the world. Here you can become a drunk driver without ever leaving the comfort of your automobile.

We ordered a couple of burgers, and while we waited for them, I briefed Tess on how I planned to approach my second interview with Ruth Barnes. "Our primary purpose is finding out why she lied about Diana Dean last night. It would also be nice if we could get something out of her about Miss Dean's romantic interest or interests."

"That might be tough. Girls tell each other that sort of thing in confidence. If Ruth is a loyal friend, she won't volunteer anything she might know about who her friend is seeing."

I nodded agreement and said, "I pretty much figured that, so I might have to play it sort of rough with her."

"What do you mean by rough?"

"When I talked with her this morning I went out of my way to make her feel easy about our conversation. That was a chore, because she clearly wasn't enjoying the experience. Tonight, I'll start off easy again, but if Ruthie is being loyal, I'll pull a switcheroo by smacking her with some tough talk—something along the lines of the third degree cops use in dime pulp novels."

Tess frowned. "That might scare her into spilling whatever beans she has to spill, but it could just as easily turn her into a sobbing wreck, which isn't going to get you what you want, either."

I smiled. "That's where you come in, Sweetheart. If she falls apart, your role is to be the sympathetic pal who comforts the sobbing little girl and reprimands me for being such a brute."

"I thought I was just along to observe."

"That, too, but if Ruthie isn't cooperative and I have to drag out the tough-guy act, I'll need your help to make it work. Is that okay with you, or would you rather I dropped you off at home and tackled the job on my own?"

Tess gave my question a lot of thought. Finally she threw a look of sadness at me and said, "No, Johnny, you don't have to take me home. I'll help you." Then she added, "Sometimes your job isn't much fun, is it?"

"Sometimes it isn't."

We finished our burgers more or less in silence. Tess might eventually accept the seamier side of my work, but it would take some time. Assuming, that is, she ever accepted it.

I pulled out of Carpenter's and pointed us west on Sunset. It was nearly seven, and traffic was thinning out. I cruised out Sunset a dozen or so blocks and negotiated a right turn onto Orange Drive just beyond my old alma mater, Hollywood High School.

Orange jogs half a block west at Hollywood Boulevard and then dead ends at Franklin Boulevard a few blocks later. I pulled to the curb just before we got to Franklin. The faintly illuminated turret and towers of a massive turn of the century chateau built by banker Rollin Lane glowered down at us from above the trees across Franklin.

Ruth Barnes' apartment building was on our left, and it didn't glower. Typical of the apartments in this part of town, it was a two-story, L-shaped structure that wrapped around the corner onto Franklin. We walked across Orange and up a concrete walk that ended at two apartment doors with an opening between them for a stairway to the second floor apartments on the Orange Drive side of the L. The apartment door on the left was dark brown and wore the brass numbers 1-7-9-1. I picked a spot on the door just below the numbers and knocked on it.

Ruth opened the door a few inches and peered out at us. Even in the gloom she recognized me. I could tell that because of the disappointment that immediately washed over her face.

Sounding as friendly as I know how, I said, "Good evening, Ruth. I apologize for barging in unannounced like this, but I thought of a few more questions I need to ask you."

She nodded and, looking resigned to her fate, opened the door wider to let us in. As Tess stepped over the threshold ahead of me, I made introductions. "Ruth, I'd like you to meet my friend, Tess Gallagher. Tess, meet Ruth Barnes."

Tess smiled a friendly smile and said, "I'm pleased to meet you, Ruth."

Mumbling something that might have been "Nice to meet you, too," Ruth closed the door behind us. She was barefoot below a faded pink housedress that fit her better when it was new. Now it emphasized bulges she didn't have back then.

Over the years I've had occasion to visit several of the many apartment buildings scattered along this section of Franklin Boulevard, so Ruthie's living room was about what I expected. The entry door was at the extreme right edge of the room, which extended across the width of the apartment. The walls were painted a dingy apartment house white, and the floor was scuffed hardwood. The furniture—all fine examples of the cheap apartment house modern style—included a gray sofa against the windowless front wall to our left, two similarly gray armchairs facing the sofa with a blond wood end table between them, and a blond wood coffee table in front of the sofa. The room was lit by a ceiling fixture with two bulbs. Only one of them was lit.

A hallway that lined up with the front door extended back through the apartment, passing doors that presumably opened onto a bedroom and a bathroom and ended in the kitchen. A back door, also aligned with the front door, opened out onto whatever was behind the apartment. It was the Hollywood version of a shotgun house.

Still not having a lot to say, Ruthie gestured toward the sofa. Tess and I sat on it, and as I took out my notebook, Ruthie deposited herself into one of the armchairs opposite the sofa. I said, "Ruthie, we have a lot of people out looking for Miss Dean, but so far there is no sign of her. I'm hoping you can give us a little more to go on."

As if I'd pushed a button, she quickly replied, "I already told you everything I know about last night. We left Barney's Beanery at nine-thirty, and I followed . . . ."

"No, Ruthie. That's not what happened."

Her mouth slammed shut and her eyes flashed panic. I continued, "We know that's not what happened because someone at the restaurant clearly remembers seeing Miss Dean's Cadillac turn right out of the parking lot onto Route Sixty-Six and you turning left. That means you could not have followed her back to Hollywood the way you told us you did."

I was expecting Ruthie to at least say the witness wasn't remembering right, but she didn't even put up that much of a fight. Instead her eyes filled with tears and she buried her face in her hands. I glanced at Tess and she took the cue.

Kneeling next to the sobbing girl, Tess put a hand on her shoulder and said, "Ruthie, we're not trying to make trouble for you or your friend, but we know Millie didn't really mysteriously disappear last night. She disappeared all on her own, and there's nothing wrong with that. I'm sure she had a good reason.

"The problem is you told the police a fib, and they know it. Lying to the police when they're investigating a crime will get you into big trouble. It could get Millie into trouble, too. But there's still time to fix all that before things get any worse than they already are."

Ruthie's sobs quieted a little. She looked into Tess's face, saying, "How can I fix things?"

Tess took a handkerchief out of her purse and handed it to Ruthie. "By telling us where Millie is hiding and why she's hiding. Johnny and the police will protect Millie if she's in danger, but they can't do that until they know where she is."

Ruthie used Tess's handkerchief to dab at the tear streaks on her cheeks, but new ones appeared as quickly as she wiped the old ones away. I heard a note of desperation in her voice as she said, "But I don't know where Millie is. I really don't."

Tess said, "Okay, Ruthie. I believe you. Can you tell us what Millie said to you last night?"

Interrupted by an occasional sob, Ruthie spilled her guts. "She said she had to hide out until . . . until it was safe to go back to the studio because someone was trying . . . trying to kill her . . . but her boss would fire her if she just left . . . so she was going to disappear mysteriously . . . like maybe someone kidnapped her. That way . . . that way her boss couldn't fire her."

Gently, Tess said, "But she didn't say where she was going?"

"No . . . no. Millie said it would be better if I didn't know."

Tess looked over at me, sort of shrugging like she didn't know what to ask next. I picked it up from there. "Ruthie, if you had to guess, where do you think Millie might go? I mean, is there any place you can think of where she's gone before—someplace she feels safe?"

Still dabbing at her tears, Ruth Barnes sat back in her chair a little, and Tess moved to the second armchair next to the girl. After appearing to think about my question, Ruthie shook her head and said, "I can't think of anyplace like that . . . where Millie would go."

I tried a different tack. "Do you think Gladys Grebb knows where Millie went?"

She didn't have to think about that one very long. "I'm sure she does, but I don't think she'll tell you. I think this whole thing was Missus Grebb's idea, and she can be very stubborn, especially if she thinks she's right. So I don't think she'll say where Millie is."

Knowing Gladys Grebb, I tended to agree with her about that. I said, "Okay, Ruthie, one more question. Does Millie have a boyfriend? I mean one she sees more regularly than anyone else?"

Ruthie nodded. "I think so, but I don't know who he is. Millie once told me about this fellow she met that she really liked, but she was kind of secret about him."

"Do you remember when it was that she mentioned this fellow?"

Ruthie was thinking again. For a girl who didn't seem very good at thinking, she spent a lot of time doing it. Finally she said, "It was a few months ago, back when she was still working at Universal Studios, before she went over to where she is now . . . Warner Brothers, I think."

I made a note of that and stood up. I was suddenly very weary of the dreary Miss Barnes. Tess took my not-so-subtle hint, and giving the girl one last reassuring pat on the back, she said, "Chin up, Ruthie. You did the right thing by telling the truth. Don't worry, Johnny will find Millie and make sure she's okay."

Ruthie looked up at Tess and, with another sob, said, "I sure hope so."

Back in my car, I turned to Tess. "Thanks, Kiddo. You saved the day in there. If you hadn't stepped in, I think Ruthie would have gone completely hysterical on me."

Tess leaned over and gave me a kiss on the cheek. "You're welcome, Johnny. You know, I feel sorry for Ruthie. I really do. She tried so hard to be loyal to her friend, but Ruthie is an emotional girl. She's just not cut out to be devious."

From Ruth Barnes' place we were only a few minutes from the Montero Apartments on Yucca. I saw Tess to her door where she gave me a squeeze and said, "Go upstairs and get yourself some sleep. I want you nice and rested for tomorrow night."

My brain was foggier than I thought. It took a minute for me to shift gears and figure out what she was talking about. "Oh, you mean Bogart's party."

Tess looked surprised. "You forgot?"

"Honey, at this point I'm lucky to remember my own damned name. I've been going full speed for sixteen hours on about four hours' sleep."

Tess responded with a kiss on my cheek. "Go to bed, Johnny."

Upstairs at my kitchen table, I poured myself two fingers' of cheap Scotch, intending to review the day's events. That turned out to be like trying to watch a blurry, out-of-focus movie while standing on my head, so I swallowed the Scotch and headed for my bed. Everything would still be there tomorrow.

Sixteen

Montero Apartments – #201, Hollywood
2:10 A.M. – Wednesday - November 22, 1939

The telephone in my nightmare rang and rang and rang. Then I woke up. The hands on my wind-up alarm clock pointed to ten minutes after two, and the telephone was still ringing. I groped my way down the hall to the little wall niche where the telephone lives and picked it up. "Spicer."

"Hi, Johnny. Bob Winfield here. Sorry to roust you out of bed two nights in a row, but we just got a homicide call that will interest you."

I have to give Winfield credit; he called at strange hours, but he sure knew how to wake a guy up in a big hurry. "Who's dead?"

"Diana Dean's friend, Ruth Barnes."

That one caught me completely off balance. I wasn't even sure I'd heard him right. "Did you say Ruth Barnes is dead?"

"That's what I said. I just got the call, and I figured you'd want to be in on this one. I'm on my way over to her apartment right now. You want to meet me there?"

Still dumbstruck, I said, "I'll be there."

I loaded up the percolator and shaved with a razor I should have thrown out half a dozen shaves ago. Dressed and ready for action—well, almost ready since I didn't bother with a tie—I poured coffee into a hefty ceramic mug imprinted with "Golden Gate International Exposition" in gold letters.

Why the hell would anyone kill Ruth Barnes? She was about as harmless as a human being could be. I lit a Lucky Strike and took a swig of the Maxwell House in my mug. Unless Ruthie was tied into some other mysterious goings-on, which seemed highly unlikely, her murder had something to do with Diana Dean's disappearance, but what?

Finally deciding there were no answers to be found in my kitchen, I stubbed the Lucky out in my snazzy Roosevelt Hotel ashtray, gulped down the rest of the coffee in my mug, and headed out. I didn't stop to leave Tess a note this time. The news of Ruthie's demise was going to shake Tess up some, so it would be better told in person.

I squeezed my Chrysler into a spot between two L.A.P.D. cruisers on Orange Drive around two-forty-five. In all, I counted five city vehicles plus a black sedan delivery belonging to the county coroner crowding the curb space in front of seventeen-ninety-one. Lights were showing in the windows of neighboring apartment buildings. Ruthie Barnes was receiving a lot more attention in death than anyone ever gave her in life. That's the way of things in Hollywood. If you want to get noticed, get murdered.

A rookie patrol officer was standing guard out in front of Ruthie's door to keep the morbidly curious away. I showed him my photostat and said I was invited to the party by Chief of Detectives Winfield. He'd been told to expect me and stepped aside to let me by. Inside the apartment was a beehive of activity. Several uniformed officers were milling about, a police photographer was popping flashbulbs, two guys in the white uniforms of the coroner's office lounged against the wall next to a stretcher in the far corner of the room, and Bob Winfield was discussing things with another official-looking fellow in a suit.

At the center of it all was Ruthie. She was on her side next to the same armchair she'd occupied when Tess and I were there, only now the armchair was tipped over and Ruthie was wearing a simple white nightgown instead of her housedress. A large purple discoloration covered her cheek on the side of her head I could see, and her hands were tied behind her back with about a foot of clothesline rope. Ruthie's nightgown was immodestly bunched up nearly to her waist, revealing a pair of dimpled knees, chubby thighs, and a pair of practical white cotton panties. Her skin matched the color of the panties.

Winfield finished with the guy in the suit and walked over. He stood there for a moment looking at Ruthie. "If you've seen enough, let's go out front and have a talk."

I followed him out onto the dew-damp lawn, and he offered me a Chesterfield from his pack. I took it and offered him a light in return. I said, "What do you have so far?"

"A disturbance call came in around one from an upstairs neighbor, and a patrol officer was dispatched to see what was up. When nobody answered his knock, he checked around back—there's a little courtyard place behind the building—and found the back door to this apartment standing open. The lock had been jimmied. He announced himself and went in, found the woman on the living room floor, and called it in.

"Judging by what I saw in there, it looks like somebody tied her up in a chair and was beating the hell out of her when the chair tipped over. She apparently hit her head on that little table between the chairs. I'm guessing that was the blow that killed her, but we won't know for sure until the coroner is through with her. You have any ideas about this, Johnny?"

I flicked an ash from my cigarette onto the lawn and shrugged. "Not at all. She was fine and dandy when I saw her last night."

"You saw her last night? What time?"

"Tess and I came over here around seven-thirty to see if I could get anything more out of Ruthie about where Diana Dean has gotten off to."

"Any luck with that?"

"Some. I pushed a little, telling her we knew the bit about her following Dean home was hogwash, and she fell apart. Tess calmed Ruthie down enough to get her talking, and she admitted that Dean put her up to lying about what happened Monday night."

Winfield was paying close attention. He wanted to know everything there was to know about Ruthie Barnes. "Did you get anything else out her?"

"A couple of minor points. For one, Ruthie thought Dean's mysterious disappearance gag was Gladys Grebb's idea and that Gladys knows where her daughter is. The other thing I learned is that Dean has or had a boyfriend. She met him when she was at Universal, and they started dating about the time she moved over to

Warner Brothers. But Ruthie never met him and didn't know his name. She said Dean was kind of secretive about him. That's the sum total of it."

Winfield nodded, then said, "You know, once we knew for sure Dean disappeared on her own, I wrote the case off. There's no law against disappearing, unless you're wanted for something. But now I have to put the whole mess back on the front burner again."

"I take it you think Ruthie's death has something to do with Diana Dean disappearing."

He looked up. "Don't you?"

"I'm pretty sure it does. It may even have something to do with the sabotage over at Warner's. It could all be tied in together, but I don't know how."

Winfield nodded again. "From the looks of things in there," he gestured to Ruthie's apartment, "Somebody was torturing her, like they were trying to get information out of her."

"Like the whereabouts of one Diana Dean?"

"Like that. Whoever did this beat the hell out of her, and the most likely reason is they thought she knew something they wanted to know. In fact, I'd bet money her death was kind of an accident. Whoever was trying to get her to talk pushed things too far and ended up killing her."

"That's pretty much what I'm thinking, especially since I now believe Ruthie didn't know anything to tell. She would have said that to whoever beat her up, but they wouldn't have believed her. If that's what happened, it means somebody besides us wants to find Diana Dean, and they want to find her in the worst way."

Our conversation was interrupted by one of the coroner's boys. He said, "They're through with the pictures and stuff in there. Okay if we take the woman now?"

"Yeah, you can take her. And tell 'em down at the morgue this might be part of a high-jingo case. We need good answers and we need quick."

The coroner's guy said, "Will do."

While that was going on, a particularly relevant thought bobbed to the top of my brain. Winfield turned back to me and I said, "Tell me, Bob, you still have someone out at the Grebb residence?"

Shaking his head, he said, "No. I told Danny to pack it in and . . . ."

I could almost see a cartoon lightbulb blink on over his head. "Wait! You think whoever did this might be headed there next?"

"If we're right about what happened to Ruthie, I'd say that's a good possibility. He might have already been there."

"Damn! I should've thought of that! I'll send a couple of patrol officers over there right now. In fact, I think I'll go check on Gladys myself."

"I'll meet you there."

Winfield went back into Ruthie's apartment to let them know he was leaving, and I beat it over to my car. I took a left on Franklin and ran down to La Brea, which I took south to Sunset. I didn't push my speed too hard because there were still a few cars on the streets of Hollywood, probably folks just heading home after a night on the town.

A moment after I turned west on Sunset, I heard a siren and saw a flashing red light in my mirror. Winfield's unmarked car, with a cruiser right on his tail, roared by me, and I put the accelerator pedal down hard to stay with them. We ran a red light at Fairfax, and five blocks later our little parade turned right and followed Monteel Road up behind the Chateau Marmont.

Winfield doused his red light and his siren died as we pulled off the road opposite Gladys Grebb's place. Getting out of my Chrysler, I heard Winfield giving his men their marching orders. They were to take a look around to be sure everything was okay, and if it was, they were to position themselves front and rear to be sure things stayed okay. That done, I followed Bob up the two flights of stairs to the porch, and he gave one of the heavy oak doors a hard rap with his fist. We waited there while nothing happened.

Winfield had just banged for the third time when a light over the porch blinked on and the little wrought iron peek-out panel in the door opened. Winfield held his shield up and said, "Police, Missus Grebb. Please open the door."

The deadbolt clicked and the door swung open to reveal the hefty Gladys Grebb wrapped in a maroon silk bathrobe that might have been a product of Omar the tent maker. There was a touch of panic on her face and in her voice as she asked, "What is it, officer? What's happened?"

"I'm afraid I have some bad news, Missus Grebb. May we come in?"

She quickly stepped back and swung the door wide. "Yes, yes, of course. What's wrong?"

Standing in the foyer, Winfield said, "There's been a murder. Your daughter's friend, Ruth Barnes, is dead."

Gladys Grebb reacted to Winfield's news with a momentary flash of relief—probably relief that we weren't there about her precious Millie. This was followed by an expression of shock that might or might not have been genuine. Dramatic performances were a Grebb family specialty.

In an appropriately shaky voice, Gladys said, "That's terrible! Poor little Ruthie! Who on earth would hurt her?"

Winfield said, "That's what we're here to find out. Perhaps we should sit down somewhere so we can talk."

Gladys Grebb studied Winfield's face warily for a brief moment. "Yes, of course. Let's go back to the library."

We followed in the broad wake of her maroon bathrobe as she led us down the hall. Once we were all seated in the library, Winfield said, "Missus Grebb, we think Miss Barnes' death is related to your daughter's disappearance."

Her reaction was almost startling. Gladys glared at Winfield and vehemently declared, "You're wrong! Ruthie's death couldn't possibly have anything to do with Millie!"

Gladys was on a small settee opposite the pair of chairs in which Winfield and I were seated. He glanced at me and I took the cue. "Gladys, cut the crap! The jig's up!"

That shocked the hell out of her, and I fired off another round. "We know for a fact your daughter disappeared of her own free will. There was no kidnapping or foul play involved. We're also pretty sure we know why she disappeared, and we have good reason to believe the whole scheme was your idea. And now your tomfoolery has gotten an innocent young woman murdered. It's time to can the act and tell us where Millie is before someone else gets hurt or killed."

Most liars give up the game when confronted with the truth, but not Gladys. She screamed, "How dare you speak to me like that! My poor Millie is out there somewhere in danger, and instead of doing your jobs and finding her, you come into my home and accuse me of awful things!" As an afterthought, she turned to Winfield and said, "Your superiors will hear about this outrage, I assure you!"

Almost as if we'd rehearsed it, Winfield stepped smoothly into his good cop routine. "Please, Missus Grebb, calm down. I didn't come here to accuse you of anything. I'm quite sure you and your daughter have a good reason for what you've done, and strictly speaking there is no law against disappearing. The problem is we think Ruth Barnes was tortured and killed by someone who is trying to find Millie, and . . . ."

In a voice loud enough to wake the entire neighborhood, Gladys shouted, "That's absurd! We had nothing to do with poor Ruthie's death!"

Winfield stood. "Alright, Missus Grebb, if you are sure of that, I will take the officers I've placed outside for your protection and leave. I apologize for the intrusion."

I also stood and was following Winfield to the library door when Gladys Grebb said, "Wait! What do you mean you have officers outside for my protection?"

Hat in hand, Winfield turned to face her. "We know Ruth Barnes didn't know where Millie is. If we'd been right about her being killed by someone who wanted to find your daughter, you would be in the same danger because it's certain the killer didn't learn what he was after from Ruth. But since you're quite sure we're wrong about that being the motive for the beating she took, you are in no danger, so there's no reason to waste taxpayers' money by leaving police officers here."

I wanted to give Winfield a pat on the back. He played it perfectly. I could almost see the gears turning in Gladys Grebb's head. She'd been so busy sticking to the story that her daughter's disappearance was the real McCoy, it never occurred to her that whoever Millie was hiding from was now taking desperate measures to find her, and that both she and her daughter really were in mortal danger. Winfield had cleverly planted that idea in her head and the reality of her situation was dawning on her with terrifying clarity.

I honestly expected that revelation would be enough to make Gladys see the error of her ways and make her tell us where Millie is, but Ruthie had been painfully right when she said Gladys was stubborn. Despite the danger that was now clearly apparent to her, Gladys Grebb still wasn't about to spill the beans. I watched her expression go from defiance to panic and back again. Calmly she said, "That's right, Mister Winfield. Now stop wasting time and put those men to work finding my daughter!"

That was that. Two minutes later Winfield and I were standing by his unmarked prowl car. He said, "Damn! For a minute there I thought we had her—that she was finally going to own up to the truth to save her own neck."

"So did I. What are you gonna do now, Lieutenant?"

He'd apparently already given that question some thought because his answer came without hesitation. "Well, as much as I'd like to, I can't in good conscience leave that woman in danger, so I'm going to pull my officers from the premises and park them someplace where they can keep an eye on things. Maybe my idea of scaring the hell out of her will still work if she actually sees us leaving."

I shook my head in disagreement. "That's a lost cause, Bob. What she's going to do is pack up and head for wherever Millie is hiding to let her know what's going on and to do something on her own to save their hides."

If Winfield hadn't already thought about that possibility, he was thinking about it now. After a moment he said, "You could be right, but if she does take off, there's not much I can do about it. Unless Millie is hiding somewhere within the city limits, which doesn't seem likely, I can't have my guys following her all over the county and beyond."

"But there's nothing stopping me from following her."

He looked thoughtful again. "I don't know about that, Johnny. Technically you're a civilian; plus, if something went wrong, I have no way of backing you up. You'd be on your own."

"I've been on my own before. As I see it, you've only got two choices. You can take Gladys into protective custody, which doesn't get Millie out of harm's way, or you can call in the Highway Patrol to shadow her, but by the time they get moving, she'll be long gone."

Winfield let out a long sigh. "Okay, Johnny, we'll play this your way, but only to a point. If you're right and Gladys takes off, you follow her, but the minute she lights somewhere, you give me a call so I can bring in the local authorities from whatever jurisdiction she's in. Agreed?"

With a little grin, I said, "Sure, Bob, that's the way we'll do it."

I didn't intend for him to like my reply, and he didn't. "Damn it, Johnny, I don't want any cowboy stuff! You play this straight like I said!"

"Okay, okay, but take your time about leaving. I need to make a quick phone call. Oh, and tell your guys to report in if Gladys takes off so you'll know she's on the move."

"Will do."

We'd passed an all-night drugstore during our caravan to Monteel Road, and I made a beeline for it. Inside, I bought a pack of Luckys and a cardboard cup of semi-hot coffee. Then with change in hand, I stepped into the phone booth just outside the door and called Tess. It was a few minutes after four o'clock, and I figured it would take a moment for her to answer the phone. I was wrong. Tess answered after the first ring.

"Hi, Tess, it's Johnny. What are you doing up at this hour?"

"I heard you leave a while ago, and I figured something was up. What's going on?"

There was no time for delicacy, so I came right out with my news. "Ruth Barnes was murdered a few hours ago."

"Oh, no! What happened?"

I gave her a brief summary of what I knew and added, "Winfield and I went over to see Gladys Grebb, thinking the news that she could be next might scare her into telling us where her daughter is, but that didn't work. Now I figure she'll bolt and head straight to wherever Millie is hiding, and I plan to be right behind her when she does. Will you please call Will Gardner so he'll be up to speed? I'll call and check in with you as soon as I can."

"Yes, I'll call Will, then I'll get dressed and go over to the office. Johnny?"

"Yeah, Doll?"

127

"Please be careful."

"Count on it." I hung up feeling guilty about worrying Tess and reminding myself why a guy in my business is better off single.

Seventeen

Anyone who thinks the life of a Hollywood private eye is glamorous and exciting has read too many dime novels. Sure, the job has its moments, but most of the time it's a boring, lonely business.

At the moment, I was being bored and lonely in my car parked about fifty feet down Monteel Road from Gladys Grebb's mansion. The cops Winfield left to keep an eye on things were pulled into a dead-end street that intersected Monteel a little further down the hill. And there we sat.

Given Winfield's new habit of telephoning me at all hours of the night, my greatest challenge was staying awake while waiting for Gladys to do whatever she was going to do, if she in fact was going to do anything. The drugstore coffee helped some, but not enough, so I kept myself busy by thinking about whatever came to mind.

I thought about the early morning chill. I thought about the celebrities, like Clark Gable, Greta Garbo, and F. Scott Fitzgerald, who might be peacefully slumbering at the ritzy Chateau Marmont down the hill. I even thought about my wristwatch, which I was consulting with some regularity.

The watch on my wrist was a holdover from my days with the Army Intelligence Police. It was Swiss, made by an outfit called Dorex. Dorex military watches were standard issue for Army folks to whom knowing the exact time might be important. The watch is round, bulky, and not nearly so elegant as the ritzy Longines and Bulova timepieces worn by vogueish gents of style and means. On the plus side, the Dorex's face was black with large, luminous numbers and hands that made it easy to read at a glance, especially in the dark.

When my trusty Swiss ticker told me I'd been parked on Monteel Road for almost an hour, I thought about something else: The possibility I'd been off-base with my hunch about what Gladys Grebb would do next. Still, I was fairly certain, in light of Ruthie Barnes' death, Gladys would be anxious to see Millie face-to-face.

When watching for something in the dark, your eyes play tricks on you. So when I thought I saw some movement in the shadows, I closed my eyes for a moment, then looked again. This time there was no doubt about it—someone was descending the stairway in front of Gladys Grebb's house, the stairs that led down to her street-level garage. A moment later, she was clearly visible against the lighter colored garage doors. Gladys was on the move, and she was taking a suitcase with her.

One of the garage doors opened, and at precisely five-twelve a large estate wagon backed out. I couldn't tell the make, but it was a dark color with lots of ritzy wood trim. Gladys got out, locked up her garage, and drove off down the hill toward Sunset Boulevard.

I ducked down out of sight as she passed, then started my engine and used Gladys' short driveway to turn around. Rolling down Monteel road with my lights off, I passed the squad car parked in the dead-end street. The cops flashed their headlights at me as I passed to let me know they'd seen what was going on. Up ahead, Gladys turned left on Sunset. Once she was around the corner, I switched on my headlights and sped up to the intersection. I made the same turn and caught sight of the wagon a block or so away.

Following someone at that hour of the morning is tricky because there's no other traffic for cover, and falling too far behind risks losing your subject in the dark. I let her open up the distance a little more, but kept a close eye on the distinctive twin taillights of her snazzy station wagon.

As I followed along, I pondered the significance of the direction in which we were going. My theory was that Gladys would head straight for her daughter, but Diana Dean was last seen driving west toward the coast, and we were traveling the opposite direction. Four blocks later, she turned right off Sunset onto Fairfax Avenue, and we were heading south. When we got to Santa Monica Boulevard, Gladys threw me yet another curve ball by turning east again.

Finally she turned right onto La Brea Avenue, and her meandering route through Hollywood made some sense. I now suspected Gladys Grebb's ultimate destination was some distance to the south because all of her zigging and zagging was for the purpose of getting to one of L.A.'s major north-south arteries.

The geographic area most folks think of as Los Angeles encompasses something like four thousand square miles, and that doesn't include the neighboring counties of Ventura, Orange, San Bernardino, and Riverside. In all, metropolitan L.A. is actually larger than several of the 48 states.

If you look at a map showing the population centers within that huge area, it would appear as if someone shook a wet paintbrush at it, spraying splotches of population all over the map with vast open areas between them. As a result, long thoroughfares like La Brea, Sepulveda, and Sunset, to name just a few, stretch out across those open areas to connect the paint splotches. I settled back in my seat for what could be a very long drive.

We rolled through the Wilshire and Hancock Park districts and on toward Baldwin Hills. Next came the town of Inglewood. There we crossed Century Boulevard, a major east-west artery, and La Brea Avenue turned into Hawthorne Avenue. We'd been on the road for about forty-five minutes and covered more than twenty miles. The time was five-thirty-five, and the sky to the east was turning gray as dawn approached. It wasn't going to be much of a sunrise, though, because the basin in which Los Angeles sits was thickly blanketed with coastal fog. The fog is a normal condition for these parts, and the sun usually burns it off after a few hours, but this morning's fog blanket was unusually heavy, meaning that we wouldn't be seeing much of the sun until noon or later.

Traffic along our route was also heavier now, so I eased up a little closer to Gladys Grebb's station wagon, keeping a couple of cars between us as we continued to travel south. I was also keeping an eye on my rearview mirror. The last thing I wanted to do was lead Ruth Barnes' killer straight to Diana Dean, still assuming that's where Gladys was taking me.

Beyond Inglewood we passed through the suburban communities of Lennox, Hawthorne, Lawndale, and El Nido. To folks in other parts of the world, those names have little meaning, but to Angelinos, they are important because it is to those little communities they return to sleep after a hard day's work in the big city.

While the names of L.A.'s suburban hamlets are unique, there is little about the towns themselves to differentiate one from another. Typically they consist of many residential blocks surrounding a small central business district in which are found grocery markets, eateries, small department stores, service stations, and purveyors of the other goods and services necessary to living the southern California style of life.

L.A.'s high-class shopping district, the place you find exclusive department stores like the May Company and Bullock's, was some distance behind me on Wilshire Boulevard. Thus, those who could afford to shop in such swanky establishments typically made a day of it, including lunch somewhere like the penthouse Tea Room at Bullock's.

The next community along Gladys Grebb's route was Torrance, where we crossed Sepulveda Boulevard—possibly the longest city street in the entire country—and kept on going. According to the odometer numbers below my speedometer, we were approaching the thirty-mile mark as we entered the outskirts of Lomita. There I closed up the distance between us a little more in anticipation of the turn Gladys would have to make within the next couple of miles.

The California coastline runs generally southeast as it passes Los Angeles, but at one point it takes a sharp turn to the east for a short distance before turning southeast again. Our southerly course was taking us directly toward that east-west section of coastline, meaning Gladys couldn't go much further without ending up in the Pacific Ocean. The next major artery we would encounter was Pacific Coast Highway, which, as its name implies, parallels the coastline. My guess was Gladys would turn left at PCH in the direction of Wilmington.

That guess proved to be correct. The coast highway was becoming a busy thoroughfare as the six o'clock hour approached, and I kept a close eye on the station wagon ahead. I suspected we were getting close to Gladys Grebb's destination, and I sure as hell didn't want to lose her after coming this far.

Just beyond Wilmington, Gladys made another turn. This time it was a right onto Pacific Avenue toward downtown Long Beach. A moment later she made one more turn—a left onto Ocean Avenue— and after driving another block or so, she pulled into the circular driveway of the Hilton Breakers Hotel. I was pretty sure Gladys had just led me to her daughter. Diana Dean was no piker when it came to selecting hideouts.

The Breakers is a Long Beach landmark. Built about fifteen years ago, the hotel is a swanky fourteen-story art deco cube situated just above the beach, the ritzy hangout of movie stars and other prominent folks who, for whatever reason, happen to find themselves in Long Beach.

I pulled to the curb at the end of the block just before The Breakers and watched Gladys step down from her fancy wagon while a bellboy dragged her suitcase out of the rear compartment. She and the bellboy then strolled through the hotel's opulent entrance. Apparently Gladys planned to take up residence at The Breakers with her daughter—that is, assuming Diana Dean was actually there. I figured she was, but I needed some solid proof to be sure.

I was debating about the best way to find that proof when a young fellow in a maroon valet's vest slid behind the wheel of Gladys Grebb's wagon and drove it around the circular drive back to Ocean Avenue. There he turned in my direction for a moment before swinging left onto the short street that ran down my side of the hotel and dead-ended at the beach behind The Breakers. Just before reaching the barricade marking the end of the street, the valet turned left into an automobile entrance in the side of the hotel. The Breakers, it appeared, had a parking garage in its basement, a garage that might hold the evidence I needed to prove Diana Dean was really where I thought she was.

Leaving my Chrysler at the curb, I trotted down the side street and casually walked through the garage entrance like I was Conrad Hilton himself. Taking up much of the hotel's basement area, the garage was dark and gloomy, but not so dark that I couldn't make out the shape of a Cadillac convertible parked nose-in against the far wall. The sight of it stirred a small sense of elation—the feeling I get when the pieces of the puzzle finally start fitting each other.

A car door slammed in the next row, and the valet who'd just parked Gladys Grebb's station wagon spotted me. Heading in my direction, he said, "Good morning, sir. Can I help you with something?"

The kid knew damned well I wasn't a guest in his hotel, but he threw in the "sir" because he'd been taught right. I held up my photostat. "My name's Spicer. I'm working with the Los Angeles Police Department on a missing person case."

He took a look at my license and said, "Yes, Mister Spicer, what can I do for you?"

I showed him one of my four-by-five publicity shots of Diana Dean. "I'm wondering if you've seen this woman here at the hotel."

A quick glance at the photo was all he needed. Diana Dean was the sort of dame guys remember. "Sure, I've seen her around here." He gestured a thumb over his shoulder toward the back wall of the garage and added with admiration, "She drives that swell Caddy roadster back there."

My feeling of elation grew stronger. "Do you remember when she arrived at the hotel?"

The young fellow had to give that question a little more thought. He frowned with concentration and then said, "The first time I saw the Caddy was when I came on duty yesterday morning. I come on at midnight, so I guess she must have checked in sometime Monday night."

I gestured toward Gladys Grebb's vehicle in the next row and said, "That estate wagon you just parked belongs to the woman's mother. I'm guessing she checked in to spend some time with her daughter. Does that sound right?"

"I wouldn't know that, sir."

"But I bet you could easily find out if they're in the same room."

Frowning again, he said, "I could, sir, but it would be better if you talked to the hotel manager. We're not allowed to give out that kind of information about our guests."

I nodded my understanding of the rules. "I would do that, but there's a small problem. The woman who owns that Caddy is in motion pictures, and her studio is trying to keep this situation out of the newspapers to avoid a scandal. The more people I talk to about her, the more likely it is that someone will spill the beans. Now, you seem to be an honest fellow, so I'm not worried about telling you what's going on, but I'd like to keep this just between us."

Then I pulled a couple of singles out of my wallet and added, "I can make it worth your while."

He glanced at the bills in my hand, but shook his head. "I appreciate that, sir, but I'd be risking my job if anyone found out I told you."

It was just my luck I'd found the only hotel employee in Los Angeles County with scruples about taking a bribe. I said, "I understand, and I certainly don't want you to lose your job, but the woman's studio would be very appreciative of your help." I put the singles back into my wallet and held up a fiver.

The prospect of a quick five bucks made my offer harder to resist. Finally he said, "Okay, sir. I'll go up to the valet station and check the room number on the Caddy's key tag against the number on the wagon's tag. Then I'll come back down here and let you know if they're the same or not."

I thanked him, and after he hurried off to complete his mission, I walked back to the Caddy and checked the license plate against the number Winfield had given me for Diana Dean's car. They matched. Things were looking up.

Since I'd followed Gladys Grebb from a distance on our trip from Hollywood to Long Beach, I'd never gotten close enough to read her license plate. I walked over and wrote the number in my notebook.

The red octagons on the car's bright chromium hubcaps told me Gladys drove a Packard. I added this information to my notebook along with the vehicle's general description, black four-door estate wagon with wood trim.

When my valet pal returned to the basement garage he was nervous as hell. After carefully looking around to be sure we were alone, he said, "The woman with the Packard wagon and the Caddy gal are registered in the same room, just like you thought."

Holding up the fiver he'd just earned, I said, "And the number of that room is?"

He hesitated and looked around garage again. I was pushing my luck because the room number wasn't part of our deal, but he was so anxious to get rid of me, he blurted, "Fourteen-thirty-one." Then he grabbed the portrait of Lincoln from my hand and took off like a scalded dog.

I strolled back out into the cool early morning air and stood watching the rolling surf for a few minutes while I contemplated my next move. I'd found Jack Warner's wayward starlet. Now the question was what do I do about it.

From a strictly business point of view, my responsibility was to my client, Jack Warner. From the legal and ethical points of view, however, I had also a responsibility to Lieutenant Bob Winfield. I weighed those responsibilities one against the other.

Since Jack Warner fired Dean from the Thunderstruck cast, his interests in her were down to two. One was learning whatever Dean knew about the production's sabotage. I had a strong hunch she knew more about that subject than she or her mother were admitting, but they weren't talking, so that was a dead end, at least for the moment.

Warner's other interest in Dean was keeping this whole sordid mess out of the newspapers. I'd successfully forestalled FBI involvement in the case, and I'd prevailed upon Winfield to keep Diana Dean's disappearance under wraps as much as possible. Of course, Ruthie Barnes' murder meant all bets were off on that score.

So under the circumstances, it appeared meeting my obligation to Warner simply meant telling him I'd located Dean and then getting back to finding his saboteur. But it wasn't really that simple. Ruthie's death also meant Diana Dean and her mother were likely to be in danger themselves. If I told Warner where they were, I would be increasing that danger because I couldn't count on him to keep their location under his hat.

On the other hand, Winfield's interests in Millie and Gladys Grebb were weightier matters. They were material witnesses in his investigation of Ruthie Barnes' murder, even though they had thus far shown little willingness to cooperate in that investigation. Winfield's second interest in Millie and Gladys was closely related to the first. He was obligated to protect them from Ruthie's killer, regardless of whether or not they wanted his protection.

When I looked at the situation in those terms, it was clear that my next step had to be letting Winfield in on where Millie and Gladys were hiding. Once I'd done that, they were his problem. I would decide how to meet my responsibility to Jack Warner when I knew how Winfield planned to deal with Millie and Gladys.

That decision made, I walked back up the side street and headed for a coffee shop I'd noticed across Ocean Avenue. The little eatery had a public telephone booth out front and would also serve as a good observation post from which I could keep an eye out for Millie and Gladys should they decide to leave the hotel.

In the phone booth, I dialed "o" for operator and placed a long distance, person-to-person call to Robert Winfield at Sixth Precinct headquarters. I deposited the required coins and waited. When Bob came on the line, the operator verified that he was the person I was calling and then said, "Go ahead, please."

"Hi, Bob, Spicer here."

"Hi, Johnny. Any news?"

"Yeah, I have some good news for a change. I've located the missing Miss Dean. At the moment she and her mother are across the street from me at The Breakers hotel in Long Beach."

Winfield was almost jumping for joy. "Good work, Johnny! I'll head out there right now. Can you keep an eye on them until I get there?"

"I can do that. I'll be in a little coffee shop kitty-corner across Ocean Avenue from the hotel."

"Thanks, Johnny! I owe you."

That made me feel a little better about my decision to call Winfield first. It was always better to have a cop owe you than vice versa.

Eighteen

I finished my call to Winfield and checked the time. It wasn't quite seven, but Tess had said she was going into the office early this morning, so I gave it a try. I dialed "o" for the operator again and placed a long-distance, collect call to my office.

Tess answered before the second ring and the operator said, "I have a long distance call for anyone from Johnny Spicer in Long Beach, California. Will you accept the charges?"

Tess said she would and the operator said, "Go ahead, please."

"Hi, Tess."

"Hi, Johnny. What on earth are you doing in Long Beach?"

"I'm here because Diana Dean is here. She's holed up at The Breakers Hotel."

"You found her! Congratulations!"

"Don't pop the Champagne corks just yet. We still have a couple of big questions to answer before we can close the book on this one. Have you talked to Will yet this morning?"

"Not yet. I was just about to call him."

"Good. Tell him to come into the office instead of going over to Warner's lot. I'm waiting for Bob Winfield to get here, but I don't know what's going to happen when he shows up. I might need Will, so I'd like to have him where I can get in touch with him."

"Okay. Anything else?"

"Not that I can think of. I'll call you back after Bob gets here and I know what he has in mind."

"Alright, Johnny. I'll talk to you then."

My telephone duties out of the way, I walked into the coffee shop. To say the joint was tiny is an understatement. They'd jammed six small tables and a counter with four stools into a space not much larger than your average clothes closet. The only customers in sight were a couple of old-timers sitting at the counter reminiscing about the good old days over cups of coffee.

I plunked myself down at a table next to the front window that gave me a clear view of The Breakers' entrance and the dead-end street leading to its basement garage. The old wooden table was covered in a cheery yellow and white checkerboard tablecloth. In addition to settings for two, the table held a glass bud vase with a couple of yellow carnations poking out of it. Very homey.

A young fellow in a chef's apron came out of the kitchen to set a glass of water and a menu in front of me. He asked if I wanted coffee, and I told him that would be fine.

The menu, a single sheet of paper with a neatly hand-printed bill o' fare on it, proclaimed homemade roast beef hash with eggs as the specialty of the house. When the combination cook/waiter returned with a mug of steaming coffee, I told him I'd try the hash and eggs. After being up and on the go for five hours, breakfast was long overdue.

With the ordering chores out of the way, I took a swig of coffee and stared out at The Breakers. The coffee was fresh and strong. Aside from a few passing cars on Ocean Avenue, there wasn't much going on outside my window. The oceanfront in Long Beach catered to tourists with folding money in their pockets, and it was still too early for that class of folks to be out and about.

I lit a Lucky and wondered what was happening up at Warner Brothers on this foggy Wednesday morning. With Jack Warner's sacking of Diana Dean, it figured the production of Thunderstruck was in an even greater state of chaos than it was before. At least I was pretty sure Dmitriy Volodin saw it that way. He'd been in a state of near panic when I last saw him on Tuesday.

All of the scenes already shot in which Dean appeared would have to be re-shot with her replacement, whoever that might be. Warner had ordered production to continue on the scenes without Dean before he'd fired her, so it made sense they'd go ahead with that plan while her replacement was chosen and prepared for the role.

The efficient managing of a motion picture production was tricky business. Costumes, sets, props, actors, and the technical stuff, like lighting and sound recording set-ups, all had to be in place before any film rolled through the camera. And since putting all that in place took time, the production manager had to stay several steps ahead of production at all times. Now much of that preparation for Thunderstruck was out the window. I'm no expert on the subject, but it seemed unlikely Warner could achieve his goal of finishing the film before the end of the year so Bogart would be available for another project. If that was the case, it seemed the saboteur would be successful in halting production for a while anyway.

Either the hash and eggs were the best I'd ever tasted, or I was so hungry it didn't matter how they tasted. I dug in and was just wolfing down my last bite when the little bell over the coffee shop's door dinged and a hefty guy in a gray suit that didn't fit very well walked in.

He glanced at the two old guys at the counter, then at me. It took him no more than three steps to reach my table, and as he did, the fellow asked, "You Spicer?"

It always makes me a little nervous when people I don't know show up in places where nobody should be looking for me in the first place. I stood. "Yeah, I'm Spicer. Who might you be?"

The fellow flashed a Long Beach Police Department Detective Sergeant's shield at me. "I'm Buchholtz, Long Beach PD Homicide. Bob Winfield called and asked me to meet him here. He said you'd be here, too, and you'd tell me what's going on."

"Sure, Sergeant. Pull up a chair."

He'd no sooner seated himself when the cook/waiter showed up with a cup of coffee, saying, "Morning, Sergeant. You eatin' this morning or just drinkin'?"

Buchholtz said, "Hiya, Robby. Just drinkin'. Gotta watch my waistline, ya know."

"Sure thing, Sergeant." Then Robby turned to me and added, "I'll get you a refill for your coffee, mister."

Since I like to know who I'm talking to, I asked, "You know Bob Winfield, do you?"

"Yeah, we go way back. I used to be on the L.A. force, and when I first made detective, I was assigned to the Hollywood Division. Bobby was my boss. We've stayed in touch since I left L.A. and moved here."

It was as much the way he said it as what he said that made me think Buchholtz was on the level. I said, "Okay, Sergeant, what would you like to know?"

He swallowed some coffee and said, "Everything. Bobby was in a big hurry to get down here when he called me, so he didn't tell me much except he needed my help and you'd fill me in."

It made perfect sense that Winfield would call someone he knew on the Long Beach force before driving all the way down here. The City of Long Beach was outside his jurisdiction, and cops tend to be touchy about unannounced visits from other departments. So, keeping an eye on The Breakers, I gave Buchholtz the Reader's Digest condensed version of the case and why Winfield was interested in Gladys and Millie Grebb.

When I finished, the sergeant said, "Got it. I liked workin' in Hollywood, but I sure don't miss dealing with those movie people. Most of 'em are nothing but a pain in the butt."

Smiling, I said, "You'll get no argument from me on that score."

"So what's the lieutenant want to do with these dames? Question them or haul 'em in or what?"

"I don't know what he's thinking, Sergeant. We've both questioned the mother a couple of times—most recently about four hours ago—and she hasn't budged an inch from her original story that her daughter mysteriously disappeared. Of course, since she just drove straight to where her daughter's holed up, we know that's a bunch of malarkey."

Buchholtz took another sip of his coffee. "Then I guess we'll just wait 'til Bobby gets here to find out what he plans to do. Whatever it is, I'll back his play. I owe him that much and a lot more."

"It looks like we won't have to wait much longer. Winfield's undercover car just went by."

The sergeant and I swapped a few minutes' worth of small talk while Winfield found a parking place. Then the lieutenant walked into the coffee shop with Detective Danny in tow. Robby's joint was getting downright crowded.

Buchholtz stood and shook hands with Winfield. "Hey, Bobby. Pull up a couple of chairs. The coffee's pretty good here."

Winfield looked about as tired as I felt, maybe more so. He said, "I'd like to, Andy, but I need to get back."

The sergeant nodded. "Okay, what's the plan?"

Winfield said, "Well, it's not much of a plan, but I need Diana Dean and her mother where I can protect them and hopefully get them talking so we can find out what the hell this is all about. Since they haven't been what you'd call cooperative, the only way I know to do that is haul 'em in and lock 'em up."

I piped up and said, "That's gonna make you real popular with the Grebb family."

Bob looked at me and said, "You got a better idea?"

"Nary a one. Tell me, what charge are you planning to hold them on?"

"For one thing, they're uncooperative material witnesses in a homicide investigation. I can hold them for a while on that alone. Then there's filing a false police report, impeding a police investigation, and probably a few other things I could come up with. I'm not letting either one of those gals out of my sight again until they give us some answers."

Buchholtz said, "Okay, Bobby, let's go round 'em up. You know what room they're in?"

I said, "Yeah, I got the parking valet to find out. Millie Grebb is registered in room fourteen-thirty-one, and the parking ticket stub for her mother's car has the same room number on it."

The sergeant said, "Okay. I'll go in with you and show the hotel manager my tin, then we can go up and roust these dames."

Winfield said, "Thanks, Andy. Is there a back way out of that place?"

Buchholtz said, "Yup, a couple of 'em. The best way would be to take 'em down to the garage floor in the elevator. The garage entrance is right down that short street there." He pointed toward the side street. "At this hour of the day we should be able to get 'em out without much fuss."

Winfield chuckled. "Oh, there's gonna be a fuss from Gladys Grebb no matter how we do it. There's no getting around that." Turning to Detective Danny, Winfield said, "You go get our car and bring it down to that garage." Then looking in my direction, he said, "You want in on this, Johnny?"

I shook my head. "Not unless you think it's going to take more than two of you to drag Gladys and Millie out of their room. I've still have Jack Warner's sabotage case to solve."

Winfield said, "I think we can handle Gladys and Millie."

I said, "Good luck. I'll check in with you later to see if you've gotten anything out of them, if that's okay with you."

"Sure, Johnny. And thanks for your help this morning. We'd still have no idea where Miss Dean disappeared to if you hadn't followed that Grebb woman down here."

While I paid Robby for my breakfast, Winfield, Buchholtz, and Detective Danny left the coffee shop. By the time I got to my car across the street, Detective Danny was walking south on Ocean Avenue toward wherever Winfield had found a parking place, and the other two were just walking up The Breakers' circular drive.

I slid in behind the steering wheel of my Chrysler and was cranking the engine over when I heard the sound of screeching tires somewhere to my right. I looked down the side street just in time to see Diana Dean's bright red Cadillac convertible burst out of the hotel's garage entrance and swing in my direction. I heard the powerful sixteen cylinder Caddy engine straining under full throttle as it accelerated up the hill, then there was more tire squealing as Diana Dean shot into the intersection and wrenched the big steering wheel around to her left.

The Caddy's engine was almost up to full steam by then, and it propelled the massive machine past me and up Ocean Avenue like an express freight train. After a quick look for oncoming traffic, I cranked my steering wheel all the way around into a U-turn on Ocean and pushed my accelerator pedal to the floor. Diana Dean's Cadillac was already halfway through the next block. I leaned hard on my horn button as I shot through the next intersection to give any approaching drivers fair warning.

My Chrysler is no slouch when it comes to power, but the Cadillac had a ten cylinder/eighty horsepower advantage on me. I thought I could hold my own, but if Diana Dean kept up at the rate she was going, I wasn't going to overtake her.

I watched the Caddy slew around to the right at a major intersection up ahead. A young man on the sidewalk jumped back as Dean cut the turn too tight and her right-side tires jumped the curb. I made the same turn and noted the street sign she'd barely missed. We were northbound on Pacific Avenue. I was still nearly two blocks behind the Cadillac when it arrived at PCH.

Without slowing, Diana Dean flew past the stop sign and fishtailed through a left turn, narrowly missing a Studebaker that skidded to a stop just in time. The Studebaker driver was still trying to restart his engine when I sailed by a few moments later. Now Dean had open road ahead of her, and the Caddy had room to stretch its legs. She was easily opening her lead on me.

With my speedometer pointer dancing close to the eighty mark, I barely managed to keep the red convertible in sight as we roared through the open fields and past short stretches of industrial buildings on PCH. Then just passed Figueroa Street I lost sight of the Caddy. PCH angles right from westbound to a northwesterly direction, and when I made the turn, the big, red car was nowhere in sight.

With all hope of catching Diana Dean gone, I slowed to the speed limit and kept going on PCH, planning to make a U-turn at Sepulveda Boulevard and head back to Long Beach. My throttle-to-the-floorboard chase of the Cadillac had lasted nearly ten miles, and I hadn't seen a single police vehicle in that entire distance. There's never a cop around when you need one.

Pacific Coast Highway with a sharp right turn onto Sepulveda. Approaching that intersection, I saw several cars pulled to the shoulder of the road and two fresh, black skid marks leading straight to the edge of the beach beyond Sepulveda. Halfway between the road and the water, a big red Caddy convertible lay upside down on the sand.

I parked and jogged to the wreckage. The windshield and the cloth top had collapsed, so the car was resting on its hood and trunk lid. A young man in swimming trunks and an older fellow in a suit were pulling at the driver's side door, trying to get it open. The twisted metal was resisting their efforts, but the door finally came loose just as I got there. Through the opening I could see Diana Dean sprawled across the shredded remains of her convertible top. From where I stood, she looked to be in about the same shape as her mangled red Caddy. Maybe worse.

Nineteen

The young man in swimming trunks was kneeling in the sand feeling for a pulse in Diana Dean's limp wrist. After a minute or so of breath-holding, the growing crowd around Dean's wrecked Cadillac let out a collective sigh when the fellow announced, "She has a pulse. It's weak, but she's alive."

I was wondering if anyone thought to call an ambulance when the wail of approaching sirens answered that question. The first siren to arrive was attached to a California Highway Patrol motorcycle. The motor patrolman, decked out in leather from head to foot, dismounted his trusty steed and walked briskly across the beach. The young man who'd found Diana Dean's pulse repeated his pronouncement that she was alive for the benefit of the newly arrived officer.

Running his eyes over twenty feet of wrenched and battered sheet metal, the motor cop shook his head in what was probably amazement and said, "That's a miracle." Leaning to look at Dean through the driver's door, he added, "Don't move her. She may have back injuries. An ambulance is on the way."

Then he returned to the highway and went to work clearing the traffic jam threatening to completely block the intersection of two major arteries. A white panel delivery ambulance arrived next. The driver and attendant pulled a stretcher out of the back and headed across the sand toward the wreck. While they were doing that, two more sirens arrived, both belonging to black and white squad cars of the Torrance Police Department.

Two of the newly arrived Torrance cops set to work clearing the crowd of onlookers from around the wreckage, me included. I thought about flashing my photostat to see if they'd let me stick around, but I could see no reason to do that. I'd seen all there was to see. Setting off across the sand in the direction of my Chrysler, I asked one of the Torrance cops where the ambulance would be taking the woman in the car.

Brusquely he said, "Torrance Memorial. Now move along, pal."

Back in my car, I gave a moment's thought to what needed to be done next. The odds were good that Winfield didn't know what had become of Diana Dean yet. After picking up Gladys Grebb, assuming she hadn't escaped The Breakers as her daughter had, Bob and Detective Danny would be high-tailing it back to Hollywood, so he wouldn't know Dean wrecked her car. Letting him in on that news seemed like my first priority.

Since he was probably still on the road, though, I couldn't reach him until he got back to the precinct. This was one of those times when I really envied Dick Tracy his two-way wrist radio. Not being so equipped, however, I did the next best thing and pulled into a Shell Oil Company service station on Sepulveda and used their public telephone to place another collect, long-distance call to my office.

When the operator completed the connection, Tess said, "Hi, Johnny. What's new?"

"Nothing good. Diana Dean took it on the lam before Winfield could catch her. She was in such a hurry to get away, she lost control of her car and flipped it over on a beach near Torrance."

"Oh, my! Is she okay?"

"Not very. She was in pretty bad shape and still unconscious when the ambulance took her away. Listen, I don't think Bob Winfield knows about the accident yet, and right now he's still on the road heading for Hollywood. So am I, but if he calls there before I get back, please tell him what's happened and let him know they took Diana Dean to Torrance Memorial Hospital. Okay?"

She repeated, "Torrance Memorial Hospital. Got it. Anything else?"

"Is Will there?"

"Yes. You want to talk to him?"

"No, I need to get back on the road. Just tell him what's happened. I'll fill him in on the details when I get back. I'm going to telephone Jack Warner first, though, and give him the bad news. Any calls for me this morning?"

"No. It's been quiet here."

"Okay, Kiddo, I'll see you in half an hour or so."

Reaching deep into my trouser pocket, I dug out all the change I could find and got the operator back on the line for a long-distance, person-to-person call to Jack Warner. The operator got as far as Esther Smith and hit a roadblock. I heard Esther say Mister Warner was in a meeting and couldn't be disturbed. I said, "That's alright, operator, I'll talk to this party."

The operator said, "Very well, go ahead, please."

"Esther, this is Johnny Spicer. I have some news for Mister Warner."

"Hello, Mister Spicer. I really don't think I can interrupt Mister Warner right now. Can you call back?"

"Not for a while; I'm on the road. Will you take a message for him?"

"Certainly. What's the message?"

Remembering that my call was going through a switchboard with big ears, I chose my words carefully. "Tell Jack the missing party I've been looking for has been in an automobile accident and was seriously injured. That party has been taken to Torrance Memorial Hospital. Also tell him I'll come by to give him more information in about two hours. Got that?"

"Yes, Mister Spicer. I will give Mister Warner that message as soon as possible."

"Thanks, Esther."

I took Sepulveda Boulevard north to State Route 14 where I turned right and cut over to Hawthorne Boulevard. From there I retraced the route Gladys Grebb and I had taken from Hollywood nearly four hours earlier. It was a few minutes after ten when I pulled into the First National Bank Building's parking lot.

In my office, I found Will reading the morning edition of the L.A. Times and Tess talking on the telephone. When she saw me,

Tess said into the phone, "Oh, hold on, Lieutenant. Mister Spicer just came in."

Covering the mouthpiece with her hand, she said, "It's Lieutenant Winfield."

I took the handset and said, "Hello, Bob."

Tess vacated my desk chair and I occupied it as Winfield said, "What's this about Diana Dean being in an auto wreck?"

"She lost control of her Caddy and missed the turn at PCH and Sepulveda out by Torrance. The car flipped a time or two and ended up on the beach."

"And she's at Torrance Memorial Hospital?"

"That's where a Torrance cop said the ambulance was taking her. She's in pretty bad shape. It looks to me like she'll be lucky to pull through."

After a pause, Winfield said, "That's not good news. How the heck did you find out about it before we did?"

"I was close on her tail when she crashed. I saw her bolt out of The Breakers parking garage as you guys were going into the hotel, and I took off after her. She headed west on PCH, and once she got out on the highway where she could open that Caddy up, I had no chance of catching her. I lost sight of her a couple of miles before the coast highway hits Sepulveda, and when I got to the intersection I saw her car out on the beach. Were you able to grab Gladys, or did she get away, too."

"We got her, but just barely. When Buchholtz told the manager why we were there, he said Missus Grebb was out in front of the hotel waiting for the valet to bring her automobile around. If Danny hadn't been in the garage and recognized Gladys Grebb's car when the kid came down to get it, we'd have missed her. Danny told the valet to leave the car right where it was, and that's why Gladys was still out in front of the hotel when we got back out there."

I asked the question that had been troubling me ever since I'd seen Diana Dean leave The Breakers. "How the hell did Gladys and Millie know you were there?"

Winfield chuckled. "You won't believe this. The valet you bribed to find out what room Millie and her mother were in had an attack of conscience and told the hotel manager what he'd done. Can you beat that?"

Winfield continued, "So naturally, the manager called up to let Millie know there was a suspicious private eye named Spicer asking questions about her. That's what put them on the run. Apparently Millie had a spare ignition key for her Cadillac because the valet still has the one she gave him. Gladys wasn't so lucky, if you want to call it that. I guess she saw us coming and ducked out of sight somewhere when we went into the hotel because we sure didn't see her until after we talked to the hotel manager."

I said, "I guess that'll teach me to trust an honest hotel employee. Has Gladys explained why she and Millie ran from you?"

"Gladys hasn't said a word about anything except how she's going to have my badge before this is all over. I've got her locked up in one of our cells for now, but I still haven't figured out what I'm going to do with her. As you can guess, she's not very happy right now."

"Just wait until she finds out what happened to Millie."

"Yeah, I know. Believe me, I'm not looking forward to telling her that piece of news." After a short pause, he added, "Before I do that, though, I need to call somebody at the Torrance P.D. and arrange to get Millie some protection there at the hospital."

Glumly I said, "Sure, if she's still alive enough to need protection."

"I'll let you know. Thanks for filling me in on the situation."

I set the telephone handset in its cradle and looked up at Will and Tess. "Did you get all that? I mean about what happened to Diana Dean."

Tess nodded and Will said, "Got the gist of it. What do we do next, Boss?"

"The first thing I'm going to do is switch places with Tess so she can use the phone to call Torrance Memorial and find out if Diana Dean is still with us." To Tess I said, "She'll be listed as Millie Grebb, and if the hospital gives you the stall, tell 'em you're her long lost sister or something."

Tess and I switched places, and I sat in one of my new guest chairs for the first time. It was pretty comfy.

While Tess went to work on the telephone, I turned to Will and said, "As for what we do now, I need to see our client. I left a message about Dean with his secretary, so Warner knows about her accident. I'm a little surprised he hasn't called by now."

Will said, "Maybe he's already written her off. Remember, he fired her yesterday. She's probably old business to him."

"That could be, but there's still the newspaper publicity angle. Technically Diana Dean is still an employee of his. I'd bet Warner has already called his publicity department and told them to get some doctored-up stories ready for the papers, stories that will make her crash sound like just a tragic automobile accident without any reference to her running from the police when it happened."

"That sounds about right. So what do you want me to do while you're talking to Warner?"

I thought about that for a minute, then said, "We need to get back to concentrating on the original case—the sabotage of Thunderstruck. All my chasing around after the Grebb gals has gotten us nowhere."

Will said, "You think Diana Dean knows who's been trying to shut Thunderstruck down?"

"I do, or at the very least, she knows something that would put us on the right track. The same goes for her mother, but she ain't talking either. And they aren't the only ones involved in this thing who know more than they're saying, including our client."

Will looked surprised. "You think Jack Warner knows who's messing with his picture? If that's true, why wouldn't he tell you? For that matter, if he knows who the culprit is, why would he hire you in the first place?"

"I don't think he knows who's causing the trouble, but I'm pretty sure he's keeping something from us that might point us in the right direction. I got a strange reaction out of him the other day when I pressed him on the question of who might benefit if Thunderstruck got shut down. I'm guessing he pulled a fast one somewhere along the line and got somebody mad—maybe mad enough to want revenge. But he isn't talking, probably because he doesn't want anyone to know what he's been up to."

Will asked, "Anyone else?"

"This might be grasping at straws, but when Dmitriy Volodin found out Diana Dean had been fired, he seemed a hell of a lot more upset than he should have been. That makes me think he's another guy who knows something about all this he isn't telling us."

"I suppose that's possible, but you'd think he'd cooperate to get his film back on track."

"Yes, you would. That's what makes me wonder if there aren't some things going on behind all this that we're missing."

Will nodded. "So, again, what do you want me to do next?"

"Go back to your original plan for today. See if anyone on the lot recognizes the rags used to start the New York Street fire and talk to Dean's wardrobe assistant to see if she can shed any light on the boyfriend situation. Then head out to Universal and see if you can uncover any dirt on Dean there. Hopefully you'll come across some kind of a lead for us to follow."

"Will do. You want me back here when I'm done with all that?"

"Not unless something breaks. Just check in by telephone. Tomorrow is Thanksgiving, so we won't be able to accomplish anything because there won't be anyone around to talk to. We can pick it all up again Friday morning."

"Alright, Johnny. I'll get started . . . ."

Tess had just hung up the telephone and she interrupted Will, saying, "Before you go, the hospital says Millie Grebb is still in surgery and her condition won't be known until sometime this afternoon. That's all I could get out of them."

I said, "Thanks, Tess. At least she's still among the living."

Will said, "I wish we could talk to her while she's coming out of the ether. She might spill something without realizing she's doing it."

I said, "That would be a neat trick, but I suspect the hospital takes a dim view of giving patients the third degree under those circumstances . . . unless you want to masquerade as a nurse."

Tess chimed in, "I'd like to see that! Will would look just darling in a nurse's uniform."

Will glowered at us. "Okay, Abbot and Costello, I'm hitting the road. I'll check in later."

With Will gone, I stood and said, "I'd better get going, too. I want to see Warner before he disappears for lunch. I shouldn't be more than a couple of hours."

Tess leaned back in my desk chair and said, "Okay, Johnny, I'll be here. What's on the agenda for this afternoon?"

"Probably a nap. I'm seriously behind on my sleep."

Looking at Tess I could see there was something on her mind, something she was hesitant to bring up. "Hey, Kiddo, what what's going on in that pretty head of yours?"

"Oh, I was just wondering if we were still going to Humphrey Bogart's party tonight."

"Sure. That's the least I can do to repay you for all the help you've given me this week and for the swell remodeling job you've done on this dump."

"Well, if you don't feel up to it . . . ."

"I feel fine. We'll put on our glad rags and make a night of it, hobnobbing with the Hollywood elite."

Twenty

I walked into Jack Warner's outer office at eleven-fifteen and flipped my fedora onto the clothes tree next to the door. Esther Smith held up an index finger meaning "wait a minute" while she finished the sentence she was typing. Then she looked up and said, "Go right in, Mister Spicer. Mister Warner is anxious to see you."

Esther's facial expression said a lot more than her words. It told me Warner was definitely in a rotten mood. That came as no surprise. He didn't have much to be happy about.

As I walked in, Warner looked up from some papers on his desk and said, "Dammit, Spicer, don't you ever bring good news with you?"

"Not lately. I take it you got my message about Diana Dean?"

He nodded with irritation. "I got it. Now tell me what the hell happened to my star?"

I restrained myself from saying, "You mean the star you fired yesterday?" Instead, I sat in one of the chairs opposite his desk and gave him an account of the day's activities thus far, beginning with Bob Winfield's early morning call about Ruthie Barnes.

The whole sordid tale took a few minutes to tell, and when I finished, Warner said, "So you finally find Diana, but you let her get away again, and now she's in some damned hospital dying. Is that about the size of it?"

I ran out of restraint and diplomacy. "I didn't 'let her get away again.' She managed that all on her own. And if she's dying in some damned hospital, it's because of her own damned stupidity!"

Warner's face was getting close to purple again. "Don't use that tone of voice with me, Spicer! I hired you to find whoever is trying to shut down Thunderstruck, and all you've managed to do is make matters worse!"

"I made matters worse? That's hogwash! If your precious star had cooperated with me, I'd have nailed your saboteur by now. Instead I've wasted a hell of a lot of time chasing her and her damned mother all over Los Angeles county! On top of that, her shenanigans got an innocent young woman killed—an innocent young woman who was just trying to be a good friend to that conniving dame!"

Of all the responses I could have come up with, I'd inadvertently picked one of the few that actually made an impression on Warner. He wasn't used to being bawled out by his subordinates, and my little tirade made him stop and think. At least that's how I interpreted what happened next.

Warner made a palms-down calming gesture with both hands and said, "Okay, okay, Spicer. None of what's happened is your fault. I know that. Now how do we find our culprit so I can get my film made?"

I mentally counted to ten and said, "I'm not sure. I've got my assistant following what few slim leads we have, but I don't have much faith in any of those. The best thing that could happen right now would be for Gladys Grebb to tell us who the hell her daughter was running from, but she's up to her ears in hot water with the cops now, and they're damned sure not going to get anything helpful out of her."

"So you think whoever frightened Diana into running away is the same person who is sabotaging Thunderstruck? And her mother knows who he is?"

"I'd bet money on it."

Jack Warner nodded almost absentmindedly. I got the feeling he was hatching an idea, but if he was, he didn't share it with me. All I got from him was a dismissal. "Okay, Spicer. You're doing a good job. Keep me informed."

With that he turned his attention back to the paperwork on his desk, and I left. On my way through the outer office, I shook my head at Esther in frustration, grabbed my hat off the rack, and headed for my car.

I thought about tracking Will down to see if he was having any luck, but I was pretty sure he wasn't. It was time to play the last card in my hand, so I drove back through the Cahuenga traffic jam to my office.

By the time I pulled into the First National Bank parking lot, the lunch hour had come and pretty much gone. But that didn't mean much when it came to Saul Cohn. If he lunched with a client or some studio exec to whom he was trying to hustle one of his actors, there was a good chance he might not be back for hours. I gave it a try anyway.

Bypassing the stairs I usually take to my second floor office, I took the lobby elevator up to the tenth floor. Stepping out of the elevator, the first thing I noticed was the lack of sound; it's church quiet in the rarified atmosphere of the First National Bank Building's upper stories. This phenomenon is due in part to their lofty location far above the racket of Hollywood Boulevard, but it's also due to a thick layer of posh. The hall in front of my office is covered in some sort of linoleum that makes footsteps echo off the lath and plaster walls. Up here carpets cover the hall floors and absorb sound before it ever reaches the rich wood paneling on the walls.

Light in the lower floor halls is provided by glaring, industrial-style overhead fixtures, while the high-rent upper floor tenants enjoy soft indirect lighting from decorative wall sconces. The office doors are different, too. No frosted glass door panels with painted-on company names for these folks; they have ritzy solid wood doors with names spelled out in individual gold letters. The gilt letters on the door to number 1002, for example, said, "Saul Cohn Theatrical Agency."

The lobby behind that door—up here the office suites include lobbies—held a classy semicircular, deco-style reception desk with a similarly classy-looking redhead behind it. She gave me the once-over through a pair of specs with snazzy black and white frames and, probably figuring me for another down-on-his-luck actor, put on the most unwelcoming expression she could muster.

I relieved her of that impression by saying, "My name's Spicer. I'm one of your downstairs neighbors. Is Saul back from lunch yet?"

Carefully sidestepping a direct answer to my question, Miss Redhead opened a snazzy leather bound appointment book and said, "Do you have an appointment with Mister Cohn?"

"Nope."

"Then perhaps I can schedule one for some future date?"

"Nope."

"Then I'm afraid we can't help you, sir. Mister Cohn is extremely busy this afternoon."

"I sincerely doubt that, so just pick up your fancy telephone do-dad there and tell Saul Johnny Spicer is out here and I'm going to throw his annoying receptionist out the tenth-floor window if he doesn't see me."

Her very green eyes, magnified by her glasses, widened to the size of saucers, and Miss Redhead grabbed the handset of her telephone. Keeping a wary eye on me, she pressed a button and said in a frantic tone, "Mister Cohn, there's a terrible man out here who says his name is Johnny Spicer, and he says he's going to throw me out of the window . . . Mister Cohn?"

The inner office door burst open, and Saul Cohn appeared with a big grin on his kisser. "Johnny, you *goyisher mensch*! Stop already terrifying my poor secretary and get your *tuches* in here!"

I removed my fedora, smiled my sweetest smile at Miss Redhead, and walked into the man's inner sanctum. Saul Cohn is the stereotypical Hollywood talent agent. Usually resplendent in custom-tailored suits of shiny silk, he's as wide as he is tall. He smokes fat, foul-smelling cigars from a gold-trimmed humidor on his desk and wears a pinky ring that, if hocked, would feed the entire population of Glendale for a week. Needless to say, Saul Cohn and I travel in different circles. I rated his jovial welcome because I rescued a couple of his clients from nasty blackmailers in bygone years.

Saul gestured me toward one of the red leather chairs opposite his desk and walked over to a well-stocked bar set against one wall of his office, saying, "What would you like to drink, my friend?"

"Nothing, thanks. I'm working."

He grinned a toothy smile at me. "Then I take it this is not a social visit?"

"You take it right. I've got a case that's not going anywhere, and I came up to swap some information with you."

Settling in behind a mahogany desk as big as a billiard table, Saul said, "I see. And about whom are we going to swap information?"

"Diana Dean."

Saul looked a little surprised. "Jack Warner's little darling? What has Miss Dean done to warrant the attention of Hollywood's most illustrative private investigator?"

"That's part of what I have to swap, Saul."

He leaned back in his massive desk chair and clasped his hands loosely in front of his ample belly. I had his attention. He said, "Alright, my friend, tell me what it is you think I might know about Miss Dean that would be of help to you."

"To put it bluntly, I'm wondering about the men in her life. Are there any, and if there are, who might they be?"

Saul Cohn gave my question some thought. Actually he gave it a lot of thought before saying, "Off the top of my head, I can't think of anyone to whom Miss Dean has been linked romantically. That certainly doesn't mean there isn't a man in her life. It just means that, if there is she's been very discreet about it."

It wasn't what I wanted to hear, and that must have shown in my expression because Saul quickly added, "But don't give up hope, my friend. I will make some inquiries and something may turn up. May I ask for whom you are working? Might it be Jack Warner?"

"What makes you think that?"

Saul gave me a knowing smile. "It's no great secret that Jack has turned to you for your special brand of help on more than one occasion in the past. But more to the point, there are rumors in the air of some trouble on the Warner lot—trouble having to do with a film Jack is making, a film in which Diana Dean plays a leading role."

Saul Cohn and I were now playing a game—a game in which he attempted to worm information out of me, and I let him. In accordance with the unwritten rules of our game, I looked surprised and said, "Is that so?"

"Yes, my friend, that is quite so."

"And do any of those rumors say who's responsible for the alleged trouble Jack Warner is allegedly having?"

"Alas, they do not. The rumors simply say there have been some 'accidents' that caused delays in this film's production. The natural conclusion, therefore, would be that someone doesn't want the film to be made. So, knowing you are Jack Warner's favorite gumshoe, I might also conclude he hired you to find the someone who doesn't want the film to be made. And considering your question about Diana Dean, I am led to the further conclusion you suspect Miss Dean is in some way connected with the trouble in the happy little kingdom of Warnerland. Am I on the right track?"

I was still thinking up a snappy reply when Saul added, "No, my friend, you do not need to answer that question. Instead, please tell me what juicy tidbit of news you brought to trade for whatever I will learn about Miss Dean's romantic affairs."

Figuring Saul would make good on his promise to find out what he could about Diana Dean's love life and knowing it was only a matter of time until the news hit the papers anyway, I gave him his tidbit, but not before building a little more suspense. "Okay, what I'm about to tell you is still under wraps, and a lot of people are anxious to keep it that way, including my client, so this has to be between you and me. Okay?"

Looking a lot like the cat who was about to pounce on an unsuspecting canary, Saul nodded, and I said, "Diana Dean was involved in a serious automobile accident early this morning. At this moment she is hanging by a thread in the hospital."

Saul looked genuinely shocked. "Heavens! That certainly is an interesting piece of news! How reliable is your source?"

"One hundred percent."

Staring intently at me, he cocked his head slightly, and I could almost see the gears turning in his brain as he asked, "And in which hospital is Miss Dean hanging by a thread?"

"Torrance Memorial."

"Torrance? What in heaven's name is she doing way down there?"

"That falls under the category of classified information. If you're thinking about checking on her condition, you should know Miss Dean was admitted under her real name, Millie Grebb. That won't do you much good, though, because the hospital is only talking to family at this point."

Raising his bushy eyebrows, Saul said, "Millie Grebb? No wonder she changed her name!" After a short pause, Saul got a cagey look on his face and said, "So might it be safe to assume Jack Warner will be replacing Diana Dean in his currant project?"

"I can't say for sure, but even if Dean survives her injuries, it's not likely she'll be back to work any time soon." Saul didn't need to know Warner had already fired Diana Dean for running out on Thunderstruck. His interest was the same either way. At that moment he was deciding which of his clients could take her place and how he was going to sell whoever that might be to Jack Warner.

Saul stood abruptly, saying, "Okay, Johnny, I'm going to get busy finding out what I can about Diana Dean for you. I'll let you know as soon as I come up with something."

I doubted very much that the phone calls Saul would be making as soon as I left his office would have anything to do with Miss Dean. He saw an opportunity, and he was jumping on it with both feet.

We shook hands, and as I turned to go, Saul stopped me. "Johnny, I'm throwing a small soiree up here Friday night for the Santa Claus Parade. You are invited. We have a great view of the parade on Hollywood Boulevard down there, so it will be a festive occasion. I might even have some news about Miss Dean for you by then. About seven?"

"Thank you, Saul. I'll be here."

Twenty-One

Leaving the elevator on the second floor, I returned to the reality of Hollywood. Down here were the sounds of the work-a-day world—a symphony of ringing telephones, clattering interurban streetcars, clacking typewriters, and newsboys out on the corner shouting for me to read all about it in the Times. I like the racket; it makes me feel alive, a kindred spirit with an entire city full of real people facing life as it came.

In the decidedly less ritzy offices of the Jonathon A. Spicer Investigation Agency, I found Tess with a bottle of glass cleaner and a rag, industriously scrubbing one of my windows. She looked up and said, "When was the last time you cleaned these windows?"

I looked back innocently and said, "It wasn't that long ago, maybe nineteen-thirty-seven or thirty-eight."

She held up a brown rag that was once white and said, "I believe it! There's at least two year's worth of cigarette smoke and grime on them!"

I plunked myself down in my desk chair and looking at the now gleaming glass, said, "Not anymore. Thanks, Tess, but I never expected you to paint the place and clean the windows. All I had in mind was a little filing and a few telephone calls answered."

"I had the filing done three days ago, and you've got the deadest telephone in Los Angeles. I had to do something to keep busy."

"Well, I appreciate it, Tess, and to show my appreciation, I'm taking you to a swanky parade-watching party Friday night. That is, if you want to go."

"A parade-watching party? What in heaven's name is that?"

"Saul Cohn, my talent agent client up on the tenth floor, is throwing a party to watch the annual Santa Claus parade. His office is on the Hollywood Boulevard side of the building and the parade passes by right under his windows."

"I see. I didn't know you spent so much time hobnobbing with the upper crust."

"As a rule, I don't. This is sort of business, but it still might be fun. Saul spares no expense when it comes to celebratory festivities."

"Okay, it's a date. Good thing I made an appointment at the hair salon this afternoon. I would hate to embarrass you by showing up at all these classy events without a coiffure of the very latest style."

I looked up and winked at her. "I think you look swell just the way you are."

"Men! You say that now, but you'll be singing a different tune when you see me in my glad rags and a new hairdo."

Stifling a yawn, I said, "Okay, if you say so. But while you're getting all dolled up for Bogie's shindig tonight, I'm going home for a few hours' rest. Winfield's late-night telephone calls are interfering with my beauty sleep. Speaking of telephone calls, any news from Torrance Memorial?"

"Not much. I called them about thirty minutes ago. Millie Grebb is out of surgery, but she's still in critical condition. The doctors aren't offering a prognosis yet."

"After what I saw of Millie at the scene of her crackup, I'm surprised she's made it this long. I'm going to give Winfield a call to see if he's gotten anything out of Gladys, although I'd bet money he hasn't."

Tess turned to put the finishing touches on her window cleaning job and I dialed the Sixth Precinct. "Hi, Bob. Spicer here. Anything new?"

"Nothing that gets us any closer to finding Ruth Barnes' killer. You have anything for me?"

"Only that Millie is out of surgery. The doctors aren't making any promises about her future, though."

Winfield sounded surprised. "How the hell did you get that news? The Torrance P.D. lieutenant we're working with said he had the hospital put a lid on all information about Millie Grebb."

Grinning into the telephone handset, I said, "I got it from Millie's sister."

"Wait a minute! Millie Grebb doesn't have a sister!"

"Sure she does—at least she does until Torrance Memorial gets wise to us."

"Oh, I get it. Well, don't count on that gimmick working much longer. I just sent Danny Collins and a patrol officer down there with Gladys Grebb so she can see Millie. If the hospital says anything about Millie's sister calling, she'll set 'em straight in a big hurry."

"Yeah, I suppose she will. How did Gladys react to the news about Millie's car wreck?"

"About like you'd figure. Gladys flew off the handle and demanded to be taken to the hospital immediately. I was hoping she might get emotional and tell us what's going on, but I didn't get a single a tear out of that gal. She's got ice water in her veins."

"Hell, all Gladys sees is a good chance that her meal ticket might die on her."

Winfield sighed audibly. "I'm afraid you're right about that. I briefed Danny on the situation, though, and gave him instructions to press her if she shows any signs of weakening. I hate to be as cold as she is, but Gladys is the only lead we've got, especially if Millie dies."

I asked Bob to keep me informed and promised to reciprocate. Then we exchanged wishes for a happy Thanksgiving and ended the call. As soon as I hung up, the phone commenced to ringing. I grabbed the handset and said, "Spicer."

"Johnny? Will Gardner."

"Hi, Will. You just caught me. I was about to run for home and catch some sleep."

"I'm not surprised. You haven't gotten much of that lately. I won't keep you long, but I wanted to report on what I accomplished, or more accurately, what I didn't accomplish today."

"Okay, I'm all ears."

"A gal in the costume department I talked to thought the scrap of cloth from the New York Street fire looked familiar, but she wasn't sure where she'd seen it before, so no joy there. Then I talked to that Klein dame, Diana Dean's wardrobe gal. You sure had her pegged right. The way she pumped me for information, I wasn't exactly sure who was interviewing who!"

"Did you get anything useful out of her?"

"Sort of. She's certain Diana Dean was, as she put it, 'involved with some guy,' but Dean was playing it close to the vest; she never named her lover."

"Hell, that's the only sign of good sense we've seen out of Diana Dean in this whole mess."

"Klein also told me she thought something had been upsetting Miss Dean the past week or so—said she seemed off in another world somewhere or words to that effect."

Jotting Bessie Klein's observation in my book, I said, "Good job, Will. You got a good deal more out that dame than I expected. How 'bout Universal? Pick up anything useful there?"

"I didn't get past the front gate. I think the guard made me for a newspaper reporter. He told me to make an appointment with the publicity department, for cryin' out loud." Will paused a moment, then added, "Something interesting did happen on my way out to Universal, though."

Tired as I was, something in the tone of Will's voice got my attention. "Yeah, what's that?"

"I picked up a tail."

"No kidding?"

"No kidding. But the guy isn't very good at it. I spotted him right after I left the Warner lot, and he was behind me all the way to Universal and all the way back to my apartment, which is where I am now. For all I know, the fellow is still out there, parked about half a block down Olive. It's just one guy by himself in a thirty-seven model Chevrolet two-door sedan . . . light brown with California plates. I couldn't get the number."

"Ya know, Will, it might be worth our while to find out who's suddenly taken such an interest in you. Maybe I should come out there so we can introduce ourselves to this guy."

Will said, "Maybe you should. But first let me take a look through the window to see if he's still out there. Hang on."

No more than fifteen seconds later he was back on the line. "Too late. The guy must have gotten tired of waiting for me to do something interesting. There's no sign of him now."

While I was disappointed we'd missed an opportunity to find out who the hell had suddenly taken an interest in Will, I thought it might be just as well. My eyes were already drooping so much I wasn't sure I could make it over the Cahuenga Pass again without falling asleep at the wheel.

I said, "Alright, but keep your eyes open. You still have a permit to carry?"

"I do, and I've already dusted off my Walther. It's right here handy."

Surprised, I said, "Geez, you pack a Walther?"

"Sure. Why not? The Germans build fine quality guns. It shoots straight and packs a wallop."

Yeah, I thought, and Walther nine-millimeters were also heavy enough to give a guy a sore shoulder just packin' one around. But I kept that to myself and said, "Okay, okay. Far be it for me to tell another fellow what heat to carry. Just be sure it's loaded in case your pal in the brown Chevy comes back for a visit. Remember, we're dealing with a killer now."

By the time Will and I ended our conversation with Thanksgiving wishes and an agreement to meet at my office first thing Friday morning, Tess had finished her window cleaning and was sitting in one of the new chairs opposite my desk. I said, "Nothing new from Winfield except he has a couple of his men escorting Gladys Grebb down to Torrance so she can see Millie.

"Will, however, had some interesting news. It seems he picked up a tail this morning. It would be nice to know who the hell was following him and if the guy fits into Jack Warner's problems."

Tess looked a little nervous, and I guessed she might be remembering the night a few months back when she and I picked up a tail out on The Strip. That turned out to be a rough night for her. I tried to put her mind at ease.

"On the other hand, the guy following Will might not have anything to do with our case. Either way, it's nothing to be concerned about. Will can handle himself."

She nodded without much conviction, and I said, "Oh, and you were on the right track when you said we should look into Diana Dean's love life. Her wardrobe gal seems to think Dean had something going on in that department, but no name was ever mentioned."

Tess was pleased with that news. "See, a woman's point of view comes in handy sometimes."

"You'll get no argument from me on that score."

"Good. You'd lose that argument anyway. Now go home and get yourself some sleep. I want you wide awake tonight."

"Okay, Doll, I'm on my way. You need a ride home?"

"No, thanks. My hair appointment is at four. I'll hang around here until then just in case Lieutenant Winfield calls or something."

"Okie-dokie. See you about six-thirty?"

With a smile, Tess said, "I'll be ready!"

On my way home I took a good look around the First National Bank Building's parking lot and up and down Yucca in front of the Montero Apartments just in case the guy who followed Will around for a good part of the day decided following me might be more fun. I saw no brown Chevies or villainous-looking characters lurking about, so ten minutes later I set my trusty alarm clock for five-thirty and caught the next train to dreamland.

Twenty-Two

A few hours sleep, a shower, and a shave had me feeling almost human again. According to my mirror, a pair of brown trousers, a fresh white shirt, a brown tie with pale blue diagonal stripes, and a tan sport coat in a conservative houndstooth pattern had me looking almost as human as I felt.

With a little time to kill, I got a fresh pot of coffee started and sat at my kitchen table to contemplate the day's events. As days in the detective business go, it was a busy one, starting out fifteen hours ago with Winfield's call about Ruth Barnes' murder. Since then I'd followed Gladys Grebb to Long Beach and found Diana Dean. From there things went steadily downhill. Diana Dean had wrecked her shiny red Cadillac on a beach and was hanging on by a thread at Torrance Memorial, Jack Warner had given me what-for, Will Gardner had picked up a tail that might or might not have anything to do with anything, and I'd threatened to throw Saul Cohn's receptionist out a tenth-floor window of the First National Bank Building. It was, all in all, an eventful day that didn't bring me one step closer to finding out who was sabotaging Thunderstruck.

Thinking about the guy shadowing Will Gardner reminded me I'd be smart to heed my own advice—the advice I'd given Will about taking precautions because our investigation was now a homicide. I stripped off my sport coat and retrieved my Smith & Wesson Police Special from its hiding place.

It's an ugly little revolver, dull gray metal with a short barrel and hard rubber handgrips. Some guys go for the showy chrome-plated jobs with carved hardwood grips, but not me. Maybe all that razzle-dazzle gives them confidence. Personally, I don't much care for firearms, shiny or otherwise. Sure, I carry the Smith & Wesson when it seems prudent to do so—it's a necessary evil at times—but I'd rather talk the bad guys to death.

I gave the revolver a quick once-over to make sure it was loaded and ready for use. Then I strapped on my shoulder holster and slipped back into my sport coat. Another look in the mirror showed me I wasn't bulging too badly. I studied the guy in the mirror for a few seconds. He bore no resemblance to a hardboiled crime fighter. He just looked like the sort of silly sap who packed heavy artillery to a dinner party. Well, you never know when you might have to plug a waiter for trying to foist off an overdone steak on you.

I knocked on the door of the apartment directly below mine at precisely six-thirty. Tess opened the door with a flourish, performed a fashion show pirouette, and said, "What do you think?"

She was decked out in a green lace cocktail dress a few shades darker than her eyes and revealing enough to make most guys look twice. It started at the top with puffy sleeves and a wide V neckline that came damned close to being risqué and ended in a hem short enough to prove she had great gams.

Tess's auburn hair was a little shorter than it was the I last saw her and it had a new wave and sheen to it. The overall effect was stunning. I gave her the only answer that came to mind, "Wow!"

Tess smiled. "I told you you'd be singing a different tune when you saw me tonight." Her eyes went down to my sport coat, and her smile disappeared. "You're carrying your gun, aren't you?"

"Is it that obvious?"

"No, not really. I just know how that jacket fits you. Otherwise I wouldn't have noticed. Are you expecting some sort of trouble?"

"No, not at all. Bogart makes a big deal out of me being a real-life private eye; he even calls me Shamus. I just put the shoulder holster on for window dressing. You know, playing the part."

Tess nodded, but her expression said she didn't believe a word of what I'd said. She knows me too damned well.

Donning a matching green wrap to ward off a slight chill in the November night air, she took my arm and we sashayed to my Chrysler at the curb. I opened the passenger door for her, and once she was comfortably seated, I walked around to the driver's door, scanning the street for suspicious vehicles as I did so. Everything looked normal and peaceful. I climbed in behind the wheel, and we set off for an evening of fun and frivolity.

Chasen's is a relatively recent phenomenon in these parts, having only been around for a few years. Still, the joint already had a reputation as a ritzy hangout for movie folk. Technically, it was located in West Hollywood, but it was close enough to Beverly Hills to claim some of the Hill's snazz appeal.

I took Highland down to Sunset and followed Sunset west until it hit La Cienega where I turned south. Then I turned right on Santa Monica Boulevard and headed west again to Doheny. A few blocks south on Doheny brought us to Beverly Boulevard and Chasen's. During the drive I kept one eye on my rearview mirror for some sign of a tail. Nothing.

Chasen's is a big white slab of a building on the northeast corner of Beverly and Doheny. They stuck a peaked section of roof over the entrance and threw up a sidewalk awning to add some character, but nobody will ever confuse Chasen's exterior with a Stiles Clements design. I pulled into the parking lot that wraps around the joint so Chasen's customers don't have to leave their classy chariots out on the street.

Inside, Chasen's is pure swank. The main dining room sits under a low beamed ceiling and is lined with cushy red leather booths. Glittering deco wall sconces and huge mirrors line the walls—the mirrors creating the illusion of a dining room twice its actual size.

At a few minutes past seven Chasen's was full to overflowing with a goodly number of folks jammed into a tiny foyer while waiting for tables. With Tess in tow, I shouldered my way through the crowd to a podium where a scrawny maitre d' with slicked-back hair and a tux that looked better from ten feet away held court. After giving Tess the eye, he sized me up as a poor prospect for a sizeable tip that would get us moved up to the front of the line. Sounding like a holier-than-thou preacher addressing the lowliest sinner in his flock, the guy said, "Good evening, sir. Welcome to Chasen's. Do you perhaps have a reservation?"

I gave him the bland expression I reserve for hired help with snooty attitudes and said, "We're with the Bogart party."

That piece of news didn't do a whole lot to improve his opinion of me. In a tone that told me Bogie's money was good at Chasen's, but he wasn't on their roster of upper-crust customers, the guy said, "Yes, sir. Please follow me."

As we passed through the crowded main dining room, I ushered Tess ahead of me and watched her gawk here and there at the joint's celebrity clientele. I'm sure she recognized more of the rich and famous than I, but if it matters, I did take note of Jack Benny with a dishwater blonde who might have been Mary Livingstone and, at another table, Warner's public enemy number one, James Cagney.

After passing through a smaller second dining room—this one paneled in wood with framed paintings adorning the wall—we came to a pair of double doors through which could be heard sounds of great merriment. The maitre d' held one of the doors open and said, "Through here, sir."

Chasen's private dining room was a cozy space crowded with maybe thirty folks. So much for Bogart's dinner party "for a few friends." Some of the guests were already seated at the tables that took up most of the room's space, and the rest were standing around socializing. A trio of Negro musicians playing some quiet jazz were crammed into one corner of the room near a bar that was doing a land office business.

Any concerns that I might be underdressed for the occasion evaporated when I saw our host. He was hard to miss decked out as he was in black and white wingtips, black trousers, black shirt, scarlet tie, and a white sport coat. The word "stylish" didn't begin to cover his outfit.

Bogie spotted us almost immediately. From across the room he shouted, "Hey, Shamus! Come on in and join the party!"

I tossed Bogart a casual salute. He raised a glass of dark amber liquid in reply and set sail in our direction. A few steps away, his eyes admiringly fixed on Tess, he said, "Well, now, Shamus, who do we have here?"

"Bogie, meet Tess Gallagher. Tess, this is Humphrey Bogart."

Bogie took her hand and bowed politely. Then, in a pretty fair Irish brogue, he said, "Ahh, a wee lass from the Emerald Isle. Pleased to make your acquaintance, my dear."

Tess twinkled her green eyes at him and said, "Likewise, I'm sure, Mister Bogart."

Still in character, Bogie said, "Now we won't be havin' any of that 'Mister Bogart' blarney. It's Bogie to me friends, and I would surely be honored to include you among that number, Miss Gallagher."

She was clearly charmed. "Then you must call me Tess, Bogie."

He gave her another little bow, and finally releasing her hand, Bogart turned to the crowd and said loudly enough to get the room's attention, "Hey, everyone. I want you all to know my good friend, Johnny Spicer, and his lady, Tess. Johnny's a genuine private eye, and if he hadn't been on his toes the other day when there was an accident at the studio, we'd be havin' this party at Hollywood Memorial and I'd be doin' a hell of a lot less drinkin'. So treat Johnny right or you'll answer to me."

Turning back to Tess and me, Bogie gestured to the attractive brunette who appeared at his side, and said, "Tess, Johnny, I want you to meet my wife, Mayo."

Mayo Methot Bogart had a round face with a quick smile. She also had a quick wit. Looking me straight in the eye, Mayo said, "So you're the guy, huh? I almost got rid of this bum," she jabbed a thumb at Bogie, "and you had to go and louse it up. I won't forget you for that, Shamus."

Putting on an appropriately contrite expression, I said, "It was just a momentary lapse in judgment. I'll do better next time."

Apparently pleased that I knew how to play the game, she gave me a satisfied nod and wandered off into the crowd. Bogie, on the other hand, did a respectable job of playing host, introducing us to a few of his guests, including some with slightly familiar faces. The only guy I can honestly say I recognized was a diminutive British actor named Niven. I remembered him from a movie I saw a year or so ago. I think it was an Errol Flynn film about World War One aviators. Niven played one of the fliers.

Dinner was announced about eight o'clock and started off appropriately with a bowl of Chasen's famous chili. After that I lost track of the courses, but take my word for it, there were a lot of them, including a fish course of trout, followed by lamb chops, and some stuffed undernourished chickens they probably called squab. It was an eclectic bill o' fare to say the least.

When the dessert course finally arrived—a peach slice over ice cream with some sort of berry sauce, which in combination, Tess informed me, was called peach melba—I was pretty sure I wouldn't need to eat again for at least a week. After that, the drinking resumed in earnest. Bogie's friends seemed to specialize in that particular sport.

While I was trying to avoid a long-winded conversation with a well-lubricated dame who was just fascinated beyond all reason by private detectives, Tess excused herself and strolled over toward the trio of musicians in the corner. They'd just finished their version of *Wrap Your Troubles In Dreams*, and when Tess arrived, the tall, slender piano player jumped up and embraced Tess like she was his long lost sister. Then the bass player and guitar man joined in the enthusiastic conversation. When I thought about it, the scene shouldn't have surprised me. After all, Tess was a fellow musician, and musicians tend to be birds of a feather despite the color of their plumage.

By the time Tess returned to our table, the gal with the private eye fetish had gone off in search of a powder room and the band disappeared on a break. Taking a short pull on the scotch I'd been nursing for half an hour, I said, "It looked like old home week over there. I take it you know those guys?"

She smiled at a memory. "Yes. Before I signed on with Betsy I found a few jobs in Long Beach, and that's where I met them. The piano player's name is Nat Cole. I love his style . . . I even got to work with them a few times. That was a thrill!"

I was wondering how the hell a trombone fit in with a piano, bass and guitar, but before I could ask the question, a dark-haired fellow wearing thick, black-framed glasses and feeling no pain stumbled over and, sloshing some of his drink on the white tablecloth, introduced himself. His speech was slurred, so I didn't catch his name, but it sounded something like "cuckoo," as in the clock with the bird inside.

We shook hands, and he commenced to thanking me profusely for some great deed I'd performed. I finally figured out that he was expressing his appreciation to me for saving Bogie's life. I said I was pleased as punch to have been of service, and in the wise and all-knowing tone of the inebriated, he said, "Yer a brave man an' i's a plesher to know ya."

Having successfully performed his mission, Mister Cuckoo left our table and followed a meandering path to the bar for a refill. Grinning, Tess said, "You certainly impressed that fellow!"

"Yeah, you meet the most interesting folks at . . . ."

I was interrupted by our host, who was standing at the end of the room where the band members were returning to their instruments. "Ladies and gentlemen, if there are any of those present, it is my great pleasure to make a very special announcement. I've just learned that we have in our midst tonight a very talented gal singer, and I'm going to prevail upon her to sing a number with the band."

Bogie paused for effect, and in a quiet voice Tess said, "That rat! I told Nat I didn't want to . . . ."

Continuing his announcement in grand style, Bogart said, "She is none other than the shamus' lady friend, Tess Gallagher!" Placing a hand above his eyes in the manner of a man shielding his vision from the sun, he searched the gathered multitude and added, "Tess, wherever you are, come up here and sing for your supper!"

That Tess was a singer, talented or otherwise, was news to me. Like everyone else in the room sober enough to remember who the hell Tess Gallagher was, I turned to stare at her. For a moment I actually thought she might dive under the table in humiliation, but some fellow nearby shouted "Here she is, Bogie! Over here!" And the jig was up.

Bogie walked quickly to our table and, taking Tess by the hand, said, "Come on, doll. Everybody pitches in at a Bogart clambake!"

With that, Bogie pulled Tess to her feet, and she gave me an apologetic look as he dragged her up to the band. "Okay, everybody, here she is—Tess Gallagher! What are you gonna sing for us?"

With a little shrug, Tess turned to the piano player. He made a suggestion I couldn't hear and she nodded. Cole then said something to the two guys behind him, and they took off with an up-tempo introduction that smoothly resolved itself into *Pennies From Heaven*. After a piano chorus, Tess took a deep breath and joined in:

"Every time it rains, it rains pennies from heaven.
Don'tcha know each cloud contains pennies from heaven?
You'll find your fortune fallin' all over town.
Be sure that your umbrella is upside down."

I sat there with my mouth hanging open. Tess wasn't just good, she was damned good. I'd heard Betsy Lind's all-girl orchestra in which Tess played her trombone a few times, but Betsy did all the singing on those occasions. Tess had blonde Betsy beat hands down and then some.

Tess was getting into the swing of things now, and Bogie's guests were right there with her, even those who were well beyond any semblance of sobriety. She belted out the final chorus with an air of confidence I'd never seen in Tess before:

"Trade them for a package of sunshine and flowers.
If you want the things you love, you must have showers.
So when you hear it thunder, don't run under a tree;
There'll be pennies from heaven for you and for me."

She held the final note while Cole played some tricky notes on his piano, and the applause began. Even the guys in the band joined in, clapping enthusiastically. Tess took a quick bow and trotted back over to our table.

Bogie took center stage again and said, "Now that was something! How 'bout one more number, Tess?"

Smiling, Tess said, "Thanks, Bogie, but not tonight. I'm quitting while I'm ahead!"

After several folks came by to congratulate Tess on her song and we were more or less alone again, I said, "Well, now, do you have any other talents you haven't bothered to mention?"

Tess gave me a wink that was almost bawdy and said, "Well, maybe just one or two."

The reserved, sometimes almost meek Tess I thought I knew had vanished like a puff of smoke in a windstorm, and in her place was a confident, talented gal who was clearly more comfortable with the Hollywood crowd than I would ever be. I wondered if the transformation was alcohol-induced, but it wasn't that; she hadn't had that much to drink. No, it had to be the recognition of the spotlight. This kid was a born performer; adoration was her booze.

Then the old Tess was back as quickly as she'd left. Looking at me with something like concern in her eyes, she asked quietly, "Is everything okay, Johnny? Are you upset with me for singing?"

I liked the other Tess better. "Hell, no! What makes you think I'm upset with you?"

"I don't know. You're kind of quiet, and I thought . . . ."

"Well, stop thinking. You just surprised the hell out of me, that's all. I didn't even know you could sing, and you just put most of the singers I ever heard to shame. I'm not upset; I'm impressed as hell!"

Most of the concern I'd seen in her eyes was gone, but the new Tess was also gone. She reached out and took my hand. "Johnny, I want you to be proud of me, but I wouldn't ever want anything I do to come between us. You are much too important to me."

I felt a familiar discomfort, a nagging something I couldn't quite put my finger on. I didn't let it show, though. "You've got nothing to worry about there, Kiddo." I grinned a big grin as I said it, but somewhere inside I had the distinct feeling I'd just told her a fib.

By this time the shindig was starting to get rowdy, and I was beginning to understand why Chasen's maitre d' hadn't been impressed when I told him we were with the Bogart party. There was a small commotion across the room, and I distinctly heard Mayo Methot's voice shrilly say, "You no good drunk! You shut your trap or I'm leaving!"

Bogie had something to say in reply, but I didn't catch it. Not more than a moment or two after that outburst, I watched David Niven and his wife—an attractive redhead with a whole lot of British accent he'd introduced to us as Primmie—said their goodbyes and left the party with a haste that made me suspect there might be more unpleasantness in store.

Tess apparently had the same impression. "Johnny, would it be okay with you if we went home now?"

"I was just about to suggest the same thing."

Another shouting match erupted just as I was about to head over and thank our host and hostess for a lovely evening. Since I figured neither of them were likely to remember my good manners, I took Tess by the arm and we quietly slipped out the door while everyone else's attention was on the brewing storm.

When Tess was comfortably seated in my Chrysler, I took a look around. There were no signs of anything out of the ordinary in Chasen's parking lot, nor did I see any suspicious headlights in my rearview mirror on the way home.

When we arrived back at the Montero Apartments, I asked Tess if she'd mind coming upstairs and making another of her sisterly telephone calls to Torrance Memorial Hospital before we said goodnight. Using my telephone, I pointed out with reason, would avoid adding long-distance toll charges to her phone bill.

She said she wouldn't mind at all, and Torrance Memorial said there had been no changes one way or the other. Miss Grebb's condition was still considered critical.

When Thanksgiving Day dawned brightly outside my bedroom window, Tess was still there, and her pretty green lace cocktail dress hung neatly in the closet next to my tan sport coat with the conservative houndstooth pattern. If nothing else, we were a tidy pair.

Twenty-Three

Montero Apartments – #201, Hollywood
6:30 A.M. – Friday – November 24, 1939

I awoke Friday morning to the splattering of big raindrops against my bedroom window. In damper climes rain is a nuisance, but in sunny southern California it is generally considered a welcome change; it scrubs the sidewalks, purifies the air, and makes everything fresh and new again.

The weather gods had shown proper respect for Thanksgiving, favoring us with a clear, sunny day for the occasion. From my point of view, Thanksgiving turned out to be more pleasant than expected.

Tess and I started out for her aunt's home in Compton after a leisurely morning spent drinking coffee and reading the Times' early edition at my kitchen table. The home counties section carried the story of a spectacular automobile accident down the coast near Torrance. The three paragraph article reported that the lone occupant of the car, a Miss Millicent Grebb of Beverly Hills, was rushed to a local hospital where doctors were guardedly optimistic about her chances of recovering from the severe injuries she'd sustained during the horrible crash. The Torrance cops were doing a good job of helping Bob Winfield keep a lid on the details. Jack Warner would pleased.

Tess's Aunt Jean turned out to be a delightful lady with a dry sense of humor and a quick wit. She was also an excellent cook. The turkey dinner she prepared, complete with all of the traditional accompaniments, was the best I'd tasted since the holiday feasts Mom had cooked up during my childhood.

Dressing for work Friday morning, the fit of my trousers was a little snugger than usual. Aunt Jean's Thanksgiving dinner and the previous night's spread laid on by Chasen's hadn't done my waistline any good.

I picked Tess up downstairs around seven-thirty, and we made a quick dash through the downpour to my car. The biggest drawback to a heavy rain in our part of the world is flooding. Any precipitation greater than a heavy dew causes the storm drains to back up, creating lake-sized puddles at every low point in the road, especially intersections.

I eased the Chrysler through an axle-deep pond at Yucca and Highland and forded another at the entrance to the First National Bank Building's parking lot. From there we made another dash to the building's alley entrance. Tess survived the ordeal quite well; she had the good sense to wear a raincoat and hat. I don't even own a raincoat. Who the hell needs a raincoat in Los Angeles? In the office Tess further dampened my mood by observing that I looked like a drowned rat.

While Tess called Torrance Memorial for the latest on Millie Grebb, I hung my jacket and soggy fedora on the coat rack and squished across the floor to watch the chaos at Hollywood and Highland from my office window. The accumulated rainwater in the intersection below was already encroaching on the sidewalks. A big red interurban car—running on tracks and heavy enough to be relatively unaffected by the flooding—roared by, throwing up a rooster tail of spray higher than the traffic signals. An older Ford roadster was stalled in the eastbound lane of Hollywood Boulevard, bringing the already slow-moving traffic through the intersection to a complete halt.

I wondered what Santa Claus thought about this deluge. He was scheduled to arrive via Hollywood Boulevard in twelve hours or so. Can reindeer swim? Was Santa's sleigh equipped with pontoons? It would be a tough night for the jolly old elf, in spite of himself.

Will Gardner strolled through the door wearing a spiffy bright yellow rain slicker and carrying a folded black umbrella. Umbrellas and raincoats are for sissies. I bet Santa wouldn't been seen with either.

Will looked at Tess, who was still on the telephone to Torrance Memorial, and then he looked at me. "Geez, Johnny! You look like a drowned rat. You should have worn your raincoat this morning."

I glowered at him. "I loaned it to Blitzen."

"Huh?"

"Skip it. How was your Thanksgiving?"

"Nice. Betty and I went to my folks' place out in San Berdoo. Mom fixed a lollapalooza of a turkey dinner. How 'bout you?"

"More or less the same, except it was Tess's Aunt Jean in Compton, and I ate too damned much. Any sign of your shadow since Wednesday afternoon?"

"Nope. I kept an eye out for him, but he hasn't shown up again."

Tess returned the telephone handset to its cradle and announced, "Millie Grebb is doing better this morning. She's conscious and the doctors are now optimistic. She won't be receiving visitors for a while, though."

"Don't bet on it."

Will asked, "You going down there?"

"I'd never get through the front door by myself, but I'm pretty sure Winfield will be headed that way. I'll see if I can tag along."

He nodded. "Maybe she'll feel like talking after her close brush with death."

"Don't bet on that either."

Will nodded again and said, "What do you want me to do this morning?"

That was a good question. We were fresh out of leads to follow, so I came up with the most productive thing I could think of. "Go over to the Warner lot and find out what's going on with Thunderstruck. See if they've recast Diana Dean's role yet and if they have a new shooting schedule. Get a copy of it if they have."

Will glanced through the window at the downpour. "Okay, Boss. At least the rain's put a halt to the construction traffic jams over the pass. Anything else?"

"I wish to hell we could get in to ask some questions at Universal. I'll talk to Esther Smith about that. She might know a way in, but I'm not counting on it." Then an idea I should have had days ago finally popped into my head. "Will, you know anybody at the Times?"

"Sure, a couple of guys."

"Eddie Carr?"

"In the Times' morgue? Yeah, I know him."

"See what he's got on Diana Dean. Maybe there's something there to give us a handle on her mystery man. How 'bout the Hollywood Reporter? Know anybody there?"

Will gave that a moment's thought. "Well, sort of. A while back I crashed a party at the Garden of Allah to keep an eye on the wife of a high-jingo client, and while I was there, I met this gal who turned out to be a gossip columnist at the Reporter. Her name was Kathryn something . . . Kathryn . . . Massey. That's it. Kathryn Massey. She lives, or lived, at the Garden."

"Okay, see her, too. But be careful. Remember, this gal gets paid good money to dig up dirt. If you suddenly show up asking questions about Dean, she's sure to smell a juicy story. The last thing Jack Warner wants right now is his protégé's name smeared all over the gossip columns."

"Got it. I'll cook up a cock-and-bull story to explain my interest. She won't suspect a thing."

I had doubts about that. "Better make it a good one."

"Got it. Anything else?"

"Not that I can think of. Come back here when you're done. And check in with Tess later by telephone just in case something pops."

"Will do. See you later."

Will picked up his trusty umbrella and headed out. I picked up the telephone and dialed the Sixth Precinct.

"Chief of Detectives Winfield."

"G'morning, Bob, Johnny Spicer here."

"Hello, Johnny. You heard the news from Torrance?"

"I heard that Millie Grebb's condition has improved. That what you mean?"

"Yeah. I'm just about to head down there. You want to ride along?"

"I thought you'd never ask."

"I'll pick you up in about fifteen minutes."

"That'll be fine. Come out Franklin. Hollywood and Highland is under a foot or two of water. I'll meet you in the alley behind my office."

I hung up the handset and glanced out the window again. The earlier torrential downpour had simmered down to a steady rain, and the clouds to the northwest were noticeably lighter than they'd been. I mentioned this to Tess.

She said, "I noticed. Maybe the sun will come out and dry things off for tonight's parade."

"It will take a while for all that water to run off, but Santa might just make it down Hollywood Boulevard after all."

"I hope so. I've lived in Los Angeles all my life, but I've never seen a Santa Claus parade. I'm usually working."

"I've got my fingers crossed for both you and Santa, then. Bob Winfield is picking me up in a few minutes for a trip down to Torrance Memorial. Hopefully, I'll be back by lunch time." I laid the keys to my Chrysler on the desk and added, "Here are the car keys in case you need to go out."

"I don't think I'll need them, Johnny, but thanks. And good luck with Millie."

"I'm not expecting to get much out of her, at least not anything that will get us any closer to Jack Warner's saboteur, but I'm down to grasping at straws. See you in a while."

Donning my damp jacket and still-dripping fedora, I headed down the back stairs and watched for Winfield from the alley entrance. He was driving his unmarked city car, a dark green Oldsmobile two-door sedan. Being a precinct chief of detectives has its advantages.

I climbed in the passenger door. Winfield looked at me and said, "Hell, Johnny, you look like a drowned rat."

"Yeah, so I've heard. What have you done with Gladys Grebb?"

Pulling the shift lever into first gear, he headed south down the alley toward MacCadden. "I turned her loose after Danny took her down to Torrance Wednesday afternoon. Gladys made it pretty clear she had nothing to say about Ruth Barnes' murder, and with her daughter all busted up in the hospital, I couldn't justify keeping her locked up even for her own protection."

We turned right on McCadden, and I asked, "Where is she now?"

"Danny took her back to that ritzy hotel in Long Beach. Gladys told him she wanted to stay there so she'd be closer to Millie in Torrance. I called Andy Buchholtz and talked him into putting some patrol officers at the hotel to keep an eye on her. Andy wasn't happy about wasting the taxpayers' money that way, but he figured it was cheaper in the long run to give her protection than to have a homicide case on his hands."

Winfield followed MacCadden south to Sunset and turned right again. At La Brea he made another turn to the south, and we were headed toward Torrance. He said, "I'm hoping this isn't a waste of time—that Diana Dean is scared enough to open up and tell us who the hell she's running from."

"I wouldn't count on it. For her to take off from The Breakers Hotel the way she did, Miss Dean was already scared out of her wits, and that wasn't enough to make her open up. I don't know if that's because she doesn't have any faith in your protection or there's something else going on we don't know anything about. I'd put my money on the latter, but whichever it is, I can't see how wrecking her car is likely to change things. If anything, it would have the opposite effect."

We rolled into Torrance about nine-thirty. Overhead, the clouds were thinning and the sun was earnestly attempting to make its presence known. My fedora was even beginning to dry out.

Torrance Memorial Hospital was a sprawling, mission-style building smack dab in the middle of a quiet residential district. The wing on our right was two stories and ran perpendicular to the street. There was a similarly shaped wing on the left that was only a single story. The two wings and their connecting structures were built around a courtyard. The grounds were tidy, and the whole place had a clean look to it—not a bad place to be sick, if you had to be sick.

Beyond a pair of tall entrance doors, Winfield stepped up to a reception counter and flashed his tin. He said, "Robert Winfield, L.A.P.D. We'd like to see the doctor in charge of Millie Grebb's case."

The receptionist, a pleasant woman in her fifties, looked through some papers attached to a clipboard. "That would be Doctor Emmet Hamilton. One moment please."

She picked up the telephone and clicked the cradle button a couple of times. When the hospital operator came on the line, the receptionist said, "Extension two-zero-four, please."

We all waited for a few moments, after which she said, "Doctor Hamilton, there are two gentlemen from the Los Angeles Police Department here in the lobby, and they would like a word with you." There was a short pause, then, "Yes, Doctor, I'll send them right up."

Hanging up her phone, she said, "Doctor Hamilton is in his office, but he only has a few minutes to spare. He asked that you come right up. His office is on the second floor." She pointed to a staircase off to one side of the lobby and added, "The stairs are right over there. Doctor Hamilton's office will be the second door on your right at the top of the stairs."

Winfield thanked her and we climbed the stairs. Our steps echoed around the quiet lobby as we went up. Torrance Memorial was definitely one of the quietest hospitals I'd ever been in. Winfield opened the door to room 204 and in we went.

Doctor Emmet Hamilton was a large man with a ruddy complexion, and a white beard, and wire-framed glasses. Attired in a white doctor's coat, the kind with buttons on the shoulder, looked like he might be in his fifties. In a deep, but pleasant voice, the doctor said, "Good morning. You are the gentlemen from the Los Angeles Police? I'm sorry I don't have much time to chat with you."

Winfield shook the doctor's hand. "I'm Lieutenant Bob Winfield, and this is Johnny Spicer, a private operative who is assisting us with a murder investigation. We'll make this as quick as we possibly can."

I also shook the doctor's hand, a soft and delicate hand, but one with a firm grip. Staring intently at Winfield, he said, "A murder investigation, you say? How can I help you?"

"One of your patients, Miss Millie Grebb, is a material witness in the case, so naturally, we're concerned about her condition and chances of recovery."

"Oh, yes, the young woman from the automobile accident. Material witness, you say? That would explain the police officers who've been keeping an eye on her room." Removing his glasses, he rubbed the bridge of his nose and said, "As for her condition, Miss Grebb sustained some rather severe injuries in the accident. Her left clavicle is broken in two places, as is her left femur.

"Those injuries will mend with time. I'm afraid, however, that I cannot be as optimistic about her head injuries. Miss Grebb has a severe concussion, how severe I cannot yet say, but it is severe enough to affect her eyesight and her thought processes. To put that in layman's terms, at the moment she is totally blind and responds very slowly, if at all, to verbal stimulus. Time alone will tell the extent of the brain damage.

"Also, Miss Grebb's face received extensive lacerations. Reconstructive facial surgery, or plastic surgery as it is sometimes known, may help some, but deep scarring will remain. There is no help for that. It's a shame. It appears she was quite a lovely woman before the accident."

Winfield said, "We need to ask Miss Grebb a few questions. Is she up to that?"

Doctor Hamilton shook his head. "Not yet. Oh, you could try asking your questions, but the patient is still in a confused state. Her answers, if she gave you any, would be somewhat incoherent and unreliable. Wait a few more days. She's a strong young woman, and her mental state may improve with time.

"Now, gentlemen, I must ask you to excuse me. I have to be going. If I can be of further assistance, you know where to find me."

We shook hands all around as the three of us left the doctor's office. Doctor Hamilton hurried off toward the stairway, and when he was out of earshot, Winfield said, "Looks like we jumped the gun by driving down here this morning. That's too bad. I could really use some answers."

I nodded in agreement. "So could I. As long as we're here, though, maybe we should look in on Millie. It couldn't hurt."

"I was thinking the same thing."

Back downstairs at the reception counter, Winfield asked for Millie Grebb's room number. The receptionist consulted her clipboard and told us that Miss Grebb was in the northeast wing, room number 1109. She added a polite reminder that Miss Grebb was not yet allowed visitors.

Winfield thanked the woman and told her that because this was official police business, he needed to at least look in on Miss Grebb. He assured the receptionist that we would not disturb her rest.

We went through a short connecting hallway that ran in front of the courtyard and entered Torrance Memorial's northeast wing. Room 1109 was easy to spot because of the uniformed patrol officer standing next to its closed door. Winfield showed his badge to the officer, and we slipped quietly into the stark white room.

Millie was sleeping. At least I assume it was Millie Grebb in the bed. I couldn't tell for sure because her face was completely obscured by bandages. I looked at Bob. He looked back at me with a grim expression, and we tiptoed out of the room.

Out in the hallway Winfield turned to the patrolman outside the door. "Has anyone besides the hospital staff been to see Miss Grebb?"

"Only her mother. Missus Grebb was here yesterday, Thursday, for a short time, maybe fifteen minutes, and she showed up again about an hour ago, but she only stayed for a few minutes. Otherwise it's been quiet."

Winfield and I looked at each other again. Then he thanked the Torrance cop, and we hiked back to his Oldsmobile. Bob started the engine, and we sat there for a few minutes listening to it idle. Finally he said, "Interesting."

"What's interesting?"

"That Gladys Grebb hasn't spent more than twenty minutes with her severely injured daughter during the past two days."

"Yes, that is interesting, particularly since Gladys told Detective Danny she wanted to stay in Long Beach so she'd be closer to Millie."

Winfield looked perplexed. "I talked to Andy Buchholtz in Long Beach on the telephone this morning and he said Gladys was still at The Breakers and everything was quiet there. Also, Gladys' car is in the hotel garage. She can go out anytime she wants. So why hasn't she spent more time with her daughter?"

"If I had to guess, I'd say Gladys is suffering from acute depression."

"Depression? I can understand her being concerned, but she should be pleased with her daughter's improvement. Doctor Hamilton seems to think Millie will recover from most of her injuries. That sounds like good news to me."

"That's not what I meant. Think about it, Bob. With all that scarring on her face, Diana Dean's film career is over and done with and so are Gladys Grebb's dreams of fame and fortune as the mother of a big movie star. Gladys is back to being nobody. That's why she'd be depressed."

Bob looked almost shocked. "Geez, Johnny, that's a damned cynical way of looking at it!"

"It's a realistic way of looking at it. Would you mind stopping at a public telephone? I need to call my office."

Winfield put the Oldsmobile in gear, and we headed west. After some zigging and zagging, Bobby turned right on Hawthorne Boulevard. A few blocks later he pulled into a Flying A and parked next to the station's public telephone booth.

I dialed "o" for the operator and made a collect call to my office. When Tess accepted the charges, I asked if Will had checked in yet. She said he hadn't. I told her when he did to have him wait for me behind the administration building at Warner's. I'd be there in an hour or so.

I climbed into the Oldsmobile, and Winfield pointed it north. We were on our way back to Hollywood, the land of fragile dreams.

Twenty-Four

Bob Winfield dropped me off at the Highland Boulevard entrance to the First National Bank Building around eleven o'clock. Hollywood looked quite different than it did a few hours before. The clouds had gone off to make puddles elsewhere, and the sun was out in all its glory. The lake covering Hollywood and Highland had receded to a manageable depth of six or so inches, and traffic once again moved smoothly through the intersection—well, as smoothly as it ever did.

Up and down Hollywood Boulevard city utility crews were busy hanging the traditional Christmas tree decorations on the streetlight poles, transforming the glamour capital of the world into a holiday wonderland. Santa Claus would arrive in Hollywood tonight come hell or high water.

I climbed the stairs and walked down the second-floor hallway to my office. Tess was sitting at my desk sorting the morning mail. I said, "Hiya, Kiddo."

She held up an advertising postcard. "Are you interested in the investment opportunity of the century?"

"Nope. I've already made all my investments for this century."

She dropped the postcard into my wastebasket and said, "Will called about half an hour ago. I gave him your message. You want your desk back?"

Flopping into one of my new guest chairs, I said, "No, thanks. I'm only here for a minute."

"How's Millie?"

"She's been better." I gave Tess a summary of our conversation with Doctor Hamilton, concluding with, "It's a pretty safe bet Diana Dean's movie-making days are over."

"That's a shame. She's really a very pretty girl."

"The key word there is *was*, and in this town *was* isn't worth a plugged nickel. Slide the telephone over here, would you, please?"

Tess pushed the instrument across the desk, and I dialed Warner Brothers' number. The switchboard put me through to the office of the president, and Esther Smith said, "Mister Warner's office."

"Hi, Esther. Johnny Spicer here. I need to see Jack. Will he be there in about half an hour?"

"I'm afraid not, Mister Spicer. Mister Warner left for a luncheon meeting. He won't be back for a few hours. Would you like me to give him a message when he gets in?"

"No, thanks. What I have to tell him would be better said in person."

In a cautious tone indicating she got my meaning, Esther said, "I understand. Should I put you on the schedule for about two-thirty this afternoon?"

"That will be fine. Thanks."

"Is there anything else I can help you with, Mister Spicer?"

"Yes, there is one other thing. I would like to look into a couple of things at Universal. By chance, do you have a contact there who could get me past the gate?"

Esther was quiet for several moments. "I might, but that is something we should probably clear with Mister Warner, don't you think?"

She was dragging her feet on the subject of my visiting Universal Studios, and I wondered why. I pushed a little harder. "It might be, but I have some time to kill before Jack gets back from his luncheon, and I'd like to do something productive with it."

"I see." A few more seconds of silence came down the telephone line. "Would it be possible for you to stop by the office here before noon?"

The hands on my wristwatch were pointing to eleven-twenty. I said, "I can be there in about twenty minutes."

"Very well, I'll see you then."

I hung up the telephone and pushed it back across the desk. Tess opened the top drawer of my desk and retrieved my key ring. She handed the keys to me, saying, "Sounds like you'll be needing these."

"I guess I will. I'm not sure exactly when I'll be back, but it will be in plenty of time to grab some dinner before we go up to Saul's shindig."

Tess smiled. "Thanks, Johnny. I'm looking forward to it."

Ten minutes later, as I started up the pass on Cahuenga Boulevard, I got one of those feelings. It wasn't exactly psychic, just an uneasy feeling that something was out of whack. I automatically glanced up to my rearview mirror and got a reminder of why I put stock in such feelings.

The third car behind me was a light brown, two-door Chevrolet sedan. Was it the same light brown Chevy that tailed Will last Wednesday? Maybe or maybe not. There really are such things as coincidences, but they're rare in my line of work. I kept an eye on the sedan and gave myself a pat on the back for remembering to wear my shoulder holster this morning.

The Chevy stayed behind me when I turned onto Barham and was still there as I approached Warners' Barham gate. It passed me when I turned, and I got a glimpse of the young man driving it. Will was right; the guy wasn't very good at tailing. He was looking directly at me as he went by. All I could see was a silhouette in the driver's seat, not enough to recognize the guy if I saw him again, but the fact he was looking in my direction convinced me Will's tail was contagious, like influenza. I had it now.

There wasn't much activity on the Warner Brothers lot the Friday after Thanksgiving. A few cars and a small truck were parked next to Sound Stage Three, and a couple of guys were unloading a large wooden crate outside the power station on Avenue C. Other than that the place was quiet as a tomb.

Turning left on First Street, I saw Will, arms folded and lounging against the rear fender of his car—a dark maroon and black, two-door Hudson Terraplane coupe that looked to be about two years old. I pulled up behind him, and Will strolled over to greet me as I stepped down off my running board. "Hi, Boss. What's up?"

"A couple of things, but first I need to run up and see Esther Smith for a minute. Then we'll get some lunch and compare notes. This shouldn't take long."

The clock on the wall in Warner's outer office said I'd made Esther's deadline with a few minutes to spare. She looked up. "Hello, Mister Spicer."

"Hi, Esther. I hope I'm not keeping you from lunch."

"No, not really. Around here lunch hour is when you can get it, and it's very seldom actually an hour. Please sit down."

Esther indicated a chair next to her desk, and I sat in it. Then, with an uncomfortable expression on her usually calm face, she held up a folded piece of typing paper and said, "Mister Spicer, I have some information here that may be helpful to your investigation, but before I give it to you, I must ask you to agree to a condition."

Puzzled, I asked, "Alright, Esther. What's the condition?"

She took a deep breath and said, "I must ask you to keep this information strictly confidential. By that I mean I would prefer that even Mister Warner not know how you came by it. Is that agreeable to you?"

I knew Esther Smith to be extremely loyal to her boss, and for her to offer me information with that condition attached to it both surprised and intrigued me. "I think I can agree to your condition, but before I do, perhaps you should tell me why you think Jack would not approve of you giving me whatever is on that piece of paper."

Esther thought for a moment, perhaps choosing her words carefully. "I'm sure you understand that the motion picture industry is a very competitive business. Sometimes deals or arrangements are made by one studio that another studio might view as . . . well, let's say, unethical.

"Now, I'm not implying that Mister Warner has done or would do anything unethical, but he sometimes plays his cards, so to speak, very close to his vest. He treats all of his dealings as trade secrets never to be made public.

"The information I have for you has nothing to do with any such secrets directly, but it may lead you to the discovery of dealings some might consider shady. Under normal circumstances I would not choose this course of action, but at the moment the situation here is far from normal. It is extremely important to Mister Warner that you find out who is trying to stop the production of Thunderstruck as quickly as possible, and having weighed the risks against the possible rewards, I believe the ends will justify the means, although I'm not entirely sure Mister Warner would agree. I have faith in your discretion, Mister Spicer, but I must know I can count on you to keep this under your hat. Does that explain things for you?"

"It does, and I agree to your condition."

Esther looked relieved. "Thank you, Mister Spicer. What I have typed on this piece of paper are the name, address, and telephone number of a woman who worked here in administration for quite some time until five years ago when she took a job as Carl Laemmle's personal secretary at Universal. We got to be good friends while she was here at Warner Brothers, and we still get together once in a while."

She offered me the folded paper. I unfolded it and read: Frances Sorenson, 10371 Moorpark Street, Toluca Lake. CHapman 5817.

"Then when Mister Laemmle became ill four or five months ago and no longer came in to work at the studio, Carl Laemmle, Junior, dismissed Frances. He could have given her a different position there, but he didn't. Frances thinks Junior wanted her gone from the studio because over the course of time she learned a great deal about the company's business . . . confidential things they didn't want spread about."

I shook my head. "Now that seems pretty dumb to me. If you want to keep a loyal employee from blabbing, you don't run them off; you keep them close by and happy."

"That's the way most would see the situation, but Carl Laemmle, Junior, is . . . well, let us just say he has a reputation in some circles for not being terribly bright, He is known for sometimes doing things rashly or on a whim without considering the ramifications of his actions."

"I've heard similar tales about Junior Laemmle, except the tellers of those tales didn't put it nearly as diplomatically as you did. So, do you think Miss Sorenson can tell us something about what Diana Dean was up to before she came here?"

Esther nodded. "Yes, I believe she might. I took the liberty of calling Frances to see if she would be willing to help us out. I told her I didn't know specifically what you were looking for, but that you wanted to learn more about Miss Dean's past.

"Frances said she would do whatever she could to help us out. She's that kind of person, especially where her friends are concerned. I told her you might be calling this afternoon. She said she would be home all day. Frances is looking for another job, but she hasn't found one yet. I've put her name in for the next opening here. Her husband died of heart failure shortly after Frances went to Universal, and she needs the money."

"Thank you, Esther." I held up the paper with Frances Sorenson's information on it. "This may turn out to be a big help."

On my way back to where I'd left Will, I practiced saying Carl Laemmle's name the way Esther had pronounced it. Even though Laemmle had been the powerful head of a major studio for many years, his was the most mispronounced name in Hollywood. Most people said it something like "la-meal," but Esther pronounced it "lam-lee" so it rhymed with the word "family." It seemed likely that a person in Esther's position would know how to say his name correctly, and if I was soon going to talk to the man's former secretary, I figured I'd better get it right, too.

Will was back to leaning against the fender of his Hudson when I returned. I said, "Alright, mission accomplished. Let's go over to the commissary and get some lunch."

Since we weren't on the VIP list, Will and I found a table in the main dining room, which like the rest of the lot was quiet. After a young woman took our orders—a roast beef and cheddar for Will and a ham on rye for me—I said, "How'd your morning go?"

"It wasn't terribly productive. I started out at the Hollywood Reporter office. The gal I know was there, but it got me nowhere. She knew nothing about Diana Dean beyond the fact that Dean left Universal a while back and was now at Warner Brothers. Strike three.

"Next, I came over here and did a little better. A woman I know in casting told me off the record that Volodin wants an actress by the name of Dennie Moore to take over Dean's role. The studio is negotiating with Moore and will probably get her for the part."

The waitress showed up with our sandwiches, but reversed the orders when she set the plates down. She wandered away, we swapped plates, and I asked, "Who the hell is Dennie Moore?"

"She's a freelancer, not a contract player, but she's made a couple of films for Warner in the past few years. Young, perky type . . . usually blonde."

"If you say so. Anything on a new shooting schedule?"

Between bites of his sandwich, Will said, "Yup. The production department has Thunderstruck shooting resuming on Monday. They're concentrating on the scenes with Bogart and Sondergaard and the others until Dean's replacement is on board. They have the idea they can wrap up everything but the scenes with Dean's character by the end of the year. Then Bogart will do double duty, filming the remaining Thunderstruck stuff at the same time he starts his new project, an Errol Flynn western, or so I'm told."

I said, "No surprises there. I kind of figured they'd have to do it that way. Did you find out anything about Dean from Eddie Carr?"

Will swallowed a bite and shook his head. "I haven't been there yet. Unless you've got something else for me, that's my next stop."

"No, I can't think of anything that would be more productive. Go see what Eddie's got next. And starting Monday, plan to be on the set for every Thunderstruck scene they shoot. I'll keep working the other angles while you make sure nobody blows up a sound stage or anything like that. Okay?"

"Got it. Did you get to see Diana Dean at the hospital down in Torrance?"

"Yeah, I went down there with Winfield. It was pretty much a wasted trip, though. Dean's still pretty dopey. We did talk to the doctor handling her case, though. He says she's a mess—broken bones, a concussion, and her face is pretty badly cut up. The doc thinks she'll recover from most of her injuries, but there's going to be a lot of permanent scarring on her face. It sounds like Diana Dean's movie career is over."

Will looked sympathetic. "Too bad. She was a looker. How's Mama doing?"

"Winfield turned Gladys loose so she could be at her daughter's bedside, but according to one of the Torrance cops guarding Dean, she hasn't been there much."

"That's a bit surprising. You'd think she'd would want to be there all the time."

"Not if you know Gladys, but that's another story." Changing the subject, I said, "Listen, Will, we've got another little problem to work out."

"What's that?"

"You remember that brown Chevy you said was shadowing you on Wednesday?"

"Sure. What about it?"

"I'm pretty sure the same Chevy followed me over here from the office."

Will grinned. "Now isn't that just swell? I guess I was too boring for him."

"Well, I want you to get unboring, but quick. When we leave here I'm going to an appointment Esther Smith set up for me, but it's a hush-hush deal. Nobody is supposed to know I'm talking to this person, so I can't have this numbskull following me over there."

Will nodded. "I get it. I'm just going downtown to the Times building, no big deal about that."

"That's exactly right. I came in through the Barham gate. Go out that way, and maybe the guy will pick you up again. I'll hang around here for a few minutes after you leave; I need to make a telephone call anyway. Then I'll sneak out through the Warner Avenue gate. With a little luck he'll be following you by then or he won't see me leave. If not, I'll just have to lose the guy before I go where I need to go."

"Okay, I'll hang a sign on my back bumper that says, 'Hey, stupid, follow me!'"

"Whatever it takes. When you're done at the Times, head back to the office. If I'm not there, Tess will know what I'm up to."

We polished off our lunches and hiked back to our cars behind the administration building. Will drove off in the direction of the Barham gate, and I made use of a public telephone booth on the other side of First Street next to the building in which Dmitriy Volodin had his cluttered office. I told Frances Sorenson I'd could be at her place in about fifteen minutes. She said that would be just fine.

Then I slipped out through the Warner Avenue gate and wandered around the residential areas northwest of Olive for a few minutes. Seeing no Chevies, brown or otherwise in my rearview, I figured I was clear and made a beeline for 10371 Moorpark Street, a mile or so to the west.

Twenty-Five

Frances Sorenson lived in a tidy little development house alongside other tidy little development houses in a quiet neighborhood. Her modest, single-story home was some architect's idea of a Spanish hacienda with a pinkish stucco exterior and a partially enclosed entry porch. The hacienda theme was enhanced by a few southwestern embellishments like the exposed ends of wooden beams poking out of the walls here and there. The two chimneys sticking out of the roof had double-arched tops. A driveway down the left side of the house led to a detached garage out back. It was all very tasteful, if a little stark.

A concrete walkway bisected a neatly trimmed lawn and took me to three brick steps. I climbed the steps and entered the covered entry area. The front door was on my right, perpendicular to the street. I pushed a little white button that rang some chimes somewhere in the house. The door opened almost before the chimes stopped chiming.

The tall, slender woman who opened the door looked to be in her late forties. She wore wire-rimmed glasses perched on a rather pointed nose. That nose and a pair of thin, very prim lips went with a narrow face. The color of her eyes was a close match to her curly, dark brown hair. She looked me up and down with those eyes as I said, "Good afternoon, Missus Sorenson. I'm Johnny Spicer. We talked on the phone a few minutes ago."

"Good afternoon, Mister Spicer. Please come in."

She stepped back and opened the door wide. I removed my fedora and stepped through the opening into a fair-sized living room that was a little deeper than it was wide. The textured walls were painted stark white. A small dark wood table was positioned squarely beneath three multi-pane windows facing the street. The table held a perfectly centered brown ceramic vase on a perfectly centered white doily. Going by her living room, I suspected Frances Sorenson of being one of those fussy folks who spend a lot of time straightening pictures on the wall that don't need straightening.

A long couch covered in a dark brown, tweedy fabric sat along the exterior wall, centered below two more multi-paned windows facing the driveway. A dark wood coffee table was centered in front of the couch, and centered on it was a sparkling square glass ashtray. The windows were hung with wood-slatted Venetian blinds tipped in such a way as to cast shadow stripes across the highly polished hardwood floor.

Against the wall opposite the couch were two overstuffed chairs upholstered with tweedy brown fabric that was a close match for the couch. Positioned precisely between the chairs was an end table supporting a lamp with a light brown shade. The space between the chairs and the front door was taken up by a Zenith console radio in a cabinet of wood that was slightly lighter than the tables. At the back of the room the curves of an arched fireplace and an arched opening leading to a formal dining area seemed out of place among the horizontal and vertical lines of the room.

Frances Sorenson said, "Please take a seat, Mister Spicer. May I get you something to drink? Tea or coffee?"

"No, thank you, Missus Sorenson."

I sat on the couch, set my hat on the cushion next to me, and removed my notebook and pencil from my inside jacket pocket. Missus Sorenson sat in one of the chairs across from me and said, "How can I help you, Mister Spicer?"

"Esther Smith suggested you might be able to tell me something about Diana Dean's private life while she was at Universal."

Florence Sorenson put on a puzzled frown. "Her private life? Heavens, I wouldn't have the foggiest notion about any of that. What on earth does Diana Dean's private life have to do with anything?"

Feeling as puzzled as she looked, I said, "Perhaps we should back up and start again. Did Esther tell you the nature of my investigation?"

"Esther said you were trying to determine the identity of someone who is interfering with the production of a film being made on the Warner lot. Is that not correct?"

"That is exactly right."

She tilted her head slightly to one side and said, "Then what do Diana Dean's private affairs have to do with your investigation?"

"After the most recent incident—a spotlight was intentionally dropped on the set last Monday morning—Miss Dean stormed off the lot and disappeared. For a while we thought she might have been kidnapped, but it turns out she went into hiding, apparently fearing for her life. We suspect someone in her personal life might be responsible for the sabotage, perhaps a man with whom she was involved, but Miss Dean refuses to explain her actions or say anything about who scared her into hiding."

Florence Sorenson nodded sagely. "I see your point, Mister Spicer, but if you will forgive me for saying so, I believe you are barking up the wrong tree."

"Oh? What makes you think so, Missus Sorenson?"

"I think that because I was privy to several items of correspondence between Mister Carl Laemmle and others, including Mister Jack Warner, concerning Miss Dean's defection, if I may use that term, from Universal Studios to Warner Brothers."

Florence Sorenson watched me intently through her wire-framed spectacles, presumably to see if I caught her meaning. I knew what she was getting at, but if she expected me to be surprised, I disappointed her. The subtle signs of evasiveness I thought I'd seen in Jack Warner's responses to my questions about him knowing of anyone who might have a motive for sabotaging Thunderstruck already had me wondering if there wasn't another angle to the case, an angle related to his business dealings concerning the film or its cast. Missus Sorenson had just pried the lid off that can of worms.

I said, "I see. Can you be more specific about the contents of that correspondence?"

She shook her head. "Unfortunately, I cannot. You must understand, Mister Spicer, that despite the disappointment I feel over the way in which I was treated by Mister Carl Laemmle, Junior, after his father passed away, I still have an ethical responsibility to maintain the confidentiality of sensitive information I learned while in the employ of Universal Studios. Can you understand that?"

"I can. However, you may agree that if you have knowledge pertaining to a crime—specifically a murder—you also have a responsibility to reveal that knowledge."

Florence Sorenson looked puzzled again. Bringing her narrow eyebrows together in a frown, she said, "A murder? Esther said nothing about a murder in connection with your investigation."

"Esther may not have made the connection, but it is there nonetheless. A young woman named Ruth Barnes, who was Diana Dean's closest friend, was murdered the other night during what the police believe was an attempt to make her reveal Miss Dean's whereabouts. Since Miss Dean's disappearance seems to have been a result of the effort to stop the production of the film she was making, Ruth Barnes' death is directly related to my investigation. It is quite possible that the same person who is causing the problems on the Warner Brothers lot is also responsible for killing Miss Barnes."

Missus Sorenson gave the matter a long moment's thought. Finally she said, "What you've told me definitely puts the matter in a different light; however, I do not see why the saboteur, if I may call him that, would find it necessary to locate Miss Dean. I should think the mere fact that she was scared into hiding would have accomplished his purpose."

She made a good point. I said, "I don't yet have an answer for that, Missus Sorenson. But the fact remains that there is a connection between Miss Barnes' murder and the trouble on the Warner lot. If you could at least give me some general idea of how the correspondence you mentioned is related to the case, it may well lead to answers for all our questions."

Florence Sorenson stared off into space, and I wasn't sure if she was talking to me or simply thinking out loud when she said, "Yes, I guess it could." Then she looked me square in the eye again and said, "Alright, Mister Spicer, you have persuaded me. I will give you correct answers to whatever questions you ask regarding what I know about the matter."

Missus Sorenson was a sharp cookie. By agreeing to answer my questions rather than volunteering information she was, in her mind, protecting her ethical position. The onus was now on me to come up with the right questions. I gave it my best shot.

"Missus Sorenson, you used the word 'defection' when describing Diana Dean's departure from Universal Studios. I also know that Miss Dean left Universal without completing the terms of her contract. Would it be correct to say Mister Laemmle was upset about that turn of events and blamed Jack Warner for luring Miss Dean away?"

She gave me a single nod of her head. "That would be a more or less accurate description of Mister Laemmle's feelings on the matter. It would be even more accurate to say Mister Laemmle was furious with Mister Warner for what he termed underhanded and unscrupulous dealings."

I took another step in that direction. "Under those circumstances and considering Jack Warner's reputation for . . . shall we say questionable ethics, it seems likely Mister Laemmle would feel justified in seeking some sort of compensation from Mister Warner for the loss of Diana Dean. Was that the case?"

"It was. Mister Laemmle demanded the sum of fifty-thousand dollars in exchange for releasing Miss Dean from her contract."

"Fifty grand seems like a great deal of money when you consider that Miss Dean's contract only had a few months left to run. I am guessing Jack Warner refused the demand and either offered a smaller amount or told Laemmle to go fly a kite."

"The latter would be correct, Mister Spicer. In his final letter on the subject, Mister Warner told Mister Laemmle he would pay nothing for Miss Dean's remaining contract and that if Mister Laemmle didn't like it, he could take the matter to court."

I grasped at what I hoped was the next link in the chain of events. "Of course, Mister Warner said that knowing full well that the actual compensation a court might award would hardly be worth the legal costs of obtaining it. Unless Mister Laemmle was willing to spend more than the case was worth just to prove Jack Warner was a crook, I assume Mister Laemmle chose not to sue Warner Brothers. Is that correct?"

"You are exactly right, Mister Spicer."

"That being the case, did Mister Laemmle plan some other means of getting even with Jack Warner?"

Florence Sorenson said, "No, he did not; at least I was not privy to any such plan."

I'd hit a dead end. Mentally cursing Florence Sorenson for making me play guessing games, I backtracked. "Are you telling me Mister Laemmle simply dropped the matter? I find that hard to believe."

She hesitated for just a split second. "I am telling you Mister Laemmle, Senior, washed his hands of the matter."

I saw the glimmer of a clue in what she said, and remembering that all this happened shortly before Laemmle died, I grabbed ahold of it. "Then, did Mister Laemmle, Senior, turn the matter over to someone else; say, perhaps, his son?"

A faint smile crossed Florence Sorenson's lips. "You catch on quickly, Mister Spicer."

She made me feel like a school kid being awarded a gold star for a term paper. "So what did Laemmle Junior do about the matter?"

"I cannot say much about what steps Junior took from firsthand knowledge because he was already pushing me out the door, so to speak, by that time. I did pick up a few more bits and pieces of the story before I left.

"For example, I received a telephone call from Junior's secretary, a Miss Martha Benson, instructing me to send all correspondence pertaining to Diana Dean's departure from the studio to her office. Then Miss Benson called back a few minutes later and said Leo Kurtz was on his way to my office and I was to hand over the Dean correspondence to him."

Furiously taking notes, I interrupted her to ask, "Who is Leo Kurtz?"

Making a face like she'd just swallowed a mouthful of sour milk, Frances Sorenson said, "Mister Kurtz is an employee of Universal Studios. He has no official title that I know of. He reports directly to Mister Laemmle, Junior, and is paid a very large salary. I've heard Mister Kurtz referred to as a 'troubleshooter' and a 'fix-it man.'"

I looked up, took note of her expression, and said, "Got it. Please continue."

"Well, Mister Kurtz showed up in my office—actually the former office of Mister Laemmle, Senior's—and took the correspondence files. He demanded to know if there were any other carbon copies of the correspondence. Mister Kurtz is the sort of man who demands, rather than asks for, what he wants. I told him there were and that the additional carbons were in a separate file folder. He demanded that folder as well.

"The only other information I can offer on the subject is a short piece of conversation I overheard on the final day of my employment. I left early that day because Mister Laemmle, Junior, and Miss Benson were moving into the offices Mister Laemmle, Senior, and I had occupied. I packed up a few personal items and was on my way down the hallway to leave when I remembered a small potted plant I had forgotten. I walked back to my former office, and as I entered, I heard Mister Laemmle, Junior, speaking over the telephone. He was saying, and please forgive my language, 'That will teach that bastard Warner a lesson! He's had one coming for a long time!'"

I asked the obvious question: "Do you know who he was talking to?"

"I do not. At the time I thought he might be speaking with Leo Kurtz, but that is just a feeling. I have no evidence to support it."

Frances Sorenson fell silent, and when I glanced up from my notes, she wore a slightly wistful expression. I thought she might be feeling nostalgic about the days when she was top dog among the hired help at Universal. Whether or not that was the case, Missus Sorenson had said all she had to say on the subject.

Glancing back through the notes I'd taken, I asked, "Do you happen to know where this Martha Benson lives?"

"I do not know her address, but I believe she lives in Glendale. You should be able to find her in the telephone directory."

"What about Leo Kurtz? Any idea where he lives?"

She thought about the question for a moment, then shook her head. "No, I do not. Mister Kurtz is sort of a mystery man around the studio. His name was seldom mentioned in casual conversation."

"Could you describe him for me?"

"I've only seen him a few times, but I would describe him as short, under six feet, but broad and stocky . . . muscular. His complexion is dark, perhaps swarthy is the word, and his hair is dark and curly. His eyes are dark, maybe brown, and I always noticed his hands; they are large with thick fingers. Also, the times I saw him he was wearing loud sport coats—the sort with large plaid patterns in bright colors."

I added her thorough description of Kurtz to my notes and slid my notebook and pencil back into the inside pocket of my jacket. Standing, I picked up my fedora and said, "Alright, then, Missus Sorenson, I'll be on my way. Thank you for the information you've provided. It may prove to be very helpful."

"You are quite welcome, Mister Spicer." Then, as she stood to see me to the door, Frances Sorenson added, "I trust I need not say that my name must not be mentioned in reference to what I have told you today. It would not help my chances of securing a new position if word got around that I cannot be trusted to keep confidences."

"I assure you, Missus Sorenson, you may rely on my discretion. Your name will not be mentioned."

"Thank you, Mister Spicer. Good luck with your investigation."

Back in my Chrysler, I started the engine and looked over at Frances Sorenson's tidy little home. It hardly looked like a place where you'd expect to find information that would bust a case wide open. I wasn't sure that's what I'd found there, but at the very least I'd come away with a solid lead in a case where leads of any sort were damned scarce.

Twenty-Six

I walked into Jack Warner's outer office at two-thirty on the nose. Esther greeted me with, "Hello, Mister Spicer. Mister Warner just came in a few minutes ago. He's expecting you. You may go right on in."

Sticking my head through the doorway to Warner's inner office, I said, "Good afternoon, Jack."

He looked up from the papers on his desk. "Oh, it's you, Spicer. Are you here to give me my daily dose of bad news?"

I sat myself in one of the chairs opposite his desk and said, "It's not all bad, Jack. I went down to Torrance this morning to see Diana Dean."

With a note of concern in his voice that almost sounded genuine, Warner said, "How is she?"

"Well, I didn't actually get to see much of her because she's not up to visitors yet, but I did talk to her doctor. The good news is he's confident Miss Dean will recover fully from her injuries."

"And the bad news?"

"Unless you plan to make a horror movie, Diana Dean's acting days are over. The doctor said her face will be deeply scarred and there's nothing they can do about it."

Warner took the news surprisingly well. He simply nodded and said, "I was afraid of something like that. Too bad. I could have done a lot with her—that is, if I could have gotten her mother stop interfering."

Jack Warner looked thoughtful for a moment, then hollered, "Esther!"

Esther poked her head into the office. "Yes, Mister Warner?"

"Call legal and tell them Diana Dean won't be able to fulfill the terms of her contract due to disfigurement resulting from her automobile accident. They'll know what to do."

"Yes, sir. Anything else?"

"Yes. Send some flowers—something nice—to Diana Dean at that hospital she's in. Put a personal note from me with them. Say something about how we're all behind her and wish her a quick recovery. You know the kind of thing to say."

"Yes, sir. I'll take care of it immediately."

"Good, but call legal first."

Esther nodded and disappeared. Warner looked at me and said, "You got any other news, like maybe you've found the guy who's causing me all this grief?"

I wasn't going to tell him about my interview with Frances Sorenson, but I wanted to say something positive. Figuring he was just about out of patience with my lack of progress, I said, "I have a new lead that seems hopeful, but I just got it, so I need a day or two to find out where it takes us."

With more enthusiasm in his voice than I saw on his face, Warner said, "Good! Go get cracking on it. We're going back to shooting Thunderstruck Monday. I don't want any more problems."

I said, "Will do," and left him to the stacks of paper on his desk.

On my way out, Esther looked at me questioningly. I smiled and gave her a thumbs-up gesture indicating my interview of Frances Sorenson had been productive. She smiled knowingly and returned my gesture.

When I got back to Hollywood around three-thirty Tess told me Bob Winfield called around two and wanted me to call him back. I put Tess to work hunting down telephone numbers and addresses for Martha Benson and Leo Kurtz in the dusty collection of directories taking up space in my office bookcase while I called Sixth Precinct headquarters.

"Hi, Johnny. I thought you might want to know that Gladys Grebb has left The Breakers in Long Beach. She's gone back to her house on Monteel Road."

"I can't say I'm too surprised at that turn of events."

"Me, neither. For the moment I have a couple of patrol officers over there keeping an eye on the house, but there haven't been any indications of a threat to her since Ruth Barnes was killed, so I'm thinking of pulling the protective detail. I can make much better use of the manpower I'm wasting on her."

"That makes sense to me. Gladys is a material witness of sorts, but she flatly refuses to cooperate, even when telling us what she knows could save her life—that is, assuming someone is really out to do her harm. I'd say to hell with her. If she gets bumped off, it's her own damned fault and no great loss."

Winfield chuckled. "You sure have a swell way with words, my friend."

"I calls 'em as I sees 'em. Anything else cooking?"

"No. We're at a dead standstill on the Ruth Barnes killing. I still have Danny talking to anyone and everyone we can find who knew the woman, but other than that, I've got nowhere to go on the case. You have anything new?"

I'd debated telling Winfield about my conversation with Frances Sorenson. If what she told me had merit, I didn't want the LAPD stepping in and tipping my hand to Leo Kurtz. On the other side of the coin, Winfield's resources were much more extensive than my bookshelf full of dusty telephone directories. If Kurtz had any sort of history with the police, Winfield could dig up the dirt a lot quicker than I could. I decided to take a chance.

"I might have, but this is a little tricky. In exchange for the information I got, I agreed to keep my source confidential. Is that okay with you?"

"That depends on what you got from whom, but you know I always try to work with you if I can."

"Okay, let me lay it out for you. What I have fits with the theory that Ruth Barnes' murder is tied into Diana Dean's disappearance, which in turn is tied into Jack Warner's sabotage problem. If those connections aren't real, what I have won't be worth much to you."

Winfield said, "Alright, I follow you."

"What I have is a statement from someone who was in a position to know what goes on behind the scenes at Universal Studios. This person says Carl Laemmle, Junior, has a grudge against Warner for stealing Diana Dean before her contract was up and probably for other affronts that go back even further."

I could almost see Bob nodding as he said, "Okay, that makes sense so far."

"My contact thinks Laemmle told one of his employees to teach Jack Warner a lesson."

"Oh, yeah? You got the name of this employee?"

"Leo Kurtz. That mean anything to you?"

Winfield seemed to be giving my question some thought. After several seconds' worth of silence, he said, "I don't recognize the name, but I can do some checking. You have an address for this Kurtz character?"

"Not yet. My secretary is searching the county telephone directories as we speak. My source described Kurtz as short and muscular with a swarthy complexion and dark, curly hair—goes in for loud sports jackets."

"He sounds like an east coast import. Okay, I'll get somebody on it at this end and let you know what we find out. And thanks for the tip. I appreciate all your cooperation."

Winfield said it in a way that made me think he was surprised I was being cooperative. Maybe he was. Maybe he had good reason to be surprised. I told Bob he was welcome for the tip and hung up the telephone.

Tess looked up from one of the telephone directories she was perusing and said, "Forgive me for eavesdropping, but it sounds as if you've had a productive afternoon."

"Thanks to Esther Smith we might finally have something to go on. I'll tell you all about it when Will gets here."

"I'm here." I looked up as Will walked into my inner office. "I'd have been here sooner, but there's still some street flooding downtown. Traffic is all messed up. You have something good?"

"I might have, but tell me what you've got first."

Will plunked himself down in the chair next to Tess and said, "Well, I might have a little something, too, but it might also be nothing.

"Eddie Carr at the Times pulled all the clips he could find on Diana Dean. Mostly they were publicity articles planted by Universal and Warner Brothers, but she's also mentioned in a story about the Academy Awards ceremony last February."

He pulled a large, neatly folded newspaper clipping from his coat pocket and spread it out on the desk for me to look at. Somebody had penciled "Friday-2/24/39" in the margin at one edge of the clipping. The story included four two-column photos.

Will said, "Don't bother with the article; there's nothing in it. But take a look at the picture in the lower right."

The photo showed a group of people in the Biltmore Hotel's grand hallway—I recognized the joint's ritzy inlaid ceiling. I also recognized a couple of the people in the photo. I read the caption:

"The Universal Studios contingent arrives at the Eleventh Annual Academy of Motion Picture Arts and Sciences awards ceremony, including (from left to right) Deanna Durbin, Herbert Marshall, Diana Dean, and Gail Patrick. Miss Durbin's film 'Mad About The Music' was nominated for Best Story and Best Musical Score."

Diana Dean looked stunning in a snazzy evening gown with a plunging V neckline. Gladys Grebb could be seen behind Dean. She didn't look stunning.

I said, "Okay, what's here that I'm missing?"

"Look at the guy to Dean's right."

Only part of the fellow was visible because Herbert Marshall was in front of him. All I could tell for sure was that he was a young man and he wore a full beard and mustache. "What about him?"

"The way she's holding on to his arm, it looks like he was Diana Dean's date for the Oscar ceremony."

Removing the Sherlock Holmes-style brass magnifying glass from my desk drawer, I took a closer look. The glass just made Herbert Marshall bigger without revealing anything about the guy with Diana Dean. "She might be on his arm, or the crowd might have just pushed them together."

I slid the clipping and magnifying glass across the desk to Tess so she could take a look. She studied the image for a moment and said, "I think Will is right. It looks to me like Miss Dean is holding the man's arm."

Shrugging, I said, "Okay, I'm outnumbered two to one. Will, if this guy was Dean's escort to the event, his name should be on a guest list somewhere. Your first job for Monday morning is finding out who the hell he is."

"Okay, Boss. I'll see what I can dig up."

Changing the subject, I asked, "What happened to the guy who tailed me to Warner Brothers this morning? Did he pick you up when you left?"

"He sure did. His car was parked across Barham from the gate, and he saw me pull out. I turned left toward the pass, and he trotted right along behind like an obedient puppy. Then he stuck with me all the way downtown, but he was gone by the time I left the Times Building. I haven't seen him since."

"Good. Thanks for taking him off my back. I spent some of the afternoon talking with a woman Esther Smith thought might be helpful to us, but the woman's identity needs to be kept strictly confidential. Okay?"

Tess nodded and Will said, "Mum's the word."

I got out my notebook and summarized my interview with Frances Sorenson. I finished by saying, "So, in Missus Sorenson's opinion, our culprit is someone Carl Laemmle, Junior, sent to get even with Jack Warner for stealing Diana Dean away from Universal before her contract was up. This guy Kurtz seems to be the most likely candidate for the job."

Will had been taking notes. He looked up from his notebook. "Any handle on where this guy can be found?"

I shifted the question to Tess. "Any luck finding him in the telephone directories?"

Shaking her head, she said, "I've got a couple of directories still to check, but no luck so far. I did find a listing for that secretary, Martha Benson. She's in the Glendale book." Tess checked her notes and added, "Twelve-hundred-forty-B Orange Grove Avenue. From the address, it must be an apartment building of some kind."

Will said, "That would be north of Colorado Boulevard at the east end of town. It's a mixed neighborhood with small houses and apartment buildings, kind of a working man's neighborhood."

I said, "Okay, I don't know that calling on Miss Benson would accomplish anything at this point, but we know where to find her if we need to. This guy Kurtz is another matter. I'd like very much to get my hands on him. I gave Bob Winfield the dope on Kurtz, and he said he'd look into it. If the guy has ever been in Dutch with the law, Winfield will find out about it—might even get us an address from the Department of Motor Vehicles. That will take some time, though, so whatever we can do to speed things up would be a big help."

Tess said, "I might find him in one of the directories I haven't checked yet. I'll get back to that."

Will was staring at his notebook. "The guy's description sure sounds familiar to me. I wish I knew why."

I said, "Think you might have seen him on the Warner lot?"

He was frowning with concentration. "No, I don't think that's it. I'll keep thinking on it, but I could be remembering ten other guys. I'll also make a few discrete inquires. We don't want to tip Kurtz off that we're looking for him."

"One thing's for sure; the man in the Times photo you guys think escorted Diana Dean to the Oscar awards isn't Kurtz."

Will nodded. "Agreed. Anything you want me to do tomorrow besides finding Kurtz?"

"Nothing I can think of right offhand. He's our number one priority."

"Okay, I'll see what I can do. Do you need me to come into the office tomorrow?"

"I don't see any reason for you to do that. Just check in by telephone once in a while if you aren't at home where we can reach you."

"Will do. It's almost five, so if you don't need me for anything else right now, I'm going to hightail it over the pass before traffic gets too bad."

"Alright, Will. Have a good night. I'll talk with you tomorrow."

Will left and Tess closed the telephone directory in her lap. "That's the last directory we have, and I didn't find a single listing for Leo Kurtz, L. Kurtz, or anything similar."

I shrugged. "Thanks for trying. I was just hoping to get lucky. We'll find him eventually."

"I know, but it seems to me we're running out of time if they're going to start shooting Thunderstruck again on Monday."

"On the other hand, if Will and I are at the studio and this mug Kurtz shows up to cause more trouble, we might just as easily nab him that way."

"Yes, but what if he shows up there and you don't see him in time?"

I smiled. "Oh ye of little faith!"

Tess looked at the tiny gold watch on her wrist. "Not to change the subject, but it's getting late, and I'd like to clean up and change before we go to dinner, if that's alright with you."

"I guess so. I don't think Saul's shindigs are formal, though, so don't get too dolled up."

She grinned at me. "Just enough to get the attention of all the handsome men at the party."

"Hey, you've already got my attention. What more could a gal ask for?"

Tess had her back to me, getting her overcoat from the coat rack. She half turned and looked back at me over her shoulder with a sly expression. "A gal can never have too much attention."

Twenty-Seven

The night air outside Eli's Delicatessen was full of a fine mist that felt more like San Francisco than Hollywood. It gave the pavement just enough shine to reflect the sparkling Christmas lights and surrounded each bulb with its own softly glowing halo, giving the whole scene an air of holiday enchantment. Hollywood glittered with the Christmas spirit.

Tess and I stopped in at Eli's for a light supper before Saul Cohn's party. We covered the half block between Eli's and the First National Bank Building's Highland entrance at a brisk pace lest the misty air dampen our holiday finery. Up ahead, Hollywood Boulevard's sidewalks were already teeming with children and parents anxiously awaiting the festivities.

It was a few minutes past seven when we stopped off at my office to deposit Tess's overcoat. Even though she groaned a little about the damp air wilting her hairdo, I thought Tess looked quite festive in her ivy green sleeveless dress trimmed in white. She even had a sprig of holly and berries in her hair. I complimented her outfit and was rewarded with a kiss and a hug.

Demonstrating the full extent of my own holiday spirit, I'd donned a red tie for the occasion. Thus outfitted, we boarded the elevator for a trip to the tenth floor. The festivities were already in full swing up there.

The receptionist I'd threatened to throw out the tenth-floor window greeted us at the door, albeit somewhat dubiously. Saul's lobby and meeting room, both with large windows overlooking Hollywood Boulevard, were decked out with boughs of holly or, more accurately, cardboard representations thereof. The large meeting room table was pushed against one wall and sagged under the weight of every imaginable sort of hors d'oeuvre. A self-service bar was set up in a corner of the lobby. The lobby was also equipped with a small upright piano on which a bored looking chap was making Christmas carols sound like cocktail lounge music.

When I asked what she'd like to drink, Tess said it seemed to her like a vodka and tonic sort of evening. I made my way to the bar, assembled a vodka and tonic for her, and poured a double shot of a pretty decent Scotch over ice for myself.

Saul's guests added up to about twenty people, most of whom were clients or in-between level studio brass. The most notable of the studio executives was Harry Cohn, the head cheese at Columbia Pictures. Harry, I learned, was somehow related to Saul, although the exact relationship wasn't entirely clear to me.

While Saul and most of the studio brass were Jewish, they seemed to have no qualms about participating in a Christmas party. I'd heard that most of them celebrated both Christmas and Hanukah. Why not? Two holidays are twice as much fun.

A few of Saul's clients looked vaguely familiar to me, but the only one I knew anything about was a brunette with an animated face and a wicked sense of humor. I remembered her as playing sidekick roles in movies staring the late Thelma Todd. Tess put a name to the face for me—Patsy Kelly. Miss Kelly was a one-gal party all on her own.

Before long, brassy strains of *God Rest Ye Merry Gentlemen* played with gusto by a marching band made their way up the ten stories between Saul's office and Hollywood Boulevard. The music drew everyone to the windows. Hollywood's Santa Claus parade was beginning, and the long awaited arrival of Santa Claus would soon follow. Tess and I squeezed into a group at one of the lobby windows to watch the spectacle.

Led by an inordinate number of baton-twirling young women, the parade passed below us from west to east. In addition to the Hollywood High marching band which was playing the aforementioned Christmas carol, three other local high school bands added enthusiastically to the parade's soundtrack.

Of course, there were horses. For some reason parades always have horses, in this instance ridden by fellows in colorful Spanish caballero costumes. With the horses came floats bearing toy-building elves, characters from Dickens' Christmas Carol, and a bevy of scantily clad Christmas fairies courtesy of MGM. Interspersed among the floats, horses, and bands were a scattering of top-down convertible automobiles carrying the obligatory film celebrities. This is Hollywood, after all. Harold Lloyd, Jack Benny, Gene Autry, Leo Carrillo, and a few others I didn't recognize bravely endured the damp air to wave lovingly at their adoring fans.

Near the end of the parade a pair of reindeer showed up. They were led by smiling young women in scanty elf costumes. The reindeer looked rather dubious about the whole affair.

Then came the big moment everyone was waiting for. Santa Claus made a grand entrance aboard his sleigh, which was carried atop a flatbed trailer pulled by a truck. Apparently his reindeer were not licensed to fly in these parts.

Santa waved and shouted, "Ho, ho, ho, merry Christmas!" Alongside his trailer, more scantily clad elves distributed candy canes to the cheering crowd. The elves looked a little chilly. Perhaps they'd worn their summer elf outfits expecting the warm California weather they'd no doubt heard about up at the North Pole.

As the crowds lining Hollywood Boulevard dispersed in the wake of the parade, Saul's guests returned to the serious business of eating his food and drinking his booze. I'd been keeping an eye on our host, looking for an opportunity to get him aside and find out what, if anything, he'd learned about the men in Diana Dean's life. He beat me to the punch.

A few minutes after the parade passed, Saul tapped me on the shoulder and gestured for me to follow him. We went through the lobby and into his private office. There Saul settled into his desk chair and gestured for me to take a seat. He said, "I have a little something for you Johnny."

"Regarding Diana Dean?"

"Yes, but first, please tell me how she is recovering from her automobile accident."

We were playing another round of the dirt-swapping game. He'd dug up something worth swapping on Diana Dean, but to get it out of him, I would first have to give him something in exchange. I gave.

"I saw her doctor in Torrance this morning. Confidentially, he believes she will recover from the worst of her injuries, but her recovery will take some time." I waited a moment, and then told Saul what he really wanted to know. "The worst of it is Miss Dean suffered severe facial damage in the accident. Word is she will have scars so deep they cannot be repaired. The implication is that Diana Dean will not be making any more films."

Saul put on an expression of sympathy with about the same sincerity a bookie has for a customer who drops a bundle on a long-shot nag. "That is truly a shame. Miss Dean had a promising career."

"So I'm told. Now what do you have for me?"

Saul looked a trifle disappointed, like maybe he thought I wasn't showing proper respect for the game by crudely coming right out and asking for the dirt he had on Diana Dean. To hell with the rules; I needed answers.

"Well, what I have for you is this: Until a short time ago Miss Dean was definitely and most intimately involved with a young man. They started keeping company regularly just after New Year's and became, according to all accounts, quite serious about each other, but they kept it all a deep dark secret. Then it seems Miss Dean and the gentleman had some sort of falling out about a month ago, and he suddenly disappeared from the picture."

"And the name of this mystery man is?"

Saul leaned back in his chair, which didn't squeak like mine. "Eugene Alexander. He is a freelance script writer. Ever hear of him?"

I shook my head. "No, should I have?"

A sly smile tugged at the corners of Saul's mouth. "No, there's no reason you should know Eugene Alexander, but . . . ." He paused for dramatic effect, and I waited patiently for the punch line. When it came, it was a doozy. "Eugene Alexander is his nom de plume— his pen name. His real name might have a more familiar ring to it: Aleksandr Volodin."

Like I said, a doozy. "Some relation to Dmitriy, I presume?"

"His nephew."

"So Diana Dean was making a movie directed by the uncle of the man with whom she'd been intimately involved and had just broken up with. Is that it?"

"That is it, my friend."

Remembering the Times photo of Diana Dean at the Biltmore Will turned up, I asked, "Do you happen to know what this fellow looks like?"

"In fact, I do. I was actually introduced to him at some function or other. I recall him being tall and rather slender. He wore a beard and mustache, and I particularly remember his eyes; they were very blue and very intense—one might even say piercing."

His description, at least the build and beard parts of it, fit the guy in the Times photo quite nicely. I felt that familiar little tingle in my stomach I get when I stumble across something significant. "Any idea where I can find Mister Alexander?"

Saul opened his top desk drawer and took out one of his business cards. He handed it to me face down so I could see the address written across the back of it. "I got this from a friend in the script department at Paramount. It seems Eugene Alexander worked there for a short time as an assistant script writer. This is the address they had for him then."

I looked at the card. The address was up in the hinterlands of Tujunga—9927 Haines Canyon Avenue, to be specific. I asked, "You say he worked—past tense—for Paramount? Does that mean he's no longer there?"

"He is not. As I understand the situation, he was hired as temporary help because the script department was falling behind on some projects. When they caught up, Alexander was no longer needed."

Now jotting notes in my book, I asked, "How long ago was that?"

"I suppose I could find out, but my impression is that it was not long ago, perhaps late last Spring."

"Do you have any idea what he's up to now?"

"Only that he seems to be doing what most out of work writers do—freelancing. My friend at Paramount told me Alexander submitted a pretty fair script last summer. According to this friend,

Paramount was negotiating to buy it, but they suddenly walked away from the deal without any explanation. That sort of thing is not uncommon, but I have the impression there was some unpleasantness associated with this particular incident. I do not know the details."

I looked up from my notebook. "But you could find out the details?"

Saul got a suspicious look on his face. "I suppose I could. Why are those details important?"

"They're important because they might tie Aleksandr Volodin to my client's problem."

Now he looked surprised. "You think young Volodin is behind the incidents causing delays in Warner's film—a film being directed by the boy's uncle?"

"Stranger things have happened."

He thought about the situation for a long moment. "I guess they have, at that. And Diana Dean's mysterious disappearance from the Warner lot, along with the breakup between her and Aleksandr Volodin, might also have something to do with it."

I nodded. "They could, but that's all guesswork until I have some details tying all the pieces together."

Saul scribbled something on a notepad. "I see. Well, Johnny, given the circumstances, I will see what I can find out that might help you in that regard. In exchange, however, I will expect you to provide me with all the gory details when you figure this out."

The game again. Well, if he came up with the information I needed, he deserved the gory details. I simply said, "Agreed."

Outside Saul's office, the party was waning. I rescued Tess from the regalements of a tall, gray-haired studio exec who was old enough to be her grandfather. We thanked our host for his hospitality and rode the elevator down to the real world.

Back in my office, I told Tess what I'd learned from Saul Cohn. She said, "That sounds promising."

"Yes, it does. It's ironic, too. This morning we were fresh out of leads, and now we have two. Unfortunately, they point in entirely different directions. I think I'll leave Will to following up on Leo Kurtz, and I'll take a drive out to Tujunga in the morning and see what I can learn about Mister Eugene Alexander, aka Aleksandr Volodin."

Tess asked, "What can I do to help?"

"I'm sure you must be tired of hanging around this joint, but would you mind coming in again tomorrow to man the telephone and help me keep in touch with Will?"

"I wouldn't mind in the least. Actually, I've enjoyed being here all week. I'll miss the place when I have to go back to my regular routine on Monday."

Tess looked as if she meant it. I said, "Well, I'm glad it hasn't been too tough because you've sure been a big help to me, to say nothing of spiffing this place up. I still have to check the number on the door to be sure I'm in the right office."

She grinned. "It is quite an improvement if I do say so myself. I'm happy to help."

On that note we locked up the office and headed for the Montero Apartments. Hollywood Boulevard was all but empty now except for the Christmas lights and a scattering of debris left by the parade watchers. The lights still twinkled merrily, apparently oblivious to the fact that the parade had passed and left them behind.

Twenty-Eight

Tujunga
8:00 A.M. – Saturday – November 25, 1939

The tiny community of Tujunga sits in the rocky foothills along the southern slope of the San Gabriel Mountains about ten miles north of Hollywood. Back when Tujunga was first settled around the turn of the century, the founding fathers claimed it was the healthiest place in the world.

Unlike like the hogwash dished out by most real estate developers of the day, that claim had some truth to it. Tujunga is isolated from the crowded San Fernando Valley by the Verdugo Mountains, a small island of low peaks running from the northwest to the southeast above Glendale and Burbank. This natural barrier, along with Tujunga's slightly higher elevation, keeps the stink of civilization at bay, resulting in some of the cleanest air in Los Angeles county.

One by-product of this unique feature was the growth of a major industry catering to the needs of people suffering from illnesses requiring rest and recuperation in a locale with clean air. Today there are dozens of facilities around Tujunga catering to those suffering from asthma, tuberculosis, and even alcoholism. In southern California there's money to be made in the clean air business.

In addition to having breathable air, Tujunga is quiet, and the price of living there is considerably less than in Burbank or Los Angeles, exactly the qualities a struggling screenwriter like Eugene Alexander would find appealing. Oh, in case you were wondering, Tujunga is pronounced Tuh-HUNG-gah.

My route from Hollywood took me over the Cahuenga Pass and along U.S. Highway 101 past Universal Studios to Vineland Avenue. I turned right on Vineland and followed it north past San Fernando Road, otherwise known as U.S. 99. Across San Fernando Road, Vineland turns into Sunland Boulevard, which skirts the northwestern edge of the Verdugo Mountains and dead-ends at Foothill Boulevard.

Foothill is another one of those long thoroughfares connecting distant communities in the Los Angeles area. It runs mostly west to east, beginning at the southern end of the Grapevine portion of U.S. 99 and continuing all the way out to San Bernardino, a total distance of about seventy-five miles. I turned right on Foothill and a few minutes later I was in Tujunga.

The address scrawled on the back of Saul Cohn's business card was 9927 Haines Canyon Avenue. Having no idea where that might be, I pulled into a Flying A service station, and while the attendant filled my tank, I asked directions. The fellow told me to go east a few more blocks until I passed the Sunny Hills Sanitarium. The sanitarium would be on my left, and the next cross street was Haines Canyon.

The fellow's directions were right on the money, and not knowing which way the numbers ran, I took a guess and turned left onto Haines Canyon. It was a lucky guess. Number ninety-nine-twenty-seven was one block up on my left.

I pulled to the shoulder across from my destination and sat there for a while getting the lay of the land. It was a quiet workingman's neighborhood. The vehicles parked along the street were older sedans and pickup trucks showing signs of hard use. The residences were little bungalows and small duplexes, most of them separated by a weedy vacant lot or two. There was plenty of room left on Haines Canyon Avenue.

Eugene Alexander, also known as Aleksandr Volodin, lived in half of a small, corner lot duplex. It was an off-white, wood-frame building of no particular architectural style. The half of the duplex Alexander lived in faced Haines Canyon Avenue, and the other half faced the cross street. Even from my vantage point I could see signs of neglect, among them a dying lawn badly in need of watering.

I climbed down out of my Chrysler and strolled across the street. The paint was peeling from Alexander's front door. I knocked. Nobody answered and nothing moved inside the duplex. I knocked again, a little louder this time. There was still no answer. After a third knock that rattled the door in its frame got no response, I walked around the corner to the duplex's other entrance. The dry grass crunched under my shoes.

This time my knock got a response. The gent who opened the door was well along in years, slightly stooped, and leaning on a cane. He scowled at me from under bushy gray eyebrows and spat out, "Who the hell are ya and whatcha want?"

I responded with a healthy dose of my winning charm. "I'm sorry to bother you, sir, but I'm looking for Eugene Alexander. Nobody answered my knock next door, so I . . . ."

"You a friend of his, are ya?"

One of the most valuable skills a guy in my line of work can have is the ability to size someone up and pick an approach that will gain cooperation. Sensing that no friend of Eugene Alexander was a friend of this fellow, I said, "No, sir. I'm a private investigator." I showed him my photostat. "I would like to ask Mister Alexander some questions about an investigation I'm working on."

He squinted at my license and said, "Well, you're wastin' your time, Bub. That bum skipped out on me a while back. Left owing me two months' rent!"

"Oh? When did that happen?"

"A few days ago . . . Tuesday, it was. He woke me up in the middle of the night bangin' around over there. I went over in the morning to give him what-for, and he was gone—lock, stock, and barrel. Left the place in a mess . . . stuff scattered all over."

The old guy had it wrong. I wasn't wasting my time. Just finding out that Eugene Alexander disappeared the same night Ruth Barnes was killed made the trip worthwhile. I might even be able to learn more if I could take a look at what the guy left behind.

I said, "You know, Mister . . . ." I hesitated and he filled in the blank.

"Owens. Elmer Owens is my name."

"You know, Mister Owens, if Alexander left in a hurry, he might have unintentionally left something behind that could tell us where he went. Any chance you'd let me take a look around his place?"

"Ain't nothin' in there, 'ceptin' trash, but if ya wanta take a look-see for yourself, it's okay by me. Wait right here a minute."

He closed his door and I waited. When Owens opened the door again, he was holding a brass key. "Here's the key to next door. Just bring it back when you're done lookin'." He dropped the key into my hand and added, "And if you find somethin' that says where he's got to, I'd be obliged if you let me in on it. Two months' rent is a fair piece of change."

I said, "Fair enough," and hiked back around to the duplex's other front door. The old deadbolt lock was cranky, but I kept fiddling the key around until it clicked.

Owens had spared considerable expense furnishing the front room of his rental. It held a sagging couch and a beat-up armchair at which even the Salvation Army would look askance. The scarred walls had been painted cactus green sometime within the past century. Two grimy casement windows were mounted high in the wall to my left. A dining nook and kitchen opened off the back of the room. The doorway to my right, alongside a chintzy art print in a cardboard frame thumb-tacked to the wall, led to the bedroom. I decided to start in there.

The bedroom had another high-mounted casement window on the outside wall. A large, unfinished wooden wardrobe cabinet sat against the wall opposite the window. I examined the inside of the wardrobe and found nothing but dust and a few clothes hangers imprinted with the names of various cleaning establishments that probably went out of business no more than a decade ago.

The unmade bed smelled like a gymnasium locker room. I found nothing concealed under its sagging mattress but a crumpled Chesterfield cigarette pack. A nightstand between the bed and the outside wall held a small table lamp with a tear in its paper shade and a tin ashtray full to overflowing with cigarette butts. The nightstand drawer revealed more cigarette butts, apparently left over from the last time the ashtray was emptied. The only other piece of furniture in the bedroom was a narrow chest of drawers on the wall next to the living room door. I pulled all four drawers out and found absolutely nothing.

A door in the wall next to the wardrobe led to a bathroom with a clawfoot bathtub, a sink that drooped slightly from where it was attached to the wall, and a badly stained toilet. A medicine cabinet was attached to the wall above the sink. The mirrored cabinet door didn't do much reflecting anymore because most of the silver behind its glass was gone. The cabinet held nothing more interesting than an empty Bayer aspirin tin.

I went back through the living room to the combination dining room/kitchen. A cockroach the size of my thumb scurried away from a pile of dirty dishes on the chipped tile counter. The cupboards on either side of a window centered over a filthy sink were mostly bare, save for a nearly empty box of saltine crackers, a sticky jar of grape jelly, and a can of Campbell's chicken noodle soup.

The light in the small fridge at the end of the counter was burned out, but that was okay because I really didn't want to look too closely at the moldy contents of two glass bowls that had been in there since Grover Cleveland left office. There was also a milk bottle about half full of something that looked like lumpy cottage cheese.

A little two-burner gas stove sat opposite the kitchen counter. The sauce pan over one of the burners was caked with what might have been chili at one time, and the inside of the oven was spattered with who knows what. A kitchen wastebasket next to the stove overflowed with a collection of soup, hash, and bean cans, along with a couple of empty pint-sized bourbon bottles.

So far all I'd learned from my search was that Eugene Alexander was a pig. My last hope was the small dining nook in the corner between the living room and the kitchen. Its sole pieces of furniture were a spindly table and one wooden chair. The floor around the table was littered with crumpled sheets of typing paper, empty cigarette packs, and other debris from a tipped-over wastebasket under the table.

On the table itself were a grimy drinking glass, another empty booze bottle, another overflowing tin ashtray, and the stub of a yellow pencil that showed signs of having been chewed back when it was long enough to chew. The way all this debris was arranged on the table left a conspicuously open space in the middle that I surmised might once have been occupied by a typewriter.

I knelt next to the table and gathered up the crumpled sheets of typing paper, hoping one of them might be a piece of correspondence or something else that would tell me about the activities and current whereabouts of Eugene Alexander. One by one I straightened the sheets and found only bits and pieces of screen direction and dialogue that meant absolutely nothing to me. Strike three.

On my way out of Alexander's pig sty, I stopped in the middle of the living room and took one last look around in case I'd missed something. The only places I hadn't searched were in and behind the living room furniture.

I walked to the armchair, lifted the cushion, and found nothing. I tipped the chair forward and looked behind it. There, between the chair and the wall, was a wad of paper. I picked it up and was about to dismiss it as more pieces of discarded script when I realized the wad consisted of three pages and they were something different.

For one thing, they were on onion skin rather than regular typing paper. For another thing, they were carbon copies of some original typewritten pages. I looked more closely at them. The top page was a letter:

September 12, 1939

Mr. Cornell Ward
Script Department
Paramount Pictures
5451 Marathon Street
Hollywood, California

Dear Cornell,

I have attached the rewrite you requested of Scene 13 of my screenplay, Revolver. I trust the improvements will meet with your approval. I anxiously await your response.

Sincerely yours,
Eugene Alexander
9927 Haines Canyon Avenue
Tujunga, California

The letter was accompanied by two carbon copy pages of dialogue and stage directions. They weren't enough to tell me what the screenplay was about. All I could get from what I had in my hand were the names of the two characters in the scene and a sense that the story was a period piece, maybe set in civil war times or thereabouts. The names of the characters were Caroline and Sam W.

Yes, indeed, this was something entirely different. Saul Cohn told me Paramount was negotiating with Alexander to purchase a script. What I'd found behind the chair appeared to be confirmation of that. There was more to it though. The script rewrite had a bell-ringer in it—something that set off alarm bells in my head. What started my bells ringing was the name of the female character in Alexander's screenplay. I'd heard or seen the name Caroline in a similar context somewhere else recently, but at the moment, I couldn't remember where or when.

There was one other piece of significance attached to the letter and screenplay rewrite. Alexander had taken the trouble to make carbon copies when he'd typed them, but then he'd wadded them up and thrown them away. That also fit with what Saul told me. Paramount ultimately rejected Alexander's script. It made sense that, after going to all the effort of rewriting at least one scene at Paramount's request, Alexander would be upset when they told him they weren't buying his work. He might very well have wadded up his copies of the letter and rewrites in anger and thrown them away.

I smoothed the wadded pages out, folded them, and slipped them into my inside jacket pocket. Even though they only confirmed what Saul Cohn told me, the bells set to ringing in my head by the female character's name made me think I should hang onto what I'd found. The memory I was missing would come back to me eventually. In the meantime, I needed to find Eugene Alexander, and my search of his former residence hadn't given me the slightest clue about where to look for him.

Relocking the door, I walked back around to Elmer Owens' apartment and knocked. He answered my knock promptly. "You find anything over there to tell where that no-good bum has got to?"

"I'm afraid not, Mister Owens. But I do have another question or two."

"Okay, Bub, fire away."

"What kind of car does Alexander drive?"

"He's got him one of them Chevrolet cars—a brown one with only two doors."

"I don't suppose you would know the license plate number?"

"Nope, never had any call to remember it."

"That's okay. It was just a long shot anyway." Then a thought struck me. I reached into my side coat pocket and pulled out the publicity photos of Diana Dean I'd gotten from Esther Smith. I picked out one of the head shots and held it up for Owens. "Did you ever see this woman with Alexander?"

Owens took the photograph and turned it into the light to see the image better. Then without hesitation he said, "Sure did. I seen her pull up out front a couple of times. She was drivin' a big red roadster . . . a lot of machine for a little gal like that." He took another look at the publicity photo and handing it back to me, he asked, "This gal anyone famous . . . like one of them motion picture people?"

"Yes, she's a movie actress."

"That figures."

"How so?"

"It figures cuz them motion picture people is the kind of trash that would hang around a strange duck like Alexander. None of 'em are worth spit."

Suppressing a grin at Owens' high regard for actors, I said, "What makes you call him a strange duck?"

Owens looked like he was trying to think how to put his answer. Finally he said, "Just the way he looks at a person. He stares at ya like he doesn't quite get what you're sayin' and he's tryin' to figure it out. If you want my opinion, I'd say that Alexander is nutty as a fruitcake."

Sensing I'd gotten all there was to get from Alexander's former landlord, I said, "Well, Mister Owens, I'll get out of your hair now. I'm sorry to take up so much of your time, but you've been very helpful and I appreciate it."

"That's okay, young man. If you find that worthless bum, it will be well worth the time spent."

"I'll let you know."

I climbed into my Chrysler, headed back toward Foothill Boulevard, and contemplated what I'd just learned. For one thing, Elmer Owens' statement that Diana Dean frequently visited Eugene Alexander's duplex added credibility to Saul Cohn's information about Alexander being the mystery man in her life. Of course, I didn't know the purpose of her visits, but contemplating how much sweat Miss Dean contributed to the gymnasium stench of Alexander's bed didn't seem terribly productive.

From Owens' description of his former tenant's car, I also now knew Alexander was probably the guy who'd followed Will and me around off and on for the past few days. That connected him in some way to the job I was doing for Jack Warner and made him look guilty as hell, but guilty of what?

Most importantly, I'd discovered a connection between Alexander and the murder of Ruth Barnes. What connection? He'd packed up and skedaddled the same night Ruthie Barnes was killed. That was no coincidence.

Did Alexander kill her? That was another question yet to be answered, but he was certainly a strong suspect. His relationship with Diana Dean meant he probably knew Ruth Barnes was her closest pal, so if he was trying to find Dean, it made sense he'd go to see Ruth Barnes. But the relationship between Dean and Alexander was over and done with, so why would he be looking for her?

I'd figured Dean was running from whoever was sabotaging Thunderstruck because she thought her life was in danger, but was Alexander the saboteur? Why the hell would he try to louse up a film his uncle was directing? Besides Alexander himself, the only two people who could answer those questions—Diana Dean and Gladys Grebb—weren't talking.

I was having a relatively productive morning, but what I'd learned about Alexander left me with more questions than answers, and the most pressing of those questions was where the hell is Eugene Alexander now? The only person I knew who might have the answer to that question was Uncle Dmitriy.

Twenty-Nine

I pulled into a Shell service station with a public telephone booth near the intersection of Vineland and U.S. 101 and set about the task of finding Dmitriy Volodin. On a Saturday that could be difficult.

After getting the station attendant to turn a couple of quarters into nickels, I called Tess and gave her a quick rundown on what I'd learned in Tujunga. Then I asked her to check the Glendale and Burbank telephone directories to see if she could find a home address and number for Esther Smith. I told Tess I'd call back in fifteen minutes or so.

My next call was to Will Gardner. He answered on the second ring, and I recited the same report on Eugene Alexander I'd given Tess.

He said, "Sounds like we're finally making some progress on this thing! What's our next move?"

"I figured to pay a call on Uncle Dmitriy this morning, but I have to find him first. Any chance your gal, Betty, is at the studio today?"

"I'm afraid not, Johnny. In fact, she's right here. You want to talk to her?"

"Not unless she happens to know Dmitriy Volodin's home address."

"I doubt that, but I'll ask her if she has any ideas how we can get it."

Some muffled conversation came down the line, then Will came back on. "Betty says she's sure Volodin's address is on file in the

228

security office, but you'd have to go over there and coerce it out of 'em ."

"I'll save that as a last resort. I'm not especially anxious to tangle with your former boss again."

"I can't blame you there. You want me to give it a try?"

"No thanks, Will. I've got Tess tracking Esther Smith down. She'll know where Volodin lives. I'd like you to keep working on Leo Kurtz. Any luck locating him yet?"

"Not so far. I've called everyone I can think of except the cops."

I gave that a moment's thought, then said, "Tell you what, Will; call Bob Winfield at the precinct office. I don't know if he'll be there today, but if he is, find out if he's had any luck tracking Kurtz down."

"Okay, will do."

"One thing, though, don't mention Eugene Alexander to Winfield. I plan to let him in on what I found out, but I'd like to talk with Dmitriy first. Okay?"

Will sounded reluctant. "Okay, but are you sure that's smart?"

"What do you mean?"

"Well, I don't know Winfield like you do, but most cops don't take kindly to being left out of the picture, especially by a P.I."

Will had a point. The same thought had occurred to me, but one of the first things Bob would do was the same thing I was doing—tracking Dmitriy Volodin down to see if he knew where his nephew was. I sure as hell didn't want one of Winfield's ham-fisted cops muddying up those waters before I talked to the man. Volodin was the nervous type by nature. Getting his nephew's location out of him, assuming he even knew where to find Aleksandr Volodin, was going to take some finesse, and finesse sure as hell ain't in the LAPD handbook.

I said, "Let me worry about that, Will. I think it'll be okay."

"Alright, you're the boss. Say, I just had a thought. Ya know, Volodin might be at the studio today. They're cranking up production of Thunderstruck again on Monday, so he could be there getting things ready."

I'd already thought of that possibility, too, but I let Will think it was his idea. "Good thinking, Will. I'll swing by Warner's and see if he's there."

"Okay, Johnny. I'll let you know if I get anything from Winfield on Kurtz."

Then I called Tess back. When she answered, I said, "It's me again. Any luck finding Esther Smith's home telephone number?"

"Maybe. There are a lot of Smiths living in Glendale and Burbank, but only one E. Smith. If that's Esther, she lives at eight-two-one North California Street in Burbank. The telephone number is THornwall-four-one-seven-zero-five."

Balancing the telephone handset on my shoulder, I jotted the number into my notebook. "Thanks, Tess. I'll give it a try. After I make that call, I'm going over to the Warner lot to see if Dmitriy Volodin is there. I'll check back in a while."

Thinking the telephone company must make a lot of money off of private eyes, I dropped another nickel in the slot and dialed what I hoped was Esther Smith's home number. It was. Though her tone lacked the formality of her office demeanor, I recognized Esther's voice right away and said, "Good morning, Esther. This is Johnny Spicer."

Esther didn't sound at all surprised to hear from me. "Good morning, Mister Spicer. What can I do for you?"

"I apologize for interrupting your day off, but I need a favor."

"You aren't interrupting anything important. I was just doing some laundry. I assume the favor you're asking has something to do with the job you're doing for Mister Warner?"

"It does. I need to talk with Dmitriy Volodin as soon as possible, but I have no idea where to find him. I plan to check the studio first to see if he's there, but if he isn't, I need his home address or telephone number. I was hoping you might be able to get that information for me."

She hesitated, but only for a second or two. "I don't have that sort of information here. I would have to go to the office for it, but I've delivered papers to Mister Volodin's home for Mister Warner on a few occasions, so I know how to find his house. Would that help?"

"Yes, it would be a big help."

"Mister Volodin's home is in the Coldwater Canyon area of Beverly Hills. From Sunset you take Beverly Drive north until you come to Coldwater Canyon Drive. You take Coldwater Canyon to a short street called Heather Road. It will be on your right. Mister Volodin's house is the first one to your right on Heather Road."

Once again, I was balancing the telephone handset on my shoulder while I made notes in my book. I repeated her instructions to make sure I had them right. "Beverly to Coldwater Canyon Drive to Heather. First house to the right on Heather. That right?"

"That's correct, Mister Spicer. Mister Volodin's telephone number might be in the Beverly Hills directory, but that's unlikely. Still, it would be better if you could call and let him know to expect you. Would you like me to drive over to the office and get his number? I could meet you there since you're going to the studio anyway."

"Thank you, Esther, but I don't think that will be necessary. Is Mister Warner available this weekend in the event I need to reach him?"

"Mister Warner is out of town until Sunday evening. He will be back in the office Monday morning."

"Okay, Esther. As usual, you've been a big help. I'll stop by the office Monday morning to bring Mister Warner up to date. Thanks."

At 10:25 by my wristwatch I drove up to Warner's Barham gate. The guard, another ex-cop type, checked me onto the lot, and I asked, "Is Dmitriy Volodin here this morning?"

He checked his clipboard and said, "Mister Volodin signed in at eight-oh-five, and he hasn't signed out, so unless he left by the other gate, he should still be on the lot."

"Any idea where he might be?"

"I wouldn't know that, sir. He might be in his office or he might be anywhere."

"Alright, I'll hunt him down. That might be a little easier if I knew what kind of car Volodin drives."

The guard nodded. "When he came through the gate this morning, Mister Volodin was driving some kind of sporty foreign job. I don't know the brand or anything, but it's real low to the ground and painted black with blue trim. You can't hardly miss it."

I thanked the guard and drove ahead. I turned left on Avenue A, figuring to try Volodin's office first. When I turned right on First Street, the first thing I noticed was a low-slung, black sedan parked in front of the building that housed Volodin's office in the next block. The guard was right; you couldn't hardly miss it.

As I drew closer, I recognized the make of Volodin's sporty foreign job. Anyone with an interest in fast motor cars would know the stylish little sportster by its horseshoe-shaped grill and swooping lines. Dmitriy Volodin had himself a French Bugatti Type 57 Coupe—a very sleek, very fast automobile. Even in a town like Hollywood where expensive automobiles are a dime a dozen, a Bugatti is a rare sight. As I pulled up next to it for a closer look at the exotic machine, the man himself burst out of the office building. He looked to be in a dither. He was also in a very big hurry. The little red-faced man was taking very big strides toward his car. I lowered my passenger window and shouted, "Mister Volodin, I need a word with you."

He looked startled, as if he hadn't even noticed my Chrysler pulled up next to his Bugatti. Puffing, he shouted, "Not now, please, Mister Spicer. I am being in a terrific hurry."

Volodin yanked open the coupe's driver's side door. Unlike most American cars, the Bugatti's doors are hinged at the rear and open toward the front of the vehicle. For a man my size, this arrangement makes entering a low-slung car an awkward affair, but Volodin performed the feat smoothly. The last thing he said before he slammed the door sounded like, "I must stop him!"

The Bugatti's robust eight-cylinder in-line engine burst into its precision song, and for a very brief moment the rear tires spun, searching for grip in the loose dirt. Then the tires found the traction they wanted, and the sleek coupe jumped forward like a tomcat in hot pursuit of a doomed mouse. Dmitriy Volodin roared away in the direction I'd come, leaving a cloud of dust in his wake.

Rather than waste time turning around, I sped up First Street to Avenue C and turned right. At Third, I tapped the brake pedal, pulled the shift lever into first, and pulled the steering wheel hard around to the right, letting the Chrysler's rear end slide through the turn. Just as I got everything straightened out again and mashed the accelerator pedal to the floorboard, I saw the Bugatti barrel past a very startled gate guard and swing left onto Barham Boulevard in the direction of the Cahuenga Pass.

Volodin had hit a lucky break in the traffic on Barham. When I got there, however, I encountered a steady stream of cars. I waited while a slow-moving Plymouth rolled by, and then shot out onto Barham between it and a delivery truck. Somebody tooted a horn at me, but I was long gone by the time I heard it.

For a moment I was afraid I'd lost Volodin, but I caught a glimpse of the Bugatti's distinctive rear end up ahead. The traffic heading toward the pass had slowed him down, too. That was when I wondered what the hell I was doing chasing a famous motion picture director through the streets of Burbank. I'd acted on instinct when Volodin took off, and upon further consideration, I decided my instincts were spot on the money. Something big was about to happen, and Dmitriy Volodin was my ticket to the show.

Approaching Cahuenga Boulevard, I saw Volodin turn right and join the long parade of cars heading north. I followed, managing to keep the Bugatti in sight, but I had no illusions of being able to keep up with a Type 57 Bugatti on the open road—its light-weight body and eight cylinder engine were built for racing. The heavy holiday weekend traffic I would have cursed under different circumstances balanced the odds.

Officially designated U.S. Highway 101, Cahuenga Boulevard became Ventura Boulevard at the north end of the pass and headed more or less west and north along the northern edge of the Santa Monica Mountains, connecting the San Fernando Valley towns of Studio City, Sherman Oaks, Encino, Thousand Oaks, and so on until it came to the Pacific Ocean around Ventura. From there, U.S. 101 followed the coastline up to Santa Barbara and points north.

Through the valley, the highway alternated between four lanes of concrete in the busier commercial areas and two lanes in the less populated portions of the route. Volodin did his best to get around slower moving traffic in the four-lane sections, but I had no difficulty keeping him in sight. If things continued the way they were going, all I had to do was follow along until he got to his destination, wherever that might be.

Volodin was on a mission to stop somebody from doing something somewhere up ahead. I had the idea the somebody was his nephew, Aleksandr, but the something and somewhere were still unknown. With nothing more to do than keeping the black and blue Bugatti in sight, I settled back and reviewed the case in my mind once more, hoping to trip over some small piece of the mystery I'd missed that last ten times I'd been through it all.

My involvement in Jack Warner's problem began in Sound Stage Fifteen last Monday. The scene was very clear in my mind. Dmitriy Volodin calmly said, "Camera . . . action," and Bogart said the first line in the scene—something like, "Caroline, what does this mean?" At almost the same moment my attention was drawn to the Klieg light's movement up in the rafters and . . . .

That was it! That's where I'd heard the name Caroline recently! Diana Dean's character in Thunderstruck was named Caroline, the same as the female character in Eugene Alexander's screenplay. By itself, that didn't mean much—Caroline isn't a particularly uncommon name—but with that as a start, other similarities began falling into place.

The male character in Alexander's script was named Sam W. Since the Caroline character's name wasn't identified with a last name initial but Sam was, it might be reasonable to think there were two Sams in the cast. Thunderstruck was the story of Samuel Colt. Was the other Sam in Alexander's screenplay by any chance Sam C. for Colt?

Both stories seemed to be set in the same era, and then there was the name Alexander chose for his script: Revolver. Samuel Colt's claim to fame was perfecting the mechanism that made the revolver pistol possible.

The similarities between Thunderstruck and Revolver were so damned obvious, I couldn't imagine why I hadn't seen them before. Thunderstruck and Revolver were the same damned story! Okay, if I accepted that as fact for the moment, what were the odds of two screenwriters independently coming up with stories about Samuel Colt at the same time? Of course it was possible, but highly unlikely. That might mean one of the screenplays was plagiarized, but which one? Who came up with the idea first?

Saul Cohn said Paramount was considering a screenplay submitted by Alexander last summer. Based on the cover letter with the script rewrites I'd found in the writer's former apartment, that screenplay was Revolver and the letter was dated the twelfth of September. If Paramount had the script long enough to suggest rewrites, Alexander must have submitted it weeks or even months before that date.

Next question: Did Alexander submit his Revolver script to more than one studio—to Paramount and maybe Warner Brothers? Did Jack Warner swipe Eugene Alexander's script and put a new name on it? Jack's reputation for questionable ethics certainly did nothing to make that possibility less likely. If that's what happened and Warner beat Paramount to the punch by immediately starting production on his version of the film, it would explain why Paramount suddenly lost interest in buying the Revolver screenplay from Alexander.

Okay, the pieces of my scenario were fitting together pretty well, so take it further. For example, how would Eugene Alexander react to Paramount's rejection of his work when he discovered the reason for it? For that matter, how would he have found out Jack Warner stole his screenplay?

That was easy. He might have found out in one or both of two ways. For one, his Uncle Dmitriy was directing Thunderstruck and might have mentioned the new project Jack Warner had given him. Also, Alexander and Diana Dean were a hot item then, so it was even more likely she would have excitedly told him how she'd just landed her first leading lady role at Warner Brothers. Dean must have told Alexander all about the wonderful film, and it would not have taken him long to suspect there was something fishy going on.

So back to the previous question: How would Eugene Alexander react? He would be furious. What would he do? Alexander might think about suing Warner Brothers for stealing his story, but Jack Warner has clout and an entire legal department full of shysters to back it up, so the odds of winning such a lawsuit would seem impossible. What was the next best alternative? Sabotage Warner's production of Thunderstruck so he would drop the project, thus leaving the door open for Paramount to produce Revolver?

Yeah, that might well have sounded like a good plan to Eugene Alexander, and the first step in that plan would be demanding that his girlfriend, Diana Dean, walk out on the project. Knowing Dean and her mother, however, it doesn't take much imagination to figure how she would respond to the idea of voluntarily walking away from her first starring role. She would have told Alexander to take a hike, and that could explain their sudden breakup.

Then as Alexander went ahead with his sabotage plan, Dean had to know he was behind the problems on the Warner lot, and when the Klieg light almost killed Bogart, Dean figured she was next. Ruth Barnes gave credence to that conclusion when she told Tess and me Dean staged her kidnapping/disappearance because she was afraid for her life.

Yes, all of the pieces of my little scenario fit together quite nicely, but the credibility of any scenario declines in direct proportion to the number of "ifs" in it, and my swell little solution had enough ifs in it to sink a battleship. And even if I was on the right track, how did Dmitriy Volodin's panicky trip up U.S. 101 to stop someone, possibly his nephew, from doing something fit into it all?

An answer to that question began forming in my mind, and I didn't like it at all. Elmer Owens, Eugene Alexander's former landlord, described him as a strange duck who was nutty as a fruitcake. Saul Cohn said the man had intense eyes. Diana Dean was apparently terrified of Alexander. And there was a good possibility Alexander killed Ruthie Barnes, maybe in a fit of rage when she couldn't tell him what he wanted to know.

So what would a strange duck with intense eyes do when he discovered that his efforts to stop the production of Thunderstruck were in vain, that Jack Warner was forging ahead with the film? If my conclusions about Alexander were more or less correct, he would see Warner as the evil cause of all his grief, and since everything else he'd tried had failed, his anger and frustration might make Alexander see his last resort as facing that evil man-to-man and destroying it once and for all. Did Eugene Alexander plan to confront Jack Warner or worse? Is that what Dmitriy Volodin was talking about when he said, "I must stop him?"

I stared at the Bugatti half a dozen cars ahead of me. If I had Eugene Alexander figured right, and since I had no idea where Jack Warner was, keeping that little sport coupe in sight might quite literally be a matter of life and death.

U.S. 101 began climbing and winding its way through the foothills separating the western end of the San Fernando Valley from the coast, and the traffic in front of me started to string through the curves. Up ahead, Volodin was pouring the coal on, risking life and limb to pass slower cars on narrow two-lane sections of the road. I was falling behind, but I got a break when traffic bunched up again in the rural community of Thousand Oaks.

Once through town, though, the twisting highway ahead was wide open, and Volodin gave the Bugatti its head. I did my best to stay with him, but this was the kind of road the Bugatti was made to race on. My Chrysler was never intended to race on any kind of road, and after going around a couple of tight curves on two wheels, I had to back off. It was either that or end up careening down a hillside. By the time the highway straightened out again approaching Camarillo, Dmitriy Volodin was nowhere in sight.

I hotfooted it another fifteen miles into Ventura, hoping to spot him again. But when I pulled into town without seeing hide nor hair of Volodin, I knew I was fresh out of luck. Assuming Ventura wasn't his final destination, Volodin had four routes open to him. He could turn south along the coast to connect with the Pacific Coast Highway at Point Mugu, he could turn east toward Santa Paula, he could head northeast through the mountains toward Bakersfield, or he could continue north on U.S. 101 in the direction of Santa Barbara.

I could take a guess, but if I got it wrong, Jack Warner could end up dead. Since letting clients get bumped off isn't good for business, it was time to stop guessing and get hold of some hard facts, like where the hell Jack Warner went for his weekend "out of town."

Thirty

Hoping Esther Smith was still home, I wheeled into a Flying A station at the south end of Ventura, and while the guy filled my tank, I made use of the public telephone hung on the office wall. Esther answered on the second ring.

"Hi, Esther. It's Johnny Spicer again, and I need a little more information."

"Certainly, Mister Spicer. What would you like to know?"

"When we talked earlier, you said Jack was out of town for the weekend. Where did he go?"

Esther hesitated. "Is it very important that you know? Mister Warner doesn't . . . ."

"It could be a matter of life and death. I think I know who's been sabotaging Thunderstruck, and if I've got things figured right, the guy is off his trolley. There's a chance he might be going after Jack now."

"Oh! Mister Warner is in danger?"

"I think there's a good possibility he is. I'd rather be safe than sorry."

"Of course. Mister Warner is visiting an old friend in Santa Barbara, Doctor Ham Rothenberg."

Damn! I would have been much happier if she'd told me Jack was in Palm Springs or San Francisco or anywhere but Santa Barbara. Santa Barbara was only about thirty miles farther north on U.S. 101.

"Do you have the friend's address, and can you reach Jack by telephone there?"

"I have Doctor Rothenberg's address and telephone number, but not here; they're at the office."

"Then please go get them and wait for me to call. I'm about forty-five minutes south of Santa Barbara right now. I'll call you at the office when I get there. In the meantime, try to get a hold of Jack by telephone. Tell him . . . ." I paused and thought about what I wanted her to tell him. Deciding to go for broke, I said, "Tell him I have reason to believe Dmitriy Volodin's nephew, a screen writer who goes by the name Eugene Alexander, is the culprit who's causing all the trouble. The guy thinks Jack cheated him, and he may be out for revenge. Tell Jack to keep his head down until I get there. Got that?"

"Yes, Mister Spicer, I have it. I'll go right over to the office."

"Thanks. Talk with you soon."

I paid the attendant for the gas he'd pumped, and headed north. Beyond Ventura's city limits, U.S. Route 101 is a modern two-lane concrete highway with a passing lane down the center. Traffic was much lighter here than it was in the San Fernando Valley, allowing me to step down harder on the gas pedal. My Chrysler's speedometer needle hovered around 70, about twenty miles per hour over the posted limit. My eyes kept flicking up to the rearview mirror, expecting to see the flashing red light of a Highway Patrol motor cop there at any moment.

The coast route between Ventura and Santa Barbara heads northwest, following the gentle curves of the coastline. To my left, the deep blue Pacific was fringed with foamy lines of surf less than a hundred feet beyond the highway's white wooden guardrail. On my right, covered by trees and wild shrubs, were the gently rolling rises and dips of the coast mountain range's foothills. It was the sort of scene they print on picture postcards for tourists to send home.

Twenty minutes or so north of Ventura I slowed for the tiny community of Carpinteria—not much more than a few small businesses and some cottages along the beach—and then I was back up to speed. Another fifteen minutes brought me to the Summerland oil fields, an ugly jungle of derricks, piers, and railroad spurs that made investors a lot of money, but did little for the local scenery. Then the coastline and the highway swung almost due west, and I was on the outskirts of Santa Barbara.

Inside the city limits, U.S. 101, known locally as the Cabrillo Highway, parallels the beach for a few miles before making a right turn into the downtown area on a main drag called State Street. After that turn, I went another four blocks to the intersection of a street called Haley, where I spotted a Signal gas station on my right. I parked next to a public telephone booth there and used up the last of my pocket change placing a long distance call to Esther Smith's office.

Esther sounded agitated. "Mister Spicer, I've been trying to call Doctor Rothenberg's home every five minutes since I got here, but I can't get through. The telephone rings and rings, but nobody answers."

Trying to put her mind at rest, I said, "That's okay, Esther. I should be there in a few minutes. Where does the doctor live?"

I jotted Rothenberg's address down in my notebook as she read it to me. "He lives at nine-three-one Las Alturas Road. His telephone exchange is WOodland-seven-four-four-three."

"Okay, Esther, I have it. I'll go right over there and see Jack."

"Should I stay here at the office?"

"I don't think you need to do that, Esther. I'll check back with you at home after I've talked with Jack. I would appreciate one more favor though."

"What's that, Mister Spicer?"

"Would you please call my office and let my secretary know where I am and what's going on? I'm out of payphone change."

"Certainly. I'll do that right away."

I walked into the cramped little service station office where an old-timer in grimy Signal Oil Company coveralls with "Bud" embroidered on the front was sitting behind the counter studying a well-worn copy of Popular Mechanics Magazine. A Montgomery Ward radio on a shelf behind him was playing If I Didn't Care sung by the Ink Spots.

He looked up, and I said, "Excuse me, but could you tell me how to find Las Alturas Road?"

The fellow cocked his head to one side and looked thoughtful. When he was through looking thoughtful, he said, "That would be up in The Riviera."

"The Riviera?"

"Yup. That's a ritzy neighborhood up in the hills."

"I see. How do I get there from here?"

"Well, ya go on up another block on State here." He gestured toward the main drag in front of the station, "The cross street is Cota. Turn right and keep on goin' 'til Cota dead ends at Padre Serra. You make yourself a left turn there and then go on up to the next street on your right. That's Las Alturas. Whose house ya lookin' for?"

I looked up from the instructions I'd written in my notebook and said, "A fellow by the name of Rothenberg."

A big grinned covered Bud's face. "Oh sure, I know Doc Rothenberg. He's that high-tone Jew doctor with the big black Cadillac . . . brings it in here all the time for me to work on . . . has him a great big mansion way up to the top of the hill. You won't have any trouble findin' the place, but Las Alturas winds around back and forth a lot up there. Just keep an eye on the street signs so you don't get off on the wrong road. Doc's got him a great view up there. On a clear day like this you can see clear out to the Channel Islands!"

Bud knew what he was talking about. Fifteen minutes later I was slowly winding my way up a tree-covered hillside north of town. The houses scattered along the uphill sides of the road weren't all mansions, but the folks living in The Riviera, as Bud called it, were clearly in the chips. Approaching the top of the hill, I saw the flat roof of what appeared to be a two story French villa poking up above the treetops to my left. I'd been watching the house numbers, and even though this particular mansion had no number visible from the street, I figured it had to be the residence of Doctor Ham Rothenberg.

Just beyond a four-stall garage that would easily accommodate the doctor's Cadillac and three more vehicles of equal proportions, I came to a driveway protected by a pair of elaborate wrought iron gates. The gates were wide open, so I turned in and drove up the hill.

My first good look at Doctor Rothenberg's French villa was spectacular to say the least. The two-story monument to extreme wealth was painted bright yellow and trimmed in white. It sat across the far end of a rectangular-shaped parking area with a wide strip of painstakingly manicured lawn down the middle. I counted ten high-priced automobiles—Packards, Cadillacs, and the like— lined up around the edge of the drive. The last car in line was a black and blue Bugatti Type-57 Coupe.

I pulled up behind the Bugatti and took a moment to consider the situation. My guess as to Dmitriy Volodin's destination was right on the money, but what about the rest of my patched-together scenario?

I'd seen neither hide nor hair of Eugene Alexander or his brown Chevy, and the hilltop mansion before me was the very picture of tranquility. Birds chirped in the trees and soft strains of what I thought I recognized as a Ferde Grofe' composition, accompanied by snatches of gay conversation, drifted on the air from somewhere behind Rothenberg's mansion. If my guess about Alexander's evil intentions was wrong, I was going to look pretty foolish barging in on Jack Warner and his host. Well, it wouldn't be the first time, so I got on with it.

Climbing down from my Chrysler, I immediately felt the warmth of a brightly shining sun in the cloudless blue sky overhead. It was really too hot to be wearing a jacket, but I left mine on. Shoulder holsters with Smith & Wesson revolvers were probably not on the list of what the best dressed were wearing to ritzy parties in Santa Barbara this season.

I climbed the broad, tiled steps leading to the good doctor's front door and pushed a white button set in an ornate brass plate bearing the name Rothenberg in elaborate script. I'd waited there long enough to think about pushing the button a second time when the door was opened by a distinguished-looking Negro gentleman impeccably dressed in a three-piece suit. In crisp, precise English with a hint of rhythm to it that made me think of the Caribbean, he said, "Good afternoon, sir. May I help you?"

Holding out my business card, I said, "My name is Spicer. I'm working for Jack Warner, and I was told I would find him here. I need to speak with him on an urgent matter."

The butler gave my card the once-over, then gave me the same. Apparently deciding I was legit, he said, "Yes, sir, Mister Warner is a guest here. Please come in."

Removing my fedora I stepped into a rectangular foyer with a pink marble floor and large gilt-edged mirrors on the side walls. The butler asked if he could take my hat, and I gave it to him. Then a mental picture of Larry, Moe and, Curly popped into my head as he said, "Please walk this way."

We passed through a formal living room over-furnished with spindly legged chairs, tables, and what-not in a style named for one of the French King Louies with a Roman numeral; I couldn't remember which one. Most of the large, gaudily framed paintings on the walls looked authentic enough to be the real McCoy. Overall, the living room looked more like a snooty art museum than a place where anybody would actually do any living.

Eventually we ended up in a sitting room at the back of the house. Two pairs of French doors stood open, and beyond them, a party was in full swing on a curved terrace. The butler said, "If you will kindly wait here, sir, I will inform Mister Warner you wish to speak with him."

He went out onto the terrace, and I stood there taking in the festivities. About two dozen colorfully dressed folks were standing around under red and white striped umbrellas drinking pastel cocktails and daintily munching hors d'oeuvres, the dinky kind that hardly seem worth the trouble. Beyond the terrace was a long green lawn surround by trees, and beyond that was a spectacular view of the blue Pacific Ocean. Bud was right again—you really could see the Channel Islands from up there.

I spotted Jack Warner seated at a table to my right. The butler was standing patiently a few feet from him, not wanting to interrupt the casual conversation Jack was having with Dmitriy Volodin. Volodin looked perfectly calm, a far cry from the state he'd been in when I last saw him outside his office on the Warner lot. Both men laughed at something, making me wonder yet again if I was way off base with my hunch about Volodin's nephew. Could it be that Volodin rushed up the coast at high speed simply because he was late for the party? Had I misheard when I thought he said something about stopping someone?

Jack finally noticed the butler waiting to announce my arrival. The butler stepped forward and began to speak when a commotion broke out at the other end of the terrace. Everyone over there was turning to look at something that was beyond my field of vision from inside the sitting room. Suddenly a white-haired woman in a pink and white sundress pointed and yelled, "He's got a gun!"

Now everyone on the terrace was staring at whatever it was I couldn't see, and those closest to the left end of the terrace were backing away. I took two steps forward and peeked around the frame of the French doors. In that moment I knew without a doubt my guesswork about Eugene Alexander was right on the money.

The tall, slender apparition walking slowly across Doctor Rothenberg's terrace didn't look much like the tuxedo-clad fellow with Diana Dean in the newspaper photo taken at the Biltmore Hotel last February. This guy had the same beard and moustache, but the hair on his head was long and shaggy, as if it hadn't been washed or even combed in some time. The tail of his grimy white shirt hung out over gray trousers on one side, and the trousers were stained and wrinkled. The piercing blue eyes Saul Cohn described were there, though, and they were staring directly at Jack Warner. Jack's makeup department could not have created a more convincing madman.

Eugene Alexander's right arm was hanging loosely at his side, and in his hand was the biggest handgun I've ever seen. It was a revolver, and it looked to be at least a foot long from grip to muzzle.

Alexander was about twenty feet away from the house, and a few more steps would bring him opposite the French doors where I was standing. I ducked my head back behind the door frame and got my Smith & Wesson out of its shoulder holster. Compared to the canon Alexander was packing, my snub-nosed revolver looked like a toy cap pistol.

Just as Alexander came into my field of vision, his uncle Dmitriy ran through the crowd yelling, "Aleksandr! Stop! You must not do this!"

The big revolver in Eugene Alexander's hand was now pointed at Jack Warner and he didn't seem to see Dmitriy. He just kept walking and staring at Jack. Dmitriy blocked Alexander's path and said, "This is wrong, Aleksandr! Give me the gun and stop this nonsense!"

Dmitriy made a grab for the long barrel of his nephew's pistol and tried to pull it from his hand. I'll never know if Alexander pulled the trigger or if the revolver discharged as a result of Dmitriy trying to jerk it out of his nephew's hand, but discharge it did with a window-rattling boom. A couple of female party guests screamed, and the big slug from Alexander's canon went clear through Dmitriy Volodin and blew out the back of his shirt carrying a large chunk of the man's innards with it. Volodin dropped to the concrete like a sack of wet laundry.

As Eugene Alexander stepped over his uncle's body, I squeezed myself against the door frame to make a smaller target. Pointing his big revolver directly at Jack Warner, he screamed, "You scheming bastard! You will never again steal another man's work!"

Looking at him over the sights of my Smith & Wesson, I shouted, "Stop right there, Eugene! Drop the gun!"

Alexander turned slowly in my direction, and as the barrel of his revolver swung toward me, I fired two rounds in quick succession. In the same instant Alexander's revolver spit a foot-long tongue of flame at me. The wooden door frame to my left exploded into splinters, and something smacked the side of my head hard enough to jerk me sideways. I was looking for Alexander to see if I'd hit him, but something was out of whack. The colorful party scene on Doctor Rothenberg's terrace had shattered into a million pieces and now resembled the little chips of colored glass in a kid's kaleidoscope. They rotated slowly, and I was just thinking how pretty it all looked when some spoilsport turned out the sun and left me with nothing to look at but blackness.

Thirty-One

Casa Sobre El Mar, Santa Barbara
2:30 P.M. – Sunday – November 26, 1939

The first thing I saw when I woke up was a window. Outside said window there were some green pine trees and beyond them, a large body of blue water I thought might be the Pacific Ocean. I noted with interest, however, that the Channel Islands were no longer in the ocean.

Despite the missing islands, wherever I was now seemed to be a much better place than where I was last, if only because there were no madmen shooting at me with cannon-sized six guns here, at least not so far. Being a naturally curious fellow, I decided to wonder where this better place was.

Shifting my gaze slightly to the left, I spotted a clue. The clue was a pretty redhead sitting in a chair next to the window. Since she was dressed in white, softly focused, and her hair had a sort of haloish glow from the sunlight streaming in the window, I thought she might be an angel, which meant Eugene Alexander had killed me with his gigantic revolver and I was now in heaven.

After another moment of intense study, however, I observed that the angel was looking at a copy of *Life* magazine. While I'm certainly no expert on the subject of the afterlife, it is my general understanding that everybody in heaven is dead and thus would have no reason to be reading a magazine called *Life*. Did that mean I wasn't in heaven? Good question.

Needing additional information, I decided to turn my head so I could see more of my present surroundings. That decision turned out to be a big mistake. The instant my head moved on the pillow—

oh, did I mention I was in a bed and there was a pillow under my head? Anyway, the act of moving my head just a little had the immediate result of setting off an explosion of pain up there. Now I'm no sissy when it comes to pain, but this was a whole truckload of the stuff, and it made me groan. That, in turn, made the angel look up from her magazine.

She said, "Oh, you're awake, Mister Spicer."

I said, "Am I?"

With an angelic smile, she said, "It looks that way. You're alert and we're having a conversation. How are you feeling, Mister Spicer?"

Thinking it was very kind of the angel to be so concerned about my wellbeing, I took stock so as to give her an honest answer. Everything below my neck seemed to be working more or less normally. North of that point, however, was an entirely different matter. Somebody was up there pounding a big bass drum in rhythm with my heartbeat, and one of my eyes—the left one—wasn't seeing anything. "To be honest," I said, "I feel like Joe DiMaggio just mistook my head for a slow curve ball. Also, I seem to be missing an eye."

The angel smiled again and said, "Well, Mister Spicer, you'll be happy to know your eye is not missing. At the moment it's just covered with a patch because the doctor removed a few small splinters and your eye needs a little time to heal. The pain in your head is also to be expected because somebody shot you."

She stood, stepped over to the bed, and placed her fingers on my right wrist, saying, "By the way, I'm Nurse Susan."

Nurse Susan. That explained the white getup and the *Life* magazine. A nurse would have a natural interest in matters of life and death. It also explained why she was holding my wrist. Nurses did that sort of thing to check pulse rates. The angel mystery was now solved, but I couldn't help feeling a little disappointed. Mostly to myself, I said, "Too bad. One doesn't meet an angel every day."

Just then Nurse Susan finished taking my pulse and said, "I'm sorry, Mister Spicer, I didn't quite catch that. What did you say? Something about an angel?"

Lest she think I was goofy, I said "Nothing. You said somebody shot me in the head?"

She gave me another of those wonderful smiles. "I did, but the damage isn't too serious. Doctor Rothenberg will explain it all to you. My instructions are to call him when you wake up. So, Mister Spicer, if you'll just sit tight for a while, I'll make that call and he'll come over and give you all the details. Okay?"

"Well, I guess so. I was planning to go for a run on the beach, but I can put that off for a little while. Doctor Rothenberg, you said? If the rusty soup can where I store my memories hasn't sprung a leak, I seem to recall it was at a Doctor Rothenberg's house that I got clobbered. Does that seem right to you?"

"It does. And now you're at Doctor Rothenberg's clinic, Casa Sobre El Mar."

"And, if you don't mind, how long have I been at this Casa whatever you said?"

Nurse Susan glanced at her wristwatch. "A little over twenty-four hours. You arrived yesterday around two in the afternoon."

"Then it's Sunday afternoon now?"

"That would be correct."

"I've always been a whiz at deductive reasoning."

She smiled brightly. "You are indeed. Now, why don't you take a little snooze while I call Doctor Rothenberg? I'll be back in a few minutes."

I returned her smile, or at least I think I did, and said, "That sounds like a delightful idea."

I assume Nurse Susan must have left the room then, but I can't say that with any certainty because I was promptly off to dreamland. When I next awoke, Nurse Susan was back and she'd brought company with her—a short, balding fellow in wire-rimmed specs and a three-piece suit. Feeling the need to say something witty, I said, "Doctor Rothenberg, I presume?"

Nurse Susan cracked a small grin, but the guy with her just said, "That is correct, Mister Spicer. I am Doctor Ham Rothenberg."

Sensing that, despite his first name, Ham was a strictly business sort of fellow, I refrained from further witticism and said, "Pleased to meet you, Doctor."

"Likewise, I'm sure. How are you doing?"

"Thanks for asking, Doc, but at the moment your opinions on that subject are far more relevant than mine. So how am I doing?"

The good doctor looked a little bewildered, which caused me to think I wasn't following proper patient protocol. On the other hand, Nurse Susan seemed to be getting a kick out of our conversation, but she quickly erased her small smile when Doctor Rothenberg turned and said, "Give me his chart please."

He spent a few moments studying notations on a form attached to a clipboard and then said, "Well, Mister Spicer, you seem to be doing quite well—actually, better than expected—considering the trauma you've experienced. To summarize, you have a concussion, although judging by your level of alertness, not a terribly severe one. You also have a deep scalp wound in the upper left quadrant. I cleaned and stitched that wound, and I see no indications suggesting it won't heal completely."

"Your left eye," he continued, "is our biggest concern. I removed three small splinters of wood from the conjunctiva and cornea. They weren't deeply embedded, however, so it appeared to me your pupil may not have been severely damaged, and with time, the lens may heal and be restored. I've already spoken to a colleague of mine, a noted ophthalmologist with a practice here in Santa Barbara, and asked that he stop by in a day or two to examine the damage. His report will tell us what to expect in the way of recovery. Other than the items I mentioned, however, you don't seem to have suffered any serious or lasting injuries."

The possibility I might lose the sight in my left eye sounded pretty serious and lasting to me, but it didn't seem as if there was anything to be gained by questioning him further on that subject. Besides, I had several other questions that needed answering. "Doctor Rothenberg, you said the eye doctor would stop by in a day or two. I presume that means you expect me to be here a while?"

"Yes, Mister Spicer. I expect you to be here for at least three or four days, perhaps a week. When you can leave the clinic depends on how quickly your body is able to recover from the injuries you sustained."

I started to nod, but remembered what happened the last time I moved my head. Instead I simply said, "I see."

"Mister Spicer, if you are concerned about the cost of treatment in my clinic, let me put your mind to rest. You were injured while risking your life to save my good friend, Jack Warner. Jack instructed me to give you the very best care possible and to send the bills to him, regardless of the amount. Of course, I wouldn't think of such a thing. Jack was a guest in my home when . . . when this tragedy occurred. I will take full responsibility for the costs of your recovery."

"Thanks, Doc. I appreciate that. And may I assume from what you just said that Jack is okay?"

"Jack is fine. Like all of us, he was a bit shaken, but he wasn't physically injured in any way."

"Good. Now changing the subject slightly, were you out on your terrace when all hell broke loose yesterday?"

He nodded. "Yes, Mister Spicer, I was there."

"Would you mind telling how it all looked from where you were standing?"

Rothenberg hesitated. "I can understand your wanting to know the details, but I'm not sure this is the time to discuss those events. You need quiet and rest right now."

"I would rest a whole lot easier if I knew a few of those details, like what happened to Eugene Alexander."

Looking resigned, Rothenberg said, "I can't answer that question with any certainty, but at least one, if not both, of the bullets you shot at the man hit him. In spite of his wound, however, he was still able to run from the scene and escape through the trees and shrubbery along the perimeter of my property."

"What about Dmitriy Volodin?"

"I'm afraid Mister Volodin's wound was fatal. I pronounced him dead on the spot."

"I was afraid of that. So, including me, the incident resulted in three gunshot victims, one of whom is deceased. How are the local cops taking this? I assume they were called."

"Yes, they arrived moments after the incident. If you're wondering where you stand with them, there's no need for concern on that score. It happens that Chief of Police Hoelscher is a close friend and was attending the party. You could not have a better witness to what was clearly a case of self defense. Of course, the police will need a statement from you, but I've told them that will have to wait a day or two until you are up to answering their questions.

"Now, Mister Spicer, I must insist that you get some rest. Jack is leaving for Los Angeles today and asked if he could visit you before he leaves. Under the circumstances, I told him a brief visit would be okay, so you may expect him to stop in later.

"I will be back to see you in the morning. In the meantime, Nurse Susan here will be supervising your care and seeing to any needs you may have. Rest well, Mister Spicer."

After telling Nurse Susan he would update my chart and leave it at the nursing station, Doctor Rothenberg strode purposefully from the room. I said, "What a cheerful fellow."

Nurse Susan smiled her angelic smile at me. "Doctor Rothenberg may be a little short on bedside manner, but I assure you he knows his business. You couldn't be in better hands."

"I don't doubt that for a minute."

"Now, Mister Spicer, do you feel up to one more visitor? I know Doctor said for you to rest, but your secretary has been here since early this morning, and she's quite concerned about you."

"Tess is here? Yes, by all means, I would like very much to see her."

"Okay, I'll smuggle her past Doctor Rothenberg for a short visit. Be right back."

I'm not sure if it was just because my body craved rest or because they were loading me up with sedatives, but every time there was a lull in the activity, I drifted off to dreamland. When I next woke up, Tess was standing by my bed. I put on my happy-to-see-you face and said, "Hi, Kiddo."

Tess gave me a hospital smile in return. "Hi, yourself, Johnny. How do you feel?"

"Well, Doctor Rothenberg says I'm doing just swell, so everything is peachy keen."

Tess' look told me I wasn't fooling her. "You're in pain, aren't you?"

"A little—mostly when I try to do something really athletic, like moving my head. I'm sorry I couldn't let you know what was going on. I woke up for the first time just a little while ago."

"I understand. I did a little detective work of my own and found out what happened."

"Oh?"

Tess said, "Yes, Esther Smith called early in the afternoon to give me your message about where you were. When I didn't hear from you by late yesterday afternoon, I called her at the home number I found for you.

"Esther was concerned, too. She told me she'd been trying to call Doctor Rothenberg's number all afternoon, but nobody answered the telephone. Esther said she would keep trying and let me know when she got through.

"Next I called Will to see if he'd heard from you. I told him what you'd told Esther and he said he would drive up to Santa Barbara and see what he could find out. Nearly three hours later he called back from here, the clinic, and told me there was a shooting at Rothenberg's party, Dmitriy Volodin was dead, and you were hurt. He said you'd just gotten out of surgery and were expected to recover."

"I'm sorry, Tess. I didn't mean to worry you."

Suddenly her eyes filled with tears. Sobbing, she said, "I know. I'm sorry. I don't mean . . . mean to be so upset, but . . . I just don't know how to handle . . . all this."

I tried to think of something to say that would make things better, but came up blank, so I said nothing. After a moment or two, Tess dried her eyes and said, "Will was sure tomorrow's Thunderstruck shooting would be cancelled, but he said he'd go to the Warner lot in the morning anyway just to see what he could find out. He said he would call you here later in the morning."

"Thanks, Tess. I . . . ."

Taking a folded piece of paper from her purse, Tess said, "Johnny, I have to go back to work tomorrow. We have a rehearsal in the afternoon and we open a one-week job out on The Strip tomorrow night. So since I won't be at the office anymore, I signed you up for a telephone answering service. They will answer the office phone while you're away and take messages." She handed me the paper and added, "Here's all their information. They will also accept collect long-distance calls from you so you can get your messages from wherever you are. They add the long-distance charges to your monthly bill. If you don't want the service, you can call and cancel any time."

I stared at the page she'd typed. A line of capital letters across the top read, "Rosie's Professional Telephone Exchange Service." There was a bunch of information below that, but I didn't read it.

When I looked back at Tess, she was staring at her wristwatch. "I'd better start back. The traffic will be bad because of the holiday weekend."

"Yes, I guess it will."

Tess leaned over the bed and kissed me on the cheek. "Take care of yourself, Johnny."

Then she was gone, and that was that. I can't say I was surprised. We'd been down the same path before, more than once. I wasn't going to change, and Tess couldn't change. I drifted off again, thinking Tess was a good kid—too good for a mug like me.

The next time I returned to the land of the living, I had a new symptom—a lump in the pit of my stomach that had nothing to do with getting shot. Like my other wounds, I guessed it would eventually heal, but it would take some time.

Nurse Susan was back in her chair by the window, but she'd swapped *Life* magazine for a copy of *National Geographic*. I said, "What are the natives in Africa up to?"

Smiling, she looked up. "Actually, I'm reading about the nomads of Arctic Lapland, but I'm afraid they're a pretty boring bunch. How would you like something to eat, Mister Spicer?"

Until she asked that question, food was the last thing on my mind. But when she brought the subject up and I realized more than twenty-four hours had passed since breakfast Saturday morning, I was suddenly famished. "Sure, I could go for a couple of hamburgers and some French fried potatoes."

Nurse Susan thought that was hilarious. Laughing, she said, "I'm sorry to say hamburgers won't be on your menu for a while, but I'll see what the kitchen has to offer."

She left and I turned to look out my window. Moving my head still hurt, but not as much as it did before. Either I was doing better or whatever they were giving me for pain was finally doing its job. Outside, the shadows were long and a bank of fog was sitting on the horizon. The end of another day in paradise was rapidly approaching.

Nurse Susan returned with a tray, which she put on one of those hospital table gizmos with a base that slides under the bed. She turned a crank that elevated the top half of my bed so I was in a more upright position. Finally she slid the table over the bed, and I got a look at my dinner.

It wasn't much to look at—a mug of some thin, brown liquid and a tiny bowl of white pudding with lumps in it. Noting my lack of enthusiasm, Nurse Susan said, "I'm afraid beef broth was as close as I could come to a hamburger, but the kitchen turns out a pretty tasty tapioca pudding."

"I'm sure it's a gourmet delight. Do you know what's in tapioca?"

She cocked her head a little to one side and said, "No, what's in it?"

"Those disgusting little lumps are made from the root of the cassava plant, which is also an excellent source of cyanide. If tapioca isn't processed right, it will kill you deader than a doornail."

"Really?"

"Really."

"Well, all I can tell you is that none of our patients have ever keeled over dead from eating our tapioca pudding."

"Says you."

Nurse Susan grinned at me. "Yeah, says me."

As I took a swig of beef broth, a telephone I hadn't gotten around to noticing on the nightstand beside my bed rang. Nurse Susan picked up the handset and said, "Room One-Oh-Four." After a moment she added, "Alright, I'll be right out."

Hanging up the phone, she said, "You have another visitor. Are you up to seeing a Mister Warner?"

"Sure. Maybe he'd like some of my tapioca."

Nurse Susan went to get my visitor and returned with Jack Warner in tow. In typical Jack Warner fashion, he walked into the room like he owned it and said, "Hello, Spicer. Ham says you're gonna live. That true?"

My redheaded angel slipped out of the room, closing the door behind her, and I said, "He told me the same thing, so it must be true."

"Good! Then you can tell me what the hell happened yesterday. Nobody from the police chief on down seems to have any idea who the hell that maniac was or what the hell he was doing there."

Gesturing toward Nurse Susan's chair, I said, "Have a seat, Jack, and I'll tell you what I think."

He sat, and I said, "Keep in mind that much of this is conjecture based on bits and pieces I uncovered during the past few days. I'm pretty sure I have it figured right, but we won't know the whole story until the cops catch the guy, assuming they do."

Warner gestured impatiently. "Okay, so you're guessing. Who the hell was that guy?"

"His name is Eugene Alexander. That name mean anything to you?"

He shook his head. "Not a thing. Should it?"

"Maybe not. Where did you get the script for Thunderstruck?"

Looking confused, Jack said, "A couple of my staff writers came up with it. What the hell does that have to do with anything?"

"It has a hell of a lot to do with everything because your staff writers stole Thunderstruck from Eugene Alexander. I have evidence that proves Alexander submitted an identical script called Revolver about the life of Sam Colt to Paramount and other studios, probably including Warner Brothers, long before your guys came up with the idea."

Jack threw his hands up in the air and said, "That's nuts! Why the hell would my people steal this guy's script?"

"Maybe because it's a good story by an unknown writer and somebody figured they could get away with taking credit for it without much risk of being caught. That it's a decent script is proven by the fact that Paramount was negotiating to buy it. They already had Alexander doing rewrites until they learned you were producing Thunderstruck. Then they dropped Alexander's script like a hot potato."

"So this guy is pissed at me because he thinks I stole his damned script?"

"He doesn't just think it, Jack; he knows it. He's pissed, as you put it, because you cheated him out of a chance for the first big break in his career."

Warner looked honestly hurt. "If it's true that my people stole the Thunderstruck script, you gotta believe I knew nothing about it."

"That doesn't matter because your reputation precedes you."

His face was starting to turn a familiar shade of red. "What the hell is that supposed to mean?"

"Let's be honest, Jack. In some circles—actually in several circles—your tactics are considered somewhat questionable, even unethical."

He thundered, "I'm in a cutthroat business. I do what I have to do to make a profit. If a few jealous people think I'm unethical, tough shit!"

"Calm down, Jack. We're not here to discuss ethics. You hired me to find out who was sabotaging Thunderstruck, and that's what I did."

"You mean this guy, Alexander, is the one who caused all that trouble?"

"That's right. I don't have much in the way of physical evidence to prove it, but everything I do have tells me he's our culprit. And when his best efforts to stop production failed, he came after you personally. That's why he showed up at Rothenberg's party yesterday. He had every intention of blowing your brains out with that big revolver of his."

Warner looked shocked for a minute, then his expression turned thoughtful. "Okay, suppose you're right. How the hell did he know where I was, and if he was after me, why did he shoot Dmitriy Volodin?"

"The answer to both those questions is obvious when you know Eugene Alexander's real name."

"Which is?"

"Aleksandr Volodin."

"What? He's Dmitriy's kid?"

"Actually, his nephew. I've known that for several days, along with the fact that Alexander was romantically involved with Diana Dean before all this happened. She's probably the one who first told him about Thunderstruck, which he recognized as his script.

"Unfortunately, I didn't find out about his script until yesterday morning. By that time Alexander had flown the coop, so my next step was to see Dmitriy and find out if he knew where his nephew was. I caught up with him outside his office on the lot, but I didn't get a chance to ask my questions because when I when I found him, Dmitriy was rushing off in a big panic to get somewhere so he stop somebody from doing something.

"I followed Volodin from the studio, but I lost him before he got to Ventura. By that time I was starting to put the pieces together, and it dawned on me that Alexander might be out to get revenge for what he believed you did to him. I called Esther Smith to find out where you were, and when she said you were in Santa Barbara, I knew we were in trouble because Santa Barbara was in the same direction Dmitriy was heading to prevent something terrible from happening. I had Esther call Rothenberg's to warn you about Alexander, but nobody answered the telephone there."

Warner was looking glum. "Are you saying Dmitriy knew about all this and told his nephew where to find me?"

"We may never know the full answer to that question. I think it's safe to assume Alexander told his uncle where the Thunderstruck script came from, and I suppose it's even possible Dmitriy was mad enough to help his nephew sabotage the film. That would explain some things because I suspected it was an inside job early on.

"The important thing is that Dmitriy Volodin was killed trying to save your life. If he hadn't intervened at the party, there's a very good chance Alexander would have shot you before I could do anything about it."

Jack Warner shook his head slowly. He simply said, "Oh, my God."

Whatever pain medication they were giving me must have been wearing off because my head was throbbing again, and I was exhausted from my conversation with Warner. Trying to wrap things up, I said, "The worst part now is we don't know where Alexander is. My man, Will Gardner, will be on the lot tomorrow morning just in case, but I suggest you pick a couple of your best security people to act as bodyguards until the cops find Eugene Alexander. The guy is nuts. There's no telling what he'll try next."

Warner stood up and slowly walked to the side of my bed. "Spicer, I . . . well, I don't know what to say except thanks." He turned and walked toward the door, stopped in the doorway, and looked back at me. I had the idea he wanted to say something else, but he just nodded and left.

Nurse Susan must have been right outside the door because an instant later she came in. After removing the remains of my dinner, she cranked my bed down flat and gave me a pill. "This will help the pain."

I swallowed the pill, and she said, "It should take effect quickly."

It did.

Thirty-Two

Casa Sobre El Mar, Santa Barbara
7:00 A.M. – Monday – November 27, 1939

I awoke Monday morning feeling a whole lot closer to normal. The throbbing in my head was down to a mild roar, and focusing on the world around me required much less effort than on Sunday.

My only disappointment was discovering that Nurse Susan had been replaced by a male nurse named Roger who wasn't nearly as cute. Roger, however, proved quite helpful. After bringing me a breakfast of scrambled eggs and toast, he returned with warm water, soap, and a washrag so I could give myself a spit bath. It wasn't my usual shower, but it served to make me feel almost human again. My humanization process was completed with a razor, shaving cream, and a mirror. Thus, by eight o'clock I was ready to receive my first visitor.

Said visitor arrived in the form of a fit young fellow with a sincere expression and alert eyes. He was dressed in a dark blue suit and carried a small parcel wrapped in brown paper. The guy showed me a badge and said, "Good morning, Mister Spicer, I'm Detective John Walsh, Santa Barbara Police Department."

"Good morning, Detective Walsh. I've been expecting you."

Looking somewhat apologetic, Walsh said, "Well, I'm sorry to barge in on you so early in the morning, but being in a branch of law enforcement yourself, I'm sure you understand how these things work, procedures and all."

"I do, indeed."

"I must say I'm rather surprised to find you looking so well this morning. From what I was told of your injuries, I expected you to be in bad shape."

I gave him a small smile. "If you'd arrived yesterday, you would have found me in exactly that condition. So far this morning, however, I seem to be feeling pretty good."

Removing a notebook from his hip pocket, Detective Walsh said, "Good. Now, if you don't mind, I need to ask you a few questions."

"I don't mind at all."

"Last night a couple of our patrol officers were cruising up in the Mission Canyon area north of town when they noticed a broken guardrail. They investigated and found a sedan had gone off the road and down an embankment. The driver was still in the car, and he was deceased. We don't know yet whether the cause of death was the accident or the bullet wound in his chest.

"The fellow's California Drivers License identifies him as . . . ." Walsh checked his notebook to get it right. "Aleksandr Volodin—a weird spelling of Alexander with a KS instead of an X and no E before the R at the end. His address is in Tujunga, California. Does that name mean anything to you?"

"Yes, it does, Detective. Aleksandr Volodin is the man who killed Dmitriy Volodin and shot me Saturday afternoon. He was also known as Eugene Alexander, a pen name he used as a screenwriter. And if I had to guess, I'd bet the car your officers found was a brown Chevrolet."

Walsh nodded. "Exactly right, Mister Spicer. Can you describe the man you know as Aleksandr Volodin?"

"I only laid eyes on him once—that was Saturday at Doctor Rothenberg's home—but I have a pretty clear mental picture of him. He was tall and slender with a full beard and mustache. His eyes were pale blue. When I saw him at Rothenberg's, he looked rather bedraggled. His clothes were unkempt and his hair was mussed."

"That description fits the dead man to a T. Now I've got some questions about what led up to the shootings Saturday afternoon."

"Okay."

"According to Mister Jack Warner, you were conducting an investigation for him. Is that correct?"

"It is."

"What was the nature of that investigation?"

"Somebody was sabotaging the production of a film Warner was making. He wanted to know who."

"And did you discover the identity of the saboteur?"

"I am reasonably certain it was Eugene Alexander—the man you know as Aleksandr Volodin."

Walsh recorded what I told him in his notebook, then asked, "What makes you think he is responsible for the sabotage?"

"I have very little physical evidence to support that theory, but I do have evidence giving him a strong motive for stopping the production."

Detective Walsh said, "I see. What is that motivation?"

"Eugene Alexander believed the film's script was stolen from him. Evidence I discovered in his former Tujunga residence seems to prove he was right about that. The evidence I have is a letter Alexander wrote to Paramount Studios and a few pages of script rewrites, both dated well before Warner Brothers began production of their film. At that time Paramount was negotiating with Alexander for the purchase of his script.

"Also, I have knowledge that Paramount lost interest in producing Alexander's script when they heard about the Warner film. Paramount gave Alexander no reason for that decision, but it's likely he would have figured it out because he was dating the actress Warner chose for a leading role in the film.

"Finally, witnesses who knew Alexander say he was unstable to begin with, so it isn't much of a reach to think the news that he'd been cheated by Warner Brothers was enough to trigger a chain of drastic reactions that eventually led to murder."

Walsh wrote more notes and said, "Alright, I see the logic in that. Now this man and his victim had the same last name—an uncommon name—so we think they must have been related, but we haven't yet established the relationship."

"Dmitriy Volodin was Aleksandr Volodin's uncle. Dmitriy was directing the film Aleksandr was trying to sabotage."

"So it's your theory that Aleksandr shot the uncle as revenge for betraying him?"

I shook my head carefully. "No. I think Dmitriy Volodin's death was an accident. Aleksandr went to that party to kill Jack Warner.

"Dmitriy apparently knew or guessed what his nephew had in mind and went to Doctor Rothenberg's party to stop him from killing Warner. There was a struggle, Dmitriy tried to take his nephew's revolver away from him, and it discharged. I saw the incident from twenty feet away, and that's exactly what it looked like to me. Besides, it's possible Dmitriy may have actually helped his nephew sabotage the film. Aleksandr Volodin would have seen Dmitriy as an ally, so it isn't likely Aleksandr killed him intentionally."

"So it's your theory that Mister Warner was this fellow's target?"

"There's nothing theoretical about it. Aleksandr outright told Warner he was there to kill him. He pointed his revolver at Jack, called him a scheming bastard, and told him he'd never again steal another man's work or words to that effect. You must have that in your witness statements."

"I recall that we do, yes." Then after making a few more notes, Walsh said, "Okay, this fellow, Aleksandr, showed up at the party. He and his uncle struggled over the gun, and the uncle was killed. What happened next?"

"I arrived only a minute or two before Aleksandr showed up, although I think he might have been there a while. Did you happen to notice if Rothenberg's telephone line was cut?"

The detective looked surprised. "It was. How did you know that?"

"I didn't know it for sure, but Jack Warner's secretary tried repeatedly to reach him by telephone Saturday afternoon, and nobody answered her calls. When I thought about that, it made sense Aleksandr might cut the telephone line to keep someone from calling you guys for help.

"Anyway, I waited in the sitting room that opens onto the terrace while Rothenberg's butler went out to tell Jack Warner I was there to see him. That's when Aleksandr made his entrance. I moved to one of the French doors so I could see what the fuss was about and saw Dmitriy Volodin try to stop his nephew. It all happened very quickly. I had no chance to intervene before Dmitriy was shot.

"After that Aleksandr turned on Warner, and I challenged Aleksandr from my position just inside the French doors. He swung in my direction and we both fired at precisely the same time. I wasn't sure I hit him, but I was damned sure he hit me. I missed the rest of the party after that."

Nodding, Walsh said, "Well, Mister Spicer, it seems Saturday was your lucky day on a couple of counts. First, at least one of your shots hit Aleksandr. We won't know how much damage it did until the coroner finishes his autopsy later today, but it was apparently enough to make him flee the scene rather than complete his mission."

"You said I was lucky on a couple of counts. What's the other one?"

Walsh smiled. "This is where you got real lucky. The round Aleksandr fired at you went through the frame of the French door before it hit you. The wood absorbed a lot of its energy, so the slug didn't do nearly the damage it could have done had it gone a few inches to the left. If Aleksandr's aim had been that much better, we wouldn't be having this conversation."

"Yeah, but if I'd been smart instead of lucky, I would've figured out what Aleksandr was up to in time to prevent him from going after Warner in the first place. Tell me something, Detective Walsh. Have you recovered his revolver?"

"Yes, we found it in his car. Why?"

"What the hell kind of blunderbuss was he packing? That was the biggest damned revolver I have ever seen!"

Walsh smiled again. "That's one of the weird things about all this. The pistol Aleksandr had is a genuine antique. One of the guys at the station who collects old guns says it's a very rare Colt Walker, one of the first percussion cap revolvers. He thinks it might have been manufactured way back around 1847."

I couldn't help laughing out loud. Startled, Walsh said, "What's so funny?"

"Aleksandr Volodin's ironic sense of justice. The script Warner Brothers stole from him was the story of Samuel Colt and the invention of the very gun with which Aleksandr intended to kill Jack Warner. He called his version of the script Revolver."

"Well, I'll be. That is ironic."

"Yeah, ain't it? Alright, Detective Walsh, if you have no more questions for me, I have one for you. Where the hell do I stand with the Santa Barbara P.D. in all of this?"

Walsh seemed surprised at my question. "If you mean do we have any interest in charging you in connection with Aleksandr Volodin's death, you're completely in the clear. First, we don't know that your bullet actually killed him. And even if it did, we have statements from at least a dozen reliable witnesses who all say you shot in self-defense after he killed this fellow, Dmitriy Volodin. Hell, one of those witnesses is our chief of police, Fred Hoelscher! Mister Spicer, around these parts you are a genuine hero!"

"Swell. John Wayne and I can ride off into the sunset together, but before we do that, there's something else you need to do about your investigation."

"What would that be?"

"You need to call Chief of Detectives Robert Winfield at the L.A.P.D.'s Hollywood precinct. Aleksandr Volodin is a suspect in another murder Winfield is investigating. I'm betting you two can help each other out with your separate cases by comparing notes."

Walsh wrote in his book. "Winfield, you say? Okay, I'll call him as soon as I get back to my office. Thanks for the tip."

I grinned a little and said, "Always happy to help out a crime-fighting colleague, but don't be surprised if Winfield is a little miffed at me. We've been sharing information, but things happened so quickly on Saturday, I didn't have time to tell him what I figured out about Aleksandr Volodin. He probably thinks I was holding out on him."

Standing, Detective Walsh said, "I'll straighten him out on that score. For now, though, I think I have all I need from you, but we might need you to sign a statement based on what you told me this morning. I take it you'll be here a while longer?"

"That's what the doctor tells me. If not, you can reach me at my office or my home telephone number. My office number is . . . ."

"Thanks, but I already have those numbers, Mister Spicer." Then the package he'd placed on the nightstand caught his eye. "Oh, I almost forgot. That package there contains everything you had on you when you arrived here, including your Smith & Wesson. You'll find there's a round missing from the cylinder in addition to the two you fired at Rothenberg's. Our forensics guy fired that one so he'd have a slug to compare with the one in Aleksandr Volodin, assuming the coroner finds it."

It gave me a little lift to have my stuff back. I said, "Thanks, Detective Walsh. Would you mind putting the package in that closet over there? They probably frown on patients toting guns around here."

Walsh's visit left me relieved. No matter how the evidence stacks up, some local cops just get a kick out of harassing private investigators. Thankfully Detective Walsh was more interested in conducting a thorough investigation than making himself feel like a big shot.

The clock on the wall by the door to my room told me it was about nine-thirty when Nurse Roger showed up with my first pain pill of the day. His timing was good. The throbbing in the left side of my head was just climbing past the annoying level on its way up to greater heights.

A few minutes after that the phone on my nightstand commenced to ringing. I got the handset to my ear and said, "This is Spicer."

"Hi, Johnny. Will Gardner here. How are you doing?"

"I'm getting along okay. What's going on in the real world?"

"Well, I've been on the Warner lot since about eight o'clock and things are pretty quiet here. Of course, a lot of people are shocked about Dmitriy Volodin being killed, but that's not too surprising. Naturally, the Thunderstruck shoot scheduled for this morning was canceled.

"What's more interesting is what Betty told me. Donald Hanson, my former boss in the Security Department, was handed his walking papers this morning. Warner's chief of security, Blayney Matthews, stormed in and gave Hanson an hour to clean out his desk and get off the lot.

"Betty also told me Jack Warner ordered up a round-the-clock security detail for himself. I guess he figured out that Eugene Alexander was out to get him Saturday and it scared the bejeezus out of him."

I said, "Hell, he didn't figure it out. I explained it all to him Sunday afternoon, and it still took some convincing. But there's some news on that score. You can go up to Warner's office and tell him to relax. Aleksandr Volodin won't be causing anymore trouble. A couple of local cops found his body up in the hills near here. The younger Mister Volodin, a-k-a Eugene Alexander, has gone on to his reward."

"I'm sure that'll cheer Jack up. Anything else you want me to do, or are we just about wrapped up with this case?"

I thought about his question for a moment, then said, "There are still a couple of loose ends we need to tie up. Take a drive down to Torrance and have a chat with Diana Dean. Tell her what's going on, especially the part about Eugene Alexander being out of the picture, and see if she'll open up."

"She hasn't so far. You think she'll have a change of heart?"

"If my hunch that she was running from Alexander is right, she might. I'd really like to know what made her so sure he was out to get her personally. We're missing a chunk of the story there."

"Okay, I'll see what I can do. Anything else?"

"Yeah. After you see Dean, go talk to her mother and find out what she's got to say. Gladys is more a matter of curiosity than anything else at this point. I'd just like to know what her frame of mind is now."

"Will do. I'll give you another call after I've seen Dean and Gladys."

"Okay, Will. Talk to you then."

No more than ten minutes later my next two visitors of the day showed up. They were of the medical persuasion, Doctor Rothenberg and a rotund fellow with a bushy moustache, rimless glasses, and a three-piece suit. I couldn't help thinking of Teddy Roosevelt when I saw him, but Doc Rothenberg introduced him as the noted ophthalmologist, Doctor Abe Bergman.

Doctor Bergman removed the patch from my left eye and proceeded with his examination. I was disappointed at first because everything I looked at through that eye was blurry and out of focus. After checking things out with a little silver penlight and a magnifying glass, however, the good doctor assured me the blurriness was a temporary condition and that within a few days my vision would start to clear. My eye would eventually be as good as new. He applied a fresh patch to prevent me from inadvertently rubbing the eye and told me it could come off for good in forty-eight hours.

After the eye doc left, Doctor Rothenberg gave the rest of me the once-over and announced that my recovery was coming along just fine. He even told me he thought I would be well enough to go home in another two to three days. It would take longer than that for my scalp wound to heal completely, but he saw no reason why I couldn't resume my normal life as long as I didn't overdo things for a while.

That good news was followed by the arrival of my lunch and the return of Nurse Susan. Of the two, seeing my redheaded angel again did more for my spirits than my lunch. The tray she brought me held a toasted cheese sandwich and a peach half sitting on a lettuce leaf and topped with a gob of cottage cheese. Dessert was a cup of chocolate pudding. I wondered if the Pig 'N Whistle would consider delivering dinner to Santa Barbara.

After lunch I dozed for a short time. Nurse Susan woke me up around two o'clock. She wanted to know if I needed another pain pill and if I was up to another visitor. I told her I could wait a while on the pain pill, but a visitor would be just swell.

I kind of thought my visitor might be Detective Walsh again or maybe even Tess, but neither of those guesses was even close. The door opened and in walked Humphrey Bogart. "Hiya, Shamus! How ya holdin' up?"

"I'm doin' good, Bogie. What brings you up to the land of the rich and famous?"

We shook hands, and he said, "Well, bein' as how this morning's Thunderstruck shoot was called off and it's a nice day for a drive, I decided to pay you a call."

"I'm glad you did, but how the hell did you know I was here?"

"There's no big secret about that. Jack summoned me up to the mount this morning so he could tell me about Dmitriy getting plugged. He also took great delight in telling me all about the big excitement on Saturday." Bogie paused for a moment, then he grinned and added, "By the way, Pally, Jack Warner is now your biggest fan. He's told just about everybody on the lot how some lunatic tried to do him in and how you rushed in like the cavalry and saved the day. I guess that makes two of us on the lot who owe you a bunch. Anyway, he told me you got shot saving his hide and you were up here in this joint recovering."

"Did Jack give you any hints about what he's planning to do with Thunderstruck?"

"Yeah, only it wasn't a hint. He came right out and told me he's shelving the project."

That was a surprise. Now that the way was clear to finish the filming, I figured he'd put a new director on it and go full speed ahead. "Did he say why?"

"Well, he gave me a cock-and-bull story about already wasting too much time and money on Thunderstruck. He told me to forget about it and get started on the western he's got me in with Flynn."

I wondered if there might be another reason for Warner dropping Thunderstruck. Given that his writers stole the script from Eugene Alexander, maybe Jack had an attack of conscience. I didn't say that to Bogart, though. He'd have laughed at me for suggesting that Jack Warner even had a conscience. It was a pretty comical idea at that.

I said, "That's a shame. This was a pretty important role for you, wasn't it?"

Bogart shook his head slightly. "Not really. I mean, it was a good role for somebody, but not for me. Sam Colt just isn't my type of character. I don't know why I got picked for it in the first place. Hell, I wanted to turn it down, but my agent insisted I take it because it was a leading role. I shoulda stuck to my guns. Making a bad picture, even a bad B picture, can hurt a guy's career. No, I'm just as glad to be done with it."

Then he leaned forward and said, "Tell me something just between you and me, Shamus; did somebody really show up at that party to kill Jack?"

"Yup. There's no doubt about that." I almost told him more, but decided that would be letting out a cat Warner would rather keep in the bag. I just shrugged and said, "The guy was nuts, though, so it's hard to say why he did it."

Bogie cocked his head and grinned. "Okay, Shamus, if you don't want to say, I understand. But at least tell me if it was the same guy who was out to sabotage Thunderstruck."

"I think so, but we'll never know for sure. The guy is dead."

He looked surprised. "Is that so? Jack didn't tell me that."

"Probably because he didn't know it at the time he talked to you this morning. He knows now, though. I sent my man up to give him the good news."

We chatted a while longer before Bogart stood up and said he'd better be getting back to town. We shook hands and I thanked him for making the trip up to see me. He stopped in the doorway on his way out and looked back at me. "Ya know, Shamus, you're alright. I'm glad I got to know ya."

I just said, "Likewise." Bogie grinned and threw me a casual salute.

Not more than few seconds later Nurse Susan came through the door with a rather strange expression on her face. "Was that really Humphrey Bogart?"

"Yeah, why?"

"And that man who was here last night, he's one of the famous Warner brothers, isn't he?"

"So?"

My redheaded angel shrugged. "I don't know. I guess I'm not used to movie celebrities wandering in and out of this place."

It seemed Nurse Susan was a little star-struck. That surprised me. She didn't seem the type. I said, "Don't let 'em fool you, Honey. Actors and producers are no better than anyone else; they're just good at making people think they are."

Nurse Susan laughed. "You're funny, Mister Spicer. Like Mister Bogart said, "I'm glad I got to know ya."

I couldn't help smiling. "I assure you the feeling is mutual, Susan."

The telephone chose that moment to ring and Susan rushed over to hand me the handset so I wouldn't have to roll over and reach for it. I said, "Spicer."

"Hi, Johnny. It's Will again."

"Hi, Will. How did your interview with Diana Dean go?"

Nurse Susan was on her way out the door, but she must have recognized Diana Dean's name because when she heard me say it, she looked back and rolled her eyes.

Will said, "It didn't."

"She wouldn't see you?"

"She isn't at Torrance Memorial anymore."

This day was just chock-full of surprises. I said, "Well, where the hell is she?"

"That seems to be a state secret. Nobody at the hospital would say any more than she was no longer their patient. I got the idea that she was moved recently, maybe no more than an hour or two before I got there."

"She is the most disappearingest gal I've ever known. What does Gladys say about all this?"

"Damned if I know. She's gone, too."

"What?"

"The house on Monteel Road is vacant and there's a 'For Rent' sign out front."

Apparently tying up the loose ends in this case wasn't going to be as easy as I'd figured. Gladys Grebb giving up her fancy digs made some kind of sense because her daughter wouldn't be getting any more fat paychecks to pay the rent, but Diana Dean leaving the hospital in Torrance was another matter. Based on what her doctor told Winfield and me only four days ago, Dean couldn't possibly have recovered enough to be discharged. That probably meant she'd been transferred to another hospital somewhere, but where and why?

Will said, "Johnny, you still there?"

"Yeah, I was just trying to digest your news."

"Kind of baffling, isn't it? What do you want me to do now?"

Technically, I was still on Jack Warner's payroll, so I figured the budget could stand another day or two of Will's time. "I want you to track Diana Dean and her damned mother down. Find out where the hell they've disappeared to this time."

Will hesitated before saying, "Are you sure, Johnny? I mean, tracking them down might take some time, and this case is pretty well wrapped up. Does it really matter where they are?"

"You got something better to do, Will?"

"No, but . . . ."

"Then go find them!"

"Okay, you're the boss."

Thirty-Three

Casa Sobre El Mar, Santa Barbara
7:00 A.M. – Tuesday – November 28, 1939

Tuesday morning started off with more surprises. Nurse Roger was back on duty, and he arrived with an orderly in tow. The orderly was carrying clothes on hangers in one of those bags cleaners use. The clothes turned out to be mine—the stuff I'd been wearing Saturday.

Nurse Roger said, "We sent your clothes out to be cleaned because they were pretty messed up. The cleaner got most of the blood out, though, so they should do you for the ride home."

I said, "Thanks. Am I to take it then my departure from this delightful piece of paradise is imminent?"

He was carrying a beige terrycloth bathrobe and a pair of slippers. He tossed them on my bed and said, "That depends on how things go today. After breakfast you and I are going to take a walk to see how strong you are, then Doctor Rothenberg will be by to see how you're doing. He still needs to remove those stitches from your scalp, and it wouldn't hurt you to have another day or two to gain a little more strength. I'm guessing we'll probably cut you loose on Thursday or Friday."

Smiling, I said, "I don't want to seem unappreciative of your hospitality, but nothing would please me more."

I'd been up and out of bed a few times already—mostly to make use of the bathroom with Susan or Roger hovering nearby in case I ran into problems. Now it appeared I was moving on to more strenuous undertakings. I was more than ready to accept that challenge.

After completing my morning ablutions, Nurse Roger helped me into the robe and slippers he'd brought and steered me toward the chair instead of back to the bed. Then he went off to fetch my breakfast. For some reason my scrambled eggs and toast tasted better sitting in a real live chair. I devoured them with enthusiasm while the orderly changed the sheets on my bed.

Next came the walk Nurse Roger had promised. We left my room and hiked all the way down to the front lobby, a grand distance of about two hundred feet. I was a little stiff from spending so much time in bed, and I experienced a few episodes of dizziness along the way, but they subsided, and I found myself enjoying my first real look at Doc Rothenberg's swanky clinic.

The hall was floored in polished hardwood, the walls were papered in a cheerful seashell print, and chairs upholstered in a matching pattern dotted our route. Numerous large windows provided spectacular views of the ocean, and everyone we encountered along the way was smiling and cheerful. In short, the place seemed more like a classy resort than a place for sick people.

In the lobby, a modern curved reception counter faced two glass entrance doors. On the wall behind the reception area, a large sign carved in what appeared to authentic driftwood proudly displayed the words, "Casa Sobre El Mar." Below that, a line of smaller letters translated the name of the joint for those not fluent in Spanish: "House Above The Sea."

Nurse Roger was pointing me back down the hall from whence we'd come when I suggested a better idea. "It looks like a beautiful day out in the real world. How 'bout we step outside for a look at the view?"

He seemed pleased. "Sure, if you're up to it."

I said I was, and we went out the entrance doors and down three low steps to an aggregate walkway. To the left it led to a parking area, and on our right the walkway headed off between the building and the cliff edge about twenty feet away. Monterey pines between the cliff and the walkway added to the view.

After walking about a hundred feet, we came to a park bench facing the sea and I headed for it. Nurse Roger asked, "Are you getting tired, Mister Spicer?"

"Hell, no. I'd just like to sit and enjoy the view for a minute or two. You wouldn't happen to have a cigarette on you, would you?"

He joined me on the bench and held out a pack of Luckys from a pocket in his uniform shirt. We both lit up and I said, "Doc Rothenberg's got a pretty swank place here. He must do a pretty good business."

Roger nodded. "We almost always have a full house. These days a lot of well-to-do folks call Santa Barbara home, and many of them are getting on in years. They appreciate having a nice place to come when they need more care than they can get at home."

Watching the endless lines of white breakers rolling in across the deep blue ocean, I said, "I don't blame 'em. I could easily become a hypochondriac if it meant spending my time here."

He chuckled. "We have a few of those from time to time, too."

After a while I figured I was keeping Nurse Roger from patients who probably needed his attention more than I did, so I stood slowly to avoid another bout of dizziness, and we made our way back. On entering my room, I was surprised to find Bob Winfield enjoying the view from my window.

While Roger went to fetch a second chair for the lieutenant, Winfield and I shook hands. I said, "Thank you for coming all this way to see me, Bob."

He grinned. "Don't flatter yourself, Spicer. I came up to see Detective Walsh. You just happened to be on the way."

I gave him a hurt look and said, "Is that any way to talk to a wounded hospital patient?"

"Don't give me that, you malingerer. I saw you out there soaking up the sun."

Roger brought a chair in and we made ourselves comfortable. Bob said, "The way I hear it, you had yourself quite a bit of excitement last Saturday."

"I don't know if excitement is the word I'd choose, but it was certainly an eventful day."

He shrugged. "Either way. The story I heard from Detective Walsh over the telephone yesterday sounded pretty exciting to me. What I'd like to know is what hole in the woodwork this fellow Aleksandr Volodin crawled out of. When we talked on the telephone Friday afternoon, you were interested in some guy named Kurtz at Universal Studios."

"That's because I didn't learn about Aleksandr Volodin until Friday night. A couple of days earlier I was thinking about Diana Dean's strange behavior in all this, and since she wasn't talking, I got to wondering if she had a boyfriend stashed somewhere who might explain it all to us. With that in mind I asked a friend with good contacts in the movie business to find out if Dean had any romantic interests in her life.

"Friday night this friend told me Diana Dean recently broke up with a screenwriter named Eugene Alexander. That was the pen name he used. His real name was Aleksandr Volodin, and he was Dmitriy Volodin's nephew. My source even had a last known address for him in Tujunga.

"So Saturday morning I went up there to see Alexander, only the owner of the duplex Alexander lived in told me he'd skipped out in the middle of the night a few days earlier—the same night Ruth Barnes was killed."

Winfield said, "Now isn't that a coincidence?"

I said, "Yes, ain't it. I asked the owner if I could snoop around in Alexander's apartment, and he gave me the key. The place was a real pigsty with papers and garbage everywhere. I'd just about given up hope of finding anything useful when I noticed some papers crumpled up under a chair in the living room. Those papers included a letter from Alexander to Paramount Studios and a few pages of script rewrites. I didn't know whether they meant anything or not, but I took them with me. I expect they're still on the front seat of my car, wherever the hell it might be.

"Anyway, I'd gone up to Tujunga to find Alexander, and the timing of his disappearance seemed to make locating him even more important, so I decided to track down his Uncle Dmitriy, thinking he might know where his nephew was. I caught up with Dmitriy outside his office on the Warner lot, but I didn't get to talk to him because he was in a panic to get somewhere to stop someone from doing something. At least that's what I got out of his jabbering before he jumped into his Bugatti sport coupe and tore off the lot.

"On a whim I followed him. It was while we were roaring up Highway One-Oh-One in this direction that all the pieces of this thing started to make sense. The key was in the pages of script rewrites I'd found. What I finally realized was that Eugene Alexander's script was about Samuel Colt—the same damned story as Warner's film, Thunderstruck. The clincher was the date on the letter. It was dated long before Warner began producing his version of the story. It looked to me like Warner stole the script from Eugene Alexander.

"If Alexander saw it the same way, it gave him a good motive for sabotaging Thunderstruck. Following that logic a little further, it also gave Alexander a good motive for going after Jack Warner when his attempts to stop Thunderstruck's production failed.

"Then it occurred to me that the person Dmitriy Volodin was on his way to stop from doing something might be his nephew. I knew Jack Warner was out of town for the weekend, and when I found out he was visiting friends up here, I knew Warner was in serious danger. The rest of the story, as they say, is history."

Bob said, "Well, you solved the case; there's no doubt about that. I just wish you could have figured it all out before this Volodin character committed a second murder and got himself killed in the process."

Feeling a little defensive, I replied, "Yeah, I wish the same damned thing. If I had figured it out sooner, I wouldn't be sitting here thanking my lucky stars that Aleksandr Volodin's aim wasn't an inch or two better."

Sounding contrite, Winfield said, "I'm sorry, Johnny. I didn't mean to be critical. You did a hell of a job on this case. It's just that with our killer dead, we'll never be able to try him for his crimes."

"True, but the guy was certifiably nuts. A good lawyer probably would have gotten him off with an insanity plea anyway."

Changing the subject, Bob said, "So when are they going to turn you loose from this resort, or are you planning to stay indefinitely?"

"I could go for that, but the word is they're going to toss me out on my ear in a couple of days."

"Well, when you get back to town, give me a call and I'll buy lunch. I owe you at least that much for solving Ruth Barnes' murder for us."

"Lunch would be nice, but we haven't entirely solved the case yet."

Winfield looked at puzzled for a moment, then said, "Oh, you mean Diana Dean's part of it?"

"Yeah, that and the fact that she's disappeared again. Did you know she left the hospital in Torrance?"

He nodded. "Yes, the Torrance P.D. called me late yesterday morning saying an ambulance was there and they were about to haul Miss Dean away. They asked what I wanted them to do about it, but there wasn't anything I could do about it. True, she's a material witness in Ruth Barnes' murder, but I'd already tried locking Gladys Grebb up on that score, and it got us nowhere. Besides, at this point, whatever she and her mother were up to doesn't really matter much. Thanks to you, we can be pretty sure this Aleksandr Volodin killed Miss Barnes and that's pretty much that."

I nodded with more conviction than I felt, and Bob looked at his watch. "I'd better get on my way or I'll be late for my meeting with Walsh."

"Before you take off, do you happen to know anyone on the Board of Prison Directors, specifically the P.I. licensing part of the board?"

"Yes, as a matter of fact I do. Why?"

"I need a favor." I told Winfield what I wanted, and he said he'd see what he could do. After Bob left, I toddled over to my bed and stretched out for a little snooze. It had been a busy morning.

After an orderly cleared away the remains of my lunch, which had been delivered by Nurse Susan, Doctor Rothenberg showed up. With Susan's assistance, he removed the bandage and examined my scalp wound. When he was done poking and prodding, Rothenburg said, "I think we can remove those stitches soon—maybe day after tomorrow."

I said, "That sounds like good news. What happens after you've removed the stitches?"

"Well, if your head pain is manageable with aspirin and assuming no other problems show up, I see no reason I shouldn't discharge you and let you be on your way. What do you think about that?"

Glancing out my window and giving Susan a wink, I said, "I'll miss the scenery around here, but I guess it's high time I quit lollygagging and got back to earning a living."

Rothenberg gave me a rare smile. "Then we have a deal. I'll have your car brought over from my place tomorrow so you'll be all set to head home on Thursday."

Then the doctor took off with my chart to add some notes. I looked at Nurse Susan and thought I saw a little sadness in her expression. I said, "What's the matter, Kiddo?"

The hint of a frown I'd noticed was quickly replaced with one her angelic smiles, and she said, "Oh, nothing really. I've just enjoyed you being here, Mister Spicer. Things won't be nearly as much fun around this place after you leave."

I gave her a grin. "That's just about the nicest thing anybody's said to me lately. I'm going to miss you, too. And while we're at it, let's drop that 'Mister Spicer' business. You call me Johnny from now on, okay?"

Susan returned my grin and said, "Okay . . . Johnny. As long as Doctor Rothenberg doesn't catch me being so familiar with a patient."

Epilogue

U.S. Highway 101 South
10:00 A.M. – Thursday – November 30, 1939

By ten o'clock Thursday morning Doctor Rothenberg had removed my stitches, "goodbyes" and "thank yous" had been said all around at Casa Sobre El Mar, and I was back at the wheel of my Chrysler. Heading south on Highway 101, I watched familiar landmarks roll by and recalled the last time I saw them. I never imagined then that most of a week would pass before I saw them again.

All things considered, I was feeling pretty chipper. An occasional aspirin kept what remained of my headaches at bay, and as predicted by Doctor Bergman, my eyesight was just about back to normal in both eyes. That fact became painfully clear when I took a look at myself in the bathroom mirror. The area around my left eye was black and blue, turning to purple, and I was missing a fair amount of hair on the left side of my head. The hair would grow back, and in the meantime my fedora covered the problem. I was pretty much stuck with the shiner, though, until it went away of its own accord.

It was a little after noon when I came down off the Cahuenga pass into Hollywood. I was hungry, and figuring there wasn't anything edible left in my fridge at home, I pulled into the parking lot behind my office and strolled over to Levi's Deli for a bite of lunch.

Sitting at a window table with my ham and Swiss on whole wheat, I couldn't help recalling the last time I'd been there. That was the night of Saul Cohn's parade party and Tess was sitting across the table from me.

I hadn't seen or heard from Tess since her visit to Doctor Rothenberg's clinic Sunday night. I'd tried calling her half a dozen times since then without getting an answer. I'd thought about asking Will to stop by and see Tess just so I'd know she was okay, but decided against it. There had been a finality about her departure from the clinic that said she was done with Johnny Spicer. I was pretty sure I would hear from Tess sooner or later, but in the meantime I had to let her do what she needed to do.

After lunch I went up to my office. There was just about enough accumulated mail behind the door to keep it from opening. I gathered it all up and sorted it at my desk. As usual, most of the mail went into my wastebasket.

Done with that chore, I searched my pockets for the information sheet Tess gave me on Rosie's Professional Telephone Exchange Service. I called the message pick-up number and spoke to a woman with a distinct Brooklyn accent. I introduced myself and learned that I was speaking with Rosie herself. She read off a list of six messages, only one of which required prompt attention; a call from Will had come in at ten-thirty-seven that morning. He wanted me to call him. I told Rosie to keep up the good work and that I'd be out of the office the rest of the day.

I dialed Will's number and he picked up on the second ring. "Hi, Will. Johnny here."

"Hi, Johnny. I tried calling you at the clinic in Santa Barbara this morning and they said you'd left, so I take it you're back in town?"

"Yeah, I got back to the office. What's new?"

"Well, it took a bunch of telephone calls, but I've tracked down Diana Dean and her mother. Dean is now a patient at L.A. General."

"That's the USC teaching hospital in Lincoln Heights, right?"

"That's the one, but don't waste your time runnin' over there. They've got an absolutely no visitors rule in effect for her. I couldn't even get 'em to tell me how she was doing."

"Swell. You said you found Gladys, too?"

280

"Yup. She's rented herself a little bungalow less than a mile from the hospital."

"You have an address?"

"Sure. Hang on." When Will returned to the line, he said, "The house is at twenty-five-oh-nine Pomeroy Avenue. I drove by there last night, but didn't stop. I figured if you wanted to talk to her, it would be better if I didn't tip her off that we know where she is."

"You figured right, but I'm not sure if I really want to talk with her. Maybe I'll just sic Bob Winfield on her, instead."

"From what you've told me about Gladys, that sounds best. Let Winfield deal with her. Anything else you need me to do?"

"I think that about does it, Will." I did some quick mental calculations and said, "Let's see, if we don't count Thanksgiving, you put in ten days on the case. Does that sound right?"

"Well, I haven't really done anything today, so nine days is fair."

"Hell, you're talking to me today, aren't you? That makes it ten days. At twenty per day, that comes to two hundred. What's fair for your expenses?"

"I haven't been keeping close track, but I had to fill my gas tank a few times and there were some long-distance telephone calls. With a few other miscellaneous items, twenty-five should cover it."

"Okay, I'll write you a check for two-twenty-five. I can mail it to you or drop it off after I see Jack tomorrow. Which would be better for you?"

He hesitated. "Well, Johnny, to be honest, things are getting a little tight. Dropping it off would be better for me, if you don't mind."

"I don't mind in the least. I don't know for sure what time I'll be seeing Jack yet, but I'd like to get it done as early as possible tomorrow, so I ought to be done by one at the latest."

"Thanks, Johnny. I really appreciate the work."

"And I appreciate the help. You done good. Thanks."

I locked up the office and headed home. I glanced at Tess' apartment as I climbed the stairs to my place. I didn't see any signs of life.

Stepping into my living room, I saw an envelope on the floor just inside the door. "Johnny" was written on the outside in Tess' tidy handwriting. Apparently she'd slid it under the door. I sat at my kitchen table to read the note inside the envelope. It was dated Monday, the day after she visited me in Santa Barbara.

Dear Johnny,

I feel like a rat deserting you when you're down like this, but I must be selfish now and think of myself first. The truth is that I just can't go on worrying about when I might get a telephone call telling me you've been hurt again or worse.

We've talked about this before, and I understand that you can't change who you are or how you live. I wouldn't want you to do that even if you could, so I've tried to change myself, but I've learned that I can't do that any more than you can.

Thanks to a recommendation from Nat Cole, I've received an offer to sing with a band in San Francisco. I have accepted the offer and I'll be moving up there next week. In the meanwhile I've given up my apartment and I'm staying with Aunt Jean.

I will miss you, Johnny, and I honestly feel I am richer for having known you. I hope you can understand why I must leave. I don't want to lose touch with you entirely, though, so I'll send you a note when I'm settled in San Francisco. I hope that's alright with you.

Wishing you all the best,

Tess

The only real surprise in the note was that Tess was moving to San Francisco. Everything else she said was pretty much what I expected. That didn't make it any easier to take. I thought about trying to call her at her aunt's house, but talking with Tess now would only make things harder. Maybe I'd write her a letter when I had her new address in San Francisco.

Feeling washed out, I stretched out on my bed for a nap. They say all things heal with time. I hoped they were right.

First National Bank Building, Hollywood
7:00 A.M. – Friday – December 1, 1939

Feeling restless, I arrived at my office early Friday morning and went to work composing a final client report for Jack Warner. I hunted and pecked my way through a two-page typed summary that was as accurate and diplomatic as I could make it.

The truth of the matter was, even though there was no doubt in my mind about his guilt, I had not found a single shred of solid evidence proving Aleksandr Volodin was responsible for Warner's Thunderstruck troubles. Fortunately, evidence was now a moot point because there would be no criminal trial.

Another truth of the matter was that Jack Warner's writers, the ones who stole Aleksandr's script, shared a big piece of the blame for what happened. By stealing the script, they set a series of events in motion that left three dead bodies in its wake. Without a good deal of luck on my part, that number would have been higher by at least two.

I read through the finished report, signed it, and stuffed the original into an envelope with Jack Warner's name on the front. The carbon copy went into my filing cabinet under W.

Next I typed up a final invoice addressed to Jack Warner at Warner Bros. Studios. Under charges it listed eleven days of investigative services at the rate of seventy-five dollars per day for a total of $825.00. Below that I typed in an item for expenses— $91.50. The final line showed a total due of $916.50.

I was pretty sure Warner would question me about including my hospital stay in the total days of the investigation. I felt justified in that because Will Gardner was actively working on the case then even if I wasn't. Besides, if I hadn't been working for Jack, I wouldn't have been gotten shot in the first place. I paper-clipped the invoice to the envelope containing my final report.

I retrieved my checkbook from the office safe and made out a check payable to Will Gardner in the amount of $225.00. I slipped the check into an envelope with Will's name on it.

It was twenty past eight—time to call Esther Smith and set up a final meeting with my client. Esther told me Jack was in and I could stop by anytime before noon.

I walked into Warner's outer office and tossed my fedora on his hat rack a few minutes after nine. Esther eyed my shiner and missing hair with a sympathetic look and told me to go right in; Mister Warner was expecting me.

Jack, who was usually doing at least three things at once, wasn't doing much of anything, just leaning back in his desk chair staring out the window at the back side of Mount Lee across the L.A. River. His expression was thoughtful. For a moment I wondered what he was thinking about, then I decided I really didn't care what the hell he was thinking about.

"Good morning, Jack."

Turning in his chair, Warner looked me over. "Hello, Spicer. Good to see you up and around again. Have a seat."

I handed him my final report with the invoice attached and sat. "My case findings are in the envelope, but you already know what the report says."

He detached my invoice and tossed the envelope on his desk unopened. Then he studied the bill long enough to memorize every word and number on it. I could almost see the wheels turning in his head. He was counting the days between Monday, November twentieth, and today, surely noting that I'd charged him for my time in the hospital.

Warner frowned and looked up at me. I stared right back at him. He opened his mouth as if to say something, then shut it, and we just glared at each other for a while. Finally he pulled one of the pens from his desk set and scrawled something on the invoice.

"Esther!"

She poked her head in and said, "Yes, Mister Warner?"

He held out my invoice. "Have someone hand carry this over to accounting. Tell 'em I want Spicer's payment in the mail before the end of today."

"Yes, sir."

Esther took the invoice and gave me a quick glance as she left to follow her instructions. Jack leaned back in his chair. "Anything else, Spicer?"

"Yeah, Jack, a couple of loose ends. Did you know Diana Dean has moved from that hospital in Torrance to L.A. General?"

"I oughta know about it. I paid to have her transported."

As if I didn't know, I said, "Who's idea was that?"

Leaning forward again, he said, "That woman stormed in here the other day ranting and raving about how I was responsible for ruining her daughter's career, and if I didn't want a lawsuit on my hands, I'd better start helping her financially."

"By 'that woman,' I assume you mean Gladys Grebb?"

"Who else would have the balls to talk to me like that?"

"Sounds a lot like blackmail to me."

"Of course it's blackmail!"

"And you're letting her get away with it?"

"I am, and it's costing me plenty. I paid all her expenses at that Torrance hospital, and now I'm paying her bills at L.A. General. I'm also giving her a cash settlement. But that's all confidential; keep it under your hat."

I'll admit I was baffled. I said, "All that just to keep her from going to the press?"

Warner shook his head. "No, it's more than that."

I waited to hear the more part. Finally he said, "In a way, Diana got a raw deal. I did some checking and found out you were right about somebody—actually two somebodies—in my script department stealing Eugene Alexander's script for Thunderstruck and passing it off as their own. If it weren't for them, none of this would have happened. I fired both of them, and I guarantee they'll never write another word for pay in this town, but the damage is done, and I'm stuck with doing what I can to undo the havoc they caused. I just wish Alexander had come to me about his script instead of going off half-cocked."

I didn't bother to ask Jack if he would've believed Alexander's story if the writer had confronted him. Odds are Warner would have thrown him out on his ear, possibly making things worse than they already were.

Changing the subject, I asked, "Word is you've stopped production on Thunderstruck. Is that temporary or permanent?"

"It's permanent. That damned project has cost me a fortune. I don't want anything more to do with it."

When I didn't comment, Jack picked up a letter opener, and tapping it absentmindedly on his desk, he stared off into space. The contemplative mood I was observing this morning was a side of Jack Warner I'd not seen before. Until now I'd always viewed him as a decisive, full-speed-ahead kind of guy. It was possible nearly getting his head blown off changed his attitude, but if that was the case, I suspected it was only a temporary condition.

Jack suddenly stopped tapping his letter opener and posed a question. "Spicer, I've been thinking about what you said the other night about Dmitriy knowing what his nephew was up to and maybe even being in cahoots with him. Do you really think that's true?"

"Like I told you, Jack, we'll probably never know the answer to that one. It's hard to believe he would have helped shut down his own film, but Alexander was family, so there's no telling how Dmitriy felt about the situation."

Warner nodded thoughtfully. Then he stood up and offered his hand. I took the hint and got out of my chair. As I shook his hand, he said, "Spicer, this has been a rotten deal from the beginning, and I'd just as soon forget any of it ever happened, but I'm not going to forget that you solved the mystery and, in the process, saved my ass. If there's ever anything I can do for you, all you have to do is say the word."

For a proud man like Jack Warner, that was one hell of a concession, and as much as I was sure it hurt him to make it, I knew he meant it. I acknowledged Warner's gratitude with a nod and walked out of his office.

Esther Smith looked up with a smile. She'd obviously heard what Jack said and she knew what it meant. I smiled back and said, "Esther, thank you for all your help with this. If it wasn't for you, this whole thing would have been a much bigger disaster than it was."

She just kept smiling and said, "You're very welcome, Mister Spicer. I'm glad I could help."

I said a warm farewell, grabbed my hat, and headed for my car. Driving off the Warner lot to deliver Will Gardner's check, I actually felt a little twinge of sadness. The movie business is a unique world unto itself, a world populated by a unique bunch of folks. Some of them were even pretty decent.

Musso & Frank Grill, Hollywood
12:15 P.M. – Friday – December 1, 1939

Bob Winfield already had a table for us when I arrived at Musso and Frank's for the lunch he'd promised me. After we ordered, Bob said, "You look pleased with yourself. What's up?"

"I saw Jack Warner this morning and delivered my final report. I guess I'm just happy to have this case over and done with."

Winfield smiled. "Good for you. I wish I could say the same, but I still have a bunch of loose ends and a murder investigation I'll never be able to call closed with absolute certainty. The worst part is I have no idea where Diana Dean and her mother are, so I can't even interview them again. I guess I'll have to put somebody to work tracking them down."

"Well, I can save the taxpayers a little money there."

Bob looked surprised. "You know where they are?"

"Yup. Will Gardner already tracked them down. Miss Dean is now a patient at L.A. General."

"Why the hell did she go there?"

"I can't say for sure, but I'm guessing she's there because her mother thinks she'll get better care, L.A. General being a teaching hospital and all. Regardless of the reason, Miss Dean went there courtesy of Jack Warner. He's paying the bills, and she's getting what I guess is a pretty fat settlement from Jack."

Winfield looked even more surprised by that piece of news. "No kiddin'? Sounds like Mister Warner had an attack of conscience."

"Maybe, but his generosity is also the result of Dean's mother threatening a public lawsuit if Jack didn't make a substantial donation to the Gladys Grebb benevolent fund on the grounds that he was responsible for ruining her daughter's movie career."

Bob shook his head in amazement. "That's blackmail, but I guess Warner had it coming."

"Yes, I suppose he did. As for Gladys, she's rented a little bungalow near L.A. General in Lincoln heights." I removed a slip of paper from my jacket pocket and handed it to Winfield. "Here's the address Will came up with for her."

"Thanks, Johnny. Maybe with Aleksandr Volodin out of the picture now, Millie or Gladys might open up and tell me what the hell they hoped to accomplish with their phony kidnapping."

Over lunch Winfield and I chatted about other aspects of the case, and he reported on the favor I'd asked of him. Then Bob paid for lunch and we wished each other a Merry Christmas before going our separate ways.

First National Bank Building, Hollywood
8:00 A.M. – Friday – December 8, 1939

During a week of relative inactivity, my physical wounds healed quite nicely. My hair had even grown enough to begin covering the scar on my head. The sick feeling in the pit of my stomach caused by losing Tess was also starting to heal, but that wound was going to take a while longer to mend.

Mostly I was restless and anxious to get started on a new case. Finding a larger than usual pile of mail on my outer office floor, I was hopeful one of the envelopes might be from a citizen desperately in need of a clever private eye.

I carried the mail to my desk for sorting, but before I sat down, the telephone rang. Bob Winfield was on the other end of the line. He'd called to tell me about an interview he had with Diana Dean the day before. While Gladys was still holding out, her daughter was in a mood to get some things off her chest. Miss Dean told Winfield that during my visit to her dressing room, she became convinced Eugene Alexander was causing all the trouble at the studio.

She said Eugene had confronted her with his suspicion that Warner had stolen his Revolver script and demanded that she leave the production of Thunderstruck. When she refused, Alexander became enraged and made threats.

The kidnapping ruse was her mother's idea. Gladys figured staging her daughter's disappearance would keep Eugene, who'd clearly gone nuts over the situation, from finding her and at the same time, force Warner to take action against Alexander.

Her plan had been to follow up on Diana Dean's supposed kidnapping by sending Warner a ransom letter that would appear to be from Eugene Alexander and that would accuse him of stealing the Thunderstruck script, thus making Warner aware of who was trying to sabotage the production.

The plan had fallen apart, though, when Winfield sent Detective Danny to the Grebb house to be there if Dean's kidnapper's tried to contact Gladys with a ransom demand—something that couldn't happen as long as there was a cop watching her every move.

Matters got even worse when Ruth Barnes was killed, apparently by Alexander trying to find out Dean's whereabouts. After I followed Gladys to The Breakers in Long Beach, Diana saw the cops arriving, panicked, and took off in a mad dash that ended with her Cadillac upside down on the beach near Torrance.

I thanked Winfield for letting me in on what Diana Dean told him, and when we ended the telephone conversation, I shook my head in amazement at how Gladys had managed to take a lousy situation and turn it into a total disaster. I didn't have long to contemplate the subject, though, because the telephone on my desk rang again. Still hoping for a client, I answered the call in my most professional voice. "Good morning, Spicer Investigation Agency, Spicer speaking."

My new client hopes evaporated when Will Gardner said, "Hi, Johnny. Will here. I just got some great news, and I wanted to tell you about it."

I was pretty sure I knew what his great news was, but I didn't let on. "Okay, Will, what's your news?"

Sounding as excited as a kid on Christmas morning, he said, "I got a letter from the Board of Prison Directors this morning, and guess what? They've reinstated my P.I. license!"

"No kiddin'? That really is terrific news. Did they give you a reason for their change of heart?"

"Not in so many words. All the letter says is . . . ." I heard Will unfold a piece of paper, then he read, "'The board has reviewed your case at the recommendation of Chief of Detectives Robert Winfield, Los Angeles Police Department, and based on the results of that review, we are reinstating your license to operate as a private investigator within the State of California.'"

Pleased that the favor I'd asked of Bob had been successful, I said, "Well, good for Winfield. You must have made quite an impression on him."

There was suspicion in Will's voice when he replied, "Johnny, I hardly know the man, but the two of you are great pals, so I'm guessing you had a hand in this."

Chuckling, I said, "Okay, I'll admit to discussing the subject with Bob, but he wouldn't have gone out on a limb by sending a letter to the board if he didn't think you got a raw deal."

"Maybe, but ultimately it's you I have to thank for this. Thank you, Johnny. Thank you ever so much!"

"You're welcome, Will, but it sure wouldn't do you any harm to call the lieutenant and give him your thanks as well."

"I'll do that; I surely will."

"Good. And if I helped in any way, all I ask in return is an invite to the wedding when you and Betty get hitched."

Hardly containing his enthusiasm on that subject, Will said, "Invite, hell! I want you to be my best man!"

"We'll see about that. Let me know when you two set the date and I'll check my calendar."

After hanging up the telephone, I sat back and felt good for a change. I rested on my laurels for all of fifteen seconds before tackling the mail. What didn't end up in up in my wastebasket was divided into two stacks, one for bills and one for Christmas cards. Opening holiday greetings seemed like a lot more fun than opening bills.

There were four envelopes that looked like they contained holiday cards. The front of the first card I opened depicted the jolly old elf himself busily placing presents from his sack under a brightly decorated Christmas tree. Inside, the greeting was addressed to "Shamus," and a note at the bottom read, "Have yourself a swell Christmas, Bogie."

The next card showed an English village right out of Dickens' Christmas Carol. The printed message inside wished me a Merry Christmas filled with yuletide joys. It was signed Bob and Millie Winfield.

My third card was decorated with a snow-covered rural scene in which a horse-drawn sleigh full of happy holiday visitors were arriving at a warmly glowing farmhouse. The equally warm holiday wishes inside the card were signed, "Your very good friend, Esther Smith."

I was beginning get into a decidedly holiday mood when I opened the last card in the stack. The cover featured a humorous drawing of Santa Claus wearing an old-fashioned bathing costume while relaxing on a sunny beach surrounded by palm trees. It was signed by someone named Sue Jackson, but I didn't make the connection until I read the handwritten message.

Dear Johnny,

I sincerely hope your recovery is still going smoothly. I suppose it's not very coy of me to say so, but I've missed you terribly. The old "Casa" just isn't the same without your wit. I don't remember ever smiling as much as I did while you were here.

As you might imagine, Santa Barbara is fairly buzzing with preparations for holiday festivities. I must admit, though, I'm having some difficulty getting into the spirit of things because I've learned I only have three days off for Christmas, which isn't nearly enough time for a trip to spend the holiday with my parents and sister in Milwaukee. So it seems I'll be spending Christmas in much the same fashion as the Santa on the front of this card.

I'm guessing you already have many plans for Christmas with all your celebrity pals in Hollywood, but if you should find time on your calendar for a trip to Santa Barbara, I would be delighted to share some eggnog and a slice of fruitcake with you.

Affectionately yours,
"Nurse" Susan

I closed the card and looked at the drawing of Santa on the beach for several moments. Actually, it seemed to me like a pretty swell way to spend Christmas in California.

Santa Barbara Biltmore Hotel
6:00 P.M. – Sunday – December 24, 1939

I leaned against a low wall behind the Biltmore and took in the twinkling lights up and down the beach and even more twinkles on the boats in the harbor. The air was cool, but not at all cold. Such was Christmas Eve in Santa Barbara.

Susan was up in her room changing from beach togs into something more appropriate for dinner in the Biltmore's swanky Beach Club dining room. Being a practical soul, she'd had trouble understanding why I would book her an expensive room overlooking the harbor in a hotel that was only about a mile from her apartment. In her words, such extravagance seemed like the height of decadence. My explanation that money wasn't worth a whole hell of a lot unless you spent some of it on the important things in life, like enjoying Christmas in a special place with a special person, may not have changed her opinion of my spending habits, but Susan did seem to be enjoying the experience. That's all that mattered to me.

I heard the clack-clack-clack of high heels on the stone walkway from the hotel and turned around to watch Susan coming toward me. She wore a simple white evening dress that fit her slim form like a glove. Illumination from the Biltmore's rear entrance backlit her hair, creating almost the same halo effect I remembered from the first time I'd seen her in my hospital room. I'd suspected her of being an angel then, and now I was certain of it.

Standing close beside me at the beach wall, she took my hand and stared off across the harbor. "It's beautiful."

Looking at her with a grin I couldn't help, I said, "You sure are."

She grinned back and, standing on tippy-toes, gave me a kiss on the cheek.

I said, "That was nice."

With a sly smile tugging at the corners of her mouth, Susan said, "It will do until we find some mistletoe. Then you'd better watch out, Mister Hollywood Private Eye."

THE END

Meet H. P. Oliver

H. P. Oliver began his career with a degree in journalism from San Jose State University and spent the next twenty-some years writing award-winning entertainment and educational media. Now he applies his creativity and imagination to writing historical mysteries.

About mystery writing, Oliver says, "To be truly engrossing, a mystery needs a little meat on its bones—something more than just figuring out who done the evil deed. Taking a story back in time or even basing it on actual historical events is a great way to endow a good yarn with even more color and depth. Historical periods and locations give the writer an opportunity to take most readers where they've never been before."

H. P. Oliver lives in northern California and spends much of his time working on projects throughout the western states. In addition to his love of history, Oliver's interests range from vintage film to restoring classic cars.

For more about H. P. Oliver and his mysteries in history, visit his website at www.HPOliver.com.

More Mysteries In History By H. P. Oliver

PACIFICA

In his first novel-length caper, Hollywood gumshoe Johnny Spicer plunges into the depths of international intrigue and finds himself entangled in multiple webs of conspiracy and deception. Set against the colorful backdrop of the 1939 Golden Gate International Exposition in San Francisco, *PACIFICA* finds Spicer searching for an attractive young Chinese woman who in reality is a diplomat on a hush-hush mission to promote U.S. military intervention in the Sino-Japanese War.

When the Chinese woman suddenly disappears from the exposition, everyone involved, including the FBI, believes the woman was kidnapped by Japanese agents intent on sabotaging her mission. Walk a tightrope of suspense with Spicer as he chases conflicting clues and dodges diabolical foreign agents in a case where nothing—and everything—is what it appears to be. (Available in paperback and e-book editions.)

SILENTS!

Lillian Lawrence, the silent film era's fastest rising starlet, is found shot to death in her room at the Hollywood Hotel only days after announcing her plans to leave motion pictures for the less glamorous roles of wife and mother. Lillian's many friends in the silent film industry and her legion of fans across America are all asking the same question: Who could have done such a dastardly deed?

Set in Hollywood during the golden days of the silent film era, *SILENTS!* follows two L.A.P.D. homicide detectives as they unravel deceptions and misdirection designed to conceal the truth about Lillian Lawrence's death. *SILENTS!* is a mystery in history embodying all of the action and drama that made Tinsel Town the motion picture capital of the world. (Available in paperback and e-book editions.)

www.ingramcontent.com/pod-product-compliance
Lightning Source LLC
Chambersburg PA
CBHW062127170626
46813CB00002B/595